ONE
WILL BE LEFT

DAWN MORRIS

R

RELIQUUM PUBLISHING

ONE WILL BE LEFT
First Edition Trade Book, 2015
Copyright © 2015 by Dawn Morris

All rights reserved. No part of this publication may be reproduced, stored in a retrieval system, or transmitted in any form by any means—electronic, mechanical, photocopy, recording, or otherwise—except for brief quotations in critical reviews or articles, without the prior permission of the publisher, except as provided by U.S. copyright law.

Some Scripture quotations and words of Jesus are taken or adapted from the New American Standard Bible, ® Copyright © 1960, 1962, 1963, 1968, 1971, 1973, 1975, 1977, 1995 by The Lockman Foundation. Used by permission.

This novel is a work of fiction. Names, characters, places, and incidents either are the product of the author's imagination or are used fictitiously. Any resemblance to actual events, locales, organizations, or persons living or dead is entirely coincidental and beyond the intent of either the author or the publisher.

To order additional books:
www.amazon.com
www.dawnmorris.net

Visit Dawn Morris' web site at www.DawnMorris.net

Published by Reliquum Publishing

ISBN: 978-0-9963702-0-2

E-book also available

Editorial: Arlyn Lawrence, Inspira Literary Solutions, Gig Harbor, WA
Book Design: Carrot Stick Marketing, Gig Harbor, WA
Printed in the USA by Lightning Source, Nashville, TN

Acknowledgments

As in the first book in this series, *One Will Be Taken*, much of what you're about to read is purely fictional. The story is inspired by the prophecies written in the Bible regarding the last days, known by many as the "End Times."

I'm so grateful to have been born in a time and place where I have had the freedom to follow Jesus without fear. That isn't the experience of everyone who follows Jesus now, nor will it be in the days that are coming. That freedom allowed me to study the Bible's prophetic passages in great detail and to use what I learned as the backbone for this series. Thank You, Lord!

Jane. You led me to faith in Jesus, and you didn't leave me to fend for myself! Patiently, you taught me the basics of the faith—*especially* the importance of forgiving those who hurt us. I'm forever grateful for your faithfulness.

Dennis. I've always loved watching the groom's face at a wedding, the way his whole countenance lights up when he sees his bride. You've given me the gift of that look almost daily for the last 30 years. How can I thank you enough for *that?*

The Five. Being your mom has been the most amazing, and frightening experience of my life! It's a tremendous thing to have parts of your heart walking around. I'm thankful to each of you, for your encouragement in the process of writing this series!

My friends. I can't name all of you—and I'm still waiting to meet more of you! I love the family God gives us in friends. Thank you for your encouragement in pursuing this dream!

Arlyn. I can learn more from you in five minutes than, well, than anyone I've ever met! You're an *incredible* editor and a woman of many talents.

Virginia and Al, from Carrot Stick Marketing. The two of you are an *awesome* team! I love the interior and the intriguing covers of both *One Will Be Taken* and *One Will Be Left*. I'm so grateful to work with both of you!

1

NEW BABYLON
IRAQ – 2022

Arturo heard a soft whirring noise. Turning his head, he tried to open his eyes but the effort was too much.

"I think he's waking. Should we call the ambassador?"

"Not yet. He wants to be called when his father is more cognizant."

Arturo could hear the words being spoken and was confused about what they meant. He could feel that he was lying on a bed. Where was he? He struggled to open his eyes again and caught a glimpse of a woman dressed in scrubs. Was he in the hospital? She came closer and bent toward him.

"Well, hello! We've been wondering when you would wake up. I'm Jean, Mr. Giamo. Your son has hired a private medical team to see to your needs. You are getting the very best care, sir."

Arturo tried to position his hands to push himself up but was restrained. Panic enveloped him as he pulled uselessly against the restraints.

"Mr. Giamo, you've had a stroke. You're going to improve, sir, but you are partially paralyzed. Please, be calm. I'll help you sit up."

Gently, the young woman put an arm under his shoulders and tilted him up a bit, propping him with a pillow. Arturo blinked, trying to clear his vision. The room was small. It had no windows. He tried to raise his right hand to rub his eyes but it was still restrained. He looked down, hoping the nurse would see and release him. He was horrified to see his hand resting uselessly on the bed unrestrained. He moaned.

"I know you are feeling disoriented, sir. As I said, you are partially paralyzed, but we are very hopeful you will completely recover. Your son will be here soon. He asked us to notify him as soon as you woke up. He's been very concerned for you. You've done a fine job raising that young man. You should be so proud!"

Arturo closed his eyes again to rest a moment, trying to remember the last thing that had happened before he woke up here. There was something awful, something that triggered a feeling of intense fear as he struggled to remember. Panicked, he opened his eyes again and attempted to slow his breathing. He looked pleadingly into his nurse's eyes and tried to talk.

"I have a swab here, Mr. Giamo," she offered, anticipating his desire to speak. "Let me wet your mouth with it. That's right." Arturo sucked eagerly on the small wet sponge she put into his mouth. His tongue was painfully dry.

"You've been in a coma for almost two weeks. We have a feeding tube in your stomach giving you nutrients, but I'm sure your mouth feels parched." She pulled out the swab and dipped it into a small glass on the bedside table. "I'm going to do this again a few times. Soon you'll be able to have some ice chips. We just have to be careful; we don't want you to aspirate."

Arturo felt the wet sponge move across his teeth and gums, and he closed his eyes again. He was so tired. He just needed to rest for a while.

St. Michaels, Maryland

Elena sat nervously in the car, unable to make out anything in the darkness and driving rain. Brant, her bodyguard, was checking the house and surrounding area. After two weeks in Baltimore, they had finally obtained transport papers to travel to St. Michaels. Elena's son-in-law, DC, had given her the deed to his parents' home before he and her daughter, Teo, had left New Babylon. He reasoned that its remote location outside of St. Michaels would make an ideal place to keep one-year old Olivia safe.

It had taken Elena and Brant eight long hours to drive to the house. There were security checkpoints along the way, and at each point, uniformed officials had carefully examined their papers. Thankfully, Brant had found out through a friend in the World Union Security Force where the checkpoints were located, so they were able to hide Olivia in the back of the minivan. Elena sighed, recalling how they'd had to give the little girl a dose of children's allergy medicine to get her to sleep and keep her quiet in the special suitcase they had altered for their escape from New Babylon. None of the guards along the way seemed too interested in them, and no one checked the suitcase. No one had wanted to check their vehicle either. She had prayed fervently each time they'd stopped at a checkpoint, murmuring, "Oh God, keep her safe," repeatedly as they neared the guards.

Elena gazed at the child sleeping in her arms. Keeping Olivia out of sight had been difficult, not just when they got off the plane in Baltimore but at the hotel, too. They couldn't take the chance that anyone would see Olivia alive. Her picture was everywhere in the media, as were images of her parents, Teo and DC. Luca Giamo played the mournful uncle and brother quite well. Olivia and her parents' "deaths" at the hands of terrorists had outraged the press, which was already enamored with the young Italian ambassador to the World Union. Most news outlets had broadcast the somber funeral that had been held for all of Luca Giamo's family. According to the newscasts, Luca's father, Arturo, had suffered a fatal stroke when he'd heard of the deaths of his beloved daughter and her family.

Oddly, Elena had felt nothing when she'd seen the news report about her ex-husband's death. She could only pray that Teo and DC had been able to escape the airplane in time, as they had planned.

ONE WILL BE LEFT

Brant startled her by opening her door. "It's all clear, Elena. Here, let me carry her in." He reached in and pulled Olivia out of Elena's arms.

Elena accompanied her escort across the pebble drive to the front porch. Picking her way carefully in the dark, Elena tried to make out the details of the classic Georgian-styled home. DC had shown her pictures of the lovely yellow house, with its windows framed in classic black shutters and its expansive porch that wrapped around the front and left sides of the house. Her way became even darker under the pergola, which stretched across the width of the porch. Elena could just make out the shape of the grape leaves that, she knew from photos, draped lavishly over the pergola. DC's parents had spared no effort in making their home welcoming.

Brant stepped back so she could open the glass-paneled door for him. A close friend of DC's, Brant Hughes was a highly trained member of the Babylon Security Forces and was a believer. Elena was extremely grateful for his help in this entire escapade. She never would have made it without him.

Brant flipped a switch and the lights came on. They both smiled as they looked around. This would be perfect. The hardwood floors were dusty, but their dark color still complemented the white pillars on either side of the entrance hall, which opened into expansive rooms painted a creamy yellow. It was a pleasant place.

"Let's look upstairs for a place to put Olivia," Elena suggested. She and Brant quickly found the master bedroom to the right of the stairs. Elena shook off the comforter, and Brant carefully placed Olivia down on the bed.

"I'll sleep in here with Livie, if that's alright. I'll leave her here for now. Let's go downstairs and see what we have there," Elena whispered.

They made their way to the kitchen and turned on the lights. Elena knew that in the daytime, she would be able to see the Chesapeake Bay out of the wall of windows. The property was surrounded on three sides by water, and DC's parents had built their home to make the most of the view.

Brant opened the refrigerator and quickly closed it. The smell was rancid. "It looks like they had Chinese leftovers. I guess everything spoils after such a long time."

Elena made a face, walked across the kitchen, and opened the pantry. It was completely stocked! She couldn't believe the house hadn't been ransacked. She'd seen such devastation on their trip here.

"I'm glad you thought to buy that powdered milk, Brant." When he didn't respond, Elena turned around. Brant's hands were up in the air. He was staring at a young woman with a gun in her hands, her hair wet and dripping.

"Who are you?" the young woman demanded. She looked frightened. Elena tried to reassure the woman calmly without belying the sense of fear that threatened to close up her throat.

"I'm Elena Foster. This house belongs—belonged—to my son-in-law, DC Bond. This is a family friend, Brant Hughes. He's helping me get things sorted here. We have documentation from World Union authorities, if you'd like to see some proof."

"Yes, why don't you show me your proof?" The girl's mouth tilted up on one side, sneering.

Elena moved slowly with her hands spread in front of her to the kitchen table where she'd set her purse. The woman moved in closer, watching as Elena opened the purse and pulled out the envelope containing the paperwork.

Elena handed the papers to the young woman. The woman's hands shook slightly as she took the documents.

"These look real." The girl visibly relaxed. "I'm a relative of the Bonds. I saw the lights on in the house and came to check it out. There aren't many people still in the area and I wasn't sure who could be in here. My brother and I just got here ourselves." She put the gun into the holster under her jacket. "We saw on the news that DC and his family had died. We thought we'd claim the house since this part of Maryland is secure from the Anti-Globalists. My name is

Maggie Bond. DC was my cousin."

Elena thought of her granddaughter upstairs asleep. Above all else, she had to keep Olivia safe.

"Well, I'm sorry, but you're not going to be able to stay. This house is mine now. You understand that after the death of my daughter and her family, I just want to be alone." She spoke sharply. "I'd appreciate it if you would leave immediately."

Maggie was about to speak when the backdoor opened behind Brant and a young boy came into the kitchen. Elena was stunned by how much he resembled DC. She had no doubt the boy was related to her son-in-law. He looked about nine or ten years old. He was painfully thin.

"Maggie, I wanted to make sure you were okay." He stayed by the door, wet and wary.

Maggie walked across the room and put her arm protectively around her brother's shoulders. "This is Dalton. I asked him to wait outside while I checked on things."

Elena breathed a quick prayer that she was making the right decision as she softened her demeanor. "Hi, Dalton. My name is Elena. I'm your cousin DC's mother-in-law. This is Brant, a friend of ours. Why don't you and Maggie have a seat at the table? We have a lot to talk about."

Amman, Jordan

Teo retched again into the toilet basin. She tried not to moan as she rocked back on her heels. She wiped her mouth with a corner of the towel that was draped around her neck and, breathing deeply, sat back against the wall. The tiles felt cool so she turned her face to rest against them. She was not experiencing the more severe problems she'd had in her first pregnancy, but the morning sickness had not been this difficult the first time. Thinking of Olivia brought tears to her eyes and they quickly spilled down her cheeks. It had been over a month since she had last seen her daughter. She bowed her head and sighed.

I know she is safer with Mom, God. Please take care of them for me. DC says that You aren't worried. There is nothing that overwhelms or frightens You. I'm scared, though. I'm new at this faith stuff. Thank You for being patient with me. Thanks for DC. He is helping me learn a lot about You and about what is coming. That would have really frightened me before. I'm so grateful to understand about Jesus and have a relationship with Him now. I'm still freaked out, but somehow there is hope in my heart. Thanks, God.

She heard a tap on the door, crawled over, and opened it. She smiled up at her husband. His green eyes shone brightly down at her.

"Hey, babe. I brought some water for you," he whispered, handing her a bottle. She sipped it slowly as he closed the door quietly and sat down next to her.

"Is everyone still asleep?" Teo asked.

"Yes. I don't think you disturbed anyone. But they wouldn't mind, even if you did. Please don't worry, Teo. Sam and Ticia are compassionate."

Teo nodded. Sam and Ticia Reynolds had been extremely kind since she and DC had shown up at their door late one night almost a month before. DC and Sam had served in the Marines together long ago. "*Semper fi*," she whispered, smiling. After she and DC had escaped from New Babylon, DC had remembered that Sam had taken a job in Amman, and they decided to risk contacting him for help after faking their deaths.

In a bid for public sympathy, Teo's half brother, Luca Giamo, had plotted to have their small family killed and make it look like a terror plot against him. The young Italian ambassador to the World Union had calculated that a "terrorist" attack taken out on his own family would aid him in his desire for greater power. Thankfully, Teo had overheard his plans, and she and DC had been able to orchestrate an escape for their daughter, Olivia, and themselves. Unfortunately, that meant separating from her. Olivia was safely in the United States with her grandmother, Elena.

"Listen, I finally heard from our friend. The passports are ready. We can pick them up early this morning."

"Oh, DC! Finally! Now we can make our way back home to Olivia and Mom!" Teo threw her arms around her husband's neck and kissed his cheeks.

Just then a pounding erupted on the bathroom door. Teo looked at DC in alarm as Sam began cursing through the door. DC moved Teo away and opened the door. Sam threw a Bible at DC.

"What the hell is this, DC? You're a Christian? Are you serious? You know how I feel about those fanatics. Here I've given you a place to stay and kept quiet about you being alive, only to find out you're one of them!" He spat out the words venomously.

"Look, Sam..." DC began, holding his palms out imploringly.

"No, DC. You listen. I heard all that Jesus crap from my parents. They never did a thing to help me—except disappear! I want you both out, now." Spit flew from Sam's mouth as his voice grew louder.

Ticia came up behind her husband, her face pale and eyes wide. "What's wrong, Sam?" She pawed at his shoulder timidly.

He swung at her and slapped her across the face. "Shut up, Tish!"

She cried out as she clasped her now-bleeding mouth. DC grabbed Sam's arm and swung him around. Teo gasped as her husband slammed his fist into the other man's face.

Sam fell backward into the wall. DC pushed him down to the ground with his foot. "How dare you lay a hand her! Ticia, we're leaving. You're welcome to come with us if you want."

Ticia rubbed her cheek slowly and shook her head. "No," she whimpered.

"Come on, Teo," DC said. "Let's go." He took her hand and led her back to the bedroom where they had been staying. He angrily grabbed the duffle bag he'd packed earlier and led his wife out of the apartment.

Quinteros Estate, North of Houston, Texas

Although it was only 6:00 a.m., it was already hot and humid. The covered porch of the pool house provided a welcome cool retreat. A ceiling fan circulated above the two men seated at a small, linen-covered table overlooking the pool and the back of the magnificent mansion. The armed men patrolling the perimeter were trying to be as discreet as possible.

A well-manicured brown hand placed a white porcelain coffee cup onto its saucer with relish. The hand's owner sighed with satisfaction. Nothing tasted so good as the first cup of coffee. He nodded to the servant standing by to refill his cup and, cup in hand again, turned in his seat toward the man sitting next to him.

"So, would you say the resistance is succeeding in meeting our goals for the East Coast cities?"

"Yes. We are maintaining enough violence to keep World Union troops busy. The WU has Baltimore under its control. As you know, the team we sent in to New York Harbor was successful, and we now control the waterfront. Since the outbreak of smallpox in the last few weeks, we've been able to move to take over the police force and the government facilities.

"I must say, sir, it was a brilliant idea to introduce the virus into the city, and quite fortunate that your men were able to secure vaccines for our own people. They can move about without fear of contracting the disease."

The man with the coffee cup smiled at his chief operating officer and brother-in-law, Marc Jafari. "We've come a long way since Ecuador, haven't we? Two boys, always in trouble, have become two men who use trouble to our advantage."

ONE WILL BE LEFT

Marc nodded in agreement. "Thanks to your planning, 'Mr. Smith.'"

"It is a useful name, for now. It wouldn't do to have everyone know that Andres Quinteros is Mr. Smith. We both know how important it is to keep a good name, even in these times."

"This World Union cannot keep control much longer. We must do our part to maintain enough anarchy that more localized oversight is needed. Our friends in the South have assured me that I will gain control of the North American sector. We already control great portions of Central America through the American Southwest, due to the efforts of our drug cartel and our resources in the Anti-Globalist movement."

Andres looked appreciatively at the summer loggia on the right side of the pool. The twenty-thousand-square-foot mansion he shared with his wife had been almost exclusively designed and decorated by his talented spouse. A great beauty, Patricia was a woman worthy of him and the empire he was building. For now, he pushed his thoughts of her to the back of his mind and returned his attention to his companion.

"You know, Marc, we have been made for these times. Desperate situations require strong leadership. The chaos that ensued in North America after the disappearances has given us the foothold we needed to gain power here.

"To think of how our mothers despaired of us! Soon, you and I will control most of North America, unrestrained by archaic, democratic ideas of government. We will bring peace and stability, and in return we will gain unlimited power and resources!"

Marc Jafari raised his coffee cup in a toast and smiled at his longtime friend. "Indeed, we have come a long way, Andres. Once you are the leader of North America, this continent will be unified for the first time. I am confident that you can restore the prosperity it once had."

Andres sat back in his chair, wiping his mouth with his napkin. "I also am confident of that. We have made careful plans and implemented them, dealing with our adversaries as needed. Your sister has been invaluable to me in seeing the path forward. Truly, she is a woman of astounding intellect. She sees solutions and possibilities others do not. It took a lot of convincing to get her to marry me, but it was worth every effort."

Marc carefully took a sip of his ice water. He remembered the men who had died in order for Patricia to be convinced to marry his friend. Andres used violence with no regret.

"My sister was young, Andres. Surely you have forgiven her initial lack of insight? She has proven to be a devoted wife to you."

"Yes, she has. You would do well to insure it stays so, my friend. I would hate for her to become an only child." Andres smiled. "My anger is as great as my love. She would suffer greatly if any indiscretion would cause her to lose the brother she loves."

Marc thought of the young man Patricia had loved long ago, Luis. Marc had been forced to watch Andres' torture Luis dispassionately until he was a mass of abused, bloody flesh. When his death did not cause Patricia to welcome Andres's advances, the psychopath had begun killing any man who approached the beautiful young girl. Finally, she had capitulated—"Beauty" submitting to the "Beast."

Marc put his water down carefully, keeping the tone of his voice neutral. "Indeed, you have no reason to doubt her. She loves you greatly."

"Do you have the report yet from Dominic about her activities last night?" Andres demanded.

Marc reached into the briefcase sitting on the patio next to him. He pulled out a folder and handed it to Andres, carefully schooling his expression.

Andres took the folder and opened it, examining the photos with interest. "She arrived in New Babylon safely. Dominic says they were met by the clinic's limousine. She had the treatment there and then went to the hotel, where she had dinner in her room."

"It was kind of you to allow Patricia to go," Marc offered, nodding, with a practiced look of gratitude on his face.

"She's a beautiful woman. I see no problem in preventative maintenance of that beauty. Giamo clinics are the only ones that provide that treatment, according to Patricia. She has wanted to see New Babylon for quite some time, as well. You know how she loves history, especially that ancient stuff. It bores me. I dislike being without her for the week. But I trust Dominic to see to her security."

Andres brushed his pant leg with his hands and let out a sigh, signaling that he was done with the conversation.

"You need to get going. I know you have the flight to Mexico this afternoon to meet with our friend there. Please give her my best regards."

Marc backed his chair from the table and stood up. He shook his brother-in-law's hand, took his briefcase, and headed into the house. The coolness of the air-conditioned interior made him shiver. It seemed so dark inside after the bright outdoors.

As he crossed the large gallery into the entrance hall, he was surprised to encounter a young woman being escorted up the curved staircase. Andres was usually more discreet. Patricia would be furious. *Maybe I shouldn't tell her,* he thought. *But somehow she knows what is going on—and then she's furious that I'm trying to keep things from her.* He stood in the middle of the hall and watched the escort open the door to Patricia's bedroom and lead the woman into it.

While Andres was obsessed with Patricia, he was not faithful to her. Marc thought his brother-in-law took delight in leaving evidences of his indiscretions. Every time Patricia found such evidence, Marc feared her anger over the betrayal would be her undoing. No one ever told off Andres Quinteros. Or if they did, they only did it once.

2

NARBONNE, FRANCE

Angelina Rogov walked through the grounds of the Renaissance fair on the outskirts of Narbonne, France, stunned. She had never seen anything like it. Canals, complete with gondoliers perched on shining black gondolas that looked right out of a postcard from Venice, snaked through the park. The two-hundred-acre fair had grown from a small festival in the 1990s to the multimillion-dollar theme park in front of her now.

Angelina turned down a cobblestone street to her right. The buildings were close enough that she almost could stand in the middle of the street and touch one on each side. She moved aside as the Queen of the Fair, attended by her ladies-in-waiting, swept past. A jester pranced behind them, bells jingling. If Angelina weren't in such a precarious situation, she would have enjoyed exploring the fair. But she had to find Mitch and Charlie.

At the thought of Mitch, her mouth tightened and her stomach turned over. He was the one responsible for the trouble she was in now. She saw a small sign indicating that the hotel he was staying in was just down the next street. Seeing a costume shop as she turned the corner, she realized that it might be a good idea to blend in with the fair's performers. A costume might allow her greater access to the grounds and facilities. She chuckled at the thought that wearing a large, voluminous Renaissance gown would actually make her inconspicuous.

Entering the shop, Angelina moved quickly to the rack of

dresses.

The saleswoman, dressed in period garb, approached and spoke to her in French. When Angelina shrugged and smiled helplessly, the woman sighed. "English? Would you like some help, mademoiselle?"

"Yes, sorry. So many people here are in costumes, I thought it might be fun to have one too."

"Very well, I think this green velvet would be lovely with your dark coloring. Let me show you the dressing room, mademoiselle."

Angelina entered the dressing room. The salesclerk hung the dress on a hook and offered to help her into it.

"No thanks, I think I can manage," Angelina replied.

Angelina closed the curtain to the small cubicle and sat down on the stool, grateful for a moment of rest. She stared at herself in the mirror. Her dark hair hung in curling layers around her face. The freckles on her cheeks, which she had hated as a child, actually added a lively counterpoint to her large, brown eyes.

She stood up, took off her jeans and T-shirt, and pulled on the gown. It was lower cut than she had thought. She wanted to blend in, not attract attention.

"Excuse me," she called to the clerk, poking her head out of the cubicle.

The clerk walked over with a smile, "Yes?"

"Um, is there some kind of scarf or something I can put here?" She swept her hand across the dress's neckline. "I just don't feel comfortable with the neckline this low."

The clerk stepped back to look. "Why, mademoiselle, you have a lovely figure. Why not show it off?"

Angelina smiled. "Maybe another dress?"

Shaking her head disbelievingly, the clerk said she would find something. Angelina let the curtain fall back. In a minute, a white gauzy scarf was thrust around the side of the curtain. Angelina arranged it around her neck and stuffed the ends into the bodice.

ONE WILL BE LEFT

Much better.

She left the dressing room, found a floppy leather satchel, and went to the cash register to pay the clerk. Afterward, she stuffed her clothes into the satchel and returned to the street. Now she had to find Mitch and get Charlie back, without being found by the police.

New Babylon, Iraq

The Italian ambassador to the World Union, Luca Giamo, ended the World Security Committee meeting with a quote from Emerson about peace, and the room erupted in thrilled applause. The charismatic ambassador was a favorite, a rising star among the ambassadors who made up the World Union. Despite his youth, Ambassador Giamo was considered one of the wisest and most prudent among the leaders of the new one world government.

The ambassador from the United States stood up. "Ladies and gentlemen, may I have your attention, please?" He waited for the room to quiet. "It is my greatest pleasure to announce that the World Security Committee has unanimously elected Ambassador Giamo as chairman of this committee." Again the room erupted in applause and shouts of acclamation.

Luca Giamo stood up again at his place at the long table. Graciously, he accepted the role of chairman of the World Security Committee. His speech was enthusiastic and hopeful for the success of the World Union and for peace for the nations of the world.

The meeting ended, and Luca headed out of the paneled room, stopping often along the way to accept congratulations for his new role in the governing body. As he left the committee room, his assistant, Stephen Amona, joined him. Stephen took the briefcase Luca was carrying and murmured that the limousine was waiting outside. They descended the single staircase leading from the second terrace of the capital building, an impressive ziggurat built to resemble the ancient monument found in Ur, an ancient city in southern Iraq.

They came to the first-level terrace and took the stairs to the left, which led to an outside door and a limousine parked next to the curb. The driver was waiting and opened the door for the ambassador. Stephen went around the back of the car and opened the other door for himself.

Settling in, his eyes met his master's. "World Security, Luca! Things are moving along quite well. Are you pleased?"

Luca shrugged his shoulders. "I am pleased, of course. My Father's plans are unfolding just as he foretold." He looked out of the window to his left.

The limousine lurched forward. Stephen reached out his hand to steady the briefcase between them.

He noticed Luca rolling a small gold object between his fingers. It was a tiny cross.

"Where did you get that, Luca?"

Luca looked down at the cross with a smirk. "It belonged to someone." He turned his head and looked out of the window again, balling the cross in his fist.

Stephen struggled to keep his face from showing his fear. The housekeeper at the ambassador's villa had a young daughter who had gone missing. Security forces had searched the city and surrounding area for her over the last two weeks. Stephen was certain he had seen a small gold cross on a chain around the young girl's neck. *Surely not,* he thought. He tried to control his breathing.

Luca spoke softly, "Did you know there is a reason the Temple of Ishtar was one of the first to be rebuilt? My Father wanted to ensure that the goddess would be honored. In ancient times she was known as the Queen of Heaven. Because my Father is mighty among the ancient ones, Ishtar is the compliment of his glory.

She has been known by many names. She was Inanna long before she was Ishtar. Long ago, the Jews worshipped her as the Queen of Heaven. She once told me they would bake little cakes to her for her festival."

Stephen thought a moment, obviously confused. "I don't know much about ancient history, Luca, but I thought the Jews only worshipped one deity."

"The Jews!" Luca spat out. "They were the reason she was bound. They are thorns in the sides of all who are in heaven and on earth. It is due to their stubbornness that my Father has been thwarted all of these millennia, Stephen."

"What do you mean?"

"When they worshipped Inanna as the Queen of Heaven, she grew very powerful. Some were moved in their devotion to her to secretly offer their firstborn children."

Stephen shifted in his seat and turned his face toward the window, drawing in a long, troubled breath.

Luca continued, noting Stephen's increasing distress with satisfaction. "As you know, there is a small faction among my Father's kind who oppose him and his rule. Their leader established himself among the Jews as their god. He is very powerful. My Father has explained to me that the Jews are the source of this opposing leader's power. Once they are destroyed, my Father will be able to overcome this false god who calls himself Jehovah. Then all that mankind has yearned for in its utopian dreams will become manifest under my rule, for my Father has promised me that the kingdoms of the world will be mine to rule, for his glory and for mine. We will be without opposition. There will be peace on earth and in the heavens."

Luca turned his face back to look at Stephen. "Tonight, you will see my glory revealed. Of course, a small sacrifice is required." He gestured to the front of the limousine. For the first time, Stephen noticed that someone small was sitting in the passenger seat next to the driver, Nico. It was a young girl.

ONE WILL BE LEFT

Demilitarized Zone, Alleghany County, Virginia

It was dusk, and in the thick woods the shadows grew more ominous. John Foster stuffed the rabbit he had just retrieved from the trap into his satchel. He would have to move quickly to get back to the compound in time. Blake had strict rules about everyone being inside and locked up during the night.

"Bastard," John muttered as he trotted through the woods. Sticks and pinecones crunched beneath his feet. He missed the comforts of New Babylon: showers, climate-controlled rooms, and plenty of food, not to mention his wife, Elena. He had flown into Washington, DC, months ago in order to interview the head of the Anti-Globalist movement, otherwise known as AG. Blake had been his contact. Through a series of alarming situations, they had ended up here, somewhere in Alleghany County, Virginia, in the midst of a war between the World Union and the rebels.

Somehow, Blake had been prepared for the complete chaos that had swept across the United States after Anti-Globalist forces attacked the capital city. Well before the AG became a violent terrorist organization and a well-trained resistance army opposing the World Union, Blake had purchased the retreat where John was now a virtual prisoner. It had turned out that Blake was some kind of a double agent for the World Union, providing the new government with inside information about Anti-Globalists and the movement's mysterious leader, "Mr. Smith."

John thought back to the fateful night in Washington, nine months previous., when Blake had helped him escape an attempt by AG forces to kill him. Blake's wife, Ashley, had warned her husband about the plot. The night before John and Blake met, she'd had a disturbing dream, the details of which had been sufficient to convince Blake that he and John truly were in danger.

ONE WILL BE LEFT

They had avoided the attempted attack only to return to Blake's house and find Ashley severely beaten by AG thugs. In the turmoil in the city that followed the terror attacks by the Anti-Globalists, Blake and John had escaped with Ashley and her mother to the remote cabin in rural Virginia.

It seemed like war had broken out all over the country John formerly had called home, though in reality, parts of the United States were relatively peaceful. AG forces had taken over Washington, DC, and whole portions of Virginia and south along the eastern seaboard. Maryland and points north were pretty much in the control of World Union forces, from what John and Blake could tell.

John stumbled over a rock and fell forward onto the ground, cursing softly as he rocked back on knees. A twig snapped nearby, and he froze. Forces from both sides had been skirmishing in the vicinity for the last week. John prayed that what he had heard was World Union forces and not the Anti-Globalists. He could surrender to the World Union forces and find himself on his way back home to New Babylon and Elena.

A man's dark hand clamped down on his shoulder, startling him. He stifled a yell. A voice whispered in his ear, "You are about to head into an AG patrol, John. Follow me."

John stood and turned, expecting to see Blake. The man in front of him was well over six feet tall and exuded strength. He was wearing dark clothes and had long braids pulled back neatly at the base of his neck. Definitely not Blake.

"Who are you? How do you know my name?"

"I am Talin. The rest can wait until we are away from that patrol. Follow me, John."

The man turned and strode briskly in the direction opposite the one in which John had been headed. John followed, trying to move as quietly as the tall figure in front of him. They ran for about twenty minutes before Talin stopped. Breathing hard, John wiped sweat from his face with the bottom of his shirt. Talin did not seem winded. It was dark now, except for the light cast by the moon.

ONE WILL BE LEFT

"We are safe here for a while," Talin said softly.

John sat on the ground. He still had the bag with the rabbit inside it slung over his shoulder. He flung that to the ground next to him.

"Who are you? How do you know my name?" he demanded, concerned about the possibility that he was now worse off than before. *Why did I follow him?*

Talin sat on a boulder and regarded John without speaking. John began to feel uncomfortable under the man's gaze. It was like he was being evaluated and did not quite meet some standard.

"Well?" he snapped. "I followed you out here without question. How do you know my name?"

"I know more than your name, John Foster. You have a choice before you. It is a choice you have continued to put off, but that you must soon make."

"What choice is that?" John snapped.

"Perhaps you are not ready. My duty is to get you to her."

"To whom?"

Talin stood up. "To my charge, your wife."

"Your charge? Where is Elena? Who are you?"

Talin smiled widely. "I am her guardian."

John stood up quickly. "You mean a bodyguard? Is Elena nearby?"

"She is not near, but we are going to her."

Just then, an explosion erupted a few miles away in the direction they had come from. John cursed. It looked close to the cabin where he and the others had been hiding for the last few months.

"We have to go back and help," he said. "There are two women and a teenage boy there. We can't leave them to the Anti-Globalist forces."

Talin shook his head. "No, we must go now."

John insisted, "Haven't you heard what they do to women? We have to try and get them out of there." He turned to go, but Talin restrained him, holding his arm.

"I am sorry, John. They are already gone."

ONE WILL BE LEFT

"What do you mean, gone?"

"Your friend, Blake. He saw the forces surrounding them and panicked." Talin let John's arm drop. "There is nothing you can do."

"He killed them? They're dead? How do you know all of this? Why should I believe you?"

"They were killed, but they live. I saw their spirits ascending. Two women, with their guardians."

John looked up into the eyes of the man speaking. He did not look crazy. Then John remembered the story Elena had told him when they were in Washington after the disappearances. She insisted that an angel had visited her and shown her that the only way to God was through faith in Jesus Christ.

"You said you are Elena's bodyguard. Is that right?"

"You said that, John. I told you that I am her guardian."

"As in angel?" John asked hesitantly.

Talin nodded. "Yes. Now we must go. More forces are moving into the area. Follow me." He turned and began to walk swiftly through the trees. John followed, his mind racing.

Lake George, New York

James smiled, closed his eyes, and gave silent thanks. It had been a perfect day. The crisp autumn air was invigorating. He sat on a log, watching David and Jack throwing rocks into the lake. Jack and Bess had suggested an outing after church, and a few other families had joined them. They had canoed over to Phantom Island after outfitting everyone with life jackets. James had made sure that his son's jacket was on securely before he put the toddler in the canoe with Bess. James and Jack had paddled their canoe across the lake, David exclaiming his delight the whole way. The boy's joyful squeals were like medicine to James' soul.

Lunch had been enjoyable. Some of the men had tried their

luck fishing, and the lake trout made a delicious addition to the fresh apples, homemade cheese, hard-boiled eggs, and biscuits that Bess had brought along from their stores.

James watched his son in amazement. *His son.* He could not believe how much his life had changed because of that little person tossing rocks into the lake. He had left the priesthood in shame to marry David's mother, Cynthia. However, at the wedding reception, her family had disappeared—along with so many other Christians around the world—and what had followed was painful for James to think about.

After Cynthia had given birth to David, her true colors had been revealed. James learned that she had seduced him, becoming pregnant, with the only intent of gaining access to the small fortune his parents had left him when they passed away. She had never loved him. When the beleaguered court system had finally ruled on the validity of her father's will after his disappearance, Cynthia was awarded his estate, worth millions of dollars. Empowered by her newfound wealth, she had left both James and their son, David, never looking back.

James still could not get over how gullible he had been. Good friends had tried to warn him, but he would not listen to their warnings. He had fallen head over heels for Cynthia and his passion had blinded him.

Still, David was evidence that God could bring something incredible out of his failure. James sighed and silently thanked the Lord again for his son and this place. When he had been arrested in the pulpit of his church months before, he'd had trouble keeping himself from panicking. He'd heard rumors about Christians being targeted by the World Union, but he did not consider that a possibility in the former United States until it was too late.

His holding cell had been a miserable place, and he'd worried constantly about David— and about his other believing friends. No one would give him any information. After miraculously being led out of prison in a scene reminiscent of the book of Acts, James, along with his rescuer, had made their way to the campgrounds in the Lake George area. Their hosts, Jack and Bess, sheltered James and a number of other Christians in the small cabins at the campgrounds. Once those cabins were filled, others moved into homes left vacant in the small town near the camp. Some people were led there by friends who knew of the place, while others were told in dreams to go to the place prepared for them in the mountain resort.

The sunlight sparkled on the lake surface. Trees were shrouded in their autumnal magnificence, and the brilliant yellows and oranges enthralled James. This had always been his favorite time of year. Harvest. His eyes traced the summit of Black Mountain across the lake. He was thankful. Because of Bess and Jack's wisdom and experience, the small community of about two hundred believers was well stocked for the coming winter.

Two of the younger men were struggling in an arm-wrestling match at one of the picnic tables to his left. James chuckled as Eric won, hollering a victory howl in celebration. Eric was one of the men in their small community whom James had dubbed "technocrats." It was Eric who had developed a safe means for believers to communicate on the Internet. He had ingeniously created a place within the Deep Web where users could connect without being tracked or monitored. With the rise of the World Union, all the member nations had agreed to allow a central control to be set up in New Babylon that regulated access and content on the Internet. Any websites considered dangerous, subversive, or divisive were taken down, including anything overtly Christian. Eric and the other technocrats had worked tirelessly throughout the past year and a half, transferring helpful sites to their own secret network, hidden in the "Deep Web" of the Internet, called 3:16.

James considered the threshold of history on which they stood. He was intently aware of their need to be as prepared for the onslaught as they could. He prayed daily, even hourly, for wisdom, insight, and protection. In his heart, it seemed as if he could feel the rise of evil's power.

3

NARBONNE,
FRANCE

Angelina entered the ornate Tudor-style hotel and found the lobby filled with patrons and staff dressed in full Renaissance regalia.

"Welcome, my lady!" An older man dressed in a red and black doublet sauntered toward her, his hands behind his back. "May I help you?"

"I'm looking for my husband and daughter, actually. Can you tell me what room they're in?"

The man patted her shoulder and led her over to the counter. "Certainly. What is your surname, madame?"

"Dixon."

He quickly typed the keys on the computer keyboard in front of him. "I can allow you to call the room, madame, but for security reasons, I am not allowed to give out room numbers. You will understand?"

Angelina thought desperately. She didn't want to give Mitch time to react to her being here. "Thank you. I will call the room." The clerk dialed the number and handed the phone to her. Suddenly, out of the corner of her eye, she saw a man walking towards the elevator. *Mitch!*

She handed the phone back to the clerk. "He just walked in! Thank you!" She hurried toward the elevator, arriving just as the door closed behind him and noting that the floor indicator lights stopped at two. She saw the stair door to her right and quickly dashed through it, running up the stairs with her skirt hitched high.

ONE WILL BE LEFT

She opened the door to the second floor and carefully looked. Mitch was just opening the door to a room on the middle of the floor. *But where was Charlie?*

Anger raged through her body, giving her a feeling of righteous power as she strode down the hallway and banged on the door. It opened, revealing the very surprised figure of her estranged husband. He stared at her, motionless, obviously unsure of what her next move might be. Angelina balled her hands into fists and started flailing.

Moving more quickly than she did, Mitch forcefully grabbed her arms, pinning them down and restraining her. He pulled her into the suite, shutting the door behind them with his foot.

"Well, I didn't think I'd see you here." He shoved her onto the couch. "I thought you'd be in jail by now."

"Your plan didn't quite work out. Where's Charlie?" Mitch laughed and bent over and kissed her. Angelina hated him even more. Even now, she felt her traitorous body respond, tempting her to give in to her emotions as she always had with him. Instead, she pulled back her head and repeated her question.

"Oh, I had the nanny take her to the petting zoo. I have a few things I need to work on." He bent close again and whispered in her ear, "We have the suite all to ourselves for a while."

Memories flooded her mind—terrible memories. They filled her with disgust. Pain. Anguish. Loss. All of these strengthened her resolve.

"I just want to talk, Mitch. Maybe we could have a glass of wine and just talk."

He kissed her lips softly. "Sure," he said, "I'll get the wine." He walked over to the bar and deftly opened a bottle of pinot noir. When his back was turned, Angelina took out the small vial she had stuffed in her bodice and tucked it into the crevice between the couch cushions.

Mitch came back and stood in front of her. "Here you go," he said, handing her the stemless crystal glass. She took it, and he settled next to her on the couch to her right, holding his glass of wine in his hand.

"So, how did you get away from the police?" he asked.

"A friend found me first. I guess that ruins your plans. How could you do that to me, Mitch?" She purposely allowed herself to sound needy. He loved it when she begged him because he relished the power he had over her.

"You have to understand, Angie. I've enjoyed our time together, but to be honest, you can be a drag. I wanted Charlie and freedom." He ran his hand along her thigh. "You know how I love variety. Life is short and I'm way too young to be tied down to one woman."

Angelina could not help the tear that fell slowly down her cheek. She felt discarded. Unwanted. Mitch leaned forward and sensually licked it off with his tongue and then kissed her again. "You do have the softest lips," he murmured.

She pulled away. "Why this? Why not just ask me for a divorce?"

"This way, I get custody of Charlie. I could have had you killed, but you're the mother of my child. A dead mother becomes like a saint or an angel in the mind of a child. I don't want Charlie to harbor tender feelings for you. I want you totally out of her life. If I play this right, Charlie won't want anything to do with you—a mother who gets drunk, runs down a teenager in the street, and runs away." His hand ran down the side of her face gently and traced her jawline.

The phone rang and Mitch got up reluctantly from the couch and picked up a cell phone from the kitchen counter. Angelina could hear a woman's voice on the other end. Mitch looked at her and mouthed, "Just a minute," before he went into one of the bedrooms and closed the door.

Hastily, Angelina fished the vial out from the cushions and poured the contents into his glass. She sat back nonchalantly just as the door to the bedroom opened.

ONE WILL BE TAKEN

Mitch tossed the phone on the counter and sat back down next to her. She was struck again by his roguish smile.

"No hard feelings, babe?" He picked up his glass of pinot and drained it. He always did that with his first glass of wine.

Angelina stifled a smile and went on the defense. "About what—you drugging me and putting me behind the wheel of a car? Or taking my daughter away from me?"

"My friend should be here in an hour or so. We have enough time to say good-bye properly, Angelina." He caressed her as his blue eyes began to look a bit blurry. She had been worried it would hurt him, but now she didn't care. He was disgusting.

Angelina stood up, dropping the vial back into her bodice as she moved away from the couch. She watched, fascinated, as Mitch's head began to nod and he slumped back, unconscious. She slipped quietly into one of the bedrooms and saw Charlie's teddy bear on the bed. She picked it up and stuffed it into the leather satchel still slung over her chest. Then, opening the suitcase on top of the dresser, she found some clothes and took those as well.

Back in the living room, she saw Mitch's wallet on the counter by the wine bottle. She helped herself to the money inside, along with one of his credit cards. It would take him a while to notice it was missing.

Sorrento, Italy

"So, what's the prime minister going to do?" Kate asked, rolling over and poking her husband of one week in the side. The sun was just setting outside and she could see the bay of Naples through the balcony doors. They were staying in a nineteenth-century villa built right on a volcanic cliff. The view was incredible, but nothing compared to her new husband. *Kate Benari*, she thought triumphantly. She had considered keeping her maiden name; after all, "Kate Havenstone" was a renowned reporter. However, Michael Benari was even more famous. He was the archaeologist who'd found the historical Ark of the Covenant, and taking his last name might help her become even more of a household name.

Michael grinned at her and shrugged. "It doesn't matter what the prime minister does, Kate. You should know that. The world hates Israel. He can't win, no matter what he decides to do."

"Perhaps if Israel actually joined the World Union, rather than just sending an ambassador? Maybe then your nation would have a part in determining your own future."

"You know, Kate, that the attempt to invade our nation met with no more than protests from our allies. It's evident to anyone that God defeated the invaders. He's the one who destroyed the Dome of the Rock and led us to find the Ark.

"We will not forget so soon. The World Union is weak and unwieldy and cannot last long. The prime minister is wise. It's a difficult time, but Israel has known nothing else since her birth."

"The World Union seems to be effective in meeting the needs of its citizens, Michael. They've brought peace, for the most part, to those third-world nations. People's needs are being met. When disaster strikes, help is given. We are working together for the first time in history."

"What about the Anti-Globalists? They're fighting this unification process in every way possible. Look at the east coast of the United States, for instance. What about other places throughout Europe and Africa where they are fighting?" He continued arguing. "The threats from the opposition are real and pernicious. National identity runs strong in many places, and many people resist the World Union. There's no way Israel will join it; she has fought too long and hard for a place of her own in this world."

"The Anti-Globalists will be beaten, Michael. With the new one-world currency, a unified army, and the commitment of member nations, this united government has the ability to even the playing field throughout the world. Some people just can't let their national alliances go. But that will change. Our children will view themselves as world citizens, not as nationals of the UK or Israel. The days of nations as we knew them are ending. That is a fact. Israel will have to enter into the new age that the rest of mankind is entering."

"Now you sound like Billings Mason, that miracle-working leader of OneFaith. I think you've done too many interviews with him, love."

Kate snorted, "Hardly. There is something oily about that man. I am just saying, Michael, that despite the disasters hitting our world—maybe because of them—for the first time we have a real chance for real peace. We are working together, meeting needs and helping one another. Our children will have the chance to grow up never knowing the devastations of war."

"Now that is the second time you have mentioned our children. We just got married; I want you to myself for a while, Kate." He rolled over in bed and swung an arm possessively around her.

Kate brushed the hair back from her eyes, smiling seductively at her husband. "Enough political talk for now; this is our honeymoon! We should enjoy every moment. Didn't you make reservations for dinner at that charming place we saw yesterday? I'm hungry."

"I can help you with that!" Michael bent over and kissed her slowly. Dinner could wait.

Rome, Italy

Billings Mason stood at the window of his office in the Vatican. He no longer wore the papal robes, having been successful in the last year in merging the remnants of the Catholic Church system into the new systematic religion of OneFaith. The World Council of Churches had helped prepare the way for many of the larger mainstream Protestant branches of Christianity to also embrace the universal movement. Many Buddhists and Hindus also had been brought into the fold. His miracles convinced the masses that he was leading them toward real truth and a unified faith.

He had traveled extensively throughout the world in the last year, establishing local leadership in the former nations that comprised the World Union. Some had been severely affected by the violence of terrorism or the devastation of natural disasters. In each place, thousands flocked to hear him speak, to have him heal their wounded and sick. He was the last prophet, the voice calling out in the wilderness for all to prepare for the one who would lead them into a new world of peace and prosperity.

Billings recalled with pleasure how easy it had been to gain popular support for OneFaith. Membership worldwide exceeded two billion now. He only half listened as his assistant droned on, listing the treasures they were liberating from the vaults inside the Vatican. He recalled some of the art he had seen earlier this morning. There were certain pieces he would have to make sure were crated and shipped to his office and home in New Babylon.

"Your Holiness," his assistant interrupted his thoughts. "Would you care to hear the rest of the list? Or would you like to prepare for your message tonight?"

Billings turned toward her. "I think that is enough for now, Lydia."

"Yes, Your Grace, of course." She left the room, shutting the heavy door behind her.

He turned back to look over the view below on St. Peter's Square. He heard a soft knocking at the door. "Come in."

"Most Holy Father, please forgive me for intruding on you."

"Matthews, I'm surprised to see you. I thought you were leaving for Paris today." Billings strode across the room, stretched out his arm, and raised the former cardinal, who was kneeling. Billings noted that the man was dressed in a simple black cassock. He had not seen the proud Cardinal Matthews dressed so humbly before.

"How may I help you?" Billings asked gently.

"Your Holiness, I confess I am very troubled."

ONE WILL BE LEFT

"Please, come sit down. You look pale. Would you like some water?"

"No, thank you, Most Holy Father." Matthews sat down, trembling as if he were cold.

Billings sat across from Matthews in his favorite chair. He crossed his legs, noticing a scratch on his new Berlutis. He frowned.

"Is there a problem?" he asked as he looked up from his shoes to the cardinal.

"Your Holiness, I have had a revelation and made a discovery." The former cardinal spoke quickly, his voice breaking like a teenage boy's. Billings saw a bead of sweat roll down the man's ashen face.

"What would that be, Matthews? And I do wish you would put aside those titles. You know that in OneFaith we are all spiritual guides. Each of us has been given a different gifting and role to fulfill, but we don't want the artifice of rank to separate us from one another."

"Yes, Your Holi—I mean, Prophet Mason."

"That's better! Now what did you come to tell me? A revelation and a discovery, I believe." Billings stood up and strode over to the small bar. Taking the crystal stopper out of one of the decanters, he poured himself a scotch. After sipping it carefully, he sat back down and waited.

"Last night I couldn't sleep. I was troubled because I felt I was losing the respect I deserved as a prince in the Church. Then, it was as if a light was turned on in my very soul! I saw it all so differently. It was like a mirror was turned back on me, and I didn't like what I saw. I didn't see a 'prince.' I saw nothing but the arrogance and pride that has characterized my entire life.

"When your predecessor disappeared with so many of the world's Christians, I thought they had just attained a higher level of spirituality, like they were more acceptable to God or something. But last night, I took out my Bible. I read the Gospels, really read them, for the first time in years.

ONE WILL BE LEFT

"As I read Jesus's words to the Pharisees, my heart felt heavy. Jesus may as well have been talking to me! I've deceived myself—and worse, I've deceived others. I repented in tears, Your Holiness. I gave my life to serve the Lord Jesus Christ. That's my revelation." He spoke quickly, sweat pouring down his face.

Billings drained his glass and set it down on the table between him and Matthews. "And what was your discovery?"

"This morning, when I was going over the accounts for the churches in Lorraine, I discovered that a good portion of the profits from the sale of Church property was going to other accounts—some in Liechtenstein, others in Zurich. I haven't been able to trace them all yet, but I had to let you know, Holy Father."

Billings stood up and stretched. "Have you told anyone else yet?"

"No, Most Holy Father. I felt I must first share it with you. You see, I have been guilty of doing the same. I am here to repent before God and you." He raised his tear-stained face to look up at Billings.

"Let me get you some water, Matthews." Billings walked back to the bar, tucking in his shirt in the back. He poured some water into a glass with his right hand, while pulling open a small drawer with his left. Making sure his body hid his movements, he quickly opened the small vial of clear liquid and added some to the water.

"Here you are." He handed the glass to Matthews. Matthews took it and drank the water, putting the empty glass on the table.

"Thank you," the man said. Almost immediately, he fell sideways on the couch, grasping his throat. Billings watched the white foam cover the cardinal's lips.

"You are most welcome."

Billings went to his desk and dialed his assistant's extension. "Lydia," he said with an urgency that would have sounded authentic to all but the most discerning of listeners, "call for help immediately. Cardinal Matthews has had some sort of seizure!"

He walked back to the couch and looked dispassionately at Matthews' face, contorted in death. Billings noticed some papers

ONE WILL BE LEFT

protruding from a pocket in the cardinal's black robe. Billings pulled them out and placed them on the table.

"You know, Matthews, it was just fortunate I had that poison hidden in that drawer. I've been able to do incredible things—heal people, even raise the dead—but I don't have the power to end a life at will. The poison was something I thought of a few weeks ago. Just in case.

"You are the first person I've killed." He pushed the body with his foot. "Oddly, I feel elated. Truly, I didn't know what to expect. Seeing you twitch and the life fade from your eyes was empowering. Luca has described it to me, but until now I've been hesitant.

"Your 'revelation' made it so easy to put that poison in your water." He walked back to the bar and poured himself another scotch before returning to his seat. Crossing his legs, he continued speaking to the corpse. "You see, Matthews, I knew all about your pilfering. Why do you think I put you in charge of liquidating our French resources? You were a pawn I controlled, until your 'come to Jesus' moment."

He got up and walked over to Matthews's body, again nudging it with his high-priced loafer. The body was still limp; it would be a couple hours before rigor mortis set in.

"There must be some better way to dispose of these Christian turncoats. Some manner of death that will make others afraid of turning to the enemy," Billings continued. He reached across the table and picked up the papers he had pulled from Matthews' pocket. It was a list of the resources they were liquidating in France.

"Why of course! The French had a very effective manner of execution, didn't they, Matthews? I will have guillotines built at the appropriate time! It's efficient and bloody enough to keep others from following the enemy."

He guzzled the scotch. The gold of his ring gleamed in the light blazing through the large windows. He set down the glass and removed the papal token, examining the image of the fisherman and the words *Petrus II* engraved on the surface. He rolled the ring between his fingers thoughtfully.

"We will need some sort of symbol for Luca's followers. Some way they can identify their loyalty to him. Oh yes, I know what your Bible says, Matthews. Who hasn't heard of the 'mark of the beast,' 666?

"But that is what could make it a most effective symbol," he mused, continuing his conversation with himself. "By taking it, Luca's followers will be completely turning their backs on the enemy and showing how little regard they have for such myths. What a brilliant idea!"

The door opened and Lydia came into the room with several emergency personnel. They quickly ascertained that Matthews was dead and removed his body on a gurney.

"Would you like me to do anything else for you, Your Holiness?" Lydia asked. She remained surprisingly composed.

"Yes, would you have my lunch brought in here, please?"

She nodded in agreement and left the room, closing the door behind her.

Billings picked up the phone and dialed Stephen Amona. He wanted to inform his spiritual mentor about the financial increase he would be siphoning off into the private accounts Amona had set up. Those accounts would help fund the next shift in world power, a shift that would end with their young master, Luca Giamo, gaining leadership of the world. Billings also wanted to share his epiphany regarding the mark of allegiance. He would design a symbol for Luca's followers to have tattooed on their hands or foreheads, somehow including the infamous dreaded "666." Amona would appreciate the irony of co-opting the symbol from the book of Revelation.

4

ST. MICHAELS, MARYLAND

Brant Hughes watched uneasily from the shore, leaning into the tree that camouflaged him from the boats patrolling the waterway. He moved a bit more to the left as he noted a command boat speeding toward him from the north, probably from Annapolis. There were enough military boats in the area to heighten his concern.

He and Elena had been in St. Michaels for almost a month now, after coming here to keep Olivia safe from her uncle's plot to kill her. Brant's lips tightened as he remembered promising her father, DC, that he would guard the toddler with his life. That was almost two months ago, in New Babylon.

Brant had met DC Bond in the US Marine Corps. After serving his country for four years, Brant had left the Corps and entered into the field of private security, working in some of the most dangerous places in the world. Those experiences had harmed him in ways he had not understood until later. When the opportunity came to join the New Babylon Security Force, Brant took it eagerly. New Babylon's cutting-edge technology made the security force position even more alluring.

New Babylon amazed him; no city in the world could compare to it. There were ancient temples and palaces, fountains of sparkling water, palm trees swaying in the heat, and the amazing re-creation of the famous Hanging Gardens, which made the city a true oasis in the desert. The place was old and new at the same time. He had loved his spacious apartment in the city center and his generous salary. All of New Babylon was equipped with the newest technologies for living, security, and entertainment. He had loved his new life there.

DC had been working in New Babylon for a while when Brant arrived, and had welcomed his old friend enthusiastically. Often they would meet for a beer after work, watch a game on TV, or discuss work. New Babylon had been a haven for Brant after all of the turmoil and violence he had witnessed—until the first body was discovered outside the city limits.

Brant slid down to a squat, his back against the tree. The memories still made him physically ill. That first body had been found just after millions of people disappeared from the earth. New Babylon had not been impacted by the disappearances, though many other member nations in the World Union had been severely afflicted by the loss of so many citizens. Crime was rare in the city, as well, so the murders were shocking to the few who knew about them.

The first body had been posed with arms crossed, covered by a silk sheet. She had been about seven months pregnant when she was murdered, but someone had cut the baby out of her uterus. Strange markings were carved into her flesh—it was evident she had suffered greatly before bleeding to death. It looked like she had died elsewhere and then been transported to the strategic spot outside of the city, because the ground around her was untouched and clean. No trace of the baby was found.

Every month afterward, another body was discovered, always female. To the horror of many, the victims were sometimes young girls. The bodies were always carved with the same strange markings. No matter how hard the security teams investigated, they could find no leads to a killer. There were no prints, no fibers, nothing to indicate where the women had been killed. Even the sheets with which they were covered with yielded no helpful clues. Frustrating Brant more was the command from their supervisor that the murders be kept quiet. No one wanted the citizens of New Babylon disturbed by the knowledge that a crazed serial killer was targeting women on a monthly basis for ritualistic killings.

Brant began drinking more, especially at night alone in his apartment. There was not enough beer in the world to drown out the images of the tortured women, so he turned to bourbon. He got to the point where he was taking between fifteen and twenty shots of liquor a night. It was hard to get up for work, and he did a poor job when he finally dragged himself there. DC had tried to question him, but Brant pushed his friend away.

One morning when Brant did not show up for work, a worried DC went to his apartment to check on him. If he hadn't, Brant would have died from alcohol poisoning. After Brant was released from the hospital, DC took his friend to his mother-in-law's apartment, where she and DC took care of him for the next few days. Thanks to DC's adept cover-up at work, Brant did not lose his job. That intervention had saved not only Brant's job, but his life.

Brant wiped the dampness from his eyes as he remembered how his friend had cared for him. The deep conversations they had had over those few days led Brant to see the dramatic change in DC that he'd only glimpsed in their casual get-togethers before. He agreed to go with DC and Elena when they met with other Christians. Through those meetings, Brant found what he had been missing.

Months later, when Teo found out that she, DC, and their daughter were in danger, Brant had not hesitated return the favor. Now, as he sat on the cold ground thousands of miles from New Babylon, he regretted that he and DC had not been able to foresee the escalation of fighting on the east coast of the United States. What had started as random terror attacks was now all-out war between the Anti-Globalists and the World Union forces.

Brant heard more boats behind him. Now he knew why supplies were not coming into the few local food depots the government had set up for residents.

He grabbed the backpack at his feet, took out a bottle of water, and drank. Recapping the bottle, he replaced it carefully in the pack, and stood up. It would take him a few hours to make it to the house. It was time to think through their options, because staying in St. Michaels might not be as safe as they had thought.

New Babylon, Iraq

The television flickered in the dark room. It was never off, never silent. A constant video loop played which Arturo guessed was about twenty minutes long. The first few days he'd seen it he was filled with horror and disgust. Someone had taped the ritualistic torture and murder of many women, quite a few of whom had been pregnant. Those scenes were especially traumatic to watch. Masked men, dressed in long robes and wearing surgical gloves, repeatedly performed a bizarre ceremony. The women screamed, but no one ever came to help.

Arturo tried to get the nurse to turn it off, but he still had difficulty talking. When she finally understood him, she stepped back with a worried expression and told him the television was not on. She gave him a sedative. When he woke again, the wretched video was still playing.

He closed his eyes, but he could not block out the sounds, even if he covered his ears. He could move his arms now, as well as his left leg. No one came to give him therapy, so he did it himself when the staff was not in the room. After some time, he finally realized why he was here. He was a prisoner.

A scream from the video made him wince. He was certain one of the men in the video was his son, Luca. Luca visited him regularly now, and Arturo was convinced that his son was monstrously insane.

Arturo had no idea how many days he had been trapped in this room. There were no windows and the only door out was locked. Late one evening, he took the chance that no one was monitoring him, though the light on the camera in the corner blinked red.

ONE WILL BE LEFT

He was still weak, but he managed to crawl to the door and pull on the handle. Lacking the strength to drag himself back onto the bed, he lay on the cold floor for the rest of the night. In the morning, the nurse came in with some food and was appalled to see the ambassador's father on the floor. She and an orderly put him back into the bed. From then on, he was restrained at night—for his own good, they told him.

He heard the door open and he turned his head away from it.

"Arturo, why turn your face away? Are you feeling stronger today?"

Arturo turned back his head and saw Luca standing by his side. His son's wavy blonde hair was brushed back from his forehead; his frank blue eyes looked down on his father with concern. Luca's face could only be described as angelic—a perfect specimen. Arturo could feel his heart rate rising. He tried to speak, but to his horror found he could not even make a sound.

"I thought we could have one of our talks." Luca sat on the stool next to the bed facing his father. "I hope you are enjoying the video I left you."

Arturo tried to speak, but his tongue would not move.

"Oh, I'm sure you are wondering why the staff isn't bothered by it. The thing is, Father," he mused with a mocking tone, "they don't see it. I don't want them to see it, so they don't. I told you, Arturo, there are many things I am able to do that would astound you." He smiled and crossed one foot over the other.

"Things are going well outside of this room. I am very pleased. North America is struggling to adjust to the loss of so many millions of people. Those great hurricanes that hit the Carolinas and Florida in the US wiped out entire communities. The Anti-Globalists are causing more problems farther north. Did you know there was actually an outbreak of smallpox in New York City?" Luca lounged casually on the stool and continued to speak to his father.

"With America devastated by the disappearances, natural disasters, and the war between the Anti-Globalists and the World

Union, my plan to shift power from West to East can be implemented. There is no more superpower. I'm sure you are not upset, are you? No, you never cared much for the Americans."

Arturo heard the most hideous part of the video in the background. He closed his eyes again. Luca chuckled.

"You truly are such a hypocrite, Arturo. Why should that bother you? You advocate aborting fetuses that are imperfect. I believe you even performed a few such abortions yourself. That child had a genetic disorder, so we offered him as a sacrifice. My Father was quite pleased with the dual sacrifice of mother and child."

Arturo moaned. Luca put a hand over the older man's mouth and removed the hand with a flourish. "You may speak now, Arturo. You have my permission to say what you would like."

"How can you do these things, Luca?" Arturo was stunned that he could suddenly speak clearly again. His thoughts quickly evaluated the possibilities. His inability to speak had nothing to do with his own physical condition! There was something clearly supernatural going on here.

"What are you doing, Luca? What are you doing to me? You used to be so gentle and kind. You need help. You must stop!"

"I have been given powers from my true Father, Arturo. Powers you cannot even fathom. I need no help. I am honoring my Father in the manner he requires. There is no gain without sacrifice. Every major step in mankind's evolution required a revolution of some kind, Arturo, with blood spilled in the process. It is the way of this world."

Though Arturo knew he could now speak if he wanted, he lay in silence, shocked and terrified.

"You must understand what is at stake here, Arturo. Not this one world government ruled by delegates from the nations, seeking peace through unity. This government is merely a stepping-stone for me to take my rightful place. Mankind has not evolved to the place where people can rule their baser instincts. Already, the leadership of the World Union is corrupt. You would not believe the money that has been siphoned off by the various 'ambassadors.' It's deplorable."

Another scream came from the television. Arturo closed his eyes and felt his hands begin to tremble.

"There have been other men in the past who've had a dim view of what was required to prepare the world for the next level of development. Some of them were even great, inspirational leaders. Hitler almost had it, but he made the mistake of leading the initial change. He was not the one, though. My Father has told me that only I can take charge. Only I can rule the world and effect true change.

"I have orchestrated much of the chaos that will bring the world's population to the place where people are ready to receive their savior. It is only a matter of time until they know utter devastation. Unlike Hitler, I come offering peace and safety. People are becoming desperate throughout the world, Arturo. I wish you could see it."

Arturo moaned again. "Luca, my son..."

"Oh, I am not your son, Arturo. Let's get that straight right now. I am the son of Lucifer, the bright morning star. Don't you understand? I am more than human. My life was not instigated by the manipulations of Stephen Amona. No, he is my Father's servant. He did as he was told, and my Father interacted with the elements Stephen prepared.

"My Father told me there were others like me once—strong, beautiful, and wise brothers and sisters born to the daughters of men. Those legends of strong men—like Hercules—sons and daughters of the gods in ancient times are based on truth, Arturo. But my Father's enemy destroyed them all."

Arturo listened in terrified fascination as Luca continued.

Luca got up and paced around the small room. "I am the firstborn of many brethren who will rise up once I am in power. You helped make that possible, Arturo. Did you know that? Stephen has created many others. They are not like me, of course. I am the only child of my Father. But there are others who are like him, and they too have reproduced. For centuries the enemy prevented them from touching human females, but your work made it possible for them to again seek to populate this world with their own kind."

"What are you talking about, Luca? I don't understand." Arturo shook his head to clear it. Luca's words made him feel like vomiting.

"The women who came through your clinic. You know, the ones who wanted the designer babies you offered? Stephen prepared the eggs. While the enemy kept my Father's kind from having relations with human women, preventing them from reproducing, your procedures allowed them to do so again. Thanks to you, the world will be repopulated with a new kind. Not with the weak men and women that exist now, though some of them will be kept to serve. We must have servants, after all.

"There will be world peace when my people take their rightful places under my rule. They walk among the world's people, many of them in positions of authority or influence. Cream rises to the top, don't you know?"

Arturo interrupted, "You are saying that aliens of some kind have been spawned using my clinics? My procedures? And you are going to take control of the world?"

Luca chuckled. "I wouldn't call them aliens, though they have been called many things. They were here before mankind. I suppose you could consider them aliens if it's easier for your little mind.

"When the enemy created your puny race, it was an affront to my Father's people. You have no idea how poorly you compare to them."

"Who is this enemy you keep referring to? What are you talking about?"

"Brace yourself, Arturo. You are in for a shock. The enemy is the being you would refer to as 'God.'"

"Luca, you are delusional. All of this is some manifestation. I am afraid that you are—"

Luca chuckled scornfully before Arturo could finish. "That is mankind's greatest weakness! You have deluded yourselves into believing you are masters of your own destiny. You rejected the One who created you and thereby sealed your doom. He was your only chance in this battle. My Father has shown me glimpses of the weakness of mankind through the ages. From the beginning, you were easily led. You have been led by my Father to reject the very idea of God, and now your rejection has led mankind to the place where my people will rise and dominate you."

"Who is your Father?" Arturo stuttered. The name Luca mentioned earlier sounded vaguely familiar, but the older man's mind was still foggy.

"I told you. Lucifer."

"The devil?" Primeval fear instantly coursed through Arturo. Devils and angels, gods and saviors were ideas he had consigned to the heap of superstition. Men of science, of intelligence, knew better, yet as Luca spoke, Arturo realized the young man was not insane. He had to be telling the truth. What else explained his rise to prominence at such a young age and the abilities and powers he possessed? Arturo felt a rising terror inside him. *Everything I have built my life on was a lie,* he thought. *I am a prisoner. There is no way out.*

The volume of the television seemed to grow louder. A woman's screams penetrated his thoughts, causing Arturo's horror of Luca to intensify. What was Luca going to do to him? Violent, horrific images raced through his thoughts. He groaned as his panic mounted. Luca bent over the bed and kissed Arturo gently on the forehead.

"I must go." The young man touched Arturo's mouth again and left the room. Arturo tried to call after him, but he was unable to speak.

ONE WILL BE LEFT

Quinteros Estate, North of Houston, Texas

Marc Jafari closed the mahogany door to his office on the main floor of the mansion and saw his sister, Patricia, sitting on a chair by the fireplace, waiting for him. She was dressed in black lace, her dark hair loose in massive curls that framed her beautiful face. Her clear green eyes caught his gaze.

"So, is Andres safe?" she inquired softly.

"Yes, his jet landed while you were still sleeping. He is at the new Anti-Globalist headquarters. You will love the irony."

"What is that?"

"They are set up in the White House."

He was gratified to see her smile. His sister was as ambitious as her husband, and it was difficult to please her. In the siblings' younger days, Patricia had worked hard to keep them fed after their mother died. Ecuador was far from their homeland, but they had managed to survive without the help of their relatives far away in Iran.

"Wonderful." She clapped in delight. "What is that package on your desk?" she asked.

"It is something I ordered our general in Washington to send me once the city was completely under our control. At my suggestion, Andres insisted you have it."

He walked over to the desk and picked up the leather box. He handed it to his sister with a gallant bow and waited.

Patricia held the substantial jewelry box, weighing it in her hands. She placed it on her lap and opened it carefully. Inside was the famous Hope Diamond. She gasped.

"Marc!"

"Would you like me to help you put it on?"

She handed him the necklace and pulled her dark hair off of her neck. Marc clasped the necklace gently.

"Once the Anti-Globalists had control of Washington, DC, I

made sure our men took control of the museums. I had this set aside especially for you, my beautiful sister."

She gasped, "Is this what I think it is? How did you get this? I've seen this at the Smithsonian."

Patricia went to the mirror that hung between the two windows, admiring the diamond sparkling brilliantly around her neck in the sunshine. Stepping back, she gazed at her reflection. Dark hair cascaded artfully from an emerald clasp, perfectly framing her classic features. The tremendous diamond seemed to radiate with a peculiar glow that made her tremble slightly.

"What about the curse?" she asked.

Marc joined her by the mirror. "There is no curse. We will be victorious, Patricia. When Andres is made leader of the North American sector, you will have everything you have wanted since we were children."

"I love this." She gestured to the diamond. "You knew I would. Thank you!" She hugged him tightly.

"You deserve it. I know what you have suffered to keep us safe after Mother died." He looked at her intently. "Andres is not an easy man, I know, but he worships you."

Patricia steadily met her brother's gaze. "Sometimes a woman would rather be loved than worshiped."

Marc looked around nervously. He had closed the door, but one could never be sure with Andres. He put his finger to his lips warningly. Patricia laughed.

"I've made sure that there are no listening devices in here, Marc. Don't worry."

"You need to be careful. You know what he is capable of doing." He spoke in a whisper.

"I know better than anyone. You have no idea of what I have to endure—what I have endured. But we will have everything I promised you when we were children. Not just wealth, but power. Real power. Andres is the means to an end." She fingered the diamond thoughtfully as she confided in her brother, reassuring herself as well as him.

"I never could stand him. He was always so cruel. Do you remember what he did to Raphael? He made me watch." She sat down on the couch, and her brother sat at her side. Andres had claimed Patricia as his own when he first saw her working at the bakery in their neighborhood in Quito. At sixteen, Andres was already well-known in the city, and was feared greatly. No one was certain about how he made his money, though everyone assumed he sold drugs. The authorities watched him, but they could never get enough evidence to arrest him. Patricia had been only fourteen at the time. She worked twelve-hour days trying to earn enough money to support herself and her younger brother. There was never quite enough. But soon, Andres changed that for them.

"I remember," Marc said quietly.

"Sometimes I dream about it. In my dreams I start to tell Andres that I think Raphael looks like an angel, but I stop myself. Or somehow I am strong enough to stop Andres before he…mutilates him."

Marc put his arm around his sister and pulled her in. Raphael was not the first man Andres had hurt, or the last. Patricia had learned to be very careful.

"I used to pray for God to intervene, but I gave up long ago. There is no God. We have to make our own way in this world. Over the years, I have learned how to control Andres, without him realizing it. But even so, I am a prisoner. I cannot go where I want, do what I want, say what I want."

She pulled her head back and looked up at her younger brother. "Do you remember when that man came to see Andres? That Stephen Amona?"

"The old man? Yes."

"Andres told me he represents a very powerful man, a man who is positioning himself to take advantage of the failure of the World Union when it is eventually defeated. Once that happens, the attacks and skirmishes will only increase. This man has been orchestrating unrest all over the world, using other men like Andres.

ONE WILL BE LEFT

Andres has been working for him for years, following his plans. Did you know that?"

"I did not."

Patricia smiled at him. "When Andres told me about this, it occurred to me that I could stop him. I could use his, shall we say, 'lack of restraint' to destroy him. When it comes to me…" Patricia's voice trailed off suggestively as she tried to find a delicate way to express her thoughts. "…he can lose all control at certain times. I don't know how exactly, but I am confident that the opportunity will present itself to me to take advantage of that weakness."

Marc shook his head. "You must be careful, Patricia. If Andres had any idea of what you are thinking…"

"He doesn't. And I've made sure my position is even more secure now. While I was at the clinic in New Babylon, I met Mr. Amona. He came into the treatment room to speak with me. We had an interesting discussion about Andres and my future life with him. It was quite astounding. Did you know our mother was a client of the Giamo clinics?"

"No. When was this?"

"When she and Father were living in Iran. They had difficulty conceiving, so Father sent her to Rome to the clinic there. I was the result of that visit. I learned quite a bit from Mr. Amona. What he shared with me gave me an idea about insuring my safety."

She got up from the couch and went to the desk. Picking up an envelope, she turned back and handed it to her brother. Curious, he opened it. Inside was a sort of photograph. It looked medical.

"What is this?"

"It's a sonogram. Andres has made several comments about an heir. I've prevented the possibility of conception until now. A son will ensure my security—and yours."

"It doesn't even look human. How can you be sure it's a boy?" Marc asked.

"It was tested before it was implanted. Believe me, I had to be certain. It is a boy. Mr. Amona is very efficient. Once I'd decided, it only took a few days for the necessary preparations. It's really quite an amazing process. This is my child, not Andres's. He will believe it is his, of course. There is no reason not to. I have been completely faithful to him all of these years. But he will spawn no children from me. That monster will not reproduce any more of his kind if I can help it."

Marc looked at his sister in amazement. She had put up with the psychopath for years, always carefully manipulating him to her own ends. One of Andres's greatest faults was that he never saw the bitter hatred Patricia held for him. "When will you tell him about your pregnancy?"

"I will tell him when we get to Washington. One side benefit to this pregnancy is that he will stay away from my bed."

"How can you be sure of that?"

Patricia smiled. "Doctor's orders. I made sure that there are sufficient test results included in my file to ensure Andres will not take the chance of losing his heir. He will stay away. He has his other women anyway."

She hugged her brother. "I can't tell you how happy this makes me! I finally see a way for us to get rid of Andres. This is the first step. Mr. Amona has given me great hope, Marc. There is a plan—a greater plan—in place and I am a part of it. I am to meet the very man you spoke of. I'm not sure who he is, but Mr. Amona assures me that I am an integral part of his plan. Soon, you and I will have everything we dreamed of. You'll see, little brother." She affectionately rubbed the top of his head and escorted him out of the room.

Amman, Jordan

DC looked at his watch again. The previous night he had arranged for a taxi pickup at the hotel at ten. It was almost eleven. Teo sat curled up in a chair sipping her bottle of water. She looked very pale.

ONE WILL BE LEFT

After the fight with Sam, they had grabbed their backpacks and left the apartment quickly. Sam had been so unreasonably angry that DC worried he would contact World Union authorities and tell them that DC and Teo were still alive.

DC had sold their car for cash early that morning. They did not have much after paying his contact, a Chechen immigrant, for new documents. Still, they needed to do their best to remain unnoticed. After settling in at the hotel, DC had found a small shop and bought a bottle of hair dye for Teo. Her red hair was now dark brown. Unfortunately, the smell from the chemicals made her nauseous. She had vomited repeatedly, even after rinsing out the color. Morning sickness was a lot worse this time, and they had no access to doctors.

DC stood up when he saw the cab driver enter the lobby.

"Hey, sweetie, let's go." He reached down and picked up Teo's bag, carrying it for her to the cab. She followed just behind him, keeping her eyes down.

The cab driver offered to take their bags, but DC declined. He made sure Teo was comfortable in the back on the passenger side before slipping into the seat next to the driver. Jordan was a fairly safe place to be but he found himself wishing he had a gun. Maybe the man who would provide their new passports could help him with that. He gave the driver the address and asked him to hurry. While it was less than a two-hour drive to Jerusalem, crossing the border would be time-consuming because it was Saturday, the Sabbath. He had no idea where they would find a place to stay in Jerusalem.

He reached his right arm back between the seat and the door, found Teo's knee, and squeezed it affectionately. He smiled when she put her hand over his and squeezed back. He didn't want her to know how worried he was that Sam would contact the World Union police to let them know Ambassador Giamo's sister and her husband were still alive and in Amman. DC knew his wife well enough to know how afraid she already was of being discovered and dragged

ONE WILL BE LEFT

back to Babylon.

After a short drive, they pulled up to the small apartment building. DC asked the driver to wait for them. He and Teo walked up the old, metal stairwell to the second floor in silence. He knew Teo was afraid Sam had turned them in, and if that were the case, their future was uncertain. He knocked on the door and they waited. No answer. He knocked again.

"He knew we were coming, DC." Teo looked alarmed, her eyes filled with panic.

"He did," DC said while trying the door handle. It turned, so he carefully pushed the door open. "Stay here," he told Teo.

She shook her head emphatically. "I am coming with you," she whispered.

The couple tiptoed into the apartment. It only took them only a minute to look through the small studio. DC's contact, Kadyrov, was not there. That was strange, because DC had just talked to the Chechen before they'd left the hotel. DC had used him in an investigation for Diplomatic Security years before when the Islamic State of Iraq was a threat to the US mission in Jordan, and the man had been extremely dependable, even going undercover as a mercenary to ferret out possible threats to the US special ops working in that country.

"Where do you think he went?" Teo breathed unevenly.

"I don't know, but I don't like this. We've got to get out of here."

DC noticed stacks of envelopes on the small desk by the kitchen sink. He began to search through them quickly. He found his and Teo's new last name written in pencil on one of the brown envelopes and opened it up. Inside were Israeli passports. He studied them carefully.

"These look good. What do you think?"

Teo inspected them thoughtfully. The passports looked worn, used. She opened one up and saw DC's photo.

"They look authentic, I guess. I just hope that we can make

the cover story work. I mean, posing as Jews just seems a little... weird...to me."

"I think it will work, sweetie. Really. Israel is only letting Jews immigrate now. The fact that I'm biracial means I can pose as the son of an Ethiopian Jew. We can go to Israel for "aliyah" and no one will expect me to speak Hebrew. Israel is one of the only nations to refuse to join the World Union. We'll be safe there. Once I find a job, we can figure out how to get your mom and Olivia back."

"We should go." Teo turned to the door and cried out in alarm. DC spun around to see Kadyrov standing in the doorway with a pistol pointed directly at Teo's head.

"It is unwise to enter a home without an invitation, my friend." The man entered the apartment and closed the door with his foot, keeping his gun pointed toward Teo. "And you seem to have helped yourself to something, I see."

DC stepped in front of Teo, blocking the path between the gun and his wife. "I paid you for the documents up front, Kadyrov. I'm sorry. We knocked. No one answered. We had to leave soon, so when I found the door unlocked, we came in."

"You paid up front? No, my friend, you misunderstand. That was a deposit. Now you pay the balance, or hand the documents back to me."

DC prayed quickly, asking God for a miracle. "Listen, Kadyrov. We had a deal. I have kept my part. I paid you the full amount already." He could feel his blood boiling inside of him, making his head hot and his palms sweat.

The bearded man drew closer to Teo and stroked her cheek with his free hand. "I could take payment in kind," Kadyrov said, leering at Teo.

She did not flinch. "Get your hand off of me."

DC reached out slowly and wrapped his right arm around Teo, pulling her behind him while simultaneously shifting his weight to his right leg. He spun to his right, extending his left leg in a roundhouse kick to Kadyrov's head. The Chechen crumpled to the ground, dropping the gun as he fell.

DC bent over to make sure the man was unconscious, picked up the gun, and shoved it into his waistband.

"Let's go, now." They scrambled out of the apartment and made their way quickly back to the waiting cab. DC bundled Teo into the backseat and got in the front passenger side by the driver.

"We're ready. Thanks for waiting." He tried to speak nonchalantly, slowing his breathing. "With any luck, we can make it to the border and cross today." He heard Teo's whispered, "Amen," behind him.

Amman, Jordan

Prince Zayd bin Asem was about to accede to the Hashemite throne as the new king of Jordan, a position the young man had never anticipated would be his. At birth he had been tenth in the line of succession, but in the past few years all the men before him in line to inherit the throne had either died of natural causes or been declared unfit to rule the kingdom. Under the old constitution, he would have been deemed unfit as well.

However, since the Allied invasion—or rather, the attempted invasion—of Israel, things were very different in Jordan. In one day, thousands of soldiers had fallen dead, so many that it had taken months to bury the corpses in mass graves. Israeli specialized environmental engineers were still disposing of the treacherous cache of weapons left in the wake of the attempted attack. Many attributed Israel's rescue from the armies mounted against her to an act of God. Multitudes had turned to faith in Jesus Christ after experiencing dreams and visions of the Savior proclaiming that He was the one true God. The nation of Jordan had experienced what could be called nothing other than a spiritual transformation.

The previous king, Hussein bin Abdullah, had found faith as well, having seen Jesus in a dream. King Hussein enacted new laws and procedures for the kingdom, which included the changes in the constitution that enabled Prince Zayd, a believer in Jesus Christ, to become king after Hussein died. Hussein had only been king for a short time, having taken the throne just after the disappearances.

"What do you think, Majesty?" Zayd's Uncle Rasheed asked. Rasheed had just finished sharing his concerns with his monarch.

Prince Zayd sat down heavily across the table from his uncle. He nodded to a servant, who filled his small cup. Zayd picked up the cup in his right hand, sipped the mixture of cardamom and coffee with appreciation, and watched as the man carefully poured a cup for his uncle.

"It sounds as though this Billings Mason is indeed the False Prophet. Are you sure, Uncle, that the Antichrist is to come from Rome?"

"Yes, I am certain. Since my mother disappeared and I put my own faith in the Lord Jesus, I have researched almost continually. She told me many stories when I was a child, Zayd. Once I knew that Jesus must be God, I thought those stories might have validity. I am sure they do, Your Majesty. I believe that God has made you king of Jordan for this dark time. You must guide our people and keep us free from the clutches of the Antichrist."

"But Uncle, the World Union is working! The world is experiencing a new peace; nations are actually cooperating. Maybe we will have a time of respite before the end comes?"

"My nephew," Rasheed smiled sadly, "I do not think so. Already the unrest caused by the Anti-Globalist forces grows in ferocity. Their ranks swell in number throughout the world. This one world government cannot last. There are strong men gaining power regionally. They will rise to dominance."

Prince Zayd set his spoon down deliberately. "I must know for myself what is to come, Uncle. I must pray and ask the Lord for wisdom. Jordan is a small nation. If we are to make a stand against this evil, as you say, we must be prepared.

"When I was born, this nation was Muslim. After the failed

invasion, after the destruction of the Dome of the Rock, after the disappearances of Christians worldwide, Jordan became a predominately Christian nation. My cousin, the previous king, also turned to Jesus Christ and followed Him in the few months before his death. My cousin chose me to be his successor. It's a role I never wanted, as you know, Uncle."

Rasheed closed his eyes and nodded his head. His silver-gray hair shone like a halo in the morning sunlight pouring through the window behind him. "We must pray, Your Majesty. We must fast and pray and ask God for the wisdom you need. I see you as a light in the darkness that will soon overwhelm the earth. The time of God's wrath is about to begin. His judgment will be upon the whole world. Jordan will be able to stand, with His help."

Prince Zayd bin Asem sighed, raking his hand through his hair. "Who can stand in the times we are about to enter? Will you pray for me, Uncle?" He bowed his head and prayed silently as his uncle prayed for him aloud.

After thanking his uncle sincerely, Zayd bolted to his own apartment in the Raghadan Palace to prepare for his coronation.

About twenty minutes later, Zayd straightened his tie carefully and checked his reflection in the gilded mirror. Usually his valet assisted him, but today was an important day and he wanted some time alone before the coronation ceremonies began. He flicked off the light and left the bathroom.

He sat on the silk tufted sofa and put his head in his hands. After a few minutes of quietly praying, he began to review his speech. *My declaration, really,* he thought. He was going to recall the Jordanian ambassador from the World Union headquarters in Babylon, and the Jordanian soldiers who were part of the World Union forces. His uncle was convinced that a prophecy about the singular world government splitting into ten kingdoms was about to be fulfilled. The split was happening, and there could not be much time before Israel made some sort of treaty with the man called Antichrist. Zayd wanted to insure his people's safety, and it seemed best to him to

ONE WILL BE LEFT

insist on Jordan's autonomy.

In the past year, the World Union had dominated its member nations. Although the Anti-Globalists continued to battle World Union forces, the one world government was effectively changing the world's power structure. AG forces hotly contested the former United States more than anywhere else in the world, attempting to gain power. Many stoutly patriotic Americans still believed in the "land of the free and the home of the brave" and Zayd sympathized with them. Spending summers with his mother in her homeland, Zayd had enjoyed his time in the United States.

Now he was responsible for his own people and he would not allow them to be enslaved to the Antichrist. After much prayer, he was convinced that now was the time to act before the Evil One gained more power. If Uncle Rasheed was right, then it seemed Ambassador Luca Giamo must be the Antichrist. It was a startling thought that Zayd found difficult to absorb. He had met the young ambassador at an inaugural party when the World Union was instituted. Luca Giamo had been charming and self-deprecating, and Zayd had noted nothing menacing or evil about him.

The prince looked out the window at the beautiful cityscape surrounding him. It was peaceful now. It was hard to imagine all of the horrors that would soon be unleashed on the world. *Heavenly Lord, please help me rule. I need wisdom. I need courage. Please spare my people.*

"From the moment you first began to pray, I was sent out to give you aid."

Zayd's ears rang at the gently spoken words, and he quickly turned his gaze from the window toward the voice, which had come from a tall man standing by the bookcase to the prince's right. The man seemed to have appeared out of nowhere. His white robe glimmered with light and his face radiated. Zayd had never seen such pure beauty. An overwhelming sense of peace washed over him and he fell from the couch to his knees before the awesome being in front of him.

ONE WILL BE LEFT

"Do not bow before me, Zayd. I am Chamuel, a fellow servant of the Most High. I am here to answer your questions and to give you instruction from the Lord."

The tall man held out his hand and pulled Zayd to his feet. "I was delayed. I had to battle the Prince of Jordan and needed the help of Michael."

Prince of Jordan? Michael? Zayd was confused. "Who is this prince? I was the prince. Today I officially become the king. I have no male relative left to have that title."

"I speak of principalities and powers in the heavenly realms. There are battles raging in the heavenlies, Zayd, even as there are battles raging on the earth. You are not at war with mere flesh and blood, you realize, but against rulers and principalities in the heavenly realms. The 'prince' of Jordan is a fallen angel—a demonic ruler with jurisdiction over that territory given to him by the god of this world, Satan," Chamuel explained. "And Michael is one of Yahweh's greatest warriors."

Zayd nodded with understanding as he gazed wonderingly at the angel in front of him.

"The prince of darkness is growing in impudence, but the time is soon coming when the Lamb will open the scroll, for He is worthy."

"I just read that in the book of Revelation this morning!" Zayd exclaimed. "It is my earnest desire to serve Jesus and lead my people through the tribulation to come. I need wisdom from the Lord to do this, and I have been fervently praying."

"The Lord heard your prayer and sent me with His answer. Now we have much to discuss. You will provide for the Lord's people a place in the wilderness, where they will be hidden from the evil one, the abomination of desolation, who will soon be revealed. You must make sure there are provisions for them, and for your own people. The Most High will keep you sheltered in the palm of His hand. He will sustain you. You must remain steadfast and stand firm. You were born for such a time as this, Zayd. The Lord Himself has appointed you."

In amazement, Zayd again knelt, but not to the angel before him. He prostrated himself on the floor, praising the Lord God Almighty and his Savior, Jesus Christ. As tears of joy ran down Zayd's cheeks, the angel who stood before him looked on in awe. The children of Light were able to commune with the Most High in a manner angels were not, and each time he observed one of the Lord's saints, he was struck by the wonder of it.

Virginia

The angel Talin sat with his back against a tree, watching over his charge as he slept. It was Talin's experience with humans that they responded in fear to him when his true identity was revealed. John Foster, however, had not become fearful. Instead, he had asked a lot of questions as they traveled. Yet, despite Talin's responses, the man was still not ready to commit himself to the Lord. Talin never failed to be surprised at the ones who refused the Savior. He hoped this man would not end up being one who refused the pardon.

John stirred and opened his eyes. "Don't you ever sleep?" he grumbled.

Talin did not respond.

"Oh, I guess an angel doesn't need to sleep like a man," John said, uncharacteristically irritated. "How much farther?" He sat up and stretched. It was just about dawn and he was anxious to get to Elena. Talin told him she was at DC's parents' home in St. Michaels, Maryland.

"Today we find a boat. We should be able to get there by dusk." Talin stood and began to walk through the crunchy leaves along the trail. The chill in the autumn air did not affect him. He wondered if his charge was irritable because he was cold, but decided it was more likely the result of the struggle going on in his soul.

He was also angry about the deaths of the women. Over the centuries, Talin had noticed that with those the Holy Spirit was moving, anger of some kind often preceded their acceptance of the Savior.

John stood up and picked up his backpack. Slinging it over his shoulder, he followed. He caught up with Talin.

"I have some questions for you," John said.

"I will answer."

"How do you know if Elena is still there?"

"I have heard from another who is watching. We may have trouble. There are signs that the enemy is at work."

"The World Union, or the Anti-Globalists? Who is this enemy you talk about? I'm not sure which one you are against."

Talin looked down at the man who walked next to him. The man was bold and confident. Talin wondered how confident John would remain as the fabric between time and eternity unraveled.

"Our enemy is not flesh and blood. There are spiritual forces of wickedness that wage war against the saints of the Most High and against His people, Israel. You call them demons. They were once among us, sons of God, but they rebelled, following the one you know as Satan."

Incredulous, John exclaimed, "You mean the devil? The devil is at work trying to hurt Elena? He has nothing better to do? Seriously, you expect me to believe all this?"

Talin was silent.

John sighed and continued, "Okay, so what signs do you mean? Are there hexes around the house? Things falling off the walls?"

Talin stopped walking and raised his arms above his head. John saw his lips moving, but heard nothing coming from them. Talin dropped his arms and looked down at the skeptical man before him.

"Like an unreasoning animal, you rail against that which you do not understand, John Foster. So I have asked the Most High and He has granted my request. Now behold, see with spiritual eyes the world as it is."

ONE WILL BE LEFT

Talin touched John's shoulder and immediately John fell to his knees. He gasped as he looked at Talin, glowing with a glorious light. Then he looked behind the angel and saw dark figures moving through the forest. They were as beautiful as Talin, but their faces were terrible to see. His heart raced in fear as he saw one that was closer than the others. It was dressed as a soldier, its long dark hair swept back from a face filled with rage and hatred.

Talin noted John's fear but did not acknowledge the demon that strode behind the man. That one had been there all along. It had been with John Foster for many years.

"It rages because it cannot get closer while I am here," Talin explained gently, keeping his hand on John's shoulder. "Fear not, the Lord has allowed you to see, so that seeing you may believe."

John could feel the warmth from Talin's hand enveloping him. His fear dissipated, even as another dark warrior galloped past them on a horse, its long golden hair flowing.

"What must I believe, Talin?" John struggled to ask.

"You must confess that Jesus Christ is Lord, and believe in your heart that God raised Him from the dead; then you will be saved. For with the heart one believes and is justified, and with the mouth one confesses and is saved."

John considered for a moment all the evidence he had seen since the disappearances of the world's Christians. Many had been left, though. Why?

Although John had not spoken out loud, Talin answered him. "Not everyone who claimed to call Him 'Lord' truly believed. You see those around us?"

John looked at the demon just behind Talin, and at the others around them, then looked up at Talin. "I do."

"They believe Jesus is the Christ." Talin spoke loudly, with authority, his voice booming like thunder. At the name, the demons around them began to wail and shudder as if they were being physically tormented. Talin held John's gaze. "Son of Adam, they believe, but it does them no good. Salvation through Jesus Christ is offered to mankind alone. It is not only intellectual assent you need, John Foster. You must take the gift of God's forgiveness for your sin, purchased at a great price, the blood of His Son. Do you see your need? Will you bow your knee to Him?"

In a moment of painful clarity, John saw the true state of his innermost self and he cried out in anguish. *What have I done?* he thought. There was nowhere to hide as instance after instance of his guilt was opened before him. He began to weep, overwhelmed by the exposure of his true self.

"There is no need to hide in the Light, John. Will you bow in faith and commit yourself to the Savior?" Talin asked.

"I don't see how He would accept me. If you knew what I have done, what I am…"

"He knows. Will you accept Him?"

Talin bent a knee as John whispered, "Yes," and the angel rejoiced. He bowed his head in wonder as John's faltering words addressed Jesus Christ as Lord for the first time. The angel heard angry shrieking from the demons that watched as John Foster entered the eternal Kingdom of Light, a newborn son of God.

5

TOULON, FRANCE

Angelina carried her sleeping daughter onto the ship and, swaying along with the vessel's movement, followed her cousin, Kurt, through the narrow door to her cabin. He closed the door behind her as she put Charlie down carefully on the king-size bed.

"This is nice," she whispered, pulling the down comforter around her peaceful daughter. "I don't know how to thank you for doing this. I don't know how you even arranged it."

Kurt shrugged his shoulders. "I know a lot of people in the cruise industry. I worked quite a few years on this route, and someone owed me a favor. My room is across the hall if you need anything. We should have no problems." He touched her arm reassuringly. "There's no way Mitch can track you here. You didn't use any credit cards, did you?"

"No. What do we do next?"

"We can get off the ship in Rome for a shore excursion. Anti-Globalists may have caused quite a bit of upheaval in other parts of the world, but Europe has been fairly stable, thanks to the World Union. We should be pretty safe. I have a friend we can stay with in the city until I can get some new travel documents for you and Charlie."

"I don't know how I can thank you," she said again. Her voice cracked with emotion. "If you hadn't found me, I would be in jail right now."

Kurt put his arm around her. "Angie, I'm just glad we were

ONE WILL BE LEFT

supposed to meet at your place for a late dinner. Mitch is a bastard."

"I'll come knock on your door when it's time for lunch. Why don't you lie down and rest with Charlie?" He planted a brotherly kiss on her forehead and left the cabin.

Angelina locked the door behind him. She lay down on the bed and cuddled her sleeping daughter, refusing to take their tender snuggles for granted. She kissed Charlie's soft curls and smelled the sweet scent of baby shampoo. If Kurt had not sensed something was wrong that day and broken in through the back window of the house Angie and Mitch shared in Versailles, the police would have found her the next morning and arrested her. Who knew if she would ever have had the chance to hold Charlie again?

The whole ordeal was still fuzzy in her mind. Angie and Mitch had spent the day in Paris with Charlie, just walking through the city, shopping around and stopping for lunch. Mitch had a business dinner, so when her cousin had texted her earlier in the day to say he was in town, she had invited him to a late supper at their home. In the rush to get their toddler fed, dressed, and in the car, she had forgotten to mention her plans to Mitch.

Mitch must have drugged the glass of wine he gave her when the nanny took Charlie up for her bath. Angie couldn't remember much after that. Kurt told her that when he got to the house, the lights were all out and no one answered his knocking. He had just turned to leave when he noticed the car in the driveway at the side of the house. When he saw the front bumper was smeared with blood, he went around back and peered through a window. To his shock, he could see her on the couch, an empty bottle of tequila on the floor next to her.

Thank God he was there! Angelina thought as she recapped the recent events in her mind. And now he was here again. It was Kurt who had helped her locate Mitch and Charlie and had supplied her with the drug to sedate her conniving, abusive husband. Now he was helping them escape and establish new identities.

It was ironic, really. Kurt had been the family black sheep

since his early teens when he took his father's new sports car and credit card on a road trip to Vegas. He had left the United States after high school, and no one heard from him for a few years, until he suddenly resurfaced as if nothing had happened.

Kurt was always cagey when it came to answering questions about how he made his money, but he did well for himself, whatever it was. Angelina had always been his favorite cousin, but when her family emigrated to Israel, they had not returned to the United States to visit very often. She and Kurt had become reacquainted a few years ago at his sister's wedding. Since then, he had made a point of visiting her whenever he was close enough to do so.

Angie knew that Mitch would come after her. He didn't like to lose anything and would do whatever it took to get Charlie back. As she lay in the comfortable bed with her daughter, Angelina thought carefully about her options. She could hide out for a while with Kurt, but that was not the best kind of life for a toddler, and Mitch would eventually find them. He had the time and the resources. She needed someone who had the ability to protect them. She closed her eyes and thought for a few minutes about her options. Then it hit her. Papa.

She hadn't seen her father in four years, not since she'd run away with Mitch. *He was right,* she thought. Her father had tried to talk her out of marrying Mitch, to no avail. Papa disliked everything about Mitch, foremost being that he was not Jewish. Not one argument her father could come up with had swayed her, though, not even his declaring that if she went through with the marriage, he never wanted to see her again.

Charlie moaned and kicked at the comforter Angie had placed over her. At least I got Charlie out of it, Angie thought. That was one thing she could not regret. For Charlie's sake, she would beg her father to take her back. Surely he couldn't refuse, not if he felt in the slightest way about her the way she did about Charlie. She hugged her daughter and whispered a prayer. If there really were a God, maybe He would help her.

ONE WILL BE LEFT

Lake George, New York

James finished typing in the last phrases of his online sermon on his laptop. He would send an electronic copy to Eric, who would then upload it onto their website. The generator was only run for an hour each day, long enough to upload and download the information they passed along and received, and to charge the few electric devices they needed, like his laptop.

Jack was a shortwave radio operator. He would use the time they had power to catch up with contacts throughout North America. He had found out the previous week, through a friend in New York City, that a smallpox outbreak was devastating the population there. World Union forces had the city blockaded, and nothing and no one could go in or out.

James had addressed part of his sermon to the people in that city, hoping to give some small measure of comfort. Eric could tell how many people were viewing their website; it was averaging two million hits a day from all over the world. The fact that Eric was able to keep their sites secure and hidden from World Union's Internet censors was a testimony to his skill, but also to God's provision.

A knock on the door interrupted James' thoughts. Before he could say a word, the door opened. Andie Singleton stood in the doorway, holding David on her left hip. The small boy struggled to get down. Andie let him down, and he ran to his father.

"Da-dee!" the toddler squealed and threw himself at James. James caught him up into his lap.

"Hey, Buddy! Did you have fun with Andie?"

David nodded thoughtfully. "Da-did helped, Da-dee."

"That's great, Buddy!" James caught Andie's eye, and they both smiled. David was the youngest child in the community, and there were many who loved to spend time with the little boy. Andie

ONE WILL BE LEFT

was a preschool teacher who was fiercely passionate about children. She took David three or four times a week to play. David was only two, but Andie had already taught him most of his letters and their sounds.

With an excited grin, Andie held up a plate she had in her right hand. "We made some cookies, James."

"You did! Where did you get the sugar?"

"The Framingtons found a farm down in the valley south of here when they were foraging. No one was there, but the place was stocked. They had to make several trips with the truck to haul it all back here."

Andie handed James the plate. He took one of the sugar cookies and bit into it.

David watched his father's expression.

"Wow, Buddy, these are so good! Do you want one?"

"He's already had five!" Andie exclaimed. She shook her head when James handed the delighted toddler another.

"He's going to be spoiled."

"Spoiled? Maybe, but if I can help it he won't be rotten!" James joked.

David rubbed his eyes with his free hand as he munched the cookie.

"I think he's tired. Maybe I should put him down now for his nap," James said.

"I'll wait here until you're done, if you don't mind. I...umm... have something I want to talk to you about," Andie mumbled nervously.

James carried David over to the small sink, wet a cloth, and wiped the boy's face. He walked back to the cozy bedroom and put his son down on the bed. For the next few minutes, James read David his favorite story, then kissed him and covered him with his blanket.

When James returned to the small living area in the cabin, he saw Andie sitting on the couch, so he took the seat across from her.

She looked on edge as she twirled her dark hair around her finger and stared down at the carpet.

"What's going on, Andie?"

She took a deep breath, closing her eyes for a moment. "This is really hard for me to do. I mean…to say, I guess. The thing is…I am wondering if you think it's a good idea for people to consider getting married."

"Is there someone you have in mind, or is this just a general question?"

She looked away, then back at him. "There is someone I have feelings for, but with what you are teaching us is coming, I don't know if it's wise to tell him. Would you, for instance, think of getting married again?"

James was taken aback. Images of Cynthia ran through his mind: her, dressed in white on their wedding day, walking toward him with a grin on her face—then, walking out on him years later, her face showing nothing but contempt for him and their son.

"No. I wouldn't. But Andie, I am not you. It may be that this man you have feelings for is the one God intends to help you through the next years of difficulty. I can't tell you it is wrong to get married.

"For centuries Christians have faced persecution and hardship and yet still managed to find joy in marriage and children." He thought for a moment. "Children might make it harder, though. Things are going to be more than difficult in the coming times—they will be catastrophic. We might be safer here from some of the dangers that are coming, but we won't be immune from them all.

"I think this is something you must pray carefully about. You've got to have confirmation from God that it's the right thing to do."

"I guess you're right, James. I will pray about it. Thanks for your time." Her dark eyes sparkled with unshed tears. She got up quickly and left the cabin, closing the door behind her quietly.

James let out a sad, frustrated sigh. Life and love were about

ONE WILL BE TAKEN

to become a lot more difficult. He bent his head and prayed for Andie, asking the Lord to make her way clear, if this man she had feelings for was God's choice for her. James's prayers were interrupted by David's little cries, whining that his tummy hurt. James got up quickly to tend to his son.

St. Michaels, Maryland

Elena stared at the back door, her heart pounding. She had padded down to the kitchen in her slippers for some coffee but had stopped on the stairs after hearing some strange noises. She had slowly made her way into the kitchen to find Maggie stuffing canned goods into a satchel. Elena had confronted her, and it blew up into an argument. Maggie had screamed obscenities and left, slamming the door. It seemed to shake the whole house.

Elena could hear Brant running down the stairs. He came into the kitchen, gun in hand. When he saw that she was fine, he lowered it. "What's going on? You scared me half to death!"

"Oh Brant, I was suspicious that someone was taking food. I just came downstairs for coffee and caught Maggie stealing some of the canned goods. We had an argument." Elena pulled out a stool from under the kitchen island and sat down heavily.

"She isn't settling in as well as Dalton, is she?"

Elena shook her head. "No, Dalton is a sweet boy. He's really fallen in love with his cousin. But I don't think Maggie has done more than say, 'Hey,' to Olivia since they arrived. She seems to resent her. Sometimes I catch her looking at Olivia with an awful expression. I wonder if I was wrong in letting them stay."

Brant went over to the stove and put the kettle on to boil. He pulled the coffee press from the cabinet and put four scoops of grounds in it. As the water began to boil, he thought carefully about what they should do next. When the kettle whistled, he poured steaming water into the press and replaced the lid.

"Elena, I have to say I think it would be a mistake for us to stay here. I told you my concerns the other day about the fighting between the World Union and the Anti-Globalists escalating and the lack of supplies to this area. Maggie is another complication. When she and Dalton got here, she was expecting to take over this place. But you were here, with Olivia, a cousin who was supposed to have died in a plane crash, a cousin who was memorialized in the media because her uncle is the famous Italian ambassador to the World Union—a man you and I know to be evil and powerful. Are you sure Maggie will keep our secret?"

Elena shook her head. "I'm so worried about that. But DC wanted us to come here. We have to stay here," she pleaded. "How else will they be able to find us when they get back? We must stay here, Brant. I promised Teo that I would take care of Livie."

Brant pushed the plunger down slowly into the French press and filled two coffee cups with the steaming liquid. He handed one to Elena and sat down at the counter next to her with the other. He sipped the bitter liquid, wishing they had sugar.

"I know that was the plan, Elena, but DC didn't anticipate the fighting going on here between the World Union and the Anti-Globalists. And he didn't know about Maggie. Listen, all she has to do is make one phone call and tell the world that the Italian ambassador's niece is miraculously alive. I've been thinking about this for days. We need to leave now. We can leave this place for Maggie and Dalton and get Olivia out while we can."

"But what about Teo and DC?" Elena implored anxiously. "How will they know where to find us?"

"We have the cell phones. They'll be able to call us just like they do now. We can even call them and let them know what we're planning."

"But you and DC said all conversations are monitored by World Union Security and we can't use our real names or talk about where we are. So how do we tell them where we're going? And do you have any idea where it's safe to go? Or how we're going to get there?" Elena's hysteria mounted.

"Elena."

She halted nearly midsentence, and she and Brant both turned in surprise toward the back door. John Foster stood in the opening, a tall, regal-looking man behind him. Elena jumped up instantly and rushed toward her husband. Brant stayed where he was and let them have their moment. When they finished embracing, they moved into the kitchen, the man following behind in silence.

"Hello, Brant Hughes. Thank you for caring for my charge." The tall man spoke softly and melodiously. As he walked closer, Brant found himself having to look up—not something he was used to doing. "I am Talin," the man introduced himself. "Elena's guardian."

Brant recognized John Foster, but not the strange man in front of him, despite his introduction. He stared at the man for a moment before relaxing, deciding that he was definitely not a threat.

John moved in and grabbed Brant by the shoulders, embracing him. "Man, thank you for taking care of my wife!" John stepped back with a smile. "I have a lot to talk over with both of you, but Talin says we must leave immediately. Grab what you can. Elena, get Olivia, and let's move."

Elena started to protest, but Talin put a hand on her shoulder. "Do not fear; have faith." She nodded and without asking any questions, went upstairs quickly to change clothes and get Olivia up and ready.

"What do you know?" Brant asked Talin.

"The girl, Maggie, called the local World Union Security in Baltimore a few days ago. They are checking into her story before sending someone here to investigate. We must leave quickly. The roads are monitored too closely, so we will have to go by boat."

"How could you possibly know all of this?"

"He's an angel," John responded. "I know it's a lot to believe. He's actually the angel who explained things to Elena. You know, the one she said helped her understand why Jesus is the only way to

God? I had a hard time with it myself. I'll fill you in when we get to the boat and have some time to talk.

"In the meantime, let's get some supplies together. We saw Maggie leading her brother out of the front door before we came in. We're safe for a while, but I'm not sure how long."

Brant went to the living room and grabbed his backpack. He checked the pockets in the front and pulled out a key. John followed him.

"What's that for?"

"I found a safe in the office. When I opened it, this key was inside," Brant said.

John held his hand out, and Brant placed the key into his palm. "Do you see the initials on it? The CSB?"

"Yes. It looks like a key to a safety-deposit box."

"I saw a bank not far from here," Brant explained. "Canton Street Bank. I think the key's from there. Do you think we should check it out before we leave? There may be something important for DC."

John looked at the key and thought for a moment. "I'll ask Talin. I'm not sure how much time we have. We'll have to carry whatever we find, too. Do you have an extra backpack?"

Elena entered the room as he was speaking, Olivia perched on her hip. The toddler was clinging to her grandmother. Olivia looked at John and buried her face into Elena's shoulder.

"Don't you remember me?" John asked softly. He moved closer and stroked Olivia's back with his hand.

Olivia turned again and pushed his hand away, glaring at him.

"I think she'll warm up. It's been a long time since she's seen you, honey. I think there's a backpack in the master bedroom closet."

"I'll get it." Brant left the room and went upstairs. He returned, backpack in hand, and he and Elena hurriedly followed John out of the back door, grabbing coats from the mudroom closet on their way outside. Talin stood in the driveway, scanning the street.

"You two can take the van and go to the bank," Talin said to John and Brant. "Elena and I will get the boat packed and ready. You must be quick, but the items in the box will be helpful to you."

"How do you—?" Brant started to ask, then stopped abruptly. He already knew the answer to the question. Taking the keys from his front pocket, he strode quickly to the van and got in. John kissed Elena and followed.

"Are you sure they'll be safe?" Elena asked the celestial creature.

"Yes. In the meantime, the boat is at the dock and we should get moving." Talin grabbed the bags piled in the yard while Elena picked up her own backpack and Olivia, silently praying for the safety of her husband and friend.

6

JERUSALEM,
ISRAEL

Kate Havenstone Benari pushed her hair away from her face and looked at her reflection with a frown. She had an important interview next week with the new king of Jordan, Zayd bin Asem. She took good care of herself, but that was not enough. She examined the wrinkles under her eyes with concern, leaning as close to the mirror as she could.

"I've got to do something about this." Turning away from the mirror, she went into the bedroom and opened her laptop. When the screen lit up, she quickly did a search, clicked on the link, and jotted down a number from the website onto a piece of paper. She would make a call later.

Grabbing her laptop and purse, she headed out to the kitchen. Michael turned from the stove and greeted her. "Are you heading to work? I made some breakfast for us."

"I wish I could, Michael. I've got to meet Christopher to go over some background information for the interview next week." She walked behind her husband and gave him a hug from behind.

Michael turned off the burner and kissed his wife.

"Do you want to meet for dinner somewhere?"

"Sure, honey. We should be done by four or five. Where do you want to meet?"

"I'll text you later today. I have a place in mind, but I want to make sure we can get a reservation first."

Kate smiled mischievously. "Are you kidding? The famous

ONE WILL BE LEFT

Michael Benari, discoverer of the Ark of the Covenant? You can eat wherever you want, and I bet it'll be free too. How many times here in Jerusalem have we gone to dinner or lunch and had someone pay for our meal?

"I wonder if I can use your name at the Giamo clinics and get a huge discount." She chuckled at the thought.

"Why are you going there?" Michael suddenly looked worried.

"Don't you remember? They offer the new treatment, the one your friend Ari Singleton developed."

"Oh, of course. But why are you going to do that, Kate? There's no reason...you're perfect!"

Kate kissed him again. "You're sweet, love, but in my business, looks matter. It's not a big deal. Noninvasive. I'm making an appointment once I get to work. What do you have on for today?"

"Oh, I'm meeting with the high priest. The sacrifice to dedicate the Temple is coming up, and we want to make sure we're doing everything in the proper manner. There's a whole committee dedicated to the ceremony."

"Okay, hope that goes well! Love you!"

Kate left the apartment, slamming the door behind her. Michael sighed. She was always such a whirlwind. His neighbor, Mr. Blankenship, had stopped him twice in the hall already to complain about how loud she was.

He scooped the oatmeal from the pot into a bowl and sat at the table eating slowly, taking breaks to make notes on the yellow legal pad in front of him. He couldn't believe the Jewish nation was about to reinstitute the sacrificial offering for the first time in almost two centuries. This would be a joyous and solemn occasion.

He turned to a new page and sketched a time line. Under the first bullet he wrote, "Gog/Magog war." Israel's enemies had been poised at the borders, ready with immense military strength to decimate the small nation. Miraculously, the armies had been defeated without human agency. The only explanation was God.

He put his pen down and thought as he ate. He was not an

observant Jew, but he had always believed in the God of Abraham, Isaac, and Jacob. It was his heritage as a Jew. As an archaeologist, he could not help but see the survival of the Jewish people as a nation, keeping their identity and language over centuries of Diaspora, as evidence of a higher power. Now the Temple was rebuilt and the Ark of the Covenant had been found! Truly remarkable, he thought.

Michael began to rub his forehead, something he always did when he was troubled. His parents had passed away years ago. They would have rejoiced to see the day when the Temple was rebuilt and the worship and sacrifices reinstituted. They would not, however, be happy to see how he lived, unobservant of the faith and married to a Gentile. Certainly, they would be proud of his work and that he was a benefit to his people, but not that he did not keep the Law. He thought back to the many times his father had scolded him for his lack of *bitachon*, or trust in God. Father would often remind him that everything was in God's hands—everything except the fear of God.

Michael's parents were disappointed that their only son had such nominal faith and commitment to *HaShem*. The truth was that while he believed in God, he disliked the idea that somehow he had to work to gain God's approval. So he had gone his own way once he moved out on his own. Although he did not like the restrictiveness of his parents' faith, he had great respect for them and for God. *From a distance.*

Getting up from the table, he took his bowl to the sink and washed it. He was drying his hands when he heard a knock on the door. *Mr. Blankenship.* He sighed and went to the door reluctantly. But he did not find Mr. Blankenship. Standing on the threshold instead was a burly, dark-haired man wearing faded jeans and a collared shirt.

"Hello, Michael."

Michael smiled at the man politely. "I'm sorry, do I know you?"

"You know of me. I am Elijah, prophet of the Most High."

Michael's hand tightened on the doorknob. There had been quite an explosion of lunatics in the past year on the streets of Jerusalem. Dozens of them walked around the Old City dressed in flowing robes. Some carried signs about the end of the world. Most of them were harmless, but he had not had one show up on his doorstep before.

The man in front of him looked respectable enough. There was nothing odd about the way he was dressed. He had a beard, but it was short and trimmed, not long and bushy.

"I am not sure how I can help you," Michael said politely as he tried to shut the door.

The man put his hand up, equally politely, to stop the door. "I am here to help you, Michael. I believe you know it is my role to turn the hearts of the fathers to the children and the children to the fathers."

The hair at the back of Michael's neck stood up at the scriptural reference. What the man in front of him was saying sounded crazy, but there was something about him. His words had authority and power, and Michael had just been thinking about his father. *What an insane coincidence*, Michael thought.

"My father is dead," he said flatly.

"Yes, that is true." The man who called himself Elijah stared into Michael's eyes calmly. As Michael looked back, he became uncomfortable. He felt as if every thought, every secret act, was laid bare before this man.

"So, you're too late. If you don't mind, I have to go to work now." Michael spoke harshly and began to close the door again. The door would not budge. He looked down to see if the man was barring the way with his foot, but he was not. Frustrated, Michael tried to close the door again. He could not move it even an inch.

Elijah looked at him with compassion. "So, have you always shut the door on the truth, Michael? Yes, your father has passed away, but you have a son. I am here about your son."

Michael stood dumbfounded. How could this stranger possibly know about Micah? Confused, he reluctantly stood aside and let the man in. He would listen and find out.

ONE WILL BE LEFT

New Babylon, Iraq

The fire crackled as the green and blue flames licked the dry wood greedily. Billings Mason sat on the broad velvet settee with his feet propped up. He picked up the dark glass block from the table. Inside the solid block was an incredible scene created from blown glass. A pale yellow moon glowed within it; the dark valleys and features on the moon's surface were quite realistic. Suspended below the moon was an intricately colored flower, its root system trailing to the bottom of the cube. He turned the block over carefully and saw human figures the artist had inserted into the plant's root system. The work was amazing, as was the entire collection, which had been delivered to the prophet's residence just this morning.

A soft knock on the door interrupted his inspection.

"Come in," he called pleasantly.

The door opened slowly and Sanjay, his butler, backed into the room, pulling a cart covered with a white damask cloth and loaded with a large, silver, domed platter. A small crystal vase of exquisite white roses and a pitcher filled with ice water and slices of lemon sat beside the platter. Billings carefully set down the large glass cube and stood up.

"Ah, lunch. Thank you, Sanjay! What will we be having this afternoon?" He stepped over to the large window where Sanjay had left the table.

Sanjay bowed. "Your Grace, the chef has something to start with which I believe you will truly appreciate." He lifted the silver dome to reveal a large platter heaped with chipped ice and a variety of oysters. Lemon wedges were scattered on the platter.

Billings smiled. "Are these from Cape May? You know how I enjoy those! Where are these from?" He pointed to another type of oyster on the tray.

ONE WILL BE LEFT

"They are from Chef Creek on Vancouver Island in Canada, a special gift from the International United Fellowship. Mother Tania is the head pastor there. I believe you met her when you were working with the Red Cross? You'll find a letter from her on your desk, Your Grace."

"Good, thank you, Sanjay. Is my guest here yet?"

"Yes, sir. She is upstairs changing. It was a long flight."

"Show her in when she's ready, please."

Sanjay nodded and left the room. Billings stepped into the small bathroom adjacent to his office and checked his reflection in the mirror. This meeting was important to Luca and it must go well. Billings heard the door open and went back into his study to find a woman standing next to his butler.

Sanjay introduced the petite young woman and left again.

"I am pleased you would come all this way to see me, Miss Salas. Won't you sit down? The chef has prepared something for us to nibble on before lunch."

"Please, call me Pilar." Smoothing her blue silk skirt, she took a seat at the table. "I am grateful that you would see me, Your Grace. I have so many questions."

Billings sat down across the table from her. "I suppose you must. Mr. Amona told me that he met with you, to explain."

He poured wine for them both and took an oyster from the tray.

Pilar began. "Yes, I was shocked, of course. It seemed unbelievable, but then it began to make sense to me. I've had some strange experiences over the years, not least of all the ease with which I have been able to take over my father's empire after his death."

"It's my understanding that you've done more than that. You are to be congratulated. Despite its best attempts, the World Union could not control the cartels in South America, yet you have them all in your power." He shook his head in amazement.

"Order needed to be restored. There are many men who are loyal to me, and we have been able to regain effectual control of the

ONE WILL BE LEFT

continent. The World Union is still ostensibly in power, but it is in name only." She took a sip of her wine and set it down as she continued.

"Mr. Amona said you would have some answers for me. He knew things about me that I have never shared with anyone else, things no one could possibly know. Could you enlighten me? How is this all possible?"

"Of course. I believe he spoke to you about your abilities—that we know their source and can explain much to you and answer questions you've had for years?"

"Yes," she whispered.

Billings Mason reached over and patted her hand. "I want you to know, Pilar, that you are not alone. There are others like you. The others share the abilities that you have, to varying degrees. You are one among many kindred.

"I've had the privilege of overseeing the education of the one who will lead you and the others into a new age for mankind. I'm certain you realize that the abilities you have make you immensely powerful?"

She nodded. "At first it did not frighten me. I was able to influence those around me to do what I wanted, such as my mother or father when I wanted something as a child. As I matured, I found I was able to hear what others thought. Not everyone, but many.

"My parents sent me to an exclusive boarding school. Within a month they had to come for meetings with the headmaster. My teachers were amazed at my ability to learn quickly, and they grew concerned that they could not offer me the challenges my intellect needed." She paused, squeezed a lemon wedge over the oysters on her plate, and delicately ate one from the shell before continuing.

"So at fourteen I began university. My mother and I moved to the United States to facilitate my education."

"Yes, I am aware. Impressive. And after you graduated at eighteen, you went to Oxford on a Rhodes scholarship, I understand."

"That's right. While I was in England, I began to explore matters of faith. I was intrigued by the idea that there is no real boundary between the physical and spiritual realms—that I could breach the supernatural arena and gain full knowledge. My mentor, Aimee Spencer, taught me how to actually break through the confines of my physical body."

"Indeed, I know Aimee very well. She is truly an astounding and deeply spiritual woman." Billings went on eagerly. "I suppose, like the others, you found you were able to see and influence people while you were apart from your physical body?"

"Exactly. As I received higher consciousness of my true divinity, I found I could have the same influence without projecting myself. I came to understand through my exploration that the next step in human evolution is not physical, but spiritual."

Billings stood up and toasted her. "Precisely! The ribbon of truth weaves through most religious history and thought. Until now, divergences in spirituality have been the results of human rebellion. We refused to recognize the true brotherhood of man. But now we are at the beginning of the new age, and things are finally changing.

"The others will be here to join us in the next day or so, Pilar. You will meet them, and you all will have the joy of meeting the one who has realized his divine nature completely. You and the others have only begun to plumb the depths of your evolution. He will lead you further."

"Are you one of us, Your Grace?" she asked.

Billings smiled. "I? No, I am the voice of one crying out in the wilderness—prepare the way for the Lord! He who is coming is greater than I. I am not fit to do the lowliest task for him, yet he is pleased to have gifted me as his messenger.

"You and the others will do greater things than I have done, or will do. The mission for the OneFaith movement is to usher in global unity. Man must find his proper divine nature in relation to man, nature, and the true god." Billings picked up a small fork, pulled an oyster from its shell, and ate it with relish. "To do this, we need economic and political unity. Unfortunately, the World Union cannot accomplish this alone.

"It has the same impotence with which every human leader has been afflicted throughout history, but from which you and your brethren have been freed. Under the leadership of the Coming One, each of you will help guide the world into spiritual unity, economic wealth for all the nations, and the peace of which mankind has only dreamed!" He noticed Pilar's eyes were wide with anticipation and sparkling with pride.

"Once we enable others to experience the harmony we have discovered, to embrace their innate goodness, they will realize their unity and purpose and be ready for the next stage of human development."

He flung his arms expansively as a few small tears ran down his face. He stood up, took Pilar's hand, pulled her up into his embrace, and whispered into her ear, "Pilar, you will be a pillar in his kingdom. You, like your brethren, were begotten by the ancient ones to usher in the new age and support the One they have given to mankind. He will lead us into the fullness of life we were designed to experience."

She pulled away and knelt before him reverently. Billings placed his hand on her head in benediction.

"As I bless you now, so will I bless your brethren. You will grow in knowledge and honor and power and in favor with men and women. You will be given a kingdom to rule, under the authority of the Promised One. Are you willing to pledge your life to him? To love him and to serve him?"

"Yes!" Pilar lifted her face, a look of exultation animating her dainty features. She was truly beautiful. "When may I see him?"

"I am here now."

She turned her head and saw Luca Giamo, the Italian ambassador to the World Union, standing by the study door. His blonde hair glowed like a halo and his blue eyes seemed filled with radiance. She gasped. "I have seen you in the news, Ambassador. But standing here now, I realize that I know you! I have known you since I was a young girl. You were constantly in my dreams; I am sure of it! How can this be?"

Luca walked toward her gracefully. Taking one of her hands, he pulled her up gently. "Yes, we have met. I have been leading you all along."

"I was so afraid you were just a dream. I've done everything you asked me to do," she murmured. She suddenly felt captivated, enthralled with the man before her.

"Yes, you have, and that is why I have gifted you, why you are here, and why I have chosen you to rule and reign with me." He kissed her lips softly. "I bless you now with the gift of my spirit. You will do greater things yet. Our time is at hand."

Billings Mason sank to the floor, completely outstretched in total surrender and worship. Pilar looked at Luca, questioningly. He answered her unspoken question. "As my esteemed brothers and sisters, you and the others will be honored with the worship of men. Their worship will empower you to help them, to lead them as one leads small children. They need us."

"And you will lead us all, because we need you." She sank to her knees in front of him.

"Yes, I will lead you. Under my rule, this world will become all that it was intended to be."

As Billings Mason began speaking ecstatic praises, Luca placed a hand on Pilar's head and spoke to her in an ancient tongue—a language not heard on the earth since before the great flood.

7

WASHINGTON, DC

Andres sat behind the desk, grinning. This had once been the most powerful seat in the world. Those days were done, to be sure, but he still relished the moment. He turned the chair around slowly until he looked out the window of the Oval Office. His expression grew somber as he saw his men setting up tents on the White House lawn. Gaining the city had cost many lives among them.

He swiveled his chair back around when he heard a cough behind him. Marc Jafari, his brother-in-law, stood with his general.

"Is everything settled, General?" Andres asked impatiently.

"Yes, sir," the general answered. "Our men have the city secured. There are few civilians left inside the Beltway, and the main roadways are blockaded. There have been no sightings of World Union forces near the city in the past two hours."

"Good. I have been assured by my friend that will continue to be the case." Andres turned to Marc. "Is Patricia safely settled in the East Wing?"

"Yes, Andres. We arrived less than an hour ago. By the way, she was very appreciative of the necklace."

"I hope she understands the historic significance of the gift, Marc. Now that our plans are close to being realized, I want an heir. That diamond necklace was a symbol of the French emperor Napoleon's gratitude for the birth of his son—make sure she understands this is what I expect from her." He stood up and abruptly changed the subject.

ONE WILL BE LEFT

"How is the situation in New York City, General?"

"As you know, they are three weeks into the smallpox outbreak. There is widespread panic. Clinics and hospitals thought to have the vaccine in stock have been looted, some of them even destroyed.

"Nothing is going into the city, so hunger is becoming a problem. Our sources indicate that World Union forces have blockades keeping anyone from leaving or entering the city. Violence in the city is escalating, and people are panicked."

Marc nodded in agreement. "This is just as you anticipated, Andres."

"Indeed it is. Another week should make the situation painful enough for the city to capitulate to my rule. My friend, the ambassador, has assured me that my help will be vital. The World Union will be willing to declare a truce so we may render aid to the suffering citizens.

"In the meantime, how are things going on our other fronts?"

For the next twenty minutes, the general delivered an overview of the state of the war between the Anti-Globalists under Andres' authority and the World Union forces. The WU forces were about to pull out of the North American sector with some help from the ambassador. At present, there were still some skirmishes between the two groups.

The general then moved on to discuss disasters in various parts of North America, and the opportunity for the Anti-Globalists' movement. An earthquake of 9.5 on the Richter scale had rocked California a few days earlier, and the epicenter, San Francisco, was completely destroyed. Hundreds of thousands were missing, and the death toll was rising by the minute. Fires were left burning with no attempt to put them out as people, even emergency responders, fled the area. The local government was in shambles, and the World Union had been unable to provide much assistance.

"Good, this is all for the good. Unfortunate, of course, that so many have to die. We must insure their deaths are not in vain."

ONE WILL BE LEFT

Andres sat back down behind the carved wooden desk and gave the general a few orders before dismissing him.

Putting his feet on the historic desk and leaning back in his chair, Andres spoke in a pleasant tone to Marc. "It is all going just as we planned, my friend. Within a year, all of North America will be begging for my leadership. I will be the supreme leader, with Patricia at my side, and you will be second only to me."

Marc smiled. "I think our success calls for a drink, Andres. One of our men—he said he was from Kentucky—asked me to give you this." Marc clicked a button on his cell phone. A moment later, Andres's valet entered the room carrying a silver tray and expertly balancing a bottle of bourbon along with two crystal glasses. Setting the tray on a side table, the young man poured a stout measure of the liquid gold for each man.

"Leave it there. You may go." Andres stood up and crossed the room, rubbing his hands together. "Ah, Marc! Kentucky is bourbon paradise! You know my fondness for it."

Marc joined his brother-in-law and toasted to their future together with another smile. Secretly, he wondered if he would still be a part of that future if Andres became unhappy with Patricia or found out about her plans for him.

Jerusalem, Israel

Teo sat on the intricately patterned Moroccan carpet, her legs crossed, sipping the ginger tea gratefully. Lately, she could only get comfortable sitting on the floor. She looked around the living room, noting that the warm autumnal colors suited Ari's wife, Mara. The rug Teo was sitting on was beautiful, a deep yellow tone with a geometric pattern of turquoise, red, and blue. Pillows, lampshades, and small trinkets adorned the home, adding pops of olive green and shades of gold. Mara's art hung on the walls in chunky wooden frames. The stone house in Yemin Moshe was smaller than any home Teo had ever lived in, but it was infinitely more welcoming and cozy.

"It seems to be helping you with the morning sickness, yes?" asked Mara solicitously. She sat down next to Teo and pulled a pillow into her lap. In the short time Teo and DC had been there, Teo had noticed Mara always held a pillow, or one of her cats, when she sat down to talk.

"Oh, it does, thank you. And it is delicious. How long ago did the guys leave?"

"They left about an hour ago, so they should be back soon. I'm glad you could sleep, Teo. You need the rest. The last few weeks have been very stressful for you and the baby." Mara smiled with empathy.

Teo nodded. She could hear someone playing a guitar through the doors that opened onto the terrace. She closed her eyes and listened, basking in the sunlight that bathed the room. They had been here for three days. She had not felt this safe in weeks.

"That is Rhetta, my mother-in-law. She loves to play on her terrace, and we certainly enjoy the private concerts."

"It's beautiful. The song seems familiar. Do you know it?" Teo asked, keeping her eyes closed.

"It's Bach," Mara replied. "'Jesu, Joy of Man's Desiring.' She often will play it if she knows I'm home because it is one of my favorites."

Teo opened her eyes. Mara was looking out toward the terrace with a tender expression.

"Thank you again for letting us stay here. As soon as DC can find a job—"

Mara interrupted, "Don't even think about it. We have plenty of room, Teo. Ari wants you both to stay, too. It will be safer for you here. If you have to rent a place elsewhere, that means your identity cards will be entered into the government's system. While Israel is not part of the World Union, we cannot be too careful about your image and new names being entered into any public domain. We still don't know if DC's friend has spoken to authorities about you two."

Teo nodded in agreement. "I just wish that whole thing hadn't happened. He was so furious. I've never seen a friend turn so quickly into a raging enemy."

"I'm afraid it is something we are going to see more as the time approaches, Teo. My own family tried to beat me into denying Jesus. I ran out of the house with only the clothes on my back. I was so hysterical that when I finally stopped running, I realized I was lost."

"Is that when Ari found you?"

Mara nodded. "Yes. He brought me home to Rhetta. She made me take a bath, gave me some of her clothes, and put me in bed. She has been like a mother to me ever since. I have learned so much from her...she is very wise."

"I'm sure she was happy when you and Ari fell in love." Teo patted her new friend's hand. "The two of you are so good together."

The music stopped.

"I've asked her to join us, if you don't mind," Mara said. "She wanted to meet you right away, but has waited to give you time to rest."

"That was thoughtful."

"Rhetta is that—and much more, you will find. She is the one who encouraged Ari to search Abraham's tomb to find the secret of Sarah's beauty."

"Really?"

"Yes, she funded the search and even participated in the research Ari did. Early on, Ari developed a cream he thought might stimulate the genetic 'machinery' he'd discovered, but he had a difficult time stabilizing the chemicals. According to Rhetta, he worked on it constantly. Ari wasn't just convinced this would help people look younger, he was, and still is, convinced that it can help with many of the symptoms that accompany old age, like dementia.

"Finally, he thought he had the cream stabilized, and Rhetta insisted she be allowed to participate when it came time to test on humans. She was the first test subject, and the results were exceptional. But...there was a problem with that mixture that Ari had not foreseen. Unfortunately, in Rhetta's case, it resulted in blindness. She applied the cream close to her eyes and accidently got some of the cream in both of them. Her vision was not affected at first, but gradually it got worse and worse, and eventually she became completely blind."

Teo was surprised. She had not known about this last year when she had vetted Ari's product to be sold to her father's clinics. "Why have I not heard of this before?"

"Only one person was affected—Rhetta. After she lost her sight, she insisted Ari continue his research. He developed the serum he sold to your father months later, after he was able to stabilize the main ingredients."

"It's fitting for my vanity, I suppose, that I can't see what I longed and hoped to regain for so many years," a reserved and gentle voice suddenly said behind them.

Teo turned to the archway to her right, where she saw a strikingly beautiful woman in a simple white dress. Long, dark hair tumbled about her shoulders, framing an oval face with dainty features. Her dark eyes were clouded; one could easily determine that she was blind.

Rhetta walked gracefully toward them and sat in a wing-back chair. Reaching a hand forward to locate Teo, the older woman greeted her with affection.

"I am so glad that you and your husband are here, Teo. We want you to feel at home."

Teo could not help but stare. She had never seen such a beautiful woman in person. Rhetta was Ari's mother. Teo knew Ari to be in his early thirties, but the woman in front of her looked much too young to have a son that old.

"I'm glad to be here. Mara and I were enjoying your guitar playing. I've never heard Bach played like that before. It was lovely."

Rhetta nodded her head. "I learned to play after I lost my sight, once I'd put away my bitterness—that took the Lord's help."

"Rhetta, would you like a coffee?" Mara leaned forward as

she spoke and touched her mother-in-law's arm. Teo noted the affection between the two women, and it brought tears to her eyes. She lowered her lids to hide the tears and took another sip of her tea. Mara got up from the couch and went into the kitchen to make the coffee.

"Are they tears of joy or sorrow?" Rhetta asked smoothly.

"How do you...?"

"The fact that I do not have sight does not mean that I cannot see, dear. I see better now than my eyes ever allowed me to do when I had my vision. I hear you speak and I see pain and sorrow."

Something about Rhetta's sweet expression and the peaceful certainty coming through her words opened Teo's pent-up emotions. Words and tears spilled out as she recounted her life as a daughter, then a wife, and then a mother. Mara returned with coffee for them, but Teo's sat untouched as she poured her heart out to this sympathetic listener.

She had been thinking a great deal, Teo told Mara, about the many ways she had failed in her life. DC had assured her that God had forgiven her when she prayed to give her life to Jesus Christ, but how could she forgive herself for all the awful things she had done?

"How could I do it? I didn't know, I didn't know..." she cried. "I can see how everything else can be forgiven, but I killed my own child." She sobbed so hard she could barely get the words out. DC was the only person she had ever told about her abortion.

"Now I'm afraid I'm never going to see Olivia again because I'm being punished. I don't deserve her or this baby. I'm so afraid. I don't know why my brother would want to kill us. I don't understand." Teo cried in great, wracking sobs. Her shoulders heaved as all the sorrow and anxiety and fear from the past came out in one big flow.

Rhetta stroked her hair and began to pray softly. Teo scooted backward so her body was leaning against Rhetta's legs. She stopped crying, breathing raggedly as she listened to Rhetta speak to God in such a familiar way. Warmth filled her heart as the blind woman

ONE WILL BE LEFT

prayed on, and Teo began to see the truth through those words. Jesus had forgiven her. Nothing had been hidden from Him when she had finally come to Him in faith. He had loved her all along. She could feel the weight of guilt and fear roll off of her heart. She felt quiet. For the first time in a long time, her heart felt at peace.

Rhetta finished praying. "He never shows us all at once, Teo. We would be undone if He did. You've known Him for a little while. You will find that He is surprisingly patient and kind and that there is nothing that can separate us from His love.

"It was His kindness that allowed you to overhear your brother's plot and to get your family away to safety. The Lord is not punishing you; instead, He has rescued you from the influence of great evil."

Teo took a long breath and sat up straight. Rhetta's hand rested on her shoulder like a benediction. Teo smiled, a warm peace radiating throughout her body.

"Thank you, Rhetta. I've been focusing on what I've lost and on my own guilt. DC has tried to explain to me who he thinks Luca is, as well as Billings Mason's true identity. That subject has filled me with such dread and fear that I haven't wanted to listen. I've had a problem with fear and panic. I—"

Rhetta put her hand on Teo's cheek, the way Teo recalled mother used to do when she was little. "Our God is stronger than those two men," the older woman said. "You see how He has already protected you and your family, Teo. You will see greater things yet. The time is at hand and the war has begun. What is the worst that can happen? Nothing can separate us from the love of God that we have in Jesus Christ, neither depth nor height, nor things past, nor things to come, neither angels, nor demons."

"But we can die."

"Yes, we may die. But for a believer to die is merely to exchange the temporary for the eternal. To be absent from this body is to be present with the Lord, and once that occurs we will always be with the Lord."

ONE WILL BE LEFT

"And what about Olivia? She is so young. Luca planned to…" she swallowed hard, "have her killed. What if she dies? She's too young to believe."

"Ah. Do not worry about your daughter, Teo. You have no reason to fear. As you grow in your knowledge of the Lord, you will find you have fewer reasons to fear. His perfect love removes all fear."

New Babylon, Iraq

Stephen Amona waited in dark shadows by the ornate stone fountain. The courtyard was quiet at this time of night, and an eerie calm stretched over him and his surroundings. The sacrifice had been made. To his surprise, he no longer viewed the process with dismay. The girls did not suffer unduly. Indeed, they were immediately welcomed into fellowship with the holy ones. He had witnessed their spirits be so received each time—a holy moment of reunion. They were not truly dead; they lived for eternity.

Two of the other men had taken the body for tonight's sacrifice and wrapped it in the special cloth, blessed by Billings Mason for the very purpose. With each sacrifice, the group's power expanded. Luca was now able to influence others to an even greater degree. He demonstrated this tonight, by causing the girl to take her own life, slowly cutting her own throat over the golden basin, smiling as she did so. Luca dipped the chalice into the basin and lifted the dripping cup to his lips, sipping her warm blood as her life force was reunited with the eternal. He passed the cup to Stephen, who had drunk deeply before passing it to the man next to him. Stephan had fallen into a trance almost immediately.

In the last few months, Stephen had experienced tremendous things. He laughed out loud as he looked at his hands, balled into fists, and felt the strength racing through his entire being. He felt thirty years younger. Luca had shown the deeper things of his Father

ONE WILL BE LEFT

to Stephen and had given him his own spirit guide. Not only had his guide, Utumzi, given the older man renewed vigor, but great insight and knowledge as well. Stephen had often lamented to Billings Mason that he lacked the energy of his youth in the very season of life in which he possessed the wisdom to use that vitality well. Utumzi's gift allowed him to have both the strength of youth and the knowledge to utilize it efficiently. Tonight, Utumzi had revealed something new to him that filled him with joy. Teo lived!

Utumzi was unclear as to where she could be found. He claimed he did not know, but still he was sure she was alive. Luca would help Stephen find her. Luca was kind and good; surely he would rescue his sister from her husband. Utumzi had been clear that DC had taken her against her will, seeking to indoctrinate her into the belief in the false messiah. She was not to blame for this deception, and Stephen was confident that Luca would keep his word and give Teo to him.

He shivered in anticipation of rescuing her. Teo would realize, Utumzi assured him, that she truly loved him. He would have the honor of watching the man who took her die a slow death. *It's only fair,* Stephen thought. *I should have Teo now. The child will have to die...but that is just the way things have to be.*

Stephen quickly skipped over the slight pang of regret he felt. This would be a necessary sacrifice since the whole world thought Luca's family was dead. The supposed tragedy had helped catapult the grieving young ambassador to worldwide popularity. They could not risk public exposure and the possibility of Luca's credibility being called into question. Who knew what rumors might fly if it came out that the tragic deaths of Ambassador Luca Giamo's family were a sham. Stephen would have to keep Teo from the public eye.

He whistled softly as he waited and watched for his master's return. Luca was alone with his spiritual Father. He had told Stephen that his Father intended to bless Luca's consort when the young man came to power, but Luca still had no idea which woman his Father had chosen for him. Luca had been promised to receive that information tonight. The children Luca's consort would bear were to become the leaders of an enhanced human race. Stephen smiled with pride. He had the great privilege of helping bring that race into the world.

No mere woman would be sufficiently suited for his master. With Lucifer's blessing and power, she would become more gifted than any other of the new race, aside from Luca. Such was Luca's due as the true god-man. Luca's conception had not been what his "father" Arturo believed, the result of scientific processes. Rather, he was the son of the true god. In fact, as Stephen had revealed to Luca that first day, the Lord of Light himself had come upon the egg prepared to be implanted in the young virgin girl, Serena. Stephen had done nothing but what he had been instructed in one of the dreams through which the Lord of Light communicated to him. After setting up the microscope so he could watch, Stephen had been amazed to watch light penetrate the egg and the cells divide. The rest was truly a miracle. Luca was that miracle.

Now, as the Italian ambassador, Luca had power. As Arturo's heir, he had an immense fortune, supplemented royally by Billings Mason, the leader of the Interfaith Global Union. Treasures from the Vatican had been sold off secretly and the funds transferred to Luca Giamo's private accounts. The World Union would become increasingly incapable of handling the Anti-Globalists' worldwide terror attacks and the destabilization of the Union currency. Crime had become rampant after the disappearance of millions of people, although local authorities struggled to maintain a semblance of order. The world was on the brink of economic disaster and physical danger, and wave upon wave of natural disasters and civil unrest threatened to unravel civilization. The world was about to enter another dark age. Now was the time, and the World Union would crumble just as Luca predicted.

Mankind had tried every sort of government for millennia, and all of them had failed. Humans needed to be ruled by a god. Only a god could save them. Luca had saved him and Stephen knew Luca would save the world as well. Stephen sighed as he clasped his hands with joy, anticipating Luca's day coming soon. The world would worship Luca, who would usher in a new era of peace and prosperity.

Stephen thought with satisfaction about the others. Luca was unique, of course. He was the only son of Lucifer, the Lord of Light, but other similarly sired children had also been born to human hosts. Each time Stephen had been blessed to see the angelic being reveal itself before the elements were entered, the cell division taking place before his eyes. The cells were then placed in their human hosts. Women had come to Giamo's infertility clinics from all over the world. Barren, they arrived, and many left carrying precious beings. There were thousands of them. He had lost count long ago.

One of those was the consort chosen for Luca. Stephen imagined she would be incredibly beautiful and intelligent. The children that he had managed to keep track of had excelled in every way. They were amazing—a new race of men and women destined to rule the world. That thought filled him with awe.

Scarlet shadows danced around Stephen. He looked up to see the moon glowing a brilliant crimson, casting a red glow on the earth below. Volcanic eruptions in the East African Rift Zone had filled the atmosphere with tiny particles. Those particles scattered the blue and green light while allowing the red to pass through. For centuries, uneducated men had thought a red moon was an evil omen, a sign that death and destruction were on their way. Stephen stared in appreciation at the moon's beauty and considered it auspicious.

Hearing footsteps behind him, he turned to welcome his master, but Luca's expression of rapture was too intense to allow mere conversation. Stephen rejoiced for his master and decided it would be better to share the good news about Teo tomorrow at breakfast. He led the way to the limousine quietly, opening the door solicitously for Luca.

8

ROME, ITALY

They sat in one of the few areas of the Piazza del Colosseo that offered shade. The summer sun beat down mercilessly, reflecting off the dark stone buildings and pavement, intensifying the already stifling heat. Kurt and Angelina perched on the curb just opposite the Arch of Constantine, watching Charlie enjoy her first gelato as she sat in front of them.

She licked the last bit off of the pink plastic spoon, and Angelina squatted on her heels to wipe away the sticky mess around Charlie's mouth. "Was it good?" she asked the toddler.

"More, Mommy!"

Kurt shook his head. "Remember when you let her have 'more' on the ship? I've never seen so many adults move as quickly as when she got sick in the dining room. They probably had to wear hazmat suits to disinfect the area around our table. You'd better not let her have any more, Angie," he warned.

Charlie looked up at him and shook her chubby finger at him. "Don't say no to me!"

It was all Angelina could do not to laugh. She tapped Charlie's finger. "Hey, kiddo, that's not a nice way to talk to Uncle Kurt. You be good."

She stood up with Charlie's hand in hers and led the way back toward the Coliseum. Instantly, the ground started shaking and a reverberating roar consumed everything around them. Angelina grabbed Kurt with her free hand to steady herself. It took her a mo-

ONE WILL BE LEFT

ment to realize what was happening. "Earthquake!" she gasped.

Kurt pulled Charlie in between them and told Angelina to get down. She wrapped her arms around Charlie as the ground heaved beneath. Thankfully, they were not close to any structures. They watched in horror as the Arch of Constantine crumbled with a crash, filling the air around them with dust and making it difficult to breathe. Angelina looked past Kurt's sheltering arm and saw the Coliseum in front of them sway back and forth, then collapse like a child's stack of building blocks.

Traffic in the street stopped completely; people were honking their horns and screaming. A huge cloud of dust billowed up from the ruins of the Coliseum and covered them. Angelina started coughing, gagging, and heaving. She wanted to get up and run, but the ground was still shaking. Kurt held her tightly and murmured reassurances to her and Charlie. Angelina could hear terrified screaming and crying around her, but all she could do was cling to Charlie and huddle under Kurt, praying they would be safe.

Finally, after what seemed like hours, the shaking stopped. They stood up and looked around to see with shock that almost every building around the Piazza del Colosseo had been flattened. Chaos. Complete and utter destruction. Kurt picked up an obviously shell-shocked Charlie. The people around them looked ghostly, all covered in dirt and debris.

Angelina started to cry hysterically, pawing at Kurt and begging him to take them back to their hotel. "I want to give Charlie a bath. We have to go back right now!" She broke into a frenzy. "I have to get her into clean clothes, get the dust out of her hair, and take her where it's safe, and—"

"Listen, you need to stop it!" Kurt grabbed her shoulder and squeezed it hard. Charlie started to wail. "You're making this worse. Get yourself together, Angie." He handed Charlie to her. She hugged her daughter tightly and whispered to calm her.

"We need to find a way to get out of here now. There will be aftershocks, I'm sure." He looked around for the best way out, but it

ONE WILL BE LEFT

was difficult to determine which way they should go. People were moaning, some frantically trying to dial out on their cell phones, some running around in panic, and some still trapped under large pieces of debris, visibly injured.

"But what about our things? We need to go to the hotel... where we'll be safe."

Kurt looked at her sternly. "That had to be over seven, if not eight, on the Richter scale. Look at the cracks in the ground, Angelina. Get with it! We need to get away from here. The hotel is probably gone, given the size of that quake. There's no sense in trying to go there."

Kurt took Charlie, set her on his right hip, and pulled Angelina along with his left hand toward the street next to the Coliseum. Some cars had fallen into gashes that ripped through the road, while others were left stranded as their occupants sought safety elsewhere. Quickly scanning his options, Kurt led them, weaving between cars before he found a small abandoned sedan that would work. He opened the driver's side and checked that there was enough gas in the running car.

"This will do. Get in," he ordered.

"But Kurt..."

"Get in now. We have to get Charlie away from here. It will be hours before help comes for us. The police and rescue crews will be busy with the injured. If we stay here, we run the risk of getting stuck, and there are a few people in Rome I don't want to run into."

Angelina got in the back of the car with Charlie and watched her cousin expertly maneuver the sedan around other vehicles.
"I'm going to head south along this road because there are fewer structures to block our way," Kurt explained.

"Are we going to go back toward the coast?"

"No, we'll head east as we are able. I don't know much about tsunamis, but I don't want to go anywhere near the ocean right now, just to be safe."

He cursed and slammed on the brakes. A woman stood in

ONE WILL BE LEFT

a gap between cars, her back toward them. It was the only way through. Kurt honked and honked, but the woman did not move. She didn't even flinch. Kurt rolled down his window and shouted at her. "Lady! Hey, you! We're trying to get through, can't you see? Move!"

Angelina looked down and saw Charlie had fallen asleep on her lap. *She always falls asleep when she's scared. She must be terrified*, Angelina thought.

"I'll go ask her to move," she told Kurt, moving Charlie carefully onto the seat without waking her.

Angelina closed the car door softly and walked up to the woman. "Excuse me, *signora*, would you please move?" The woman did not respond, so Angelina put a hand to her shoulder and turned her around. The older woman's eyes were downcast and she trembled. Angelina put her arm around the woman's shaking body and gently asked if she was alone, but she didn't answer.

"Do you speak English? Do you need some help?" Angelina tried to speak kindly, but panic caused her to be abrupt. The ground heaved beneath her feet. "Look, I have to get my daughter out of here! I'm sorry, but I need to ask you to move. Let me help you."

The woman moved robotically as Angelina directed her off of the street to the sidewalk. The woman whispered something in Italian. Angelina recognized some of the words. "Are you praying? Praying is good." She looked around for help and saw Kurt drive the car through the gap and stop. He rolled down the driver's-side window, motioning frantically for her to get back in the car.

"Get back in! She's fine!" he ordered.

"I can't just leave her here alone," Angelina protested. Something about the old woman kept Angelina from just leaving her alone.

Kurt looked around the cluttered roadway. "There are other people here. Let someone else help her. She probably has family who will be looking for her, if they're not already..."

Angelina nodded. There were other people walking around or standing together in small clusters. Surely someone would help the older woman. She rubbed her hand on the woman's back. "We have to go, but you're going to be fine. Just move over here off of the road."

Angelina led the woman to the sidewalk, stepping over a fallen tree. A small retaining wall ran along the length of the sidewalk. It had crumbled in some places, but Angelina found a portion that looked solid enough.

"Sit here."

The woman sat obediently, her lips still moving.

Kurt honked the horn in saccadic bursts, which made Angelina want to scream. She grimaced at him and turned her back pointedly before addressing the older woman.

"You're going to be all right. There are people who will help you." She turned to go, but the woman grabbed her arm with surprising strength, nearly knocking Angelina backward.

"Do you see them?" the woman whispered thickly, dragging her words out one by one.

Angelina patted the hand that gripped her tightly and answered, "Yes, there are people here. I'm sure help is coming."

"No. Them." The old woman raised her eyelids for the first time and stared at Angelina with a fearful gaze, her bright blue eyes wide and glossy. Angelina started to shake her head no, when she saw someone move swiftly in her peripheral vision. Turning her head slowly, she saw a dark-haired man moving toward the chaos behind them. She froze as she watched him glide, his short robes flowing behind him, sword in hand. His face was frightening, beautiful, and ferocious. He turned his head and smiled at her knowingly before turning away and continuing on. It took her breath away.

The old woman grabbed both of Angelina's shoulders. "You see?"

Angelina nodded, suddenly trembling. She could faintly hear Kurt honking in the background, but awe and fear caused her to tune out many of her surroundings. She looked around. There were hundreds of fierce-looking men marching across the street and sidewalks, navigating through the cars and even through groups of people, completely unnoticed. They were all incredibly attractive with symmetrical features, chiseled jaws, and muscular builds. But there was also something about them that made Angelina's stomach turn. She quivered as another one of them caught her gaze and scowled menacingly.

"Are they dead people?" she whispered to the old woman. "No one else seems to see them...why can we?"

The small woman pulled Angelina down to her level and muttered, "They are the fallen ones. I have seen them before, but never in such numbers. Not many humans can see them."

Angelina ignored the car horn she now heard blasting impatiently at her and looked into the woman's eyes. "What are fallen ones?"

"Demons, woman! Demons! I have seen one or two together before, usually around a human host. But this...this is a catastrophe. God help us!"

As more of the demons rushed past, a dusty breeze kicked up around them. Angelina became frantic with fear. She looked back toward the car where Kurt and Charlie were waiting. Dozens of demon warriors were gliding between her and the car. How could she pass through them to get back to the vehicle? Would they harm her?

Pulling away from the elderly woman's clutch, Angelina looked around and noticed there seemed to be some sort of a barrier around the two of them. The passing hordes broke rank to move around her and the old woman, yet they marched straight through other groups of people. Why?

Quickly, she asked the older woman if she noticed how the demons seemed to avoid them. The woman's panicked breathing slowed down as she stood up and turned in a circle looking at the evil horde. Cautiously, the woman moved into the path of an oncoming demon. He recoiled suddenly and moved away. She turned to Angelina with a smile.

"Praise God! Praise God! He has saved me and now He keeps me in the shelter of His care!" The woman grabbed Angelina's hand.

"Please, let me take you back to your car. Your husband is becoming upset. Thank you, thank you for helping me get to safety!"

She led Angelina back across the battered road to the car. They had to hop over small crevices in the broken pavement.

"Why can I see this?" Angelina asked the woman. "You see them. I see them. No one else is reacting to these creatures. Why?"

The old woman patted her hand. "Do you know the Savior? He gives each of us our own gifts. I have had this one since the day I believed, just days after my dear husband disappeared with the others to meet Him in the air."

"What savior? What do you mean?" Angelina inquired fervently as they neared the car.

"Well, perhaps He is letting you see the true reality of what is happening in the spiritual realm around us so you will come to Him. He loves you, my dear. Pray that He will open the eyes of your heart. Thank you again!"

Kurt got out of the car, yelling at Angelina to get in. She ran the last few feet to the vehicle, pulled the door open, and got in. Charlie was still sound asleep, sprawled out in the back. Kurt got back into the driver's seat and slammed his door immediately, putting the car in gear. As they drove off, he ranted about her selfish behavior, how she had put him and Charlie in danger just to help an old woman. But Angelina hardly heard him. Her attention was fixated on the creatures that continued to swarm the area, dozens passing by her window. Many of them glared at her as they moved by, their evil gaze tying her stomach in knots. Her mouth was dry and her heart felt like it was beating a million times a minute. *Demons...* she thought. *Do I really believe this?* She began to pray silently to God that the savior the woman talked about would keep them safe from the monsters that marched alongside of them.

ONE WILL BE LEFT

Chesapeake Bay

Elena lay in the small bed, her head against John's chest, staring at the empty fireplace as she listened to her husband describe all that had happened during the months they'd been apart.

"I feel terrible about Ashley and Celia. Talin said he saw their spirits rise. I know that means they're in heaven, but still, Elena! Blake killed his own wife and mother-in-law to keep the Anti-Globalists from getting them."

"Why would he do that?"

"Once when we were foraging for supplies, we went into a house we thought was empty. We found a woman there, barely alive. She'd been tortured by the Anti-Globalists..." Dismay roiled John's handsome features. "It was horrific. Blake put her out of her misery and vowed he'd never let them do that to his wife. I hate him...he's a liar and a murderer. Those were two gentle, kind women." His voice cracked with emotion.

Elena tilted her head and looked up at her husband. His face had thinned considerably. His skin was tanned and weathered, and his hands felt rough and brawny. She raised her right hand and stroked his cheek. Everyone else was asleep, and they were finally alone. She filled him in on her escape from New Babylon with Brant and Olivia, relaying how DC had faked his, Teo's, and Olivia's deaths in order to keep them safe from Luca's evil plans. John, in turn, shared with Elena about some of his own experiences. Listening to how he had been rescued by Talin, whom she knew to be her own guardian angel, filled her with wonder and thankfulness. John might have died along with those women, but God had spared him. She was grateful.

John took her hand and kissed her palm gently. "There were times I thought I would never see you again," he whispered, gently tucking a piece of hair behind her ear.

"How long do you think we can stay here?" she asked quietly.

"I don't know," he answered. "It depends on how long the fighting goes on. It's been quiet for a while." John kissed her and got up from the bed. Standing by the window, he looked outside.

"How will we know when it is safe to go?"

"Talin will let us know. I still can't believe he's an angel. I mean, I believe it, but it is so surreal. Did you ever imagine something like this happening to us?"

"I know...you must have been terrified when you saw demons." She shuddered.

"I was, and then I wasn't. After I surrendered myself to God, you know, finally laying down my pride, I wasn't afraid. I felt something else, but I'm not sure how to describe it." He shrugged his shoulders.

Elena asked curiously, "What are they like? Talin looks like a man. What do the demons look like?"

"Most of them looked like men, too. Strong, beautiful, terrifying men. The others were weird, disturbing-looking creatures that had human and animal characteristics. I could feel their overwhelming power...it seemed to have a thick, tangible presence in the air. When they surrounded me, it felt like every word I spoke needed to be pushed out with all my resolve. As I prayed, I felt my words come out with more ease." He sighed. "I'm just glad I can't see that reality all of the time."

"I hope I never see it."

"I have a feeling we are all going to see more strange things than we ever expected," John remarked.

"Has Talin told you more?" Elena felt her stomach churn. "Do you know what's going to happen next? I always believed in God, but demons and antichrists and false prophets, disasters and devastation...John, I don't know if I can cope. What else has he told you?"

John went back to the bed and sat next to his wife, pulling her over onto his arms. "He is pretty tight-lipped, actually. I think he only tells us what God allows him to—what is needed in the moment." He chuckled. "We could learn a lot from his example."

A thoughtful look crossed John's brow and he suddenly changed the subject. "Remember when the Christians disappeared? How I was doing that research?"

"Yes, of course."

"I like to be thorough when I'm investigating a story, so I spent a lot of time reading and researching what Christians believed about the end times. I read the book of Revelation, but it didn't do much for me. I couldn't understand anything past the first chapter."

A sudden explosion outside shook the window across from them, and he stopped talking. A picture fell off the wall and landed on the floor with a crash. They waited in the dark to see if someone was going to return fire, but no one did.

John hugged Elena reassuringly and continued speaking. "Then I stumbled across a book that DC had in his apartment. It was his mom's. She had obviously read it a lot because it was highlighted and marked with dozens of notes. So, I asked DC if I could borrow it."

"Oh, I remember you reading that! You said it was about Bible prophecy and the last days. I thought you didn't like that book." Elena pulled back with a confused look on her face.

"Although I didn't believe any of it, I couldn't stop reading." John shook his head and grinned at her. "I made time lines, notes, thinking I might write a book about the 'rapture,' as they called it. But after a while, no one seemed to care about the disappearances. So I set it aside."

Elena had turned to face John as he spoke. Pondering his words, she mused, "You know, that was strange, wasn't it, that everyone stopped talking about it? After a couple of months, it seemed like no one was interested in the disappearances anymore. Almost like the world was tired of the whole thing and had moved on, even people who had lost loved ones. DC and I talked about it once. He attributed it to some kind of deluding influence over the world. Apparently, it had been foretold by the apostle Paul in the Bible."

ONE WILL BE LEFT

"Then I was certainly one of the deluded!" John exclaimed. "But Elena, it's so strange. Now I can remember everything I read in that book! It's like I can see the pages I read. I've been going over and over it in my mind; I had been even before I met Talin. I think God used it to help convict me about the truth of Jesus. When I read about the False Prophet, Billings Mason immediately came to my mind. That's what he is.

"Do you remember when he came to the hospital in Rome and healed DC and Teo?"

Elena nodded.

"It really bugged me how you adored him. Now I realize that at some level, I knew there was something wrong with him. He's deceived so many people!"

"I know. I can't tell you how guilty I felt about believing he was a godly man. I honestly thought he might be a true saint—I mean, the things he can do! He heals the sick and raises the dead. He seems so truly good.

"John, when I became a believer in Jesus, I began to see how evil the plans of the enemy are. He's taken over the church! He's corrupted the truth, and millions have bought into it. Do you know that the Interfaith Global Union has more members than all the Christian denominations ever had at one time?" Elena's voice rose heatedly.

"Elena, he did not take over the church. The church isn't an organization; it's an organism. It's a living thing. The church is people." John spoke emphatically.

"I hadn't thought of it that way," she said. "The others are in heaven and we're here. Does that make us part of the 'church?'"

"Definitely," John agreed. He went on, "But really, the most disturbing part of that book was the part about the Antichrist. I couldn't figure out who he might be—that is, until earlier today when you told me about Luca's plan to kill DC and Olivia. It all fell into place—his sudden rise to power, his quick rise to position as the most influential man in the world, so rich and charismatic. Why would he kill anyone? Why risk killing his family? That's just evil."

Elena was stunned at the implications of what John was telling her. "Are there any other things about the Antichrist that fit Luca?" she asked.

"Well, there's an old prophecy that says the Antichrist will come from the people who destroyed Jerusalem and the Temple. The Romans did that."

"Hmm," Elena pondered. Then she exclaimed, "Luca is Italian!" She became very still. "John, you know I like to study the etymology of names. Do you know what Luca Giamo means?" She stared intently into her husband's eyes, troubled. "Luca means 'light' and Giamo is from the Spanish word for James—Jacob in Hebrew—which means 'supplanter.' So putting both of Luca's names together means 'supplanter of the light.'"

"That sure describes the part the Antichrist is to play, doesn't it? But we have some time, Elena. He's in a powerful position, but he's not ruling the world. Not yet, anyway."

"How much time do you think we have, John? And are we ever going to see Teo and DC again?" Tears began to roll down her cheeks. "I'm so afraid they won't find us—or worse, that they'll be caught. It's been running through my mind all day that Maggie's called the authorities about Olivia. How long until the whole plan is discovered? I've never been so afraid, John."

John pulled his wife into his arms again. "I have to think that if God sent an angel to bring me to faith and back to you again, then He is able to keep us all safe. We just have to trust Him no matter what."

9

LAKE GEORGE, NEW YORK

"I've had quite a few messages from New York," Eric continued, "begging for someone to help them. Apparently the World Union has the entire city cordoned off. Nothing comes in—no food, no help."

Everyone in the room was silent. Bess, Jack, Andie, James, and Eric made up what constituted the leadership of their small community. They sat in the office of the tiny church they used as headquarters.

"I don't understand," James said. "The US had stockpiles of the vaccine. Why didn't the World Union supply them to the people in New York?"

"Apparently the Anti-Globalists have confiscated many of the vaccines that were stockpiled. They're refusing to release them until the World Union leaves North America. No one is sure how the virus was released into the city. It was supposed to have been eradicated," Eric explained.

"Maybe the Anti-Globalists were the ones who released the virus," Jack suggested. "They've been surprisingly able to gain power in key areas of North America." He ran his fingers through his hair in frustration. "How is it that what started as a protest movement a little over a year ago has morphed into such an effective army?"

"I don't know," James began speaking deliberately, anticipating the group's reaction. "I don't know how it started, but what I wanted to discuss is how I believe the Lord wants us to respond." He looked at each of his friends in turn. "I've been praying and fast-ing for the last few days. Last night, the Lord clearly spoke to me. He wants me to go to the city and preach the gospel message. He told me He was going to 'heal the brokenhearted and bind their wounds.'"

As he expected, the others in the room all started to object. He lifted his hand and waited for everyone to be quiet. "Remember Bernard, who led me out of prison? He came to see me this morning. I asked him to tell you all what he told me. He's in the other room waiting."

James went to the door and opened it.

"Bernard, would you please tell everyone what you told me this morning?"

Bernard walked to the edge of the group. He was not a tall man, but he was an imposing figure, a striking man with a kind face.

"I had a dream last night. It was strange, not like the normal sort of dream where things are all jumbled or confusing. It was more like I was watching something real unfold in front of me.

"Pastor James and I were walking through New York City. It was strangely quiet and empty as we walked through the streets and came to Grand Central Station. I could hear the sound of many people inside, crying and screaming. We opened the door and saw the place was crowded with people clustered in groups throughout the main terminal." He paused, his voice cracking slightly before he continued.

"Pastor James cried out. Everyone we saw was infected with something terrible—like boils or something. The people we saw were really suffering. Pastor James bent to pray for a child. I couldn't believe he touched him! The boy was revolting, just covered in sores. I'm sorry, but it was…terrible," Bernard swallowed. "Anyway, I don't know what Pastor said, but when he stood up, the boy was healed—completely cleared of the sores.

"Then I heard a voice telling me to go tell Pastor what I had seen and to go with him. So, when I woke up, that's what I did." Bernard looked at James and nodded, giving him the floor.

ONE WILL BE LEFT

"When Bernard came and told me this," James said, "I knew I had confirmation that the Lord does indeed want me to go into the city. Bernard feels he is to go, as well."

Andie spoke first. "I understand that you feel badly for the people there in New York, but it's so dangerous! What about David? What if something happens to you there? Surely he and the people God has brought here are your first priority?"

Bess rubbed Andie's shoulder. "I agree with Andie, but it seems clear that the Lord has spoken to James and confirmed it with Bernard's dream."

"James, are you asking us for advice?" Jack asked.

James looked at his friends with affection and understanding. In the months he and David had been living in their small community at the campground, this group of people had become like family. He greatly respected Jack and Bess; their knowledge gave them all tremendous advantages in learning how to cope with their new reality. The couple were like grandparents to David, who had none. Eric was a genius with technology and, through the network he had developed, made it possible for James to transmit his weekly messages. Eric also made it possible for the community to get information from the outside world. Andie, too, was indispensable. She loved David and he loved her. She helped care for him daily, and James could not imagine how he could continue his work without her help.

James smiled at Jack. "Well, I guess I'm not really asking for advice. I believe it's clear the Lord is calling me to go. What I do want are your prayers as we go. I know that it's dangerous, but still, I'm called to go.

"Andie, I'm leaving David in your care. I know Bess and Jack will help you. Jack, you'll be in charge of the community while I'm gone. I'd like all of you to pray for me, for us." He turned to include Bernard and stretched his arm around the man.

"How will you get into the city when the World Union has it blockaded?" asked Bess.

"I'm confident we will find a way." James sat down on the

small stool in the room and rubbed his forehead in thought. "I don't know everything that's ahead of us. But I do know the time is short. We know the world is being shaken, literally. The World Union seems to be losing power—at least here in North America. Somehow, out of the battles and chaos that are going on, the Antichrist will come to power."

"But why do you have to go now?" Andie implored. "We need you here!"

James looked at her and leaned in closely. He could see deep concern on her face, so he explained, "We know that once Israel signs a peace treaty with the Antichrist, seven years of tribulation will begin. How much time is there until then? Not much, I think.

"We're all pretty sure that Billings Mason is the False Prophet, leading the world into one religion. The Antichrist will surely be revealed soon. He will only appear to bring peace, but we know that persecution and trouble are ahead." James paused for a moment, earnestly trying to form the right words to explain his motivation for leaving.

"What I'm trying to say is that we don't have the luxury of time. We're safe here for now, but we may not be in the months to come. We know the Bible says many of us will die during the days of tribulation. The people in New York need to hear about Jesus right now. Some are dying without the hope of salvation—hope you and I have—and God is calling me to go."

Andie began to cry softly and buried her face in her palms. Bess put her arm around the younger woman and hugged her.

"James is right," Jack agreed. "The time is short. Those folks in New York deserve a chance to hear the gospel. Let's pray for James and Bernard."

Each of the others stood up and walked over to James. Bernard sat next to him. Eric put a hand on each man, as did the others. He began to pray, whispering at first. Then, as he continued to implore the Lord for protection and power for James and Bernard, his words seemed to become infused with confidence. When he ended,

ONE WILL BE LEFT

Andie began to pray, followed by Bess. Their voices were tearful, but their words—like Eric's—expressed faith and confidence.

When they finished praying, James stood up and embraced them all, tears flowing down his face. It would be terrible to leave David, but he knew his son would be safe with his friends, his family.

Istanbul, Turkey

Billings Mason stood at the center of the dome in the famous Hagia Sophia. An altar had been erected just behind him, raised on an elevated plane. It was covered in gold cloth and exquisite lace. On the altar was a large crystal bowl; in it, bare branches supported purple-flowered vines, dripping here and there with red, orange, and green berries. Facing the cameras, Billings raised his arms upward, his black chasuble stretched out like a banner. It was embroidered in gold with symbols of the cross, the Star of David, the star and crescent, letters in Sanskrit, and the outlines of plum-colored flowers.

The hushed crowd erupted in delighted applause and laughter as the sunlight beamed through the ancient windows and focused directly on the former pope, now leader of the one world religion called OneFaith. The faithful began to weep as Billings glowed ethereally, his face tilted toward the light, receiving the light's blessing.

Softly, violins began to play. The orchestra was hidden from sight, but the peaceful strains lifted the hearts of all gathered. Billings lowered his arms, spreading them wide as if to embrace every viewer. The music faded away as he began to speak. The light of the sun and the cameras caused the silver in his dark hair to glisten and the blue of his eyes to sparkle. Wisdom and childlike wonder both found expression in his charismatic appearance.

He smiled in greeting. "Welcome, my brothers and sisters. Peace and joy be with you all."

The crowd replied, "And with you."

ONE WILL BE LEFT

The prophet nodded his head. "Please be seated." He turned in a circle so everyone in the assembly could see his smiling welcome before he turned to face the cameras. "We are gathered here at the Hagai Sophia, this place of holy wisdom, to officially inaugurate our commitment to the true faith.

"For centuries, mankind has been divided into hundreds of religions—mere versions of the true faith that have been the basis of contention, persecution, and war. Many have come saying they are the answer, the chosen, the enlightened, or even the savior, but look at the fruits of those who followed them. Were they in keeping with what is good and right and true? No. Centuries of blood speak to these religions' failure to address humanity's greatest needs. Each had aspects of the divine, but mixed with human error. We were lost and we sought to find our way."

One of the cameras panned the crowd, recording people's reactions. Some looked down, others wept, and others stared intently at Billings Mason.

"We were taught that ours was the only truth, weren't we? Then, as the beginning of a new age dawned, we were told we could achieve unity through faith. Of course, truth is always true, but our understanding of truth has to evolve. While our experience as a race has bettered, we still have suffered the ravages of war, famine, and natural disaster. The earth itself has seemed to turn against us. I know many—too many—have suffered.

"But what we have experienced are merely birth pangs, my brothers and sisters. A new age, a revolutionary age is about to begin. There will be more pangs as we near the day when the true savior of mankind is revealed."

Billings' voice rose with passion. "There is a bit of god in all of us. We are all equal partakers of the divine; we have just lost our way over the centuries. There is One coming who will help us realize this truth and unleash the divinity within us. He will enable us to find the purity and peace that lives in us all, so we can serve others with true love. There is indeed one true faith, which encompasses and eclipses all others.

"When mankind experiences the unity of true faith, there will be no more hunger, no more war. Once we have tapped into the divinity of our true selves, we will have true and lasting peace." He paused for effect, turning to face the crowd encircling him before moving deliberately and ceremoniously to the altar. Carefully, he pulled out from the vase a tendril of purple blossoms.

"This is a beautiful flower, is it not?" He held it up so the cameraman could get a close shot. "Its name is bittersweet nightshade. The truth is often bittersweet, is it not? You may have noticed this flower is woven onto the emblem of our faith. Indeed, it is woven here." He gestured to the gold embroidery on his garments. "Its berries too are beautiful, but poisonous—even deadly.

"I want to demonstrate something amazing about the true faith. Even one as young as a child may embrace the truth and be set free from the limitations we have known." He indicated a small girl standing to the right side of the door near him. "Nobuye was born with a severe heart condition. She was only two years old when her tiny heart finally failed her. Her father brought her to me in Rome during one of the summer meetings we held. Do you remember the one? Her story was celebrated throughout the world.

"Many of you wrote to me, especially to ask about Nobuye. Her story touched many hearts. She is her father's only child because her mother died in a tragic accident shortly after Nobuye's birth. Nobuye was the living memory of the love her father and his wife shared. He could not bear to lose his daughter. And you know what? He did not."

Billings Mason turned to his left with a smile and held out his hand to the dainty girl with jet-black pigtails who walked hand in hand with her father toward the prophet. The crowd stood clapping, the intensity increasing when Billings picked up the child and perched her on his hip.

He spoke to her in English. She answered in Japanese. They talked for a minute about her heart, and the crowd grew quiet again.

It was obvious that each understood the other despite the language difference.

"As you can see, Nobuye is a healthy little girl. She just told me she loves to dance and sing. Those are things she would never have experienced.

"I know there are many who believe that the healings come from me, but this is not true. I am only the channel through which the revitalizing energy comes. Only when the power given to me by the source of all things is met with faith are healings or miracles possible."

"Nobuye had the faith of a child, and she was healed. This four-year-old has greater faith than any I have seen." He paused to place a hand on her head, as if in blessing.

"She can communicate with anyone. I do not speak Japanese, yet you saw her talk with me. She has the gift of languages. She also has the gift of self-healing. Let me demonstrate."

He offered the branch to Nobuye. Carefully, she plucked the green berries and popped them into her mouth. When the last berry had been picked and eaten, Billings handed the vine to her father.

"While this is not as poisonous as deadly nightshade, it can and has killed children." The crowd gasped.

Billings gently tilted the child's face up to his. "Do you feel unwell?"

The girl moaned and grabbed her stomach. Her face turned red and her eyes shut tightly in pain. After a moment, she lifted her arms upward, palms raised toward the ceiling and smiled. Billings spoke to her softly. She hugged him and gave him a kiss before he set her on the ground. Nobuye ran dancing around the altar, laughing and singing.

The orchestra joined in as the crowd thundered with applause. When the song finished, the girl skipped away from the center of the huge room with her father.

Billings addressed his audience again. "This is the faith that overcomes!" He waited for the enthusiastic crowd to quiet, then picked up a blossom from the white altar cloth. "Even poison can be neutralized by the power available to each one of us. There is no reason for sickness for those who have such faith, no need for ignorance or hatred to reign any longer in the world of men. True faith will bring us five things, five things represented by the petals of this flower: knowledge, joy, purpose, peace, and love.

"I am the last prophet. My purpose is to prepare the way. Are you ready for the way to be revealed? Are you eager to be set free? Do you long to realize the truth? If we will come together and realize the unity of faith, the Promised One will come. He will show us how to unlock our potential as we worship him. All are welcome! Will you come?"

Billings Mason reached his hand toward the cameras entreatingly. "All you need to do is come. Counselors are waiting to speak with you. Contact information is scrolling across your screen. Please do not wait. Do not hesitate."

His gaze swept over the crowds around him before he started on yet another revelation. "It has been granted to me to lay hands on and empower others as ministers of true enlightenment—men and women who have been gifted by the true source of all and who have realized in some measure their divinity. They will be dedicated now to serve humanity. Please welcome them as they come forward."
He added, "You will notice that each has chosen to take the mark of discipleship on their foreheads or hands. This is a symbol of their dedication."

The prophet turned to his right and then left in welcome as men and women walked slowly through the enormous columns of the ancient church and mosque on either side of him. They were dressed in white robes, and each came and knelt in front of him.

He walked to the nearest celebrant, a young man. Taking his hand, Billings lifted him up. "These dedicated few here in front of you represent the many ministers of faith we are sending throughout the world. You may recognize the symbol on their foreheads and hands. We have taken this ancient six-pointed star, used in many of mankind's transient belief systems, and incorporated in its center six interlocking circles. These circles represent interconnectedness—the inseparable relation of the parts to the whole. The six circles in the center signify unity. The One who is coming will bring true unity to humanity once again.

"These emissaries will be starting their missions at local places of worship throughout the world. Each one of them has demonstrated gifts of true faith, just as Nobuye showed you. These ministers will be available to serve you in your quest for knowledge and understanding. They are identified by their marks so that wherever they go, you may easily find them.

"Now, please join me in dedicating these men and women to the service of the faithful." Billings placed his hand on the young man's head in benediction. As Billings spoke, each person in the ancient place of worship heard the prophet in his language of origin.

Jerusalem, Israel

Michael Benari stood outside across the street from his old home. He noticed the bougainvillea his mother had planted decades ago cascading over the wall in stunning shades of pink and purple. He knew his mother would have loved it. From where he was standing, he could see Devorah's home as well as his parents'.

The old, familiar sensation of despair came over him. His ears were ringing, and for a few moments, he breathed slowly to combat the nausea. Memories of his young wife, Devorah, crowded his thinking. There were so many images that tumbled through his mind, bringing up long-suppressed yearnings for her. He looked at the window in her parents' home where her bedroom had been. They had grown up together on this street; their mothers were the best of friends. He smiled, remembering his mother's reaction when he told her that Devorah had agreed to marry him. Both sets of parents had been overjoyed, despite his and Devorah's young age. The marriage had been something of which both families had dreamed.

He looked at the stairs that led to Devorah's childhood home. She had been so happy here with her mother and father, Sigal and Moshe. When Michael's own parents died on a bus in a suicide attack, Sigal and Moshe had been a real comfort to him. Then, just a few weeks after his parents' deaths, Devorah went back to bed early one morning after nursing her and Michael's newborn son, Micah, complaining of a terrible headache. She never woke up. Again, Sigal and Moshe were there to help, taking care of Micah. In his intense grief, Michael just could not cope with the infant.

Michael rubbed his mouth and turned to leave, suddenly overwhelmed with guilt. He had seen Micah a few times that first year, but excuses were easier than the pain of seeing Devorah's eyes staring back at him from his son's face. *I failed you, Devorah,* he thought. *I have not taken care of our son.*

He walked quickly, stifling sobs and overcome with sorrow. He was startled when he found himself outside of the Great Synagogue on King George Street. He wiped his eyes.

"Michael? Is that you?"

He turned to see an old friend of his mother's standing next to him. The tiny woman was a spitfire who loved to gossip yet was fiercely loyal to her friends. She had aged in the ten years since he last saw her, but her black eyes still looked sharply at him the way they always had.

"You've been crying, Michael. I suppose you heard about Sigal. It was sudden, really. After Moshe's death, she just didn't have the heart to go on, at least that's what I think." The little woman patted his shoulder in a way he knew was meant to be comforting.

Michael was confused. "What do you mean? I didn't know Moshe died!" His voice became strident. "Why wasn't I told?"

"Oh dear, I am sorry, Michael. I thought you knew. He just passed last week, and Sigal, this morning. I don't know why she didn't let you know about Moshe. She was devastated. Maybe she was afraid to let you find out the truth; it's such a scandal to so many of our old friends," the woman lamented, shaking her head in disappointment.

"What are you talking about?" Michael asked, more confused and alarmed.

"Well, after the war—the 'unwar' when our enemies were destroyed and that evil Dome was demolished by HaShem, Sigal and Moshe both became followers of Yeshua the Messiah." She looked around carefully and whispered. "I did, too. We had to be quiet about it."

"They became Christians?" Michael was astounded. There were no Jews more devout than his in-laws.

"No, not Christians! We do not belong to the Christians. We follow Yeshua. We are part of His body, but we are Jews, not Christians. The Lord was gracious to give us eyes to see the truth about Yeshua. Rest assured, Sigal and Moshe are with the Lord," the elderly woman spoke soothingly. "But since the boy also believed, they began to speak more openly about it, and many of our friends were mortified."

"Where is Micah?" Michael asked.

"I know he was at the hospital with Sigal this morning because I was there, too. She passed after I left. I was told that a child welfare officer was called to take him somewhere. That's all I know."

Michael thanked her sincerely. He turned and walked quickly back to where he had parked his car. He had to get to the hospital. His mind raced as he walked. *On the day tMicah is left alone, with no family to care for him, a man who claims to be Elijah comes to my door and tells me I need to turn my heart back to my son. Then I find out Sigal and Moshe have both died and that both of them are Jews that follow Yeshua. I don't understand what is happening!*

Opening the door, Michael got into his car and drove to the hospital. He drove on autopilot, not really focusing on where he was going, his thoughts and emotions overwhelming him. He parked and jogged into the hospital. Without too much trouble, he was able to find the floor where Sigal had spent her last moments. A high desk marked the central nursing station. One of the nurses smiled at him as he approached, and he saw the familiar glimmer of recognition in her eyes.

"Dr. Benari! What an honor to have you here, sir! Can I help you?" she exclaimed with a welcoming smile.

"Yes, my mother-in-law, Sigal Lewit, passed away here this morning. My son was with her. Can you tell me where I can find them?"

"I just got on duty. Let me find out for you, sir." The nurse crossed to the other side of the workstation and spoke quietly with another nurse. Michael saw the first nurse nodding her head before turning back toward him.

"He is still in her room. He wanted to sit with her. I'm sorry, sir, but we thought he was orphaned, so the child welfare officer has been called in."

"That's fine," Michael replied. "I will deal with them. What is the room number?"

Heading down the hallway, he felt a lump lodge in this throat; it had been almost ten years since he last saw Micah. He opened the door slowly and instantly spotted Sigal's body on the bed. Micah sat next to her reading a book out loud. No, his eyes are closed, Michael noted to himself. Tears filled his eyes as he realized Micah was praying. The father stood silently, his hand on the doorknob as he listened. He had never heard anyone pray like this boy. There were no formal, ritualistic phrases; he was just talking, as one would speak to a friend or a father. Michael felt guilt stab at his heart as he let the door close behind him.

Micah opened his eyes when the door clicked. He looked straight into Michael's eyes.

"Hello, Father," he said simply.

"You know who I am?" Michael asked.

"Yes, I have pictures of you and Mother. Savta also kept a scrapbook for me of your work."

Michael could not help but stare at his son; his resemblance to Devorah was astonishing. Surprisingly, that fact caused Michael no pain. Even sitting down, Micah looked big for a ten-year-old, healthy and fit. His clothes, though simple in appearance, were well made. *Sigal would have made sure of that,* Michael thought.

"I'm sorry about your grandmother, Micah. I just found out today about her and your grandfather." He did not know what else to say so he sat down in a chair at the end of the bed.

"Savta told me that Elijah talked to her about you, and she said you would be coming, so I shouldn't worry. The Lord would make sure I wasn't alone."

Michael could see his son was struggling to be strong.

"When she left her body, she was not afraid—" The boy's voice broke. "I was with her. She saw Yeshua as she died. She whispered His name and said, 'Beautiful Savior!' Look at her face, Father. You can still see the joy!"

Michael did as instructed. Indeed, joy illumined Sigal's pale face, and the sight startled him.

Micah stood up, reverently placing the book he had been reading in the chair, and walked over to Michael.

"Will we go to your home now?" He caught his father's eyes in his steady gaze.

Michael nodded, bemused. He didn't know how he was going to explain all of this to Kate. Early on in their dating he had told her his first wife had died suddenly and that it was not a subject he wanted to discuss, but he had never told her about Micah. In the short time they'd been married, he'd come to dread her biting anger and had quickly learned the best way to avoid it was not to annoy her.

What is she going to say? he wondered apprehensively as he ushered Micah out of the hospital room. He couldn't begin to imagine how his wife would react to a confession that began with an old man knocking on their apartment door, claiming to be Elijah, and that ended with the revelation of a long-lost son who now had to live with them because he had no one else in the world.

10

NEW BABYLON,
IRAQ

Dishes clinked as the girl carefully placed them in the tub on the serving cart. She crossed the spacious room quietly, her vintage, black lace dress clinging to her lean figure. Leaning discreetly over the Italian ambassador's chair, she asked, "Would you care for anything else, Ambassador?"

Luca smiled at the young woman and shook his head, "No, thank you, Najah." He turned his attention back to the men sitting around the conference table in his study as he sat his coffee cup back in the saucer. He began to summarize the presentation just made to the group by General Mark Tabor, head of the World Union Defense Forces. "So you believe it is only a matter of time before World Union forces in North America are defeated?"

"Yes, I am afraid so, sir," General Tabor answered tersely. "We realized about a month ago that someone was feeding classified information to the Anti-Globalists. Despite our best efforts, we've not been able to find the source. Their continued attacks have been precisely coordinated and devastating as a result. Our men have simply started surrendering whenever the enemy confronts them."

The other men at the table began murmuring.

"Please sit, General. Thank you for your service. I appreciate what a difficult task the North American front has posed," Luca commended the older man, then continued.

"Since I have taken over the security for the World Union, it has become clear to me that having one centralized government is not the most efficient or effective model to govern the entire world."

The ambassador from the former United States spoke, "Sir, when we began this great experiment, we hoped that the unification of the world's governments would achieve the peace and security we all desperately needed. As you know, not long ago the United States was the world's greatest power. However, after the disappearances of almost a third of our population and the constant barrage of natural disasters, we could barely take care of our own needs."

"And the devastation to your country gravely affected the rest of the world," interjected the ambassador from the former United Kingdom, Kurt Harris.

Ambassador Basset looked dourly at his colleague over the edge of his reading glasses. "The World Union was our best hope. All of the ambassadors have endeavored for the past year and a half to govern the nations of the world. If not for the Anti-Globalists, we might have succeeded."

Luca put both hands on the table and pushed himself to a standing position. "Thank you, Ambassador Basset. We all appreciate what you've been up against." He turned his attention to the whole group and continued. "As you all are aware, North America has been a complicated area for the World Union to govern. Despite the setbacks the ambassador has described, they have been a people used to great freedoms. Although the World Union afforded them aid and protection, many sided with the Anti-Globalist forces because they resented restrictions on those former freedoms. My intelligence sources informed me that the AG leader has taken Washington, DC, and is at this moment sitting in the White House."

The American ambassador shouted his outrage, while the other men at the table also erupted in angry exclamations. Luca waited for their attention, his left hand raised.

"We began this great experiment with every expectation of success. The rebellion in North America has been a roadblock to our goal of world peace, has it not? These people would not allow the World Union to help them by means of our peaceful rule, so they will have rule imposed upon them by this self-proclaimed dictator. It is my advice that the Ambassadorial Body send a delegation to Washington, DC, to broker a peace treaty with this leader, Andres Quinteros."

Austin Basset stood up, his entire body shaking as he began ranting about the injustices and war crimes perpetrated by the Anti-Globalists on the citizens of the former United States. He protested voraciously against any terms between the World Union and the terrorist leader of the rebel group.

Luca walked over to the livid man. Placing a hand on his shoulder, he murmured reassurances to the ambassador, whose face became calm and his body relaxed. Ambassador Basset embraced the younger man affectionately and smiled sheepishly at him before taking his seat again at the table, somewhat embarrassed at his outburst.

Luca continued walking in a circuit around the table. As he spoke, the resonant tone of his voice generated a hopeful expectancy among the assembled leaders.

"While the rebellion in the United States has had negative effects throughout the World Union, the European nations have been most enthusiastic and supportive, providing the greatest number of volunteers to our army," Luca commented. "However, the Chinese have been less helpful." He stood and politely waited while the Chinese ambassador protested. Luca responded to his objections in fluent Mandarin.

Ambassador Xi Vong smiled in response before replying in English, "You have an exceptional gift, Ambassador Giamo."

Luca continued walking around the room as he spoke to the group. "As I indicated to Ambassador Vong, I believe that what I am about to share will make the situation more palatable to each member nation. It is my hope that the few nations that declined membership within the World Union will reconsider if this proposal is passed.

"I would like to present this plan to the entire body of the World Union when we meet in session next week. I believe that by decentralizing our governing body into ten regions, we can more efficiently govern the world and meet the needs of its citizens more effectively."

The ambassador representing the former United Kingdom interrupted Luca to shout, "Hear! Hear! Brilliant idea, Ambassador Giamo! We are all aware that it has become very difficult for us to govern as a body. There's an old saying about too many cooks spoiling the stew. I believe that for this union of nations to work most effectively, we must have leaders. Surely we are still needed to help rule?"

Luca responded, "Of course the ambassadors will still continue to work on behalf of the new world order; we just need to deliberate as to how we implement the governance of it." He stopped his circuit, noting a raised hand. "Yes, Ambassador Basset?"

"It was our vision to bring peace to the world. We believed if we could remove borders and boundaries, much like Europe did at the end of the last century, we could work our way to peace." The American ambassador spoke wistfully. "As you know, we understood that national identities would still need to be recognized, so each nation appointed ambassadors to represent its interests. Member nations agreed to abide by the governance of the World Union. Unfortunately, there were citizens of those nations who would not tolerate our union, and the Anti-Globalist terror attacks began."

Luca nodded his head, pondering his answer for a moment before speaking. "In the former United States, one man now holds power. The same thing is happening in parts of South and Central America. It is my hope to engage these men, to find common ground in order to create a stable basis for the World Union to continue in a new form. The form may change, but the function remains. We will be unified, though diversified." Luca paused as the other ambassadors called out encouraging words, banging the table with the palms of their hands. When the noise dimmed enough, Luca continued speaking.

"I think we need to restructure, gentlemen. Let me show you the model I have developed. Please direct your attention toward the screen.

"I realize that this may seem self-serving, since I took this idea from my ancestors." Luca smiled at the group, the deep grooves of his dimples adding charm to his expression. "The ancient Romans may have the answer for us. Two counsels, who were elected by the people, were responsible for governing Rome. The Roman Senate advised those counsels. I propose that we hold a worldwide election to choose two counsels. The World Union Ambassadorial Body works well together as a unit, so I suggest that our body act as advisor to the counsels, much as the Senate did.

"In addition, we will have ten tribunals who will govern the ten regions under the authority of the two counsels and the 'senate.' I believe this trilateral approach will provide a more effective way of managing our resources and meeting the needs of those nations in need. It will provide worldwide peace and the prosperity that is only possible through unity."

The Australian ambassador stood up, "Ambassador Giamo, I have a question as to how you will divide up the world."

"If you will note the next image, sir." Luca picked up a remote from the table and clicked it. "This map details the boundaries of the ten regions of the World Union. As you gentlemen know, there have been too many planetary boundaries that have been transgressed by the nations, especially the first-world nations, in the past. We must act now. We see the effects on the earth. We must provide safety for human development to continue. Peace is necessary for the continued progress of mankind and is necessary for preserving the future. I've asked Ambassador Harris and General Tabor to discuss the plan we've drawn up. Gentlemen?"

Kurt Harris, the UK ambassador, stood up and walked toward the screen while General Tabor received the remote from Luca. General Tabor spoke first. If you will direct your attention to the chart, you will note that North America will be Region One. Europe will be Region Two. The Koreans have already incorporated the Japanese islands through battles and skirmishes this past year. They have brought great stability to the region, along with an incredible economic growth, so we suggest their new boundaries be Region Three. Region Four will incorporate Australia and South Africa. Region Five belongs to the Russian confederacy of nations. Region Six, Central and South America, along with the Caribbean Islands. Region Seven is Northern Africa. Region Eight is the center of the African continent, along with Madagascar. Region Nine is India, Thailand, and Indonesia, while China will be Region Ten."

Xi Vong, the Chinese ambassador, spoke. "I must say, Ambassador Giamo, that you have wisdom and insight above your years. This proposal is a good one. May I make a suggestion?"

Luca nodded in assent, and Ambassador Vong continued speaking, "I suggest that this committee adds to the proposal our advice that the North American Tribunal be offered to this Anti-Globalist leader, Quinteros, and Region Six to one of the other new dictators. We cannot afford to have more men killed in the battle over the former United States. Since Quinteros is able to dominate those people, I think it is best we utilize the man already in place. I am certain the American people will find approved leadership within the World Union to their benefit in many respects."

Luca nodded at his friend. "I hope to negotiate just such a peace treaty with them, sir."

"We do have another issue, gentlemen." The Palestinian ambassador spoke, carefully enunciating his words in English. "Israel has been bombing our people for the last two weeks, and the World Union has done little to help. Hundreds of innocent civilians have been killed and it's sheer chaos! Where's our World Union support?"

"Respectfully, Ambassador, your people have been fighting with Israel from day one."

Ambassador Basset replied quickly, "I don't know why you people can't get along. For years, the United States tried to negotiate peace, but you people don't want peace. You want Israel gone."

Heated conversation instantly broke out in the room, and all of the delegates began to talk over one another, some of them shouting. Luca raised his hand for their attention. "Please stop now!" he commanded, and they all stopped at once. The Palestinian ambassador, who had been standing and shaking his fist at Ambassador Basset, sat down abruptly.

"While I sympathize and agree with you, Ambassador Basset; Abd Alhameed is completely right. The people of Gaza are suffering. This missile war between the Palestinians and the Jews must stop or the people in Israel will suffer as well from retaliation." Luca looked up at the ceiling, paused, and closed his eyes as if in prayer. He lowered his head for a moment, then looked at each of the ambassadors one by one.

"Once we have ratified our new plan for the World Union, I suggest we try to broker a peace treaty with Israel. It is time for stability in and among all people groups. I believe we can make headway with the prime minister. He is a reasonable man who has shown great compassion in the past for the plight of the Palestinians. I believe now is the time for that situation to be addressed," Luca urged emphatically.

The men in the room applauded. Ambassador Vong rose to his feet first, clapping enthusiastically. The other men did the same, some shouting their approval of the young Italian ambassador. Luca smiled at them and bowed his head, modestly lowering his eyes toward the floor in humble acceptance of their adulation.

Jerusalem, Israel

Walking along the ancient street, DC felt the warmth of the sun on his back. Despite the heat, he felt energized and had a lightness in his step. The outdoor market was bustling. Vendors displayed their offerings on makeshift counters; old plastic boxes were turned upside down with boards perched on top, covered by a wide variety of items. He passed rows of burlap bags, folded open to reveal assortments of olives. He admired the little storefronts where one could buy a meal, sit at a small table, and watch people as they strolled through the market. *Teo would love this,* he thought. He saw a fruit stand to his left, and he turned into the alleyway it bordered.

As he looked over the fruits, he heard a woman speaking in English. He turned around to see her. The dark-haired woman was speaking to a little girl, her tone pleasant and questioning. She would say a few words in English, then point to something and say the Hebrew name. The little girl would repeat the word carefully, looking up at her mother with a serious expression.

DC watched them with a lump in his throat. The little girl looked about the same age as Olivia. He smiled at the girl's look of wonder when her mother handed her a star fruit. As he listened to the mother talk about the fruit with her daughter, he picked through the bananas at the stall. They were all green. He was hoping to find some ripe ones for dinner tonight. Bananas were one thing Teo could tolerate.

"Give me back my daughter!" He heard the woman let out a bloodcurdling scream. Turning back, DC saw her frantically chasing a man down the short alley into the street. The man clutched the little girl in his arms and was racing toward a black van waiting at the corner across from the fruit stand.

DC did not pause, but bolted after him, passing the mother and reaching the man just before he got to the van's rear bumper. Yanking the kidnapper by the scruff of hair hanging just below his collar, DC pulled, and the abductor fell backward toward him. DC grabbed the girl from his arms in an instant. The man fell quickly but jumped back to his feet in an impressive flip and began hurling punches at DC with a vengeance. DC parried the blows, trying to keep the girl away from the flailing fists.

"Give her to me now!" the woman commanded breathlessly. DC shoved the child at her while he continued to fight off the kidnapper. As they struggled, DC saw in his peripheral vision the driver of the van leaving the vehicle and heading their way. Slamming his opponent in the nose with the palm of his hand, DC turned and grabbed the woman and her child, running with them away from the men. DC scanned the crowds and noticed other men were watching them, closing in a perimeter around them.

Making a swift decision, he pulled the woman and child through the door of a rug shop. "What are we doing in here?" the woman asked, trying to catch her breath. DC imagined she must be afraid and panicky, but she seemed cool. Her dark eyes searched the shop's window, and then turned to him.

"There were others with them, in the crowd. I don't think there is a way out," he informed her.

The woman shook her head negatively from side to side, frowning. Carrying her daughter on her hip, she walked to the back of the shop where an older woman sat in a chair sleeping. Motioning DC to follow, she tiptoed around the woman and through an opening covered by a thin rug. DC followed her into a small room and watched as she put down the toddler and rifled through some things in a cupboard. She had obviously been here before, DC noted. She tossed a white robe to DC and grabbed a scarf. Quickly wrapping her hair in the scarf, she started talking.

"I don't know how to thank you. I know my father will want to thank you personally. I have no idea who these men are, or what they want, but you saved my daughter."

DC smiled down at her as he pulled the robe on over his clothes. "My pleasure. Are you thinking a disguise will help us get away from here?"

"It may help us put some distance between us and them." She turned to the little girl.

"Charlie, you are such a brave girl. I am so proud of you, baby. Listen, you know how you like to pretend?" The little girl nodded, her black curls shaking with the motion. DC noticed she had the same sprinkling of freckles across her nose as her mother and the same dark eyes, lavishly fringed with black lashes, and the same thick, curly hair. Even for a mother and daughter, the resemblance was uncanny.

"Listen," the woman continued speaking quietly, "I want you to pretend to be Bopsie, your rabbit. I'm going to put you in this big bag, and I want you to stay cuddled down inside of it, okay?"

Picking up a large canvas duffle bag, the woman opened it up and helped the little girl settle inside, leaving the bag unzipped.

"I'll carry her," DC said. With little effort, he picked up the bag and slung it on his right shoulder. Peering around his shoulder and inside the bag, he saw the tot staring back. "We're going to have a little adventure, Charlie. It might be a little bumpy, but you'll be okay," he reassured her.

He twisted back around to face the mother. "My name is DC."

"I'm Angelina," she replied, her lips tilting up at the corners in a tight smile as she spoke. "Are you ready?"

Angelina opened the rickety wooden door that led out to another alley and pulled a fringed, black shawl around her shoulders. DC watched in amazement as she took on the gait and body posture of an old, feeble woman. He followed her a few paces back, as if he were an employee carrying her purchases.

As they entered the square again, he surreptitiously looked around for any of the men he had seen earlier. He kicked a small stone so that it clattered ahead of Angelina and spoke in a low tone. "There are two men ahead, one at ten, the other at two. Just continue on the way you are."

He kept his eyes averted, hoping that the disguise was enough, and started to pray.

After they had left the marketplace and walked a few blocks, he felt more secure. It looked like they had made it out of the capture zone the kidnappers had set up. He walked a bit faster and caught up with Angelina.

"I don't see them anymore. Where do you live?" he asked her.

"With my father, you know him—Arnot Rogov."

"The prime minister?" DC asked, surprised.

"Yes." She looked up at him, the shawl dropping away from

her face. "Would you mind helping me get home? I lost my cell phone back there."

"Sure." DC thought quickly. He had told her his real name without thinking, failing to use the alias that was on his passport.

"Do you live nearby?" she asked. "We were visiting a friend in the area and stopped at the market to buy some fruit for dinner. I was going to take a taxi back. Maybe you could drive us home?" She looked at him appealingly.

"I don't have a car, but if we can find a taxi, I'll make sure you get home," he assured her.

They continued walking for a while in silence. DC checked the bag to make sure the little girl was fine. He was surprised to find her asleep.

He chuckled and showed her mother, tilting the opening of the canvas bag.

Angelina sighed. "She's been through a lot in the past few weeks. We were in Rome when the earthquake hit."

DC looked at her in amazement. "Wow, that was horrific! The devastation was inconceivable. So many people dead. How did you survive? Where were you when it happened?"

"By the Coliseum. We were very, very lucky. My cousin was visiting and was with us when it happened. He was able to get us out of town right away. He was sure the aftermath was going to be drastic, so he got us on a ship here safely with my father...at least, I thought we were safe."

"Do you have any idea who those men were?" DC asked as he studied her animated expression.

"I have an idea that my husband is behind it. He tried to take Charlie away from me and get me in trouble with the law so he could get permanent custody of her. Marrying him was the worst mistake of my life, but at least I got Charlie out of it."

"I have a daughter too." He started to say her name, but stopped himself. If Angelina heard his name and Olivia's, she might recognize him. Although, now that he thought about it, there had not been a lot of focus on him specifically in the media after their "deaths." Teo and Olivia's pictures, however, had been all over the Internet. Teo was stunningly beautiful. There was no question that she attracted attention wherever she went. Even now with her hair cut short and dyed black, she was striking. That was why, for the most part, he kept her out of sight. They both agreed that he would not be as noticeable and could go out without attracting attention to himself. *Unless I get into public brawls in the town square,* he thought. Teo was not going to be happy about this.

He turned the conversation away from himself. "Why would your husband go to such lengths?"

"My father is the prime minister of Israel. There's no way my husband can get Charlie legally, but I didn't think even he would make such a bold move." Her nose wrinkled in distain. "I'm hoping Kurt can help me do something about it," she muttered under her breath.

"Who's Kurt?"

Angelina glanced up at him and then at the canvas bag. "He's my cousin. He'll do anything to protect me and Charlie."

DC stopped walking. "Anything sounds kind of ominous. Did you mean it that way?"

Her dark eyes glinted in the sunlight. "Wouldn't you do anything if it were your daughter?"

Taking a deep breath, DC answered. "I'd do everything reasonable and moral, but not anything. At least, I don't think so."

Angelina turned and began walking again toward a taxi parked ahead of them. When they reached it, DC handed her the canvas bag and then opened the car door for her. Cradling the bag carefully, she got into the cab. DC did not follow her.

"Don't you want to come home with me? My father will be very grateful." Her voice was pleading. "I can't tell you enough how thankful I am that you saved Charlie."

"I appreciate that, Angelina, but I really have to get back to work. I think you'll be safe now." He moved to close the door, but she put her hand out and stopped him.

"Listen, if you ever need anything, please contact me." She rummaged in her pocket and pulled out a scrap of paper. Asking the driver for a pen, she jotted down a number. "This is my home number. You call if you need help. Please?"

She thrust the paper at him. DC took it and read it before putting it in his pocket. He closed the cab door and watched as the taxi pulled from the curb and drove away. Once it was out of view, he turned and headed back toward Ari's house. He was not looking forward to telling everyone about his day, especially the part about the fistfight in the marketplace and rescuing the prime minister's granddaughter!

11

BIDDEFORD, MAINE

James looked over at Bernard—asleep in the driver's seat—with envy. It had taken them all day to get to the rendezvous, and while James was exhausted and couldn't sleep, Bernard apparently could sleep anywhere. They were parked under a dense canopy of trees by a small path, which Bernard told him led to the water and a dock. There they were to meet the man who would help them get into New York City. James looked around but couldn't see much since it was dark. No lights illuminated the campus, and he wondered how long it had been since the University of New England had been abandoned.

As they had driven east, Bernard and James had not seen many other people on the roads. They had planned the route to the small town on the coast of Maine with Eric before they left home. With all the fighting going on between the World Union forces and the rebel Anti-Globalists, they knew a direct path to New York would only put them in jeopardy. Eric had a contact in Biddeford, Brian Korah.

Brian was part of a fairly large group of Christians who lived in the area. Before the disappearances, he and his best friend had run a fishing charter in town. Ironically, Brian, like James, had been at a wedding on the day the world's Christians vanished—his own. His beautiful bride and many of their friends and family had disappeared just as her father was escorting her down the aisle. Eric told James that Brian had gone "crazy" for a while, quitting work and drinking heavily all day and into the night. Brian had recognized what had happened because his fiancée had often shared her new faith with him. She had been the kind of person who gave 100 percent to whatever she did, and the Jesus stuff was no different. Her beliefs never bothered him—until she was gone.

Then one night he had been searching the Web and found one of the portals Eric had designed, where Christian content could be freely shared without censorship. Furious with God for taking his fiance, Brian wanted answers. He thought maybe he would find them at the Christian portal. What he had found instead was their little virtual community on the Deep Web, and he had begun listening to James' sermons. As it had with others, the gospel message slowly began to penetrate his heart, and Brian decided to give his life to follow this Jesus he had once scorned. Through the online community, he found other believers in the area near him.

Bernard began to snore softly, and James shook his head in slight disgust. They were supposed to meet Brian at midnight. James wanted to sleep, but his restless mind would not allow it. He thought about David and said a prayer for his son. He also began to pray for the suffering people in New York City, asking God to fulfill Bernard's dream and allow healing to take place for those in torment.

As he sat sleeplessly, he thought about the studies he'd been conducting over the last few months, about the end times. He didn't know how long it would be before the Antichrist's rise to power, but he knew things were going to get much worse. He felt a strong compulsion to prepare God's people for what was coming. It was imperative that they stand firm and do what they needed to be armed with the truth.

He smiled, remembering his friend, Joseph Levy. James had met the older man at a coffee shop just outside of Washington, DC, when Joseph had invited James to sit at his table. A Messianic Jew, Joseph gently challenged the younger priest in matters of faith—especially prophecy. It was a letter from Joseph, delivered by his attorneys after the disappearances, that had been the last tool God used to pry off the blinders from James' heart.

James missed Joseph. He also missed Bishop Ellis, his former mentor. The bishop had tried many, many times to explain faith to the proud younger priest. James liked to think of Joseph and the bishop enjoying one another's company in heaven, each shaking his head at the stubbornness of their young friend, who was now finally a fellow believer.

So many of the Christians he knew had had friends and families who'd tried over and over for years to explain the gospel to them. Like him, over and over, they had rejected it, some politely and some not.

The gospel is too easy, he thought. *Lord, if You had made it more complicated, many more of us would have flocked to You earlier. If great works and kind deeds could earn us Your favor, the whole world would probably follow You. But the humility of the gospel is a stumbling block to our pride. I guess that's why children find it easier to believe in You, Lord.*

He saw a light farther down the road. He knew that Brian was coming by boat from the other side of the Saco River and would dock the boat in the small cove at the end of the path where James and Bernard were parked. James reached over and gently shook Bernard, who woke with a start.

"I wasn't sleeping, just resting my eyes," he stammered groggily. "What time is it?"

"Near midnight. I just saw a light. I think Brian is near the cove."

Bernard yawned and stretched as both men got out of the car, quietly shutting their doors. The campus seemed deserted, but it was better to be safe. They made their way carefully down the path in the dark. James could barely discern the darker shadows of the dock ahead. A light flickered on and waved slowly back and forth. Bernard pulled out a small flashlight from his jacket and clicked it on and off three times before they carefully they made their way to the boat at the end of the dock.

Bernard's flashlight lit the back of the boat, revealing the

ONE WILL BE LEFT

name painted there, *Sea Wolf*. James didn't know much about boats, but it seemed small for traveling on the ocean. He pushed aside his reservations as Brian jumped onto the dock, his right hand extended.

"Hi, I'm Brian."

Introductions were made since Eric had insisted on not allowing photos of James and other community members on their websites. Safe as Eric had tried to make it, total security on the Internet, or their intranet, was not possible. Though James and Brian had communicated many times online, they would not be able to identify one another to authorities in case either of them were apprehended. James had been arrested once already, and that experience made them careful. Outright persecution of Christians was not happening yet, but there were people who had disappeared in the various "Humanitarian Centers" the World Union had set up throughout member nations. From what Eric could find, it was mainly outspoken critics of OneFaith and former Pope Peter II, Billings Mason, who ended up entering the centers. No one ever came back to verify the rumors, but there were frightening stories about what happened to the detainees in those centers.

Brian spoke quietly, "We'll head out in about ten minutes. Let's get on board and I'll introduce you to the rest of the men."

After they boarded the *Sea Wolf*, Brian made introductions. "These two are my cousins, Kerry and Colin. They'll provide some measure of security in the city, but don't let them start talking. Their mother was Irish, and they inherited her love of embellished blarney."

James smiled as he said hello and shook hands with each of the younger men. He was a bit above average height for a man; these two were well above average and towered over him.

"Pastor James, Bernard, if you both will follow me, I'll introduce you to the others below," Brian said. "Our pastor has an early breakfast for you. There's also a head if you need to use the facilities."

As they entered the cabin, James could smell bacon, and his mouth began watering. While they had plenty to eat at the compound in Lake George, bacon was not something readily available.

ONE WILL BE LEFT

The aroma was tantalizing.

Brian introduced them all. James shook hands with Doug Patterson, pastor of the community in the Biddeford area, and his sons, Matthew and Daniel. James guessed the young men were in their early twenties. They all found a seat on the benches at the galley table, and Doug served them breakfast.

James looked at his plate, stunned at the variety of food. He saw Bernard reverently touch a bagel smeared with cream cheese on his plate and held back a grin.

Doug turned the knobs on the cooktop and joined them at the table as he asked them all to join him in prayer. For a few minutes they ate in silence, enjoying their savory, filling meal. James tried to get a better feel for the group as they ate.

Doug Patterson was graying and maybe near sixty. His sons were built like him, small and slender. In one of James and Brian's online conversations, Brian had told James that Doug had eight sons. Eight sons and two daughters. Doug had been a fourth-generation Mormon until he was excommunicated for apostasy. His crime had been publicly criticizing another member of the LDS church who had been running for public office in the state. Doug had held a lot of influence in his community at the time, and that member had lost the race due in large part to Doug's criticisms. When the campaign was over, the failed candidate wasted no time in turning his attention on the man he blamed for his loss, making sure Doug was ousted from the Mormon Church. Shortly after the Christians of the world had disappeared, Doug began to feel that he'd been drastically misled all his life. Nothing he'd been taught made sense, so he began to search for answers. As a result of his seeking for the truth about Jesus in the Bible, he, his wife and children, and a large number of his former congregation gave their lives to Jesus as true God and true man. Now Doug and his family were strong leaders in that community.

As James ate, he turned his gaze to Brian and his two cousins. The three young men were seated next to each other on the bench across from James, their shoulders touching. *Wedged in*, he thought. They were large and obviously strong. Brian had told James that he and his cousins previously had worked for the US government in counterterrorism. Each of them had trained under masters of Krav Maga in Israel, joining in training with the Israeli Defense Forces. James watched as the three bantered quietly back and forth, the bond of familial ties evident in their looks and mannerisms.

Doug put down his fork, pushed his plate away a fraction, and addressed him. "Pastor James, it's an honor to have you here."

"Please call me James," he answered. "I'm thankful for your help. I had no idea how I would get here when the Lord first directed me to go to the city."

"Well, I'm happy to be able to help you get past the blockade. In the short time since the rapture, many have turned to faith in Jesus Christ. Your ministry has been incredibly helpful to new believers like me."

"Thank you for your encouragement, but by default we're all new believers, aren't we?" James felt uncomfortable with the praise. "Brian told me you've mapped out our travel plans."

"Yes. The 'Sons of Korah,' as I call these guys, have made a few trips to the city already." Doug nodded toward the three cousins. "The World Union would call them criminals, but they like to think of themselves as compassionate privateers. They're heroes to me."

Brian's cousin Colin spoke, "We've got a contact in the World Union Security Force, an old friend from high school. The WU is very strict about troops and alcohol. We've developed a mutually beneficial relationship over the last month or so to see that they're adequately supplied, and that they'll allow us into the city."

Kerry continued for his brother. "We load up on beer and other alcohol for our World Union friend, who then sells it. He's part of the security at the Chelsea Piers on the West Side. In return, we're allowed to continue up the Hudson with a special pass. Since the city is under strict quarantine, food is becoming scarce, and our friends rely on us to help them."

Brian nodded his head as they spoke; then he finished explaining. "There's an old pier near Riverbank Park where we meet Doug's son Devan to unload supplies. The first time, he had five guys helping him move the supplies to the school, but last week there was just one. The others had come down with symptoms of the virus."

"Why are they at a school?" James asked.

Brian answered, "When the virus started spreading, Devan thought it made sense for their group to barricade themselves in a place near the pier. He and Doug communicated and made plans to coordinate aid. The school had been closed for years, but one of the women in their group was the principal just before it shut down. She still had keys to the building, so they got in and set up. They still had running water and showers in the gym. Everyone brought supplies from their homes and hunkered down to wait it out, figuring they would have a better chance of surviving together."

Doug interjected, "Devan's lived in the city for the last twenty years and knows it pretty well. Once we get there, he'll meet us and can guide you wherever you want to go, Pastor James."

James looked at the man across from him. "Let's go to the school first. How many people are in Devan's congregation?"

"About fifty. They've been doing well until last week. One of the men snuck out a couple of weeks ago to check on his sister who wouldn't join them at the school. He didn't tell anyone anything until he started coming down with the symptoms. Devan said they isolated him right away, but others started getting sick, too.

"About a third of them are sick. Do you think you can heal them, Pastor?" Doug asked.

"I can't. God can. I believe that is what He will do. When do we leave?"

"At daybreak. Let me show you what we're planning to do." Brian pulled out a chart. Pushing the breakfast plates to the side, he spread it out and began sharing his plan with James and Bernard.

12

AMMAN,
JORDAN

Kate waited, playing a game on her phone, as Christopher set up the camera. They had about five minutes before their interview with the new Jordanian king. Putting the phone down, she checked the schedule on her clipboard. The Al-Hashmiya Palace was the first place she was interviewing King Zayd bin Asem. He was granting her and her crew an exclusive opportunity, a personal tour of Jordan. Despite the fact that most nations were willingly coming together under the authority of the World Union, people were intrigued by the handsome new king's insistence on keeping his country out of the Union. Kate was fascinated to discover the Jordanian people were just as insistent as their king that he continue as their sovereign ruler.

While his subjects loved him, King Zayd bin Asem was also popular with the rest of the world. Many bloggers and reporters online and on air followed him. Royal fever had spread throughout the world, and fans couldn't get enough information about the man who stood almost alone in opposition to the World Union, refusing to submit the sovereignty of the Jordanian nation to its rule.

He was the last ruling monarch in the world. Over the last few decades, the remaining royal families of Europe had abdicated their official roles one by one, leaving the last of the Windsor family, Queen Zara, as Europe's only monarch. At the inauguration of the World Union, Her Royal Highness gave up the throne in a moving speech and afterward retired to the family's castle on Balmoral Estate. Other monarchs, sheikhs, and the few sultans left also resigned their

ONE WILL BE LEFT

positions to allow the World Union to exercise its authority over their countries. Interestingly, the World Union had sent the young Italian ambassador to each monarch. The charismatic man had convinced every one of them to abdicate and let the World Union rule—all but the previous Jordanian king.

With his smoldering, dark good looks, King Zayd embodied the romance and glamour of royalty. Young women dreamed of catching his eye and his heart. Whole magazines were devoted to him, informing delirious readers about his favorite pastimes, foods, and music—any mundane tidbit was sufficient fodder for the masses. His popularity reminded Kate of pop stars in the early days of rock and roll in the previous century. His exotic life was a great distraction from the terror threats of the Anti-Globalists and the relentless natural disasters that shook the world. Kate sighed as she looked over her notes and the photos in her file on the king. She preferred more substantial interviews to the sort of puff pieces that gossipmongers loved, but this was part of her job, and this interview would guarantee her an audience larger than any she had previously had. That thought made her smile.

She mentally reviewed what she had learned about the young king. He was the last of the Hashemite males eligible to reign over the Jordanian kingdom. King Zayd's mother had been an American, Kathryn Chandler, who had traveled to Jordan to teach English in a private school. His widowed father, Asem, had had a young daughter at the same school. Asem and Kathryn fell in love and married before the end of the school year. They had welcomed five daughters to their family before Zayd was born.

Neither parent had any thought of their son one day taking the throne, because at his birth he had been tenth in the line of succession. Accidents, heart attacks, and various illnesses took their toll on the Hashemite family in the twenty-four years following the young king's birth. As male heir after male heir died, many speculated that there was a curse on the family.

Kate looked up as the king entered the room with an older

man. She stood as they came toward her, noting with appreciation that Zayd bin Asem was even more handsome in person. She was glad she had visited the Giamo clinic for that treatment. She was ten years older than the king, but now no one could tell. *I love technology!* she enthused inwardly. She knew it was vain, but she truly didn't care. She believed in using every asset to her advantage.

"Mrs. Benari, it's a pleasure to meet you." The king reached out his right hand and shook hers, smiling warmly. Kate looked into his dark brown eyes and grinned back coyly, grateful that she could still elicit male admiration. She caught Christopher standing behind the king shaking his head in disgust. Christopher was the one man in her life who was not swayed by her charm and good looks. She ignored him and turned to the older gentleman.

"You must be the king's uncle." She offered her right hand to him and shook his warm hand in a gentle grip.

"I am not really His Majesty's uncle. His father and I were close friends. Asem asked me to care for his children when he was first diagnosed," Rasheed explained to her.

Kate clasped both of her hands over his. "It was such a tragedy that he lost his second wife and was diagnosed with cancer so soon after she passed."

"Yes, truly. I think the sorrow of losing Kathryn robbed him of any desire to fight for his own life." Rasheed turned to the king. "Are you ready to begin, Your Majesty?"

"Yes, shall we sit?" Kate indicated the couch behind them.

The king and his uncle sat on the silk couch together while Kate took the chair to their right. Christopher had discreetly rearranged a few items in the room so the effect on-screen would be more pleasing. Kate noted an exquisite vase covered in copper flowers on the table next to the couch.

King Zayd followed Kate's gaze. "It is from the Ming dynasty, a gift from the Chinese government to my family years ago. Usually it is kept on that shelf." He nodded to the built-in shelf behind her. Kate turned to see the central cubicle was empty, and embarrassment caused her cheeks to flush. *Christopher!*

"I am so sorry, Your Majesty," she stammered, unusually at a loss for words. She knew the value of such things, and the thought that Christopher had touched the vase, let alone moved it, was appalling. The vase was not quite priceless, but it was irreplaceable. She narrowed her eyes at her cameraman.

"It is quite fine, Kate." The king was grinning. "Would you like to discuss our itinerary?"

Kate took a quick breath to calm herself. "Yes. Let me introduce you to the viewers first, then I will ask you some questions before we talk about the tour of your lovely country." She smiled thankfully at him.

As Christopher took his place behind the camera, the red light flickered on and Kate turned slightly in her chair to fully face the audience. She introduced the king and his uncle, tracing the family history briefly before touching on the tragic aspect of what many people regarded as a curse on the family line.

A look of concern crossed her features as she turned to King Zayd with a gentle question. "Are you concerned, Your Majesty, about the tragedy that seems to plague your family?"

King Zayd shook his head, "No, Kate, not at all. It is God who is the ultimate Sovereign. The Scriptures tell us He establishes kings and removes them. I believe my life is in His hands."

Kate had been hoping to add pathos to the Hashemite curse and garner some extra publicity since the gossip magazines and Internet were full of stories about the deaths of the Jordanian royals. Unfortunately, King Zayd's response was not what she had anticipated.

She thought quickly. "Then you believe that God removed all of your family members to make way for you to become king?"

"So it would seem, as I am now king of Jordan," King Zayd smiled kindly at her. "I am eager to show your viewers how God has blessed Jordan. As you know, my country has a rich history." He turned to the camera expertly as Christopher tightened the shot on the young monarch.

ONE WILL BE LEFT

"You will see how courteous and hospitable the people of Jordan are, as we explore our nation. We have much to show you about the history and beauty of our land."

Kate was a bit frustrated. She had hoped to capitalize on the family curse to boost ratings. To her dismay, Zayd had successfully parried her question and moved the conversation to what amounted to a tourist ad for the Jordanian kingdom. Stifling her irritation, she finished the interview smoothly.

As Christopher began packing his gear, she graciously thanked the king and his uncle for their time. Perhaps as they filmed their tour over the next week she might get a real interview with something significant.

Hebron, Maryland

Elena leaned back on the porch step and rested her head against the railing, closing her eyes as the sun warmed her face. Hearing Olivia's delighted laughter made her smile. The young girl and Talin had discovered a turtle. The toddler was fascinated.

"It's good to hear that sound," Brant said. He sat down next to Elena on the steps, watching Olivia.

Elena sighed. "It's been hard for her. I'm glad we found this place."

"We're going to have to move on tomorrow. There are too many people around here," he reminded her.

"I know. At least the warmer weather will make sleeping outside tolerable if we can't find shelter." She looked around at the house they had found the day before. "It's awful what's been done to this home. I bet it was spectacular at one time," she remarked.

"I'm sure it was. At least vandals didn't tear off the doors and break the windows. We won't have some kind of critter surprising us tonight." He laughed. Elena had yelped a few times on the long hike when they happened on a raccoon or large spider. She had actually screamed when they stumbled onto a coyote with her pups earlier in the day.

"Listen, I'm not a country girl. I've always lived in the city. I can't help that this whole thing is out of my comfort zone. What I wouldn't give right now for a hot bubble bath and a glass of wine…" Her voice trailed off wistfully.

Brant looked at her and smiled, standing up. "Well, I'm going to help John clean the rabbits he caught. It will be safer to cook them now before it gets dark." He stretched. "Do you want to help?"

Elena merely stared him down in response. With another chuckle, Brant turned and left.

Elena watched as Talin opened up the sandbox and Olivia picked up a bucket and a shovel from inside it. The little girl immediately got to work filling the bucket. Talin made his way over to the porch.

"You're so good with her," Elena commented.

"She is much like you were at her age."

"It's so strange to me that you look young enough to be my son, Talin, and yet you've been watching over me all my life."

Elena studied him. With his dark skin and hair twisted in long dreadlocks pulled away from his face at the back of his neck, he looked Jamaican—which is what she had thought when she first saw him.

"And you were watching over the girl in Colorado, too?" she asked, recalling their first meeting at a university in Colorado, so long ago.

"Yes. She already believed, but had been straying from the way. It was for your benefit, as well as hers, that I spoke to her."

Elena thought about that for a moment. "Do you know what's going to happen to us?"

"No," he answered. "Only the Lord knows the future for each individual. We know what is written in the Book, of course, so I know about the general future of your world from that."

"But you don't know if Teo and DC will make it here? If we'll be together again?"

"No." He shook his head.

Elena sighed. "I wish we could at least get through on the phone. John thinks the World Union has disabled the cell towers to keep the Anti-Globalists from being able to communicate. Can you tell me if they're safe?"

Talin was quiet for a moment. "Yes, they are safe. They are in Jerusalem now."

"Where are we going? John said that you two discussed it this morning before I woke up, but he had to go and check his traps."

"You will be heading south tomorrow. There is a farm there with a turf landing strip. The airplane in the hanger is in good condition. Brant knows how to fly it."

"You aren't going with us?" Elena looked up at Talin anxiously.

"I will be nearby, but I am needed for other things." He looked around the yard. He seemed extra alert to Elena. She cleared her throat and blinked a few times to hold back the tears.

"I've tried to not think about it too much, but John's description of the fallen angels he saw has haunted me. Is that the other thing you are needed for?" She struggled to speak without crying. She was tired of being fearful, unable to relax.

"You do not need to fear, Elena. Greater is He who is in you. You know the promises of Scripture. The war is already won." His deep voice resonated with power.

Elena wrapped her arms around herself. "But there are still battles to be fought. The enemy will continue to fight until the bitter end, and the fact is, many of us here are going to die.

"I'm not so upset if it's me, but DC and Teo, Olivia, John..." Her voice cracked.

Talin put a hand on her shoulder. "I have escorted many into eternity. Some feared the crossing before it came, but none when it was time to cross."

She was quiet for a moment. "DC and Teo have both given their lives to Jesus. So have John and I. So, what you are saying is that only eternity matters. But what about Olivia? She is too young to believe."

"And her angel always sees the face of your heavenly Father. That, too is a promise of Scripture. You are to teach her about Jesus. Children are more than able to enter the kingdom; in fact, more children enter than adults.

"I must go now. I will be nearby," he reassured her.

"When will I see you again?" she asked.

Talin smiled and was gone. Elena knew somehow that he could hear her soft good-bye as she whispered it.

"Hey, love."

She turned to see John standing with his arms wide open. Elena ran to him and hugged him tightly.

"We're going to be okay," he assured her. "Brant has the rabbits on the grill we rigged. The meat will be good! We've only had those bars to eat the last day of our hike."

Elena took her spot back on the stairs, watching her granddaughter while John spoke.

"We won't have far to go tomorrow. When I was checking the traps, I found an old truck with some fuel still in the tank. Brant said he could hot-wire it. So we'll take that to the farm tomorrow. It will be a lot faster and easier to drive with Olivia than to walk."

"I'm afraid we're going to attract attention in this area if we're in a vehicle. Since we left the boat, we haven't heard many cars or trucks. Won't we be a target?" Elena rubbed her forehead the way she did when she was worried.

John sat down next to his wife and took her hand. "No, we won't." She narrowed her eyes at him. "Well, maybe," he admitted. "That's why you're going to drive while I sit in the passenger seat with the .357 DC's father so thoughtfully put aside. Brant will ride in the back with the other gun. I think between the three of us we can get to the farm and the hanger safely."

"I never expected you would have found guns in that safety-deposit box," Elena commented.

ONE WILL BE LEFT

John chuckled. "Years ago, when the National Gun Safety law took effect, a lot of people hid their weapons."

"Good thing he did," Elena sighed gratefully.

"For sure. Those guns and the bullets he had stashed away are invaluable." John stood up and stretched.

Elena's mind switched gears as she surveyed their granddaughter. "I don't know how I'm going to get her clean. She really needs a bath too, especially now with the sand all over her."

"Then I have a surprise you're going to love. Brant and I found a creek running on the other side of the little hill over there. We found a couple of metal buckets in the basement, used them to fetch and heat the water, and filled the tub in the master bathroom. She can have a warm bath!"

Elena threw her arms around his neck and kissed his face. "Oh, John! It's been so long since I've been able to give her a real bath."

She walked over to the sandbox and looked down at her granddaughter. "Okay, Livie! All done with the sand! Papa has a surprise for you upstairs—a real bath!" Elena gently pulled the toddler up and led her into the house.

13

JERUSALEM,
ISRAEL

The small brunette stood before the congregation in the middle of the worship team. She was singing, her left hand raised in praise.

Teo looked around the large room filled with people. In the three months she and DC had been in Jerusalem, she had come to know quite a few of the members of this church. As the worship team sang, she studied their faces. Saleem had been a member of Hamas, but after the destruction of the Dome of the Rock and the disappearance of the world's Christians, he became convinced that Jesus was the Savior. He'd met his wife, Deborah, an Israeli, at the church. Now they were expecting their first child.

Avi stood on the other side of DC, both arms lifted up in worship. His mother and father had been American Jews who made *aliyah*, a return, to Israel in the late 1990s. Rhetta wrapped an arm around Teo's waist and squeezed her, interrupting her thoughts. Teo leaned into her friend and hugged her back. Despite the differences in their ages, she and the blind woman had become very close in the short time Teo and DC had lived with her family.

The church services were so different from what she had experienced growing up. She still found it hard to follow the Hebrew words during the singing. Thankfully, the pastor taught in English, since many in the congregation were not fluent in Hebrew. She saw DC raise his hands in praise like so many of the other worshippers. She just could not do it; she felt too self-conscious. Maybe once she understood more Hebrew she could get into the worship. DC was fairly fluent. She noticed tears running down his face as he sang.

The music ended, and Pastor Ezar Cohen walked to the front of the room and stood behind the small podium. This was her favorite part of the meeting. It was her habit to outline his sermon, writing in the margins any questions she had. Later, she would ask Rhetta or DC to explain the things she didn't understand. She took a small notebook and pen from her bag.

Pastor Ezar looked somber. "Good morning, everyone. Before I begin with the message, I want to share something that is just being reported on the news. Rocket attacks hit in southern Israel this morning, some as far north as Tel Aviv. Ashkelon has been heavily bombarded too, and it's believed thousands have been killed."

Pastor Ezar waited for the murmuring to die down. "As you know, since the attempted invasion of Israel by the armies allied with Russia, we've experienced unprecedented peace. It is as the Lord of Heaven said to Samuel the prophet, 'Behold, I am about to do a thing in Israel at which both ears of everyone who hears it will tingle.' It's been over three years since God Himself defeated those armies. You know what an impact that event had on many people throughout the world. Many of you came to faith in Yeshua as a result of seeing those armies destroyed without human intervention.

"Incredibly, the Dome of the Rock was destroyed as well, and now the Temple is almost completely restored. The Ark of the Covenant once again sits in the Holy of Holies, and the Temple will be open to worshippers soon. Many Palestinians and Israelis have turned in faith to Yeshua because of these happenings. The Bible predicted them long ago. We are watching the fulfillment of prophecy.

"What group or groups are behind this new attack is yet to be seen. Our missile defense system, however, worked well. You know that for years we have had the Iron Dome and David's Sling missile defense systems in place. Almost 80 percent of the missiles were intercepted. The problem is that the number of missiles fired from the Gaza Strip was so great, we just couldn't handle them all.

"While we've experienced a peaceful season, we all know

what is coming, and we must be prepared. Israel is not the secular nation it was a short time ago. When it was, we fulfilled Jews were tolerated; we even won equal rights to be recognized as a religious organization for tax purposes. But in the past eight months, there has been more radicalization from the Ultra-Orthodox Jews. They are gaining greater power within the government itself, and we've seen some disturbing trends." He paused to take a sip from the water bottle on the podium in front of him before continuing.

"Until last month, Messianic Jews were able to serve in the Israeli Defense Forces. As many of you know, a mob attacked the congregation that met in the reception hall in downtown Jerusalem as they left their meeting last week. The media has grown increasingly antagonistic toward us, portraying us as a cult bent on destroying Jewish culture.

"I've spent the last week studying the end-times prophecies. I want to set the results of my studies before you to give you some advice and comfort." He nodded to the men standing in the aisles at the front. They began passing out papers. DC handed one to Teo.

"What is it?" Rhetta whispered.

"It's an outline," Teo whispered back.

When the men finished, Pastor Ezar began to speak again, "We've seen the World Union crumble in the last months as the Anti-Globalist movement has gained support and power. Their tactics in North and Central America have proved effective. While the African continent is still under the World Union's control, that control is tenuous. Although Europe hasn't seen any real battles, we know terror attacks on major targets are almost a weekly occurrence.

"The Chinese people have completely embraced the Anti-Globalists, and that entire region is under their control. Real battles have taken place there. The Korean Peninsula and the islands of Japan are all entirely under the control of former South Korean general Daniel Jae-suk. I could go on, but the bottom line is that the world situation is unstable. The one world government that so many had faith in is about to collapse.

ONE WILL BE LEFT

"The splitting of this one world government into ten governments, or kingdoms, was predicted by a prophet named Daniel. If you look at your handouts, you will see the references from the Scriptures."

Teo studied the page in front of her. She found trying to understand the Old Testament very difficult, and there were many references from it on the page in front of her. Last week, on one of her few excursions out of the house with Mara, she'd found a children's Scripture storybook in an old bookstore. She'd read the entire book in one sitting. The richly colored, stylized pictures captured her imagination. She recalled there had been quite a few stories about the prophet Daniel. On the handout was a crude drawing of a statue that reminded her of the picture in the children's Bible about the king's dream. She traced the drawing with her finger.

Teo's wandering thoughts were interrupted as Pastor Ezar brought his hand down on the pulpit with a resounding thump. "His kingdom is at hand! He will return and His kingdom will be established and fill the whole earth!" One of the women in the room cried out, and others responded to her exclamation with applause and shouts of acclamation.

Pastor Ezar nodded approvingly at his congregation before speaking again. "But, my dear friends, we must still go through the time that will be the worst the world has ever known."

Teo's stomach lurched, and she felt the pull of her old terrors. DC put his arm around her shoulder and held her close. She peered at Rhetta, who was nodding her head in solemn agreement. The room became very quiet.

"God has not left us without some direction, my friends," the pastor said. "In the next few weeks I'll be sharing with you what I've found in the Scriptures. I want to prepare you as well as I can for what lies ahead. Some of you will remain in this world. Some will survive, but I believe most will not. Regardless, whether we live or die, we will *all* see the kingdom of God in this world."

Rhetta stood suddenly, surprising Teo. Her willowy figure

swayed a bit as she spoke. "I believe the Lord wants us to recall something. Before Yeshua was crucified, He warned the people that they must flee when Jerusalem was surrounded by armies. Seventy years later, that came to pass. And when Jerusalem was surrounded by the Roman armies under Titus, there was a short window of time when the armies had to withdraw briefly to get their supply lines in order. During this brief time, the believers left Jerusalem for the safety of nearby Pella, fleeing across the Jordan River.

"I am sensing the Lord wants us to know that He is preparing a place of refuge for some of us in the Kingdom of Jordan." She sat down.

Pastor Ezar thanked her. "Rhetta, we are grateful for the gift the Holy Spirit has given you. That is a good and hopeful word of encouragement."

Saleem raised his hand. "I have a question, Pastor. We all know Billings Mason is the False Prophet. You've seen the crowds that flock to the OneFaith centers—even here in Jerusalem. Daniel tells us the 'prince who is to come' is from the same people group that destroyed the city and the sanctuary. We know that was the Romans. How are we to figure out who this prince is?"

"Well," Pastor Ezar answered carefully," I believe that by using a system called 'gematria' and the Hebrew alphabet, we can figure out the identity of the Antichrist. Whoever he is, we know he must be of Roman origin and the number of his name must add up to 666."

"How does gematria work?" Saleem asked curiously.

"That's a good question," Pastor Ezar replied. "Numerical values are assigned to each of the twenty-two letters in the Hebrew alphabet. I've tried to figure out the names of several world leaders, whom I thought might fit the criteria, but none of them worked. There was one I was sure was the Antichrist, but his name failed to add up."

"Who was that?" Teo was surprised to hear herself ask out loud.

"The Italian ambassador to the World Union, Luca Giamo."

ONE WILL BE LEFT

Teo stood up, her head reeling as an onslaught of strange memories flooded her mind. "He's my half brother, Pastor Ezar." She heard murmurs in the crowd, but she ignored them. "When my stepmother secretly had him baptized, she gave him another name that not many people know about—a middle name." Teo spelled out the ancient family name given to Luca, and watched as Pastor Ezar wrote it down on the paper in front of him and did some calculations.

His face paled. "It adds up to 666. He is of Roman origin and his name adds up… this is the man who somehow will rise up to dominate the world."

"It makes sense, doesn't it?" Teo said. "Billings Mason mentored him for years. I know the two speak and visit regularly." She began to tremble. "Many of you know who my husband and I are and why we are hiding here in Jerusalem. What should we do, Pastor?" Her voice crackled with fear.

"All I can think of right now is to pray. God has revealed this to us for a reason. Teo, you are here for a reason. Let's all pray."

Teo sat down next to DC and leaned into him. "God help us," she whispered. "My brother is the Antichrist and he's determined to kill us."

14

THE WHITE HOUSE,
WASHINGTON, DC

Luca tapped his pen on the pad rhythmically. He'd been waiting in the Roosevelt Room along with the others for almost an hour. Looking down the long table to the doors on either side of the room, he knew the one to the right led to the Oval Office. *Quinteros is in there*, Luca thought. He closed his eyes to concentrate. The fool was playing a game of cards with one of his associates. Luca hissed in anger.

"Sir." Luca's assistant stepped forward. "Would you like me to inquire again whether Mr. Quinteros is ready to meet with the team?"

Luca assured him it was only a minor irritation. "No, thank you. He's trying to assert himself as the leader in this situation. Let him make his point. He will take our offer."

Just then, the door to the Oval Office opened. Luca stood as a secretary emerged and motioned for them to follow her. Luca noted that the dictator sat behind the Resolute Desk, which had been a favorite of many of the American presidents. Luca kept his facial expression still with a little difficulty. There was nothing he didn't know about Andres Quinteros, who had legions of spirits controlling him.

The first one to possess Andres had been Balun. The things he and Balun had done would appall most people. The others came quickly after Balun had accomplished the preliminary work of degeneration. Andres had no idea that many of his thoughts and decisions were not his own. *Now they are mine.* Luca was humored by the thought. The legion of spirits obeyed his will.

ONE WILL BE LEFT

Humbly, Luca shook Andres's hand and expressed his appreciation for the time the leader was giving the group to make their presentation. Once everyone was settled, the head of their delegation, the Chinese ambassador, made his opening statement. Then he introduced Luca as the architect of the substantial changes in the World Union government structure and the one who had drafted the treaty, which they all hoped Mr. Quinteros would sign, making him the leader of the tribunal over Region One.

When the Chinese ambassador finished, Luca stood up and gave a quick overview of the changes the World Union would be making in the next six to eight weeks. "And as you can see, we will be changing the governing structure to ten regions, each one led by a tribunal. The tribunals will each have a vote in the governing body, along with the senate and two councils. We believe that in this manner, each region, along with the smaller national interests, will be represented."

Andres nodded thoughtfully, then interjected, "Now tell me, why should I join this new regime? I fought against the World Union and its corruption. I already have what you are offering. Of what advantage is this treaty for me?"

Luca responded by reading off the list of advantages he had in front of him. Andres laughed, then pushed his chair back and stood up. "You're wasting your time. Good day, gentlemen."

"Just a minute," Luca spoke quietly. Andres stopped, his hand grasping the doorknob. "Everyone else may leave the room," Luca commanded with an eerie calm. Each of the members of the World Union delegation stood and walked out of the room. Even Andres' security team left their leader alone with Luca. The last man out closed the door quietly behind him.

"What do you think you are doing?" Andres snarled.

"Be quiet. You are tiresome. I want to speak to you, Balun." Luca watched in fascination as the spirit known as Balun separated himself from his human host. He stood before Luca, while Andres looked on in fear. Balun materialized in front of them, standing in a physical form that was about six foot five. Luca thought he must weigh almost three hundred pounds. His arms were like tree stumps, and his red-brown hair was pulled back, revealing a strong-looking face. A ragged scar ran from his right cheek across to the right corner of his mouth, but oddly it did not detract from his beauty. Rather, it made him appear more fearsome. Andres began to whimper and fell to his knees before the giant demon.

"Yes, my lord." Balun bowed on one knee and bent his head in supplication before Luca.

"You have done well, Balun. My Father is pleased." Luca placed his hand in benediction on Balun's head and felt a surge from the touch. It was similar to the electric shock one might get from static in dry air, but much more powerful. It energized him.

"You may stand." Luca waited a moment before continuing. "I would like you to *control that* during the negotiations." Luca nodded toward the man sniveling before them. "When I call the others back in, they will remember nothing. It will seem to them as if there had been no interruption to our discussion.

"Allow him to be combative at first, but then I want you to subordinate his will to mine. Make him see the wisdom of what is being offered to him."

"Yes, my lord. I will do just as you say." Balun bowed his head respectfully before reentering Andres Quinteros' body.

Luca watched, captivated, as Andres's head lolled forward, then whipped back upright. Andres stared blankly at Luca and stood up.

Chuckling, Luca went to the door, opened it, and called the others back into the room. When they had all taken their places, Luca spoke. "Thank you, General Quinteros for giving us this time to make our case."

Andres blinked a few times before his face took on a disdainful sneer. "I still see no reason I should entertain your offer, Ambassador. What could you possibly offer me?"

"I do understand your position, General. Please let me present the benefits you will enjoy. First of all, you will live. You of all people know how easily power is gained and lost. We can provide you with that added insurance, which will make your sleep more restful." Luca spoke slowly, staring Andres in the eye.

"Under the offices of the New World Union, each director will be absolute ruler of his or her region. Each year, taxes will be sent to the capital, Babylon, to be redistributed to each region. Each of the directors will receive one percent of the entire worldwide tribute before its distribution. North America, while still possessing vast natural riches, is suffering the results of the loss of its citizens in the disappearance and all of those unfortunate natural disasters. Yet one percent of their taxes still is a vast sum."

Andres looked at Luca and suddenly smiled, revealing stunningly white teeth. "I can see that you and I have much in common, Ambassador Giamo. Like me, you are a pragmatic man. It is getting late in the day. Please…" He looked at the men around the table. "Allow me to host the delegation tonight for dinner. I believe my assistant will find rooms for each of you. Ambassador Giamo, I would be privileged if you would stay in my personal residence."

"I would be most honored, sir." Luca smiled with pleasure.

Andres stood and left the room with his assistant and security team. The members of the commission each took turns congratulating Luca on his negotiating skills.

As the group left the room, a young woman approached Luca.

"Mr. Ambassador? I'm Jenna Franks, one of the general's personal assistants. May I show you to your room?"

Luca followed her through the West Wing to the walkway next to a garden. It had once been quite beautiful, but months of neglect had left the lawn brown and full of weeds. He could see that some roses managed to bloom anyway.

They walked up many stairs before reaching the third floor. Jenna opened the door for Luca and led him down the hall. "I've put you in this bedroom, sir, because it leads out to a solarium that is quite nice. From there, you can walk along the promenade if you would like to do so."

She opened the door to a cramped little room. "I know it doesn't look like much, but I think this will be the most comfortable for you. The other ambassadors are sharing accommodations."

"I appreciate your thoughtfulness, Miss Franks. This will be just fine. Thank you." He smiled reassuringly at her retreating back before turning with a frown to the room. He walked over to the window through the narrow space between the end of the bed and the wall. Pulling back the heavy drapes, he saw the solarium, but there was no access to it unless he climbed out of the window.

He left the room and walked down the hallway that led to the promenade. Opening the door, he walked out into the dazzling light.

"Well, Ambassador, this is a most pleasant surprise."

Luca blinked in the sunshine and saw an exquisite woman standing next to the railing to his right. Long dark hair tumbled in curls around her shoulders and down her back. She was dressed in white lace that clung to her figure in a disarming manner.

"And whom do I have the privilege of surprising?" His eyes slowly traveled from her feet upward. He stopped when he came to her dark green eyes.

"I am Patricia Quinteros." She smiled seductively up at him.

"The wife of the general. I'd heard you were an incredible beauty, but it's no wonder. You are one of us."

"One of you?" Her smile faded. "I know Stephen Amona said there were others, and that you were his protégé, but I had no idea."

"I see that you are pregnant." Luca reached forward and caressed her belly with his right hand. "It is a son. The next generation of our people."

"How could you possibly know that?" Patricia asked. "Although Stephen explained the whole thing to me, I must confess that the thought of being a hybrid bothers me. What does that mean for my son?"

Luca took her arm and pulled it through the crook of his arm. "Let's walk and talk about it." He patted her hand reassuringly. "I understand this is new information and that you have many questions.

ONE WILL BE TAKEN

I will do my best to answer each of them. You are much more than you realize."

Beit Aghion
Official Residence of Israel's Prime Minister

The fountain burbled next to the gazebo where Angelina sat as she watched Charlie play in the still, sunny garden. They had just finished dinner outside on the patio.

Angelina tilted her left ear toward the open door to the house behind her. She could hear her father speaking just inside the kitchen but couldn't make out what he was saying. He had been gone all day, but he'd left the dinner table to take an important call more than thirty minutes ago.

She poured a bit more wine into her glass and nodded when Yona, Charlie's nanny, asked if she wanted Charlie taken up for her bath. Yona had been Angelina's own nanny, and Angelina felt nostalgic watching the older woman care for her daughter with the same love she had shown for Angelina as a young girl. Yona brought Charlie over to her, and Angelina gave the girl a hug. "Now make sure you and Yona get all the stinkies out!" she joked. Charlie giggled as Yona carried her into the house.

Angelina was only alone a moment before her father returned. "Where there more bombings, Papa?" she asked.

"No, it's something else. I had to assure myself that what happened to you and Charlene in the bazaar would not happen again." He spoke sternly.

Her stomach turned and she put down the wine carefully. "What does that mean?"

"I had some agents look into your attempted kidnapping. There was surveillance video, of course, so it wasn't hard to find the men; nor did it take much to convince them to talk." He reached over, picked up his wineglass, and dumped the warm wine into the grass next to the gazebo. "Mitch hired them," he added flatly.

"What can I do, Papa?" Angelina tried not to panic. "I thought we would be safe here in Israel. I don't know where else we can go. North America is in such turmoil. Europe is pretty safe, but I know he'd find us there."

Her father sat down next to her and tenderly took her hand. "I do not want my only child to live in fear. It has been dealt with. I've just had confirmation. Mitch and his sister had an unfortunate incident in the village of Eze in France, victims of a robbery that didn't end well. It's best to avoid some places so late at night. Trouble is bound to find you." He patted her hand. "There you are. Charlene is safe."

Angelina closed her eyes and sighed. She felt slightly conflicted by the loss of her child's father and the relief she felt at being free of him at last. "I don't know how to thank you. I suppose I should be upset, but relief is the greater feeling. If that man had not intervened, I don't think I would have ever seen Charlie again."
Opening her eyes, she smiled at her father. "I know I've given you so many bad moments, Papa. I hope to do better. Would you like some more wine?"

"No, I must get to another briefing in a little while. I also wanted to tell you that we could find no record of the man who helped you."

"Oh, I'm disappointed about that. I did wish to let him know how thankful we are. Did the facial recognition not help?" Angelina asked.

"That's the odd thing. The man seemed to know where the surveillance cameras were. His face was always either turned or obscured in some way. From the man's actions, Mossad believes he is or was part of some special forces. Since he helped you, we must assume he is a friend."

"He has my friendship forever," she declared. "He saved Charlie and brought both of us safely back to you. Oh well…" She changed the subject. "What do you think will happen with the bomb-

ONE WILL BE LEFT

ings from the south?"

Arnot sighed, "They will continue. I'd hoped that the destruction of the armies and the Dome were the signal of a new era for Israel. We've had relative peace from Hamas for almost three years, but they've been reorganized. There's someone new in charge and we've not been able to discover who it is."

He grimaced in frustration. "And as always when Israel is attacked, other governments call on us to use 'restraint.' The World Union ambassador calls me daily, asking me to stop bombing Gaza. How can I do that?

"The shields are fairly effective, but not entirely—some missiles still get through. Honestly, I don't know how long we can keep it going unless we're proactive. The cost for the shields is high. We must destroy our enemies before they destroy us!"

"The new king of Jordan, isn't he coming here next month?" Angelina inquired.

"Yes, he is our one ally and has offered to help in any way he can. But in the meantime, more young men are finding their way into Gaza. Also, there is a great deal of evidence that the Chinese are arming the Egyptians—we must stand strong, as always."

"Papa, do you remember that story you used to read me when I was little? The one about the flat for rent?"

"Yes." He smiled at her quizzically.

"Do you remember how no one liked the neighbors, so none would live in the flat except the dove? Israel needs a dove. We need someone who can bring us peace. Do you believe we'll find someone like that?"

"I don't know." He stood up and patted her shoulder. "From the beginning, Israel has battled to survive. In these days, God has again intervened, so perhaps when the time is right, He will send us a dove. Surely He did not protect us as He did to let us fall into the hands of our enemies now. We live in an incredible time, Angel." Hearing him call her that once again made her smile.

"We do, Papa. I know you always hoped the Temple would

be rebuilt. When I was a teenager, I used to be embarrassed at how you would go on about the importance of the Temple—and of Israel having control of the Temple Mount. Now I see I had no idea. Who could have known that it would indeed be rebuilt? But you had the vision, Papa. You believed!

"Now we not only have the Temple but the Ark of the Covenant too. What other miracles can Israel expect?"

"Peace. I hope we can expect peace." Her father stopped speaking and listened. Charlie could be heard shouting for her grandfather from the house. Sweet pleas of "Granddad, Granddad!" rang from the upstairs windows. Arnot read to her each night, the highlight of his day. He kissed Angelina and went into the house.

Angelina put her head in her arms on the table in front of her and thought. She had rescued Charlie from Mitch. Then they had survived the terrible earthquakes in Rome. There, she had seen those terrible creatures, evil-looking spirits. She had returned to her childhood faith after that experience in Rome. Following her return to Jerusalem, her father had been overjoyed to have her join him in synagogue once again.

She sat up and glanced around the darkening garden. Clouds were covering the sun, and the change in the light startled her. She had not seen any of the evil spirits since Rome, but she was still afraid she would see them again. Her heart raced as she recalled them, and she began to talk to God in a whisper.

"I'm so afraid! God, nothing in this universe, seen or unseen, happens without Your permission. I pray You will not give permission for those creatures to touch my daughter, or Yona, or Papa, or me. I cannot sleep because I am so afraid of them. Please? Thank you. Amen."

She scraped the plates in front of her, stacked them, and took them into the kitchen to wash, feeling a little better.

ONE WILL BE LEFT

The White House, Washington, DC

Andres lit his Churchill cigar with relish. The warm, mild flavor held a slight taste of coffee and licorice, which he enjoyed. Thin smoke trailed upward as he turned his attention to the music playing softly in the background, Paganini's "24 Caprices." The challenge and complexities of the piece thrilled him.

Ash dropped from his cigar onto the yellow-and-white fabric of the chair without his notice. He leaned his head back and stared at the Lincoln bed to his left. Patricia had claimed the master bedroom on the west side of the second floor. He had chosen the Lincoln bedroom.

The kingly symbolism of the carved crown canopy over the huge bed gratified him. His goal was in sight. Anti-Globalist troops in North America had successfully pushed World Union troops to the coastal cities on the Eastern Seaboard, and Washington, DC, was in his complete control. His men from South America had swarmed north and now held every major city in the western portions of the former United States. For years, he had cultivated supporters and friends. Now all of his detailed plans were coming to fruition. As his cigar burned, Andres recalled his strategies and recounted their fulfillment, due in part to the money and resources that flowed in from his silent partner.

Patricia came into the room, interrupting his thoughts. "Andres, there you are! It is almost time for dinner."

"Please, sit and talk with me while I finish my cigar." His words were a request, but his countenance was commanding. He watched with satisfaction as her face reddened. He loved the power he had over her.

Patricia sat carefully on the silk chair across from her husband, smoothing the blue velvet of her dress.

"I see you are wearing my gift. It suits you." He gestured to

ONE WILL BE LEFT

the necklace she wore.

She touched the outer edge of the pendant. "Let's hope the curse is not real, Andres," she joked. "I have to admit, I never thought you and I would be living in this place."

"I saw it in a vision. I knew I could make it happen. As I told you, when chaos exists, people will give up their liberties to have order restored. It will not be long before the World Union troops withdraw and we have complete control of this continent," he boasted.

"How can you be so confident, my love?"

"I have assurances from our friend. Our next step will be to outlaw privately held weapons. Security and safety for our citizens will be the hallmark of our reign."

"How can you ensure such a law is followed? Surely there will be many who will hide their weapons. I know I would," Patricia said.

Andres stood up and walked behind the couch where his wife sat. She was so fiercely desirable to him. He rubbed her bare shoulders suggestively and asked, "Do we have some time before we have to go down?"

"Andres, you know what the doctor said. The baby's condition is delicate and we're not to indulge ourselves. I must remain calm and placid." She patted his hand with feigned affection. "I know seven months seems like a long time."

"It is a long time, but anything for my son." He sighed. "Let's go down and see our new friends and supporters."

By the time they arrived at the State Dining Room, a large crowd was already seated and waiting. As Andres escorted his wife to the front of the room, many of the guests stood up and clapped. He took note of those who kept to their seats.

Andres pulled Patricia's chair out and waited while she sat and arranged her gown before he raised his hand for silence.

"Thank you, all of you. Please take your seats." He waited for a moment as his guests sat down. "Thank you for joining us in celebrating with this victory dinner. Although we still have had some sporadic skirmishes with World Union troops, I expect a formal surrender soon. We are already in negotiations with Ambassador Giamo from the World Union."

Andres indicated Luca, sitting at the main table next to Patricia. As the crowd applauded, Luca stood up and bowed with a charming smile.

"Thank you, Ambassador, for joining us tonight. You and your delegation are most welcome. Ladies and gentlemen, the world is very different than it was just a few short years ago, is it not? Then, the great experiment of the World Union was just beginning. Many hoped it would offer stability and the peace we all so greatly desire. But from the beginning it was corrupt. We saw that and we stood up to it. It was necessary.

"Please, join me in celebrating our victory," Andres invited the crowd warmly. "I believe each of you has a glass of champagne on the table, please join me in a toast." He turned and nodded to Patricia, who also stood, raising her glass toward his in a salute.

Turning back to the men and women gathered in the State Dining Room, Andres raised his glass. "You are the ones who have made this victory possible. Each of you has been faithful to support the cause, each of you has a part in the success of our movement, and each of you will be rewarded according to your involvement. Tonight is our time to celebrate. Tomorrow new work begins."

He tipped his glass and drained it as the crowd applauded wildly. Andres allowed the tribute to continue a full minute before he raised his hand. When the room was quiet enough, he spoke again.

"Tonight I want each of you to have a small token of my thanks for your efforts. There are gift bags for you when you leave, gifts which Patricia and I chose individually for each of you." He waited while the crowd applauded again. "I want you to know that as the leader of North America, the head of the 'Tribunal of Region One,' I will shower my supporters with many good things. You can expect a quick return to the amenities we North Americans have enjoyed.

"Electricity will be available, and fresh food, fruits, vegeta-

ONE WILL BE LEFT

bles, and meat will be plentiful. You will once again enjoy running water in your homes. All will be restored!"

The room reverberated with the noise of celebration. Andres looked at his watch, then reached for the bottle of champagne on the table in front of him and refilled his glass before raising it once again. "Now, please join me in toasting our future! To those who have been faithful, no good thing will be withheld!" He raised his glass and finished it. The crowd followed his lead and many finished their champagne.

Andres stood and observed the crowd expectantly. People began to feel uneasy at his silent stare, and many began to look at one another with worried expressions. Then the first man fell to the ground, grabbing at his throat as white foam bubbled out of his mouth and dripped onto the carpet. His wife fell right after him.

Andres smiled as one person after another fell. From the corner of his eye, he saw Ambassador Giamo reach over and squeeze Patricia's shoulder. Andres felt the blood pound in his ears. He turned away and continued to watch each traitor fall. He waited a few minutes after the last person fell before he spoke to the survivors. "Those who cross me will experience my justice." He paused as soldiers entered the room and began removing the bodies. He beamed at the remaining people and spoke in a reassuring tone. "If you obey, you will receive great rewards, both you and your families. But, if you don't, be assured, you and your families will suffer the ultimate loss. Now, please join our liaison to the OneFaith Church, Sister Bernice, as she leads us in prayers of thanksgiving for all we have and all we are about to receive." He raised his hand in benediction.

As Andres sat down next to his wife, he noticed her pallor. "My dearest, are you well?"

Her pupils were dilated with fear. "Andres, what have you done and why?"

"I explained it quite clearly, dearest. They rebelled against me, some in greater ways than others, but each of them crossed me. You know I will tolerate no dissension. Now that I am the leader of

North America, I intend to remain so. Might makes right, my dear." Patricia stroked the diamond on her neck and swallowed. "But their wives?"

"Oh, not just their wives. Their children, too have been eliminated," Andres picked up his fork, selected a stuffed mushroom from the plate in front of him, and shook his head back and forth, closing his eyes and relishing the flavor. "Oh, crabmeat. It has been so long since I have had this pleasure!" he moaned. "You must try one, my love."

Stabbing his fork into another mushroom, Andres put it in front of Patricia's closed mouth. "I must insist you try it. Now, dear," he said lightly, his eyes narrowing. Obediently, she opened her mouth. She chewed slowly and swallowed.

"Isn't it wonderful?" he asked.

Patricia smiled weakly and nodded her approval. Andres turned to speak to the man on his right, and she shivered.

15

JERUSALEM, ISRAEL

Kate sat with her long legs tucked underneath her on the broad, red leather chair across from Christopher. She started to speak but saw their waitress making her way to the table with a fresh bottle of tequila. Kate and Christopher were well known to the staff of the Cellar Bar. Kate's habit of leaving extravagant tips ensured they were well looked after whenever they showed up. After thanking the server, Kate continued her tirade.

"I'm just ticked off, Christopher. You have no idea!" Kate threw both hands up in front of her in disgust, almost knocking over the expensive bottle their server had just placed in front of her. "Really. Michael and I are married. Did it never occur to the man to tell me he'd been married before, or that his parents died at the hands of terrorists, or that his wife died right afterward, or that he abandoned his son to her parents and that *some-bloody-hell-how* the 'prophet Elijah' himself shows up at our door to show him the error of his ways? Good Lord!" She sank back into the chair, crossing her arms dramatically in exasperation.

Christopher wisely said nothing but poured Kate another shot of tequila. She downed it, continuing on with her diatribe.

"He didn't even warn me. I got home to find out I have a stepson, who is now living with us, thank-you-so-very-much, and on top of that..." she stopped yelling and whispered, "he's terribly religious."

Christopher licked his lips nervously. "Maybe you should just go home and talk it over with him."

"I'm not going home. Hell, no. Michael is going to have to fix this somehow. I want children. I want my own children. I didn't sign up for this." She looked into Christopher's eyes, her own full of tears. "I'm not a nice person, Christopher. You know that. I know it. Michael just found out, and I think he's sorry." She started to cry in great sobbing gulps, burying her face in her hands as her body shook with sadness and anger and fear.

Christopher looked around the now-empty bar for a way out. Kate angry was something he was quite used to, but not this hysterical woman. He couldn't handle it. With relief, he saw Michael standing in the doorway of the bar, anxiously looking around. He saw them and lifted a hand in recognition.

"Hey Kate, I'll leave you two to discuss things." Christopher got up hurriedly and acknowledged Michael as he passed him on his approach to the table. "Good luck, man," the cameraman said and scurried out the door without a backward glance.

Kate looked up at her husband, tears streaming down her face. "I'm sure you hate me. I'm a horrible person, I know," she groaned.

Michael sat down on the sleek sofa where Christopher had been sitting and smiled ruefully at his wife. "That makes two of us. I don't know where to start apologizing, Kate. For being dishonest with you, or abandoning my son, or being angry when you weren't happy to come home to a completely different situation than when you left it…there's just so much." He moved the tequila bottle back and forth on the table. "I don't know what to say that will make it better."

"I just think lying made it all worse, Michael," she said, slurring her words slightly.

"I know I should have told you about Devorah. I should have, but to be honest, her death still haunts me." His voice broke as he spoke.

"No, I get that. I honestly understand it. I even get leaving Micah with her parents. He looks so much like the pictures he showed me of his mother. I truly can comprehend all of that, Michael. It's the ridiculous story about some ancient Jewish prophet returning to the earth and knocking on our door that I'm having a hard time understanding. Why did you have to go there? Why elaborate on the truth? Don't you trust me?" She pushed her blonde hair back from her face and glared at him defiantly.

Michael put the tequila down abruptly. "That's the thing. I didn't elaborate. He really did come to our apartment door. I had no idea Micah was alone. No one contacted me. I know it sounds crazy, but I do believe the man is Elijah."

Kate picked up the tequila bottle and poured another shot, slopping some of the liquid on the table. "Then we have more than one problem. There's no way that could be true, so either he's a crazy man, or you are."

"You're forgetting the third option, Kate." Michael spoke softly, but with indignation. "The third possibility is that it's true. There's a prophecy that in the last days, the prophet Elijah will come back to Israel. I've heard rumors of him doing things here for the last year or so."

"Why would he be here?" she asked, obviously trying to control her words. "Why would God send a dead man back to earth? Doesn't make any sense."

"Well, first of all, the prophet Elijah never died. He was taken to heaven in a chariot of fire, according to the Tanakh, or what you might know as the Old Testament. He told me his mission is to 'return the hearts of the fathers to the children'—that's also in the Tanakh. For years, the Jewish family has not been what it ought to be. Traditionally, our families were very closely knit, but lately, not so much. Certainly in my case that's true."

Kate stared at her husband in disbelief. "I told you my granny was very religious and I went to church with her quite a lot. I do remember the story of Elijah—that Elijah didn't die. But that's a Sunday school fairy tale meant to impress kids who don't know any better, Michael. For you, an educated man, to sit there and tell me you believe that some old man is actually a prophet from the past is just too much." Kate rolled her eyes in annoyance.

Leaning forward, she put her hand firmly on his forearm. "Look, I think someone went to a lot of trouble to get you to Micah, pretending to be Elijah so that you—the discoverer of the Ark of the Covenant—would go along. Or, maybe you on some primeval level knew Micah was alone and your psyche manufactured this 'Elijah' to help lead you to your son."

Michael did not respond; he just stared at his wife with red-rimmed eyes that were shadowed in pain. Even half-drunk, Kate could see he was upset that she didn't believe him. "You know, Michael, you're asking a lot of me. You really are. All of the Elijah stuff, and what about Micah? What are you going to do about him?"

"What do you mean?" he asked tightly.

"Look, you know all of that Yeshua stuff is not going to endear your son to your coworkers and friends. He quotes the Bible like he's a prophet instead of a boy. I think he's traumatized by his grandparents' deaths. Maybe you need to have him see someone. The way he talks isn't normal. I thought his grandparents were observant Jews.

"They were. Apparently, they decided that the Messiah was..." Michael could not bring himself to say the name. "Listen, I think we just have to leave it alone and let him get used to our home...to living with us. It's a huge adjustment."

Michael tenderly took her hand in his and kissed it softly before rubbing the back of her hand against his cheek. "Will you forgive me for not talking to you about all of this, Kate? I was wrong to just spring it on you when you got home. I'm not lying about Elijah. I wish you would believe me. It bothers me that you think that I would lie to you about it—or that I'm crazy. But let's leave that alone for now. Can we agree to try our best to make Micah feel welcomed?"

Kate sighed. "Yes. But I'm telling you right now, Michael, I'm not jumping on any religious bandwagon. I'm a reporter—a damned fine reporter with a reputation I worked hard to earn. I live in a world of facts and tangible evidence. No man who lived thousands of years ago, no prophet or messiah, is going to tell me how to live my life." Staring at him, she deliberately poured another shot of tequila and downed it, wiping her mouth with the back of her hand. She quickly bit a lime wedge before continuing. Her face puckered. "If we're going to stay together, we've got to go on the basis that we agreed to when we got married: there is no sacred or spiritual, just tangible reality. I can't have a relationship with a man who is going to go batty over prophets and ancient prophecies and all of that. You can't be one way and then change on me, okay? No bait and switch." She pulled her hand away and poured another shot of tequila for both of them, pushing his across the table to him. Michael slowly picked it up, toasted his wife with it, took a sip, and set it down.

"Let's go home." He took Kate's hand and led her out of the small bar. He steadied her as she wobbled to the cab he had waiting outside. As the driver made his way through the dark streets, Michael stared out of the car window. Kate's head rested on his shoulder. His mind raced, his thoughts jumbled and confused. When they pulled up in front of their apartment building, he shoved a wad of bills at the driver and pulled Kate out of the cab, supporting her with his right arm around her back as she stumbled up the thirty-six stairs to their second-floor apartment.

"Can you stand?" he asked as he moved her to lean against the wall while he pulled out his keys. Opening the door, he led her into the living room.

"Well, hello, Livy!" Kate exclaimed enthusiastically. She stumbled toward their neighbor, who was sitting on the couch with Micah.

"I see you found Kate," Livy said to Michael, smiling as she stood up to greet them.

Kate gave the woman a hug and kissed her. "I'm going to have a terrific headache in the morning. Michael found me just as I finished off a bottle of tequila," Kate boasted with an inebriated grin. "I'm sure you will, dear. Why don't you sit here and I'll get you some coffee?" Livy hurried to the kitchen, leaving Michael with Kate and Micah.

ONE WILL BE LEFT

"You know what, Kate? I think it might be better if you just went to bed," Michael observed. "You need to sleep it off."

"Really?" she questioned, obviously struggling to hold it together. "I think it might be nice to chat with Micah." She sat down on the chair opposite the boy, whose expression was flat. Michael could not tell what his son was thinking.

"I'm just a little drunk, dear," Kate continued. "I can hold my liquor very well, thank you very much. I'll be just fine once I've had that coffee Livy's getting." She leaned in toward the boy, who sat back farther against the couch in response.

"So, Micah. I have to say I'm sorry for yelling at your dad and running out of here earlier tonight. It was just that I was tired from my late flight and all, and, well, let me be honest, I didn't know you were here." Michael caught her eye and shook his head severely. She pursed her lips together.

Livy came back into the room with a cup of steaming coffee. "Here you go, Kate. Drink this." She pushed the mug at Kate. "I'm going to go home now. Gad is probably already asleep, and I'm tired."

Michael walked his neighbor to the door and thanked her for staying with Micah. She motioned for him to follow her out into the hallway. Once the door was shut, she shared her concerns about his marriage. It was apparent that she'd ferreted out quite a bit of information from Micah in the time Michael was gone. He tried to reassure her, secretly hoping he was not going to read about this in a gossip magazine. Since they'd married, he and Kate were often on front covers. So far, they'd been media darlings, but he knew that could change quickly. He tried to do as much damage control as he could.

When he returned to the living room, he saw that Kate had curled up on the chair and fallen asleep. Micah was standing next to her, covering her with a blanket.

"That's kind of you," Michael said quietly.

Micah smiled at his father, then rushed at him and hugged him fiercely.

ONE WILL BE LEFT

Jerusalem, Israel

Angelina felt the breeze lift her hair, cooling her neck. The Mamilla Mall had always been a favorite place of hers, a great spot to go out and be alone in a crowd. She overheard the two women in front of her talking about how long it had taken them to get used to the sun setting so early in the winter. They sounded like Americans to her, or maybe some of the many refugees who'd immigrated to Israel during the civil war in North America between the World Union and the Anti-Globalists. She saw the pharmacy to her right and hurried in. There were some special vitamins she wanted to pick up for Charlie while she was out.

Finding the aisle stocked with supplies for children, she noticed a woman looking at the diapers with a confused expression on her face as she examined the boxes. A young infant lay in a stroller next to the woman.

"Is she your first baby?" Angelina asked, noting the pink blanket with the name Juliana embroidered across the bottom.

The brown-haired woman turned to her, "No, but my first baby in Israel. The brands are different from what I'm used to, and I don't read Hebrew very well. Could you help me find the right size?"

Angelina agreed and showed her the appropriate package. Then Angelina turned her attention to the baby, crouching down to her level. "She's so beautiful! What a complexion! She looks like a little princess!"

"She's in our home," someone else spoke.

Angelina looked up to see who had joined them. The woman in front of her was easily one of the most beautiful women she'd ever seen. Angelina could not help but stare at the perfectly symmetrical features framed by shimmering dark hair. She noticed a vacant expression, though, in the woman's dark eyes and realized with a start that the woman was blind.

"Oh, Rhetta!" the brunette who had been looking for the diapers exclaimed. "This woman was very kind to help me find the right diapers. Would you mind staying here with the baby while I look for that lotion I wanted?" Thanking Angelina, the young mother turned and walked around the end of the aisle.

"Well, I suppose I should get what I came here for," Angelina said softly. Moving down the aisle a bit, she looked over the shelves for the vitamins Charlie liked. Suddenly, she heard a gasp and glanced back at the striking woman. Angelina's stomach lurched when she saw the horror on Rhetta's face, and as she looked farther down to the aisle across from them, she saw the source of the woman's fear. Angelina stifled a scream, not wanting to draw their attention to herself. It was them again—those hideous creatures. She could hardly believe it.

Rhetta pushed the baby's stroller behind her, close to the shelves, so that she stood between the baby and the repulsive beings. Although terrified, Angelina moved next to her.

"Do you see them?" she whispered brokenly.

"Yes. I may be blind, but there are things I can see. They've been all over Jerusalem lately. Right now they seem to be hunting, prowling. Something is about to happen here. Do you see the swords in their hands?"

Angelina nodded her head. "Yes." She gasped as one creature hissed at her as it passed close by. "What are they? Why do they look like that?"

Rhetta placed a calming hand on Angelina's shoulder. "They're just as Scripture describes them. They're demons.

"Now listen, please. I'm going to get Teo, the baby's mother. Please stay here with the baby. Guard her. Do you see? They won't actually touch you. They are terrifying, I know, but do you see the shining one guarding us?"

"No, I only see the dark ones," Angelina shuddered as she started to cry. Her heart felt like it was being torn apart. She'd never felt so terrified, so helpless, so afraid for her own life. Rhetta pulled her into her arms, hugging her tightly. Angelina heard her whisper a prayer in Hebrew, asking Abba to save this daughter. Then Rhetta pushed Angelina gently back, placing the younger woman's hands on the stroller.

"Watch her," Rhetta ordered before moving quietly down the aisle, turning in the same direction as the dark creatures had gone. Angelina closed her eyes briefly before she scooped the infant up out of the stroller. Cradling Juliana close, she crept down the aisle.

What she saw brought her to her knees, and she leaned away from the scene unfolding before her, clutching the infant. Teo was several aisles down, toward the back of the store, with her back to Angelina. She was examining a bottle label. Rhetta was nearing her swiftly, but three human men were standing in between the two women, oddly lurking just behind Teo. There was something off about them. Demonic guardians surrounded each of the men, and Angelina noticed others nearby fighting unseen adversaries. She gasped in awe as she saw their opponents materialize before her own eyes. A gory battle was unfolding in front of her—destruction and victory and bloodshed all taking place in a drugstore aisle. As she watched, she recalled that Rhetta had also murmured something about "allowing her to see." She was seeing, alright.

A massive warrior, almost seven feet tall, stood between Teo and the attacking horde, his sword drawn. Angelina watched in horrible fascination as the muscles rippled in his immense arms and he met every parry from the enemy with a ringing blow. As terrible-looking as the demons were, this warrior shone with a glory that could only come from God. Angelina noticed another shining warrior battling through the mass of demons and clearing a path for Rhetta to cross. Rhetta reached Teo's side just as one of the men called her name.

Teo turned around with a smile that faded instantly. Her face became ashen, and Angelina saw her mouth *No!* just as the man stepped forward, grabbed her, and forced a white cloth over her mouth. Rhetta tried to pull Teo away from his grasp, but one of the other men gagged the older woman.

Angelina watched in confusion and horror as both the gleaming warriors stopped fighting and sheathed their swords. The demons tried to jab at them with dark blades, but there appeared to be a barrier preventing the evil creatures from doing so. The men pulled the two women through a service door for the pharmacy employees, and all the others simply vanished.

Angelina looked around, breathless. There was not a single other witness to the surreal abduction she'd just observed. She let out a sigh, surprised that she even had any strength left inside of her. The baby started to whimper. Carefully, Angelina got to her feet and crept back to the service door, peering through the window. She couldn't see anything. Transferring the baby to her right arm, she tugged her cell phone out of her back pocket and quickly called her father, barely able to dial numbers because of her trembling. She knew that calling the police was not going to help those women. Mossad, Israel's intelligence agency,would have to get involved right away if there was to be any chance of rescuing them.

When her father answered, she quickly relayed what had happened. He instructed her to stay in the pharmacy near other people until his men arrived.

She thanked her father, clicked off the phone, shoved it in her pocket, and made her way with the baby back to the stroller. A small basket under the buggy had a purse in it. Angelina grabbed it and rummaged through, looking for a cell phone. She found one in an outside pouch.

Thankful there was no lock on the screen, she hit the contact button and scanned the directory. There were only a few numbers in the device, so she tapped the history button and selected the number that was used most often, for someone called DC.

Angelina heard the phone ring over and over, but no one answered. She waited for the message prompt, but it was only the standard one the phone company provided. She hesitated and hung up. What if this person, DC, had also been abducted? She thought quickly, looking over the contents of the baby bag. There were no bottles and only a few diapers.

Carefully, she placed the infant back in the stroller. She grabbed some infant formula and a baby bottle from the shelf. Moving down the aisle, she picked up the diaper package that Rhetta had dropped and made her way to the cashier.

"Don't you worry, sweet girl. I'm going to keep you safe. My papa will be here soon with men to protect us," she cooed at the little girl. "I'll do all I can to help get your momma back to you, I promise, sweetie."

She heard the sirens in the distance and closed her eyes in relief as she clutched the stroller handles. *Thank you, God!* she prayed silently. *Please don't let them come back. Please help this baby's mother and friend.* She opened her eyes, and to her utter shock, a tall, shimmery man was standing in front of the baby's stroller. Carefully, she glanced around her to see if there was anyone else around, any of the other kind.

"Can you see me?" she asked the shining man, stunned at his radiance.

"Of course."

"You're so..." Those were the only words Angelina could get out as she fell to her knees in fear. He was so unlike the others she'd seen before—not evil like the demons, but also different from the warriors who had battled them. Holy. She stared into the man's eyes, mesmerized. Her head felt like she'd been spinning in circles. What raced through her mind was too terrible, too heavy to handle. For the first time, she saw herself in the light of the pure goodness before her, and the sight was loathsome. She bent over and began rocking herself back and forth in quiet hysteria as she realized the depths of her sin.

She felt a hand touch her head, stroking it as a father would a child, and a perfect warmth enveloped her. She opened her eyes. Before her, just inches from her face, was a pair of sandaled male feet. Each foot was scarred, and the impact of seeing them was tragic and divine at the same time. Before she even looked all the way up into his face, she knew who he was. When she finally mustered up the courage to look into his eyes again, she knew she was loved and forgiven and made new. Tears of joy ran down her face as he spoke to her. It seemed only a moment, yet he told her many things. Then, in a flash, he was gone, and Angelina was left kneeling on the tile of the pharmacy floor.

She realized she wasn't alone. An angel was kneeling there too, his arms raised in praise, his face full of glory. He stood up, walked toward her, and pulled her to her feet.

"It is something we long to see!" he exclaimed. "Welcome to the kingdom."

"Are you here for this baby?" Angelina asked.

"No, I am your guardian, Angelina. I've watched over you your entire life. I'm here to protect you. The child also has a guardian, and he is there."

Angelina turned to the place he indicated and saw a sparkling warrior fiercely attacking a demon. She watched as he chased the evil one away. Then the warrior turned and approached them. His body shimmered for a moment and then disappeared as one of the first responders walked right through him toward her.

16

GRAND CENTRAL STATION,
NEW YORK CITY, NEW YORK

Standing on the east balcony with Bernard, James observed the masses of people below him. They'd spent several days walking through the terminal, laying hands on and healing people covered with the appalling pustules brought on by smallpox. Some had only black splotches on their skin, while others—it was too awful to even think about. The smell was horrific. At first, James had found it almost impossible to overcome his revulsion and touch the people. But with each healing, his heart swelled with joy and compassion, and the next person was easier to touch.

He watched as Brian, Kerry, and Colin moved through the area to his left where people were bringing others to be healed. At first only James had done the healing; then Bernard suggested that the pastor lay hands on each of the team and ask God to give them the gift of healing also so they could alleviate the suffering more quickly. James agreed, and for now, at least, all the members of their team shared this God-given ability.

"Have you noticed a change in those young men?" James asked Bernard.

Bernard paused for a moment. "Yes, they were young pups before they saw the first plague victim. I doubt any of us had ever seen anything as horrific as we have the last few days. There's a thing my granddad would say in trying situations: 'We grow under the load.' I never understood it until lately, but boy, is it true! Those boys have really grown."

ONE WILL BE LEFT

James nodded. "It's been three days, Bernard, and more infected people are coming. Doug suggested he and his boys go back for more supplies, because not many of those who were healed are leaving. It is incredible to see the way people are staying and helping others."

"I know!" Bernard exclaimed. He was in awe of the spirit of giving he'd witnessed over the last couple days. "There is a group following up after the healings, helping to clean, then burning the contaminated bedding and clothing, while another group has organized areas in restrooms where they've jerry-rigged showers. There's a group in charge of food preparation. Everyone, it seems, is involved in helping the community in some way." He paused to watch Brian bend over a young child with running sores.

"This continues to amaze me, Bernard," said James. They both stared at the scene unfolding below. Brian touched the child's head and then raised a hand above his forehead as he prayed out loud. Meanwhile, his cousins knelt on either side of the child, each holding a hand and praying silently. Incredibly, miraculously, the sores on the child were healed. Both men smiled when the little girl sat up and threw her arms around Brian.

Bernard glanced back at James. "Colin and Kerry are spreading the word that you'll be speaking to everyone at noon. Do you know what you're going to say?"

"I have some rough ideas. I've been praying and asking God to give me the message He wants me to share, but I haven't had much time to prepare."

Bernard continued to look over the crowd below them. "The new government is now in control. Did you know that some think it was Andres Quinteros who exposed New York to the smallpox virus? There's a man here, Trevor something, who claims he worked for the Anti-Globalists. He says Quinteros is the real name of their elusive leader."

"You mean the 'Mr. Smith' we've heard rumors of?" James asked.

ONE WILL BE LEFT

"One and the same. Trevor was one of the men who released the virus here in New York City when the Anti-Globalist military forces had the area surrounded. They got to officials here in the city and lied about Patient Zero being infected, giving that as their rationale for shutting the city down and basically quarantining everyone. Then they released the toxin in various places around the city simultaneously. They wanted to keep the infection under control and not take any chances with travelers spreading it to other areas. Trevor and the other men thought they would be taken out to safety and given the vaccine, but they were left here to suffer the same fate as the others."

James looked at Bernard. "How did this help their cause? I don't understand why anyone would do such a thing."

"Quinteros has the vaccine and the virus. He threatened to expose various opponents with the virus unless they supported his authority. New York City was his proof, his pawn to show that he meant business. How can anyone protect themselves from smallpox? All Quinteros has to do is infect one of his men and have him stand next to someone in a shop and cough or sneeze, or expose people more directly by putting the virus in their food or on their clothing."

"Well, that explains how he was able to quickly stop the war and take control of so much of the continent. What do you think he's going to do when he hears what we're doing here?" James asked with concern.

"I don't know. Maybe use those detention centers like the one you were in and imprison us or kill us. We're in the middle of a battle between two kingdoms, James."

James nodded his head in silent agreement, a million thoughts racing through his mind.

"Hey, I saw a broadcast on the national station before I came up here. Guess who's visiting Quinteros at the White House?" Bernard asked, abruptly changing the subject.

James guessed, "The Italian ambassador? Isn't he leading the World Union effort to divide the world into ten districts?"

"Yes, indeed! Luca Giamo is here to give official recognition

ONE WILL BE LEFT

to Quinteros and assign him to govern North America. The reporter said Giamo's heading to the Middle East next. There've been some problems on the West Bank again, and he's supposed to broker some kind of peace treaty so the world can have a 'last chance' at peace."

"So, we are close to the start," James sighed. He looked at the people below him. Happy laughter and exuberant shouts reverberated through the hall. People who had been so tragically near to death were now completely well. Many were praising God for their healing. However, amidst the victory, James still felt oppressive weariness in his heart as he considered what was ahead of them all.

"How many of these will be left at the end of the next seven years, Bernard? You know what we are facing. We must prepare them somehow."

"I've been thinking about that. I think we should try to get as many out of the city as we can. Cities are going to be bad places for us," Bernard said.

"Why do you say that?"

"Look at how easily these folks were infected with a deadly disease. Out of the cities, they have more of a chance to make it through to the end. We just have to plan. We need to figure out where they can go and how we can get them there safely."

"We can take some back with us, right?" James considered the logistics of moving so many people. What would happen to them if they stayed?

"Yes, but there will be more than we can take. We'll have to be careful to not overwhelm one community," Bernard added.

Below, a panicked man shouted James's name and interrupted them. James and Bernard both leaned over the railing. It was Colin.

"James, we need you to come down here! Quickly!" he yelled, desperation on his face.

James and Bernard both headed to the stairway, James sprinting and Bernard trailing after him.

James saw that Colin was truly distraught. "What is it? What's

ONE WILL BE LEFT

going on?"

"There's a woman over there, in the back. She's real bad. We haven't seen anyone so bad. We prayed, Pastor James, but..." he started sobbing, pacing back and forth.

James patted his shoulder and headed over in the direction Colin pointed. The pastor could see people crowded around a body on a cot, low to the ground.

Kerry and Brian were on either side of the makeshift bed; an emaciated woman lay on top. James could tell she was a woman only by the clothes she was wearing, most of which were covered in black blood. Bile came up his throat at the stench that surrounded her. She was almost disintegrating, her flesh being eaten alive by the virus. It was the worst case of smallpox he had ever seen.

Kerry turned toward him. The young man's face was red with exhaustion and sweat and fear. "We've prayed and prayed. It's not working. She is suffering so much, Pastor James. We need you to pray with us."

Despite the last few days and all the wondrous healings he had seen, it took all James's resolve to move toward the woman. He touched the top of her head, and as his hand stroked the golden-red hair, the woman opened her eyes. With shock, James instantly recognized Cynthia, his ex-wife. There was no denying it. From the expression in her eyes, he knew she recognized him, too.

She began to moan, trying to speak, but her lips were so covered with pustules that she could not form any words. She writhed in agony and anxiously began trying to move around on the bed.

James started to pray hesitantly, his voice breaking. The more he prayed, the stronger his voice grew. He clenched his eyes shut and continued on, begging God to have mercy. He remembered how, in the Gospels, Jesus had rebuked a fever. He did the same, rebuking the virus and commanding it to leave the body of the very woman who had broken his heart.

He heard someone in the crowd around them gasp, and he stopped. Opening his eyes, he saw with wonder that Cynthia's face was suddenly completely clear. He could see her familiar fair skin, dotted with freckles. Someone handed him a bottle of water. Stunned, he opened it mechanically and helped her drink.

"Thank you! Oh God, thank you!" she murmured repeatedly in between sips. She looked at him with a vindictive expression that startled him. The women who helped clean those who were healed moved in quickly. Laughing, they pushed him away good-naturedly, saying he had done his part and now it was their turn. He watched, his heart completely still in his chest as they led Cynthia off to the showers. Neither he nor Cynthia had said a word about their true relationship.

Colin, Brian, and Kerry came up and hugged him enthusiastically, and Bernard clapped him on the back.

"That was amazing! Incredible! What a miracle! She was just on the brink of death, James, and you snatched her back! Did you see the look in her eyes when she saw you?" Bernard exclaimed.

"I did," he answered softly. "She's my wife."

An awkward silence fell over the group of men, and Bernard looked at him dumbfounded. "That was Cynthia? David's mother?" He looked toward the restroom where the women had led her, then looked back at James.

"That can't be a coincidence, my friend," Bernard stated soberly.

"No, it's not. But what does God possibly mean by it?" James asked his friend, a pit in his stomach.

Virginia

Elena switched on the portable gas stove. She'd filled the bathtub with cold water from the faucet. They could not make enough electricity to run the water heater, so she set the large pot on to boil for the second time, which would make enough hot water for a decently warm bath.

She moved over to the vanity and pulled out the stool while she waited. They'd been at the house for a while, but she still couldn't believe how much she appreciated the small luxuries they had here.

As she pulled the small mirror to the edge of the counter, she began to look at the messy state of her hair. It had been a great while since she'd been able to color it, and she was well past the point where she could hide the grey by piling all her hair up on top.

Experimenting with it in a few ways did nothing but frustrate her. She grabbed a hair clip and grumbled about growing old gracefully, when it struck her that she could at least do it gratefully.

"I could, Lord," Elena said out loud. "I'm sorry." She thought of how God had returned John to her and how He'd kept them safe as they'd traveled to this refuge in the mountains of Virginia. "I know I should be more grateful. Here You've brought us all safely to this wonderful place that You obviously had that sweet man get ready for us. He did his best. I just wish there were some hair color in this bathroom, even though I know it's vain."

She went through all of the drawers again. There were all sorts of supplies the original owner had thoughtfully provided: toothbrushes and paste, floss, lotions, even some makeup and perfume—the sort of things the note said his wife had used.

"Well, Lord, You had Your servant get this house ready for people he'd never met, and would never meet, so I'm going to stop complaining about it and be thankful."

She turned off the gas, carefully grabbed the pot with two washcloths, and dumped the water into the bathtub. Using the big wooden spoon Brant had found to stir the water, she made sure it was warm enough before she got in. Leaning back, she wet her hair and washed it carefully with the shampoo. She massaged her scalp and let out a long, heavy sigh. After so many weeks without, she still relished every bath as a special luxury.

When she finished, she stood in front of the mirror, robe on and towel in hand, staring at her reflection. Pulling open the drawer beside her, she found the scissors. Before she could change her mind, she began clipping her hair, one large lock at a time. She could not bear to cut it too short, so she left a dark end on each bit of hair as she cut. She stepped back when she had finished and ran her hand through her new, shorter tresses.

"That looks very stylish!"

Elena swung around to see her husband standing in the doorway.

"Do you really think so?" she asked.

John came in the bathroom and pulled her into his arms. "You could be bald and you'd still be stunning." He ran his fingers through her hair and kissed her.

"Brant got the radio working. He was able to contact a group not too far from here," John informed her, stroking her face affectionately.

"How did he find them?"

"Apparently, when he was in New Babylon he worked in BabelCom. He and DC secretly researched for months. They were able to uncover another Internet, sort of an underground network for Christians," John said. He held Elena at arm's length, looking into her sparkling eyes.

"I can't wait to see it. Is there any news from DC? We haven't heard from him and Teo since the baby was born."

"No. There's still some sort of block on anything going in or out of Israel. Brant says others are having the same problem. Someone named Eric in upstate New York is working on it." His voice carried a distracted tone that warmed her heart. She smiled, and he kissed her slowly.

"Why don't you get dressed? I have a late dinner ready for the two of us on the porch. Olivia is sound asleep in her room, and Brant is busy." John's smile widened meaningfully as he spoke.

Elena smiled in return and nodded in agreement as she watched him walk out of the room. *He actually made me dinner!* she thought, slightly bemused. Pulling on the clean clothes she'd stashed on the counter, she faced the mirror and ran her hands through her hair—it did look good!

ONE WILL BE LEFT

"I know I'm being vain," she told her reflection and stuck her tongue out at it.

Elena left the bathroom and made her way through the bedroom to the patio. She pushed open the sliding door and gasped at the romantic scene in front of her. John had found a stash of small candles and placed them all over the porch—on the floor, the table, and the porch railings. By the dim light of the tiny flickering flames, she spied flower petals sprinkled on the patio floor.

"What do you think, love?"

Elena turned to him and smiled. "Perfect. But what's that behind your back?"

"Something Brant came across when he went into the town on one of his walkabouts." He pulled out a bottle of wine he'd been hiding behind him. "He said it's his anniversary gift to us."

"Oh, how wonderful!" she exclaimed. "A new hairstyle and a romantic dinner!"

"Happy anniversary, Elena." He kissed her again softly and poignantly, with a tenderness he never had before. Their lips pulled apart, leaving her breathless. "I'm glad I get to be with you tonight. I'm grateful for every day we have, even now, at the end of the world."

He led her to the patio table and pulled her chair out with an exaggerated bow.

"John, this is so wonderful! I love it!" Elena exclaimed with a grin as she sat down.

"Well, I'm sorry that the best pairing I have for this vintage is canned ravioli. No caviar or escargot tonight, love."

"Well, Livie did find a lot of snails and slugs down by the barn, so I might be able to create my own romantic dinner for you with a little escargot another night," she teased.

John opened the bottle of wine ceremoniously and poured a bit into her glass. Elena swirled the wine and tasted it carefully. "Perfect." He poured a bit in each glass and then sat down across from her.

She looked across the table, tears beaming in her eyes. "You know, John, I can't believe it's the end of the world. I can't believe God would go to so much trouble to help me find you, to bring us here. This place is amazing! You cannot deny that He got it ready for us."

"No, I can't. Robert, the owner, surely was a man who heard God speak. His welcome letter to us was insightful. He calculated what we would need," John agreed.

"To my *beloved* brethren," she quoted.

"You're right, Elena. To think he spent years getting this house ready for people he didn't know! It is an incredible feat of faith. He prepared this place for fellow believers—people he'd never met!"

"We have to be thankful for Talin's help too, and the other angels. Not everyone gets to see that side of reality," she added.

"That's right. You know, if you had told me a year ago that I would be practically held hostage by a lunatic and then rescued by an angel, who would lead me to faith in Jesus Christ…" his voice trailed off.

"Thanks be to God!" She raised her glass in a toast.

He raised his glass and touched the top to hers.

"There is so much to be thankful for, Elena. Yet I can't help but feel worried that things are going to get really bad, progressively bad. We don't have a guarantee that we'll make it."

They both sat in somber thought for a moment before Elena spoke.

"That's why Jesus said we're to take up our crosses daily. This is going to be very hard because we didn't believe before. Now we have to walk through the darkest days the world has ever faced. It scares me, too." She put her hand over his and squeezed three times.

"But let's not think about the end of the world tonight. Let's talk about how we fell in love and all of the days we've been able to spend with each other. We can let God take care of tomorrow."

The candles flickered as they talked, and when they got up from the table, they blew out each flame and left the smoke to rise into the night air.

17

AMMAN,
JORDAN

King Zayd wiped his forehead with the back of his hand. He'd been outside all day overseeing the warehousing of food and water supplies in a secure storage facility within the city limits. With his uncle's help, they had mapped places throughout the country where they could cache goods for the difficult days ahead.

While reading the book of Genesis one morning a few months back, Zayd had come across the story of Joseph, and the account of the young man's life had completely captivated him. That God would take a young boy and mark him out for special favor, then allow him to be sold by his own brothers into slavery in Egypt, only to end up in prison for years, seemed harsh and unjust.

But then after years in prison, Joseph's incredible ability to interpret dreams had brought him before the most powerful man in the land, Pharaoh. With God's help, Joseph had interpreted Pharaoh's troubling dream and explained to the king that God was warning him of an impending famine that would devastate the land. Pharaoh had given Joseph the responsibility to make sure Egypt was prepared. The former slave and prisoner became one of the most powerful men in the country, second only to Pharaoh himself.

Zayd wondered if Joseph understood while he was suffering that God was taking a situation meant evil and turning it for Joseph's good—good not only for Joseph, but also for his people and the entire nation. At the close of the story, it was evident he understood that God had allowed it all.

ONE WILL BE LEFT

It occurred to Zayd that he could do the same thing Joseph had done and plan for what was coming in the days ahead. Who knew how long it would be before the treaty with Israel was signed? He had to prepare, but it would not be easy. Part of the difficulty was buying massive amounts of supplies without drawing too much attention to what he was doing.

"I think this warehouse is done, Sire," one of the men came up to him and bowed, handing him a clipboard with a thick stack of paper on it.

"Thank you," Zayd replied, looking through the papers carefully one by one.

"Can we go now?" his Uncle Rasheed pleaded. "You are the king, Zayd; I don't think we need to be out here all day. I want to go back to the palace and have a bath and sit in the garden there with your sisters."

Glancing up, Zayd noticed the dark circles under Rasheed's eyes. "I'm sorry, Uncle. I've been so intent on finishing today that I forgot you were here, too." Zayd motioned for his driver and gave orders for the man to take his uncle back to the palace. Zayd thanked Rasheed for his patience and promised to follow soon. There were a few more things he wanted to check at the warehouse. He watched his uncle affectionately as the older man made his way to the sedan.

"Your Majesty, you sent for me?" Colonel Obeidat looked up sharply at him. Zayd liked the small man. He was only five feet two, but he was a man of integrity and great patriotism.

"Yes, Colonel. I wanted to make sure you have enough men to staff this site full time. I want an armed guard and a sufficient number of men at each site. There may come a time when they will have to ward off an attack."

"Yes, Sire. I have taken care of that. All of the sites are heavily guarded."

Zayd smiled at him. "Good. Now is there anything you need before I go, Colonel?"

"I do have a question for you, if it is allowed, Your Majesty."

ONE WILL BE LEFT

"Of course."

The colonel licked his lips nervously. "I've been wondering if there will be some sort of, well, allegiance required before citizens will be given rations."

"Allegiance? I'm not sure what you mean, Colonel Obeidat."

"Well, while Your Majesty and his family—indeed many—have turned from our Muslim heritage and converted to Christianity, many others have stayed true to the Prophet," the colonel stammered.

"I am aware of that." Zayd kept his tone pleasant purposefully, knowing that his Christian faith was a sensitive issue for some of his subjects.

"Some of the men have asked me if these supplies are for all Jordanians, or only for those who have converted?" Colonel Obeidat finished his question in a whisper.

Zayd responded quickly. "These supplies are for all of my people! There will be no 'test' before supplies are given to anyone, and I'm dismayed that anyone would think there would be."

"Well, Sire, you know how rumors begin. There are bound to be misconceptions, and as you are aware, there has not been an easy relationship between Christians and Muslims for centuries."

Zayd watched the sweat drip off the end of the colonel's nose and felt compassion for the frightened man.

"Rest assured, Colonel, every Jordanian will be treated equally by me. Now, if you would please see to setting up the guards here, I will be leaving shortly. Thank you, Colonel. You are dismissed."

King Zayd watched with some concern as the colonel made his way back to the side door of the warehouse. Although the king was popular with his people now, he knew how quickly that could change. Many Jordanians had turned to faith in Christ, but there was still a significant number who had not. Another rapidly growing sector belonged to OneFaith, led by Billings Mason. How long could he remain in power as king over Jordan? Since becoming a Christian, he had often read the Bible and studied commentaries until late into the night. He felt like a man with a fatal disease desperately researching for a cure. Being king was overwhelming much of the time. He began praying silently.

Lord God Almighty, it is hard to know who to trust besides my own family. I read in Your most holy Word what lies ahead of me, and I tremble. Somehow I must stand strong against the Evil One. I can only do so with Your help. I'm helpless apart from You. Please help me. Give me strength and wisdom.

He watched as the men worked, and he thought about what he had studied in the Scriptures the night before. Somehow his nation was going to be divided. That's the only thing that made sense. It appeared Amman would be destroyed, condemned because of its ancient malice toward Israel, yet part of Jordan would be a haven for Israel in the coming days. What would happen? Would he and his sisters survive?

He reached into his pocket and pulled out the map he had sketched the night before. Modern Jordan was made up of three biblical kingdoms listed in the Old Testament. From north to south they were Ammon, Moab, and Edom. The Ammonite and Moabite people were descendants of Lot through his incestuous relations with his daughters, while the Edomites were descendants of Esau, the older brother of Jacob, one of the Jewish patriarchs. Zayd stared at the map, recalling what he had learned from his late-night studies. There would be refugees pouring into "Edom" from the southeast portion of Israel. Not only did he have to prepare for his own people but also for hundreds of thousands who would be fleeing the devastation brought on in Israel by the Antichrist.

Flipping over the map, he began to list things he would need to prepare for those refugees besides food and water. Years ago, refugees from Iraq had flooded over the border into Jordan. Zayd tried to remember what some of the major problems had been, and he listed them too. If he could anticipate the future issues, he would have a better chance of having ready solutions.

When he finished brainstorming, he realized he had to find a way to finance more preparations. He recalled the British reporter whose cameraman had taken it upon himself to move a priceless work of art for their interview. The reporter had been shocked and had apologized profusely for her coworker's rudeness. He realized there were many pieces like that in his palace—and in the other palaces, too. In spite of the world's troubles, there were still enough wealthy people who were interested in acquiring valuables. Surely he could sell the pieces to which he had access and recoup enough to purchase what he needed.

He considered some of the treasures he had seen stored in back rooms of the Archaeological Museum in Amman. He recalled some beautiful frescoes from a palace that had been located somewhere near Petra. He looked at the map again. Rebuilding that palace and investing money into the World Heritage site already there could give him a reason to divert funds and goods to the area without raising too many questions. Indeed, his younger sisters, Alia and Rania, could be placed in charge of the restoration. If someone attempted a coup, they would be safer in the south.

Satisfied with his plans, he folded up his map and put it back in his pocket. His limousine pulled up, and he waited for his driver to open the door. Zayd thankfully accepted the bottle of water the driver handed to him as he sat on the cool leather seat. While he gulped the icy water, he silently asked God to either bless the plans he'd made or point him in a different direction. He watched the passing scenery as the limo powered through the city streets toward his palace; he was eager to discuss his plans with his uncle.

New Babylon

Teo opened her eyes and closed them. *What a lovely sleep!* She took a deep breath and considered sleeping just a bit longer, but was startled awake by a strange gurgling noise. Her eyes fluttered open again, and she noticed a strange green light dappled with shimmering strands of sunlight surrounding her. Panicked, she sat up. She was in the front seat of a car behind the wheel, DC next to her asleep, and they were under water!

Teo started screaming for him to wake up and saw Olivia in the backseat, clipped into her safety seat. Teo screamed louder in panicked horror.

"Honey, wake up. You're safe. Wake up, Teo."

She sat up abruptly and saw Rhetta sitting next to her. Teo flung her arms around her friend and clung to her tightly. She prayed silently for a moment before pulling back and looking around. Rubbing her eyes, she could see a bit more clearly with every passing second. She was in the middle of a large bed in a strange room.

"Do you remember what happened?" Rhetta asked quietly.

Teo nodded affirmatively as the memory of their abduction replayed in her mind. "Juliana!" Her stomach roiled with fear.

"There was a young woman there. Do you remember her?" Rhetta asked.

"You left her with a stranger? Why? Why would you do that?" Teo fought to keep the hysteria out of her voice. Her heart physically ached thinking about the danger her perfect baby girl could be in.

Rhetta put a hand on her shoulder. "Please be calm, Teo. I want you to understand that the Lord told me to do it. It was very clear that He wanted me to help you and leave her with the woman. I'm completely confident that Jules is fine." She lowered her tone of voice. "Given where we are, I believe if they knew about her, she would have been killed."

"What! Where are we?" The familiar panic rose, causing Teo to tremble. She felt like she couldn't catch her breath.

"We're in New Babylon." Rhetta paused and gave Teo a moment to take it in. "You've been unconscious for the last sixteen hours. I woke up on the airplane. I pretended to be asleep when we landed." Rhetta bit her lower lip nervously for a moment before continuing.

ONE WILL BE LEFT

"Before we were taken off of the plane, a man came into the cargo hold where we were. He was surrounded, Teo. Surrounded by demons."

"You saw demons?" Teo asked in a whisper.

"I saw them in the pharmacy, too. I've been seeing that sort of thing from the other realm for a while now, and that's how I knew you were in danger at the pharmacy. The warrior who watches over Juliana told me to leave her with the young woman." Rhetta tenderly brushed Teo's hair away from her face like her mother had when she was little.

Teo sat up against the headboard and cradled her head in her hands. Tears ran down her face, but the familiar fear did not grow as she cried silently. Instead, she felt a peacefulness quietly envelop her.

"Rhetta, I was praying one morning last week after I finished reading my Bible. I read that there were ministering angels for believers and I was thanking God for that, because I know who my brother is." Her voice became fierce. "I know he is the Evil One, and I was—I am—so afraid of him. As I prayed, I felt that God was speaking to me, to my mind. I don't know if that makes sense."

"It does. I, too have heard Him speaking to me in that quiet way," said Rhetta.

"I felt I was going to go through something terrible, but that He was promising me it would be okay and I didn't have to be afraid—He would be with me." Teo's voice broke. "I used to have a problem with fear."

"I remember."

"Then I heard these words, not audibly, but still clear: 'Perfect love casts off all fear.'"

Rhetta sighed and nodded. "I'm glad God was preparing you. The man who came on the plane had us taken off on stretchers, and when we got into the building next to the runway, we were wheeled into a large area. I heard a car's engine and then doors opening and closing.

"I kept my eyes closed, Teo. I could feel such oppression—a physical, heavy oppression—that I could hardly breathe. Then I felt a hand on my shoulder. Your brother spoke to me. He said he knew I was awake, so I opened my eyes."

"He laughed when he saw I'm blind. It was obvious from what he said to me that they were going to kill me in some sort of a sacrifice, but that since I was marred, I was unsuitable. He said he would allow me to stay with you."

"Did he say anything else?" Teo asked, running a hand through her hair.

"Not to me. He just spoke to the other man, but it was so hard to be in his presence whether he talked to me or not."

"Could you still see the others? You know…" Teo did not want to say it out loud.

Rhetta shook her head. "No, they were no longer visible."

The two women were quiet for a few minutes. Pushing off the silken covers, Teo slipped out of bed and walked over to the window. She could see from her view of the garden that they were in Luca's residence.

"Could you hear what Luca was saying to the man?" she asked her friend.

"Yes, I think I heard it all. Luca told him they were going to say you'd miraculously survived the plane crash and that Bedouins had found you and nursed you back to health. Then just recently, your memory returned and your caretakers brought you back to your grateful brother." Rhetta followed Teo to the window and gently touched her shoulder.

"He told the other man that after a short time passed, he could marry you. Luca said he knew how much you meant to the man, and you were his reward for his faithful service."

Teo stood by the window looking at the beauty of the gardens and felt nauseous. *It must be Stephen Amona he was talking to*, she thought.

"Then they brought us here?" Teo asked.

"Yes, it's a small suite. There's a small living area just through the door behind me. My room is off of that. We each have a bathroom. The door out of the suite is through the living area, but it's locked." Rhetta stifled yawn. "I haven't slept since we got here. I've been sitting in here with you. I heard someone open the door earlier, but I didn't go out."

Teo walked over to the closed door and opened it, revealing a living room as exquisite as the rest of Luca's home. She did not recall ever having seen it, but she'd never had a real tour of his residence. Now she wished she had.

Seeing a coffeepot and cups on the low table in front of the couch, along with a lavish arrangement of her favorite fruits, she strode over and deftly poured two cups, took them back into the bedroom, and handed one to her friend.

"It's still warm," Rhetta murmured. Setting her own cup down, Teo walked over to the closet and opened it, not surprised to see it filled with the clothes she'd left behind when she and DC had escaped New Babylon months before.

"I'm going to finish my coffee and take a shower, Rhetta. At least we know they aren't going to kill us. I guess that's something." Teo turned back to the older woman, smiling wryly.

Rhetta stood up, holding her cup in both hands, and walked over to Teo. "That's something. I'm not sure what is going to happen, Teo, but I do know that the Lord is in control. I'm confident He'll be with us, no matter what we have to face."

Teo put her free arm around her friend's shoulder and gave her a hug. "Yes, but I'm letting you know there is no way I'm going to give myself to that man! Stephen Amona is a fiend. He's just... sick." Teo shook her head in disgust. "We have got to find a way to get out of here."

"I'm sure that DC is going to find some way to get you back, Teo. In just the few months I've known the two of you, I know that man will not stop looking for you. He'll stop at nothing to fight for you and keep you safe."

ONE WILL BE LEFT

Teo pulled away and faced her. "I know he'll try, Rhetta, but he doesn't know what happened. I wish I knew that he had Juliana with him! Surely the woman would have looked in the stroller and found my cell phone, or DC would have called when we didn't return home."

"I'm certain Juliana is fine," Rhetta reassured Teo. "Why don't we pray?"

"Yes, it's all we can do now."

Teo grasped Rhetta's hands, and the two women started to pray.

The Italian Ambassador's Residence, New Babylon, Iraq

Luca sat in his office with Billings Mason. The setting sun illuminated the room, richly highlighting the luxurious furnishings. The ambassador sat with his feet propped up on his desk, slicking his blonde hair back from his eyes while admiring his chestnut wingtips, a gift from Billings. The costly shoes were handcrafted with the OneFaith logo, a six-pointed star surrounded by six interconnected circles. Billings sat across from Luca with a notebook in his lap.

"Despite my best efforts, there are many going over to the other side, Luca. It seems there were quite a few among the priesthood who turned to the enemy after the others were taken away. They were very well trained and have made effective leaders. There is another one in North America we need to watch, a James Martin. He's the one who was involved in the healings in New York. Thankfully, his healings did not damage the control Quinteros has on the East Coast. People are still afraid of what he has in his arsenal."

Luca sat behind his desk, listening, his distain causing his nostrils to flare. "I don't like this for many reasons, Mason. My associates tell me their numbers grow daily, these Christians." He choked on the word "Christian" and had to pause momentarily to recover his momentum. "There seems to be nothing we can do to stop it. They are becoming a thorn in my side. We must do something to prevent more from following that pretender." He spat out the last word.

"That occurred to me also, sir. When I dispatched the cardinal, I realized that we could take the very thing Christians have warned others about for centuries and use it as a proof of commitment to you and your rule over mankind. Of course, we'll have to make that public once your true identity is revealed. But those who have made the full commitment to OneFaith, and who wait expectantly for your coming, have already embraced the idea." He stood up and spread out his arms enthusiastically, reminding Luca of those ridiculous late-night TV salesmen that the Americans were so fond of. *He can be so facile*, Luca thought.

"Those who have taken up the true faith have had this symbol," Billings gestured toward Luca's shoes, "tattooed on the back of their hand, while some have gone so far as to have it placed on their foreheads. I have blessed each of those who have done so and gifted them with their own spirit guide so your new disciples can be equipped to lead others to faith in you, the Coming One."

Luca restrained himself from rolling his eyes. Billings was becoming a prima donna, but he had to be tolerated and encouraged until he was no longer useful. "Mason, you've done an excellent job using social media and the press to promote my cause. I like the 'I Am' campaign. The stories of people overcoming some terrible disease or disfigurement to become whole and wealthy are moving."

Billings Mason beamed. "Thank you! It is my delight to serve you. I've also begun targeting celebrities, and more are joining our ranks each week. In fact, one of them is James Martin's ex-wife, Cynthia Grayson. My guides tell me she may prove a useful tool against him. In fact, there is a plan already in operation." He clasped his hands together and shook them to his left side in a victory clasp, then threw them open in a priestly blessing. He rocked back and forth for a moment as he prayed in the ancient language his spirit guide used. Luca waited without showing the impatience he was feeling. While his Father, Lucifer, was all-powerful, the spirits he led could exceed themselves, and the one that controlled Billings was obviously a showman.

Billings concluded his incantation and continued detailing his plans. "Once you've taken your rightful place, we'll begin to blame those Christ followers for various problems. We'll create terror plots and crimes to charge them with, then arrest them and put them in the holding facilities that have been built on each continent."

Luca shook his head slowly, frustration causing each syllable to be clipped as he spat out his response. "Where they will become a burden for us and a source of inspiration to others as they see them suffering nobly. It has happened too many times in history, Billings; you know this."

"But we won't leave them locked up. Here, take a look at this." Billings bent over the briefcase parked next to the chair he'd been sitting in and reached across the desk, handing Luca an envelope. Luca pulled out some photographs.

"Is this a guillotine?" he asked. "Very interesting idea, Mason."

Billings grinned. "Yes, isn't it brilliant? Think of the horror mass executions will elicit. Anyone who might be attracted to those Jesus followers will certainly be discouraged by seeing their heads roll across the ground."

Luca looked up from the photograph at his mentor, equally impressed and intrigued. "That is quite a plan. You do realize much of this is straight out of the enemy's book?" He had a tone of grudging respect in his voice.

"Yes, that is the beauty of it!" Billings chuckled gleefully. "The whole 'mark of the beast' thing," he said as he made quotations with his fingers, "is the best demonstration that the recipient totally rejects any thought of God being in control over his destiny.

"And the guillotine is a terribly beautiful instrument. Its appearance is fearful. Can't you picture the scene? Many 'believers,' lined up, waiting their turn, and watching those in front of them decapitated, one by one? Surely many will turn away from their faith in the enemy and give their allegiance to you." He bowed with a flourish toward Luca, straightened, and continued sharing his plot.

"We will target the leaders first. I have men and women infiltrating these Christian groups throughout the world so that once you take power, they will be solid, trusted members who will be able to lead us to those in charge. Cut off the head of the snake, as it were."

Pulling his feet off of the desk, Luca stood up and stretched before turning back to Billings and saying abruptly, "Changing the subject, has Stephen told you his good news? That he found my sister?"

Billings rolled with it. "He did. He called me for some counsel in how to sell her 'rescue' to the media. Have you seen her?"

"Not yet. She's had some sort of a virus for a few days now. The doctors are quite puzzled. Perhaps you could check in and lay hands on those who are ill? Stephen has come down with it, too. He's miserable. Covered from head to foot with some sort of rash."

"Certainly, I will go. I would like to see your sister again. She was such a devoted follower." Billings stood and joined Luca by the window.

"Was," Luca emphasized. "I'm not so sure now. I can't read her. I used to spend hours in her mind. It was rewarding to see how easily I could manipulate her. The change leads me to think she belongs to the enemy now."

Billing placed a hand on Luca's shoulder and squeezed. "Perhaps that is not it. Stephen said she has a woman with her, a blind, beautiful woman. She might be the problem. Some of these Christ followers are quite powerful, just as you said. The former priest in New York I was telling you about not only has the power to heal, but apparently also has the ability to give others the same power. This woman might be shielding Teo somehow."

"It doesn't matter either way. I plan to use Teo to teach our dear father a few pertinent lessons. When I finish, Stephen may have her." Luca turned back to look out of the window at the magenta twilight.

"I have no love for my sister, and I won't have her making a fool out of me. Finding her husband and daughter are a priority. If they show up alive, it may harm my credibility."

Billings nodded his head slowly. "We have people looking for them. So far, we've found nothing."

"Then get more people on it. You know exactly what I want done. Whoever finds them has to get rid of them quietly. Then you need to make sure they are also silenced permanently. We can't risk people finding out."

"I will get more people on it today. It really is only a matter of time, Luca. We will find them and take care of it.

"Tell me, how did your meeting go with the new North American leader?" Billings asked, changing the subject again. "We haven't talked about that yet."

"Andres is no fool. He is quite decisive and has no compunctions about using brutality to his benefit, even if the benefit is only his pleasure in inflicting pain. He'll be quite useful in establishing a secure seat of power in North America. When the time is right, I promised Patricia I would get rid of him. It's a true testimony to her superiority that she's endured that pig for so many years. She will make a fitting leader in his place, and her son will be the first of the children born to us. I do not want that man raising him. It's essential that each region be under the control of my true brothers and sisters. After all, Billings, in the end, who do you have but family?"

18

VIRGINIA

Brant padded along the dusty path, the early morning light revealing signs of the recent drought. Brown leaves crackled and crumbled as he trampled them under his boots. It was not yet midsummer, yet it seemed like everything green was dying. The creek had dried up some, but it still managed a decent flow. Brant was out tracking deer, and when he looked ahead he could see faint tracks in the clay near the creek. On closer examination, it appeared many animals had found relief from the drought at this spot where the water widened a bit. He saw at least six different tracks.

Finding a spot upwind, Brant sat down to wait for his prey. His T-shirt clung to his body, damp from the sweltering heat. Brushing off a spider that landed on his leg, he tipped his ball cap forward to block the sun's glare. After a while, he started to get drowsy and nodded off. It was simply too hot to do anything else.

Some time later, he woke abruptly, feeling like he was falling. He looked around, confused and hazy, and was startled to see a woman not far from his perch. She was scooping water from a small pool created by the creek, drinking the water in thirsty gulps. He looked around cautiously. She seemed to be alone.

He watched her as she drank. She appeared anxious, looking from side to side after tipping the water into her mouth. As she stood, he noted how thin she was. She grabbed an elastic band from her wrist and twisted her thick curls up into a ponytail.

The young woman rifled through a backpack and pulled out

a small can. Brant watched with interest as she rolled it on a stone and then hit it sharply. Smart, he thought. She was smart. He grinned as she peeled back the top of the tin, drained the liquid and tipped the solid contents into her mouth. As she wiped the back of her hand across her mouth, he made a decision.

Debating with himself for a moment on how to approach her, Brant figured it would be prudent to move toward her quietly from behind. If he made noise and walked toward her from the front, she'd probably run. He was hot and sweaty and did not feel like running anyway.

Leaving his pack by the tree, he crept behind her. He quickly wrapped a hand over her mouth and pulled her backward, whispering, "I'm not going to hurt you. I just want to talk and not draw anyone else's attention." To his amazement, she slumped to the ground and nodded complacently.

"I'm going to let go of you now. I don't want you to scream. I won't touch you again. I just want to talk." Brant pulled his hand away from her mouth and moved to her side. She looked at him, her dark brown eyes glowing with calm interest.

"Darius told me to come here and drink from the creek. He said you would be here to help me." As she spoke, dimples appeared on one side of her mouth. Brant found himself wanting to see her smile again. "I wasn't sure how you would introduce yourself, but I didn't think you would act like a caveman. Really, did you think I was a threat to you? I thought you were expecting me."

Brant could not help but grin at her. "I wasn't expecting anyone but a deer I intended to invite home for dinner. Who is Darius?"

Confusion crossed her face. "He said a man would be here to lead me to some others. Others who would help me through the times Granny called the 'Dark Days of Wrath.'"

"She sounds just like my grandmother!" Brant chuckled. "You still haven't told me who Darius is."

"He's...." she hesitated, examining his eyes carefully.

"Are you going to tell me he's an angel?" Brant asked.

"Yes! Have you met one, too?" she whispered in a tone of wonder.

"I have. Not Darius, but another angel. What's your name?" He stood up and offered her his hand, pulling her up too.

"Annabel." She smiled at him, and Brant decided in that moment that he would help her any way he could. There was something original about her, something intriguing.

"I'm Brant. How far did you come?"

"About twenty miles," she responded casually. "I've been walking for the last couple of days with Darius. He said others are coming, too. He showed me where to find you. He was standing on the bank right up there," she pointed. "Didn't you see him?"

"No, I fell asleep. You said others are coming?"

"Yes. Darius said there were places prepared for God's people. Places of shelter—and this is the closest one to my home."

Brant thought about her words for a moment. It made sense that his small group of comrades weren't the only people God would help. It made sense that He would help others as well. Lots of them.

"Well, I'll show you the way to the house. It's kind of a strange setup. From the outside, it looks like a small rambler, but the back of the house is built into the side of the mountain. The man who owned it spent years excavating the original caves and formed a whole complex of rooms within the mountain. There's even running water from an underground stream."

"That sounds amazing!" Annabel exclaimed as they started walking. "Since the disappearances, I've tried to make it on my own, and it's been tough. My parents were believers, so I knew right away what happened. I've been staying away from populated areas as much as I can because of the danger from the Anti-Globalists and Union forces—not to mention all of the refugees. Darius started visiting me over this past year right after I fell and broke my leg. It was bad, Brant. The bone came right through the skin. I was terrified and in incredible pain. All I could do was cry for Jesus to help me, and

Darius showed up, just like that."

"Did he heal your leg?" Brant asked.

"He did! Then he took me to a safe place, an abandoned cabin by a small lake. He brought me food and water and watched over me while I slept. I hadn't felt so safe in ages. After that, I didn't worry. I knew that God was going to help, just like Granny said. I know now He's always waiting to do that for His children."

Brant peered at Annabel as they walked. She looked like she was in her mid-twenties, tall and slender. Her clothes were clean but ragged. Her shoes were held together with duct tape. He thought about the supply room back at the house. There were some things there that would work for her to replace her worn ensemble.

As they walked, he wondered how she had survived by herself. Virginia had been part of the war zone in the battle for power between the Anti-Globalists and the World Union forces. He asked her about it.

"My parents were what they used to call 'preppers.' They believed in being ready for a disaster or catastrophe. My dad made sure I could shoot a gun, catch fish, hunt, and live off the land if I had to." She seemed to have guessed what he was thinking because her voice softened to a whisper. "He also made sure I knew how to stay out of sight. Women are…well…vulnerable. That's what I've been doing: keeping out of sight. Until Darius told me to come here, I've avoided people. Seemed the safest thing to do, you know?" She looked up at him quizzically.

"It must have been lonely," Brant remarked, visibly impressed with the courage of the striking young woman walking by his side.

Annabel shrugged her shoulders and sighed. "At first I was so sad, I didn't care about being alone. I actually felt like I deserved it in a way. I mean, I knew the truth. I knew Jesus is God and that He's the only way to God. But I wanted to live the way I wanted, not the way my parents wanted. I wanted to live, you know? Enjoy life and not be boxed in by their morality and stupid rules. At least, I thought they were stupid at the time. I don't now.

"Anyway, I was out partying with my boyfriend when it happened. We were at a nightclub, and someone screamed that her boyfriend was gone. There was such uproar, chaos in only a matter of seconds. I was pretty drunk, but I knew right away what had happened. I ran out crying, took my boyfriend's car, and left.

"When I got home, Mom and Dad were gone, too. Since it was so late, I looked in their bedroom first. Their clothes were between the sheets. I broke down and sobbed hysterically on my knees at the end of their bed. I begged God to turn back time so that I wouldn't miss out. I cried for hours and fell asleep there on the floor."

She stopped talking for a moment, and they hiked in companionable silence. Brent could tell she was trying to collect herself. Tentatively, he put his right arm around her and gave her a side hug.

"The next day I got the bag Dad had me pack in case of trouble. I took as much food as I could carry and left town. I've been on my own since."

Brant listened to her story with intense interest. He had not known anyone personally who had disappeared. When it happened, he thought it was a strange thing, but it hardly affected his life at the time. After he made the decision to follow Jesus Christ, he had become more interested. He'd read accounts online by those left behind. He studied the passages in the Bible, at first with a profound sadness that he had missed the event, but later with hope.

He told Annabel his own account of coming to faith, ending with the fact that missing out on meeting Jesus in the rapture no longer filled him with regret. "I realized it happened just the way God said it would. So did the attack on Israel and the building of the Temple, and so will all the other things the Bible talks about." Brant caught Annabel's arm and steadied her when she tripped over a dry branch. She nodded her thanks, and he kept talking.

"There's an amazing guy in our group who used to be a reporter, John. He knows a lot about the end times. I can talk to him for hours. It's going to be horrendous; I have no doubt. But I have this safe feeling deep inside of me. It's hard to explain."

Annabel stopped walking suddenly, her expression animated. "I know what you mean! It's like a certainty, right? Like you know for a fact, no matter what, that it's going to be okay. Like you can't worry if you try."

"Yes! Exactly. Some people think I'm too easygoing, but that isn't it," he said.

Annabel went on, "My mom told me that when she was little and afraid, she'd pray to Jesus. When she got older and knew Him better, she found she didn't fear as much because she was so sure He would work everything out somehow."

The small house at the base of the mountain came into view as they clambered up the dusty knoll. "Here we are." Brant turned to look at her. "I didn't expect you. I mean, I didn't expect to find you when I went out this morning." He fumbled for the right words. "But it's kind of like there was something missing and when I saw you I realized it." He offered her his hand. Annabel felt a tingle of excitement when she placed her hand in his and they walked to the house together.

Jerusalem, Israel

Micah Benari raised his hands. As the tempo increased, he began gently waving his hands and swinging his body back and forth. He felt his heart leap inside him as others in the room sang praises to Yeshua. He didn't bother to wipe away the warm tears that sat on his cheeks. He had worshipped with these brothers and sisters along with his grandparents. Now that his grandparents were with the Lord, this family loved him and gave him the encouragement in the faith that he needed.

The singing ended, and everyone sat as the Messianic rabbi, Asher, stepped to the front of the room and onto the small raised platform. Micah smiled. Asher had been his grandfather's friend. The godly man reminded him of his missing grandparents; Micah loved him.

"Welcome! Welcome! It's so good to be together to worship our Lord!" Asher paused as the congregation erupted in applause and shouts.

"As you know, I've been gone the past two weeks traveling around Israel. I want you to know how much I felt the presence of the Lord as I met with other congregations. He is removing the veil from the eyes of many of our brothers and sisters!" Again he waited until the spontaneous clapping and cheering ended. "We and other Hebrew congregations are being flooded with young people who are earnestly want answers to life's most important questions. Realizing Jesus was a Jew, they are asking themselves, 'What if he really was the Messiah?' Many are coming to faith.

"When I was a younger man here in Jerusalem, we saw the beginning of the national return to the Lord Yeshua. Perhaps there were one hundred and thirty congregations then. Now there are over five hundred congregations in Jerusalem and the nearby areas! Thousands are coming to know him as Savior, our Messiah!"

Asher smiled broadly as he again waited for the enthusiastic crowd to quiet down before he continued. Micah whooped and shouted along with the others, turning mischievously and elbowing his best friend, Joel, in the ribs.

"With all that in mind, we are going to be dividing into three new congregations." Asher paused as murmurs of disapproval erupted from the noisy crowd.

"I know, I know," he said over the rumbling, waving his hands in acknowledgment of their dissatisfaction. "It is not ideal, but we draw too much attention with such a large crowd. You know that the climate is becoming more difficult, even while so many are turning to Yeshua." That fact hushed the muttering, and the atmosphere became somber.

Rabbi Asher's face mirrored the mood of the crowd. He stood before them, his eyes watery as he contemplated the group. When he spoke, his voice cracked.

ONE WILL BE LEFT

"Also, this way we leaders can care for you more effectively." He paused, pulling a handkerchief from his pocket, and wiped his eyes. "There are papers posted on the wall behind with each of your names and your new congregation. Please find your name on the way out and note where you will be meeting and at what time. Commit it to memory, but do not write it down. We will destroy the lists as soon as everyone leaves this morning. We desire to be careful for your safety. No sense in making things easy for the enemy, eh?"

Asher looked around the room again, and Micah thought his eyes seemed very sad. Famines, earthquakes, war, persecution, and a ruthless dictator were all judgments God would pour out on the earth. Asher's pronouncements made Micah feel apprehensive, yet he was not afraid. He and his friend, Joel, had had long discussions about the time ahead. Both boys prayed the Lord would give them the same courage David had shown in the ancient times. Although he was just a boy as they were, he had faced a giant alone and won, with God's help.

When the service ended, Micah and Joel made their way to the front of the room. They waited while Asher prayed for a couple. Micah noticed the woman's round belly. When Asher finished, Micah moved forward and gave his friend a hug.

"Micah! How are you?" Asher exclaimed with a smile, cupping his hands to cradle the boy's cheeks. Micah remembered how his grandmother used to pinch his cheeks in the same manner, and he felt the lump in his throat again.

"I'm okay, Rabbi. My father finally agreed to let me come back here. He doesn't understand my faith in Yeshua, though I pray for him a lot. I think he'd prefer I didn't come. And he did say he'd be a hypocrite if he stopped me from coming."

"Well, I'm glad you're here! We've missed you, Micah. Joel especially." Asher patted the other boy on the shoulder. "I've been praying your father would give you permission to come."

Asher led Micah to the front row of chairs and sat down. "Excuse me, but these old legs get weary after standing for so long." He

ONE WILL BE LEFT

leaned back and loosened his necktie. "So, how's it going for you in your new home?"

Micah sat on the floor in front of Asher, and Joel did the same. It was their custom to have a private conversation with Asher after the services. He was training both boys in the faith.

"It's different. My father has a Gentile wife now. Her name is Kate Havenstone; I mean, Kate Benari." Micah fidgeted with a rubber band he found on the floor in front of him.

"Yes, I've seen that on the magazine covers on the newsstands. She's a very well-known reporter worldwide! And your father, well, everyone in Israel knows Dr. Benari! You must be proud of all he's done for this nation."

Micah was quiet, unsure how to respond. He looked away from the rabbi for a moment before meeting his inquisitive gaze. "I'm not sure what I feel, sir. I don't really know my father. At least, not as a father."

Rabbi Asher nodded. "It makes sense. Your grandparents were very warm, affectionate people. They delighted in you, made much of you. Your father is a stranger, and so is his wife, but you will come to know them soon, Micah."

"But they're hardly around!" Micah bit his lip. He didn't want to complain.

"I'm sure they're busy with their work. Do you eat together?"

"On Fridays, but lately it's just been Father and me. Kate's been away on different assignments. She's going to New Babylon this week to interview the Italian ambassador. She seemed pretty excited about it."

Asher stiffened at the mention of Luca Giamo. The ambassador was coming to Israel in six weeks to discuss the restructuring of the World Union with the Israeli prime minister. Asher had felt a cold sweat when he heard about it on the news broadcast.

"Well, Micah, let's do the best we can. Let's keep this in our prayers. You remember the prophet Elijah? He was a man just like you or me, and he was able to stop the rain in Israel for three years.

ONE WILL BE LEFT

Surely we can ask the Lord for your father to draw closer to you and expect He will answer such a request. Is that not why Elijah has returned here to Israel at this time?" Asher asked.

Micah smiled recalling his father's account of meeting Elijah. Michael Benari still didn't know what to make of his encounter with the Old Testament prophet. Kate refused to believe it wasn't some kind of ruse to get money out of the family, but then she seemed to be skeptical of everything.

"Now, let's go over the lessons I sent you both last week. Joel, you may go first," Asher said.

Joel stood up and began reciting the first chapter of the Gospel of John from memory. Micah listened intently. He followed mentally, careful to keep his lips still while his friend recited the chapter. He and Joel were memorizing a chapter every week.

Joel finished.

"Perfect! Now your turn, Micah." Rabbi Asher nodded to him. Micah stood up. He did not put his hands behind his back as Joel had done. Since he was alone so much in the apartment, he had taken to videotaping himself with one of Kate's extra cameras. He tried to mimic the precise way she presented the news, while adding the passion he felt to the beautiful words he was reciting. They were the words of life to him, and he revered each one.

Joel and Rabbi Asher listened, entranced by Micah's beautiful recitation. Asher became emotional as he realized that the boy was speaking truth directly from memory, by heart. When he came to the end of the chapter, Micah did not stop but continued on speaking for almost thirty minutes before he quit.

"Amazing, Micah!" Asher clapped, and Joel joined him. They were stunned and moved. "You did much more than I assigned you," Asher exclaimed. "And your delivery was absolutely excellent! What chapters were those? How much did you memorize?"

"I know all of them," Micah said simply.

"All? The entire book? How did you manage to memorize the entire Gospel of John in a week?"

"I don't know how, Rabbi. I just read it. I read it, and now I can see it in my mind as if it were in front my eyes. I can tell you the page number of any single verse I've read," Micah responded humbly, his eyes downcast.

"I've known you since you were born, Micah. I did not know this about you!"

"It just started this week, Rabbi. It is true at school, as well. I seem to be able to recall everything I read or hear."

Asher thought a moment and shook his hands in acclamation. "God is preparing you, Micah. I do not know what is in the future for you, but He is getting you ready for something big."

Asher turned to Joel. "The same is true of you, Joel. What we have just heard Micah do is incredible. A gift from none other than God. I want to remind you that every believer has a gift and a part to play on this world stage." Joel nodded respectfully to Asher before giving his friend a playful punch.

New Babylon, Iraq

Arturo struggled to pull away from the intense shaking that threatened to waken him from his sleep.

"Mr. Giamo, you must wake up. Sir, your son has a surprise for you in the garden. Come on, you've slept the whole afternoon away! Please wake up!" It was Jean. He was relieved. She was kind to him. At least it wasn't the other one.

"Come on now, let me get you sitting up here. That's it." She hauled him to a semi-sitting position, half slumped over in the bed. Arturo could move his arms now, though his legs were still paralyzed. He pushed his body up farther on the bed and leaned his head back. He closed his eyes while Jean wiped his face with a warm, damp washcloth. She fastidiously made sure he was clean.

"You haven't seen your son in weeks. I'm sure you miss

him! He's just been so busy flying all over the world with this World Union reorganization he's working so hard on. I'm sure you're proud of him. He's got a way of giving us hope that things can really be different, you know?"

Arturo cringed but said nothing.

"My husband says if Ambassador Giamo can do for the rest of the world what he's doing in North America, we're going to see a time mankind has dreamed of for centuries! It's incredible the rebuilding going on there, don't you think?"

Arturo still did not respond. He had regained the ability to speak, but he chose not to. Unfortunately, Luca could force him to talk. Those conversations were always horrid. Luca would taunt him with a litany of all of his failures as a father and a man, or describe some foul deed in such revolting detail that Arturo would actually become physically ill. He wondered what fresh terror awaited him in the garden.

Reluctantly, he helped lower his body into the wheelchair next to his bed, and Jean placed his feet onto the footrests. She pulled an afghan from the end of his bed and draped it over his legs. He was very grateful for her thoughtful kindness. Arturo was sure that Jean had no idea of the horrors he endured from the other nurse, Brempton, as well as his own son. Jean had no idea what the real Luca was like.

Luca. It was sobering to Arturo to realize that the pinnacle of his scientific achievement had nothing to do with his own efforts. Rather, the miracle of Luca's creation and birth was through intervention from the spiritual realm, something Arturo had always rejected. It was so ironic. And in these last few months he had discovered just how real and how vile that realm truly was. He still couldn't believe that Luca's "enemy" was the God of the Bible. Arturo had tried calling out to God to save him from Brempton's late night visits, but no help came from heaven or earth to rescue him. The demons were real enough, though; he was sure of that.

Jean never noticed the bruises or cuts; somehow she was

blind to it all. She squeezed his shoulder and he winced with pain. Brempton had allowed his spirit guide, Legion, to manifest itself through him. Arturo moaned as he remembered the terror of the long hours under Legion's torment. There was no God, only these evil beings who called themselves angelic majesties.

Legion had many titles and loved to recount to Arturo his many conquests among humans. At first Arturo had thought Brempton was making it all up, that he was insane, but Legion had powers no human being could manufacture. When he bragged about his successes in the German Gestapo, he had actually shown Arturo many of his harrowing schemes, much as humans would play video of a favored vacation. Arturo vomited in terror and disgust, but the demon had no pity.

Arturo hoped Brempton had the night off.

As Jean wheeled him out of the room, he was mortified to see Brempton waiting for him.

"Ah, thank you, Jean dear! The Ambassador asked me to take his father out to the garden. Mr. Amona is in need of your services. His, uh, rash, has become worse," the monster lisped.

Jean put her hand against her cheek in worry. "Oh, dear! The poor thing. I wish the doctor could find the cause of that poor man's suffering. I've never seen anything as painful. Even the ambassador's friend, Prophet Mason, couldn't heal him." She scuttled away down a dark corridor to the right. Brempton wheeled Arturo abruptly around a corner.

This was the first time Arturo had left his room in the months he had been held prisoner. He tried to remember the turns Brempton made and which direction they were going, just in case.

"I see I should've put a blinder on you, old fool," Brampton snarled, as if he had read Arturo's thoughts. "I told master so, but he wants you to see it all. He said you couldn't escape even if you wanted to. They're watching you, you know, on his orders. You can't hide. There's no hiding." Brempton ended his warning with a click of his tongue.

ONE WILL BE LEFT

They came to an elevator, where Brempton hit the up arrow with his elbow. As they waited, he rocked Arturo back and forth in the chair slowly and started singing the song. *Please, not that song,* Arturo silently pleaded. Brempton sang it often, and it still chilled Arturo to the bone.

"He is the king of lights,
Our sovereign bright,
Come to war
With fear.
He'll show the world
Its death
And its emptiness.
When he gives his grace
In the secret place
Men will sing their praise
To the One who reigns."

It was Luca about whom he sang. Whenever Brempton sang the song, Arturo remembered his mother warning him as a child about demons and their schemes to replace God in the hearts of men with progress and science. Back then he'd considered her a superstitious woman. He had sneered when she knelt to pray in the small chapel in their home and had ridiculed her when she moved through their ancestral home anointing the door frames with holy oil. As a young man, he had openly mocked her, silently rejoicing when he made her cry. Now he felt regret and sorrow mingled with his fears.

The elevator door opened and Brempton had pushed him inside, positioning him facing the wall. Arturo didn't dare turn his head to see what button Brempton pushed. That would surely be a mistake.

In a few seconds they reached their floor with a lurch. Arturo tried to steel himself for what was going to happen next. Surely it would be unpleasant, grotesque.

Surprisingly, Brempton pushed him outside and along a pleasant pathway hedged with precisely trimmed boxwoods, reminiscent of a parterre he'd seen in Verona long ago. Flaming torches dotted the pathway and lit the way in the darkening evening sky. By the dim light he recognized Luca's gardens. The fountains sparkled in the moonlight, and the warm night air was refreshing after his confinement. He realized that the last time he had been in this garden was for his granddaughter's first birthday. Now she was dead, along with Teo and DC. He wondered if Elena was dead, too. Luca had told Arturo she'd killed herself.

Brempton continued to push the chair for a while until they reached the center of the rose garden. No one else was there.

"The master will be here directly," Brempton said flatly. He moved in front of Arturo and bent over, staring at him and swaying from side to side. The younger man was sly, and his mannerisms reminded Arturo of the charmed cobras he'd seen in India. Brempton reached his hand out and stroked Arturo's face gently, humming the song again. With a start, Arturo saw a new tattoo on his arm.

Brempton grinned when he saw Arturo's eyes fixate on his new marking. "All who follow the master take this mark to honor him. We are only a few now, but there will be others. It has been foretold." His voice trailed off in a whisper, and he abruptly ambled away into the darkness, leaving Arturo alone.

After waiting a while, Arturo heard whistling. It was the same melody Brempton sang. Arturo tightly gripped the armrests of his chair as his son came into view.

"Hello, dear Arturo! You look quite well, old man. I've got a tremendous surprise for you that I think you're going to love. You see, it's the first full moon. I'm certain you recall that all of our sacrificial worship centers around the phases of the moon?" He bent forward, put a hand on Arturo's shoulder, and buzzed his cheek with a loud kissing noise. Arturo couldn't help but tremble at his touch.

"Unfortunately, Stephen cannot attend. He's laid up with some horrible skin condition. We haven't been able to cure it, but I believe I've finally discovered its cause." He rubbed his hands together the way he'd done since he was a child, as if anticipating a promised treat.

ONE WILL BE LEFT

"This is going to come as something of a shock to you, Arturo. It seems my sister did not perish in that plane crash. No, it was all faked. A stunt! Can you believe it? She was able to fool me. Stephen's investigators were able to finally track her. She was in Jerusalem, of all places!" A look of satisfaction flitted across Luca's cherubic mask.

Arturo could not control his emotions, and he began to sob, overwhelmed by relief, fear, and shock.

"I was astonished, too!" Luca exclaimed. "They were so clever, too clever for their own good. I don't know how I didn't see it was all a ruse. Anyway, I told Stephen he could have her. Unfortunately, he's been struck with a strange condition."

Arturo tried to calm his racing heart. Teo was alive, but in the hands of these monsters! He wanted to kill the man in front of him, son or not. He was filled with an insatiable rage. *If I could get up at this moment, I would choke the smirk right off his face and make him beg for mercy,* Arturo thought.

Suddenly, pain seared through his head, and he cried out in anguish as something contorted his body and an unseen force jerked him violently from his chair. The agony left him limp and unable to fight back, lying helpless on the ground.

"Do not dare to even think such things, Father. There's nothing you can do to stop me. In fact, soon you will join the others and bow before me in worship. You will worship me or die. We both know how weak you are. You will bow."

Arturo was thrown back into his wheelchair by whatever dark entity his son commanded. Luca turned and began walking down a path in the dark, away from the torchlit area. Arturo's chair followed, moving of its own accord. Despite the darkness, Arturo could make out figures moving nearby in the light of the full moon. As he and Luca neared the grotto, he remembered how he had, in happier days, teased Luca that the structure reminded him of a small version of Stonehenge. Now in the moonlight he thought there was some vile significance to that resemblance.

A phantom hand continued to push Arturo's wheelchair

behind his son as he entered the stone circle. There, two women dressed in simple white dresses arranged a scarlet robe on Luca before bowing down and kissing his feet. Arturo swallowed bile as he realized they were wiping tears from Luca's feet with their hair. Even Arturo, a non-religious man, could not mistake the significance of their actions.

"Father!" Arturo looked away from his son to see his daughter, Teo, running from the opposite side of the circle to him. He raised his arms and embraced her. They cried and hugged each other tightly.

"What a tender reunion," Luca said sarcastically, his eyes dark with malice. "You may stay there for the moment, Teo. We will see to your friend now."

He nodded to the robed men next to him, who grabbed the arm of a beautiful woman at his side. Her long dark hair curled at her waist, almost obscuring the fact that her hands were tied in front of her. Arturo noted that she was dressed in the same sort of robe worn by the other women Luca had victimized. Seeing his own daughter was wrapped in the same sacrificial garment, Arturo pulled her closer to him.

Teo became still and silent in his embrace. Arturo recollected her usual anxious response to danger and was startled by the peaceful expression on her face. He'd been concerned about how to restrain her, but he realized she was in complete control.

His daughter closed her eyes and began moving her lips silently. He looked back up at the woman, Teo's friend. She was one of the most exquisite women his eyes had ever beheld. She looked... *perfect*.

Luca was stroking her face, mocking the caress of a lover. "So, it is you who has brought this painful disease on my good friend Stephen. My associates assure me that if we sacrifice you tonight, the curse you carry will end."

The woman lifted her tranquil gaze to meet Luca's. Teo gasped. "She can see!"

Although Teo had spoken quietly, the woman turned to look at her and smiled winsomely. "I do see! I see the Lord Jesus standing at the right hand of God." Her smile faded and her lips tightened as she turned her attention back to Luca.

"You are the one foretold, the abomination of desolation," she spoke clearly. "Fear is what you crave, but I do not fear you. Greater is He who is in me than the one who is in you. Your time is short. You will fail. That, too has been foretold. Jesus Christ will crush you under His feet. You and the False Prophet will be cast alive into the lake of fire."

The man to her right slapped her face and cursed. Arturo felt fear grip his bowels as Teo trembled next to him. He had seen enough of the sacrifices. He knew what came next.

Luca snorted. "You are brave now, but soon you'll scream for my mercy. Your impotent god can't save you. You'll die for the pleasure of my Father like the rest."

He nodded to the men, and they pulled the woman toward the flat stone where the other women had been tortured. Arturo moaned in fear. As Teo looked up at her father and gripped his hands tighter in hers, Luca spoke to those assembled in the grotto.

"Before the sacrifice, since this one is a follower of my enemy, each of you may exact vengeance on her as you see fit." As Luca spoke, Arturo noticed the crowd for the first time. Most of them were dressed in black robes. As he watched, they formed a circle around the woman and began striking her, one at a time. She fell to the ground after a particularly vicious blow from a large man. Arturo realized it was Brempton. He fell on her and began to pull up her robe, obviously intent on rape.

Teo began murmuring, and tears poured down her face. Arturo glanced at her and realized she was praying. Too bad it wouldn't help her friend.

His thoughts were interrupted by Brempton's screams, and the older man looked back at the scene in front of him. Brempton was standing again, viciously kicking the woman's limp body. "She's dead! She's dead!"

Teo pulled away from her father and stood. "Stop!" she shouted.

Luca turned to face Teo and strode over to her. "Curious. You dare to command me?" He ordered Brempton to cease before turning back to the indignant woman standing before him.

"Where is that fearful woman I've known all of my life?" His tone turned mocking. "Sister, you must tell me the source of your newfound courage! Is the pill white or pink?"

Teo took a ragged breath as she stared up at her brother. Arturo waited for her to speak, but she remained silent.

Luca chuckled, "Well, it seems like you are taking a page from your master's book. I believe he was silent, too; wasn't he? Like a lamb led to the slaughter."

Arturo tried to pull Teo back. The group around them exploded in derisive laughter, jeering appalling comments about how she should die.

"Kill the whore!" a voice from behind them said. The group erupted into an even louder cheer.

"No!" Arturo pleaded with his son. "You can't do this, Luca. You cannot do this to your own sister, please!"

Luca closed his left hand into a fist, an expression of disdain on his face. Arturo tried to beg for Teo's life, but found he could not speak. Luca had silenced him yet again.

Gently, Teo pulled her hand from her father's grip and walked over to where the woman's body lay on the ground. She knelt down and rolled her friend over. Gently, she moved the hair away from her friend's face. From where he sat, Arturo could see the dead woman's expression. He had never seen such perfect rapture. Teo kissed her friend's cheek before standing again. She stared at Luca with no fear, and despite his own terror, Arturo felt hope for the first time.

Luca nodded his head toward one of the men. "Take her back."

"What about the sacrifice, sir?" the man asked.

"Brempton has others ready. Use one of them. I promised

Stephen he could have her. Take my father back now, too," he commanded, emotionless. "I'll be in my office."

Arturo turned in his chair as he was wheeled away, trying to see where they were leading his daughter, but she was already gone.

Jerusalem, Israel

DC sat in the bright, sunny garden under the vine-covered pergola, holding his daughter while she slept soundly in his arms. He listened to the refreshing sound of the bubbling fountain. He closed his eyes and silently prayed for Teo and Rhetta. As he prayed, the tight band of foreboding on his heart lifted. He thought about all God had done to restore Juliana to him and thanked Him for her safe return. Surely God would help him find Teo, too.

Opening his eyes, DC studied the face of his second daughter. She looked so much like Olivia had at this tender age. Three months old. He hated to think of it, but he hadn't seen his oldest daughter in almost a year. He knew she was safe with Elena, her grandmother. They were able to communicate, but everyone had to be careful about how often, especially now that Luca had discovered their plan.

DC had come up with the plan to fake their deaths in order to keep his family safe. How Luca had found Teo was something DC could not fathom. If only he could discover how Luca had known they were still alive. If he could figure that out, he might somehow be able to locate his wife.

DC's thoughts turned to Angelina, and he shook his head with a small grin. How crazy was it that the woman whose child he had saved from kidnappers would be the one to call him and let him know his baby girl was safe?

He'd been frantic when evening came that day and Rhetta and Teo still were not home with the baby. They'd gone shopping in a safe area for some necessities. When DC had tried calling their cell phones multiple times with no answer, he began to get worried. He and Ari, Rhetta's son, had gone to the shopping mall to look for them, but they couldn't find the women.

Just when they were heading home, dejected, DC's cell rang. He had seen on the display that the call was from Teo's phone and had felt relief—until he heard the woman's voice on the other end. DC had listened, holding his breath, as the woman described the abduction and how she had ended up with Juliana. She reassured him that Jules was safe with her in her home. When he'd started to question the woman about being followed home and to express his concern for their safety, she'd quietly informed him that her father was the prime minister. She described how Mossad forces had brought them safely to her home and were guarding them there.

DC remembered the shock he'd felt as he realized that the woman he was talking to was Angelina Rogov. He'd saved her daughter, and then she'd saved his.

DC and Ari had driven immediately to the prime minister's residence, where they had been carefully searched and rushed through two metal detectors before being allowed to enter. He had sobbed in relief when he entered the house and saw his daughter in the arms of the same freckle-faced young woman he had helped weeks before. Angelina. They had both exclaimed in surprise at the coincidence.

"You look deep in thought!" A feminine voice interrupted his reminiscing.

DC looked up and saw Angelina standing right next to him, Charlie on her hip. The young mother had an impudent grin on her face that elicited a responsive smile from him.

"I was just thinking how odd it is that you were the one who saved Juliana—that you were there when Teo was…you know. I'm so grateful for all you and your father are doing to help us," he said.

"My father and I are grateful for your help too, DC. Of course we will do anything we can." Charlie's demand for juice interrupted her. Watching the interchange brought a lump to DC's throat as he recalled many such interruptions from Olivia. *Livie...* His heart ached to see her.

"Listen, Father just called," Angelina said. "He has some news from our contact in New Babylon, and he wants to see you in an hour." Angelina shifted Charlie on her hip. "Yona will help me with the girls, so you can leave Juliana here."

DC got up from the bench and gingerly moved the baby, cradling her against his shoulder, but she woke up despite his best efforts. He turned his attention back to Angelina.

"Do you have any idea what they found?" he asked her.

"No, Father just said for you to go to his office." She put Charlie down on the ground and held out her arms for the baby. Angelina nestled the infant's head under her chin and quipped, "You might want to change your shirt."

DC looked at his shoulder and chuckled. "I guess I forgot the burp cloth. I'll go get changed. I really appreciate all your help, Angelina." He gave her shoulder a squeeze before going back into the house.

Angelina's smile faded as she watched him go. She sat on the bench he had just left and watched as Charlie found the garden cat and shrieked with glee. Her daughter gathered the longsuffering feline up by the rear end, leaving the cat's head dangling downward. Yona came out from the kitchen entrance and scolded the toddler. Taking her by the hand, Yona marched Charlie into the house for lunch before her nap.

The baby murmured. Angelina wondered if she was aware enough to miss her mother. Angelina pulled her head back to gaze at the baby and stared into her eyes. They were the same shade of green as her father's, clear and light, ringed with a dark color that defied definition.

"You're amazing," Angelina whispered. Juliana yawned and closed her eyes again.

"I'll bet your momma misses you." Angelina thought about

the woman she'd only known for a few minutes. She was beautiful, awe-inspiringly so. No freckles. Angelina sighed and got up so she could pace with the baby.

DC had been staying with them for less than two weeks, yet he fit in so well. She could tell that her father relished coming home and having someone to talk to who could comprehend the complex issues he faced as Israel's prime minister. Yona blushed whenever the handsome man spoke to her, and Angelina was certain she prepared meals with extra care to please him. And Charlie! Charlie adored him.

"Maybe that's all it is. I just appreciate how much he has done for my child," she whispered to herself. "That's all it is. I hope that he finds Teo. I do." She looked down at the baby in her arms. She deserved her mother.

New York City, New York

James stood on the overpass, looking down Park Avenue. The women he'd questioned said Cynthia had thanked them, walked out the door, and headed this way. He scanned the deserted road and caught a glimpse of her as she turned to the right and out of his view. He ran down the stairs that led to street level, and then he dashed across the road. Just as he turned down the street to follow her, he saw Cynthia open a door and enter. He didn't think she knew she was being followed. He paused for a split second to catch his breath, noticing the steam of his breath in the cold winter air, before he continued jogging toward the building his ex-wife had entered.

Slowing down as he neared the door, James realized Cynthia had entered a boutique. *Fancy That?* was etched in the shop window. Peering in, he saw her rifling through a dress rack, her back to the window. The shop was abandoned and ransacked, like many of the other stores along Madison Avenue.

"What do I do?" he whispered. "I don't want to talk to her, but obviously, Father, You brought her here for a reason. Please show me what to do."

Reluctantly, James pulled open the shop door. The tinkling of the doorbell alerted Cynthia. She turned and saw him, and her face spread into a huge grin.

"Hey! So you followed me. I have to admit, I was not expecting to ever see you again." She held up the dress in her right hand. "What do you think of this?"

He honestly could think of nothing to say in response.

"You always liked me wearing white, remember?" She laughed and turned her back to him. "I think it's a bit too much for travel." She tossed it to the side.

"Travel? There is no way out of the city." He moved back toward the door warily.

"Oh, where there's a will, there's always a way, sweetie. Don't you know that?" She pulled a black jumpsuit off of the floor. She held it up and murmured her approval. "Just the thing." She arranged it facing out on the rack and walked to the back wall, which was loosely filled with shoeboxes.

James watched dumbly while she tried on various shoes. Choosing a pair, she walked back to the rack where she'd left the jumpsuit. "I'm going to get out of this monstrosity if you don't mind!" With a sultry expression, she pulled off the simple cotton dress she was wearing and dropped it to the ground.

"Oh, I suppose I do have to thank you for healing me," she quipped, turning around so he could admire her nakedness.

"How did I never see what you truly are?" A burning sourness rose in his throat.

"You saw what you wanted to see, honey; everyone does." She pulled on the jumpsuit and the shoes. "But I do thank you. I was about to die. I know it and feel that I do owe you something... but what?" She lowered her head a bit and looked up at him suggestively, raising one eyebrow and biting her lower lip.

ONE WILL BE LEFT

"I don't want anything from you." He shook his head and held up his hands to keep her away as he backed closer to the open door behind him. "And it was God who healed you, not me."

"James, I can't tell you how much I didn't miss you and your God talk! Just shut up about that damned God of yours!" she screamed, suddenly full of rage. Closing her eyes, she took a deep breath to regain her composure. "You know, I just refuse to allow any negative emotions to control me." She smoothed her hair down on either side of her face and took another breath before opening her eyes.

"Do you want to know anything about our son?" he asked quietly.

"No, I could not care less, actually. I didn't want him to begin with, so what you do with him is up to you."

"What will you do now?"

"My very dear friend is sending in some men to get me out of here. They're going to land a helicopter on the old MetLife Building, and an 'extraction team' is going to get me out." She spoke with a mocking tone. "I told them there's nothing dangerous going on in the city, just a big revival. Andres was very interested in that." She turned her attention to a shelf of handbags and began pulling them off the shelf one at a time, tossing the rejects aside carelessly.

This is why God wanted me to come in and confront her! James realized. *I'm being warned.* Carefully keeping his tone calm, he asked who Andres was.

"Uhhh, where have you been? He's only the leader of all of North America! Oh, I think I'll take this one with me! Look how lovely! I think it's real zebra hide!" She held the bag up for him to admire, grinning gleefully.

"I guess I've been too busy trying to survive to keep up," he muttered. "Why would a revival interest him?"

"Well, I suppose it wasn't so much that, but that I almost died of that horrible disease and *you* healed me. He wanted me to tell you that he is so grateful and would like to tell you personally."

ONE WILL BE LEFT

She moved closer to him as she spoke. James had to restrain himself to hide his disgust as she touched his face and brought her lips to his. She was so beautiful, but her breath smelled like death. He swallowed back the bile. He wanted to speak, to tell her to leave, but it was impossible. Something kept him from speaking, a physical presence that was overwhelmingly oppressive and weighing on his body.

Jesus, help me! Jesus, please help. Jesus! he prayed quietly and earnestly. Then suddenly he was free. James pushed her away and yelled, "No!"

Cynthia looked bemused. "Listen, Andres isn't too good about sharing his women, but we could make it work. After all, fair is fair. He's got his wife and the others."

"I don't want you," James said, rubbing his lips with the back of his hand. "When are the men coming for you?"

"Soon. But they aren't just coming for me, darling. They're coming for you too. We might as well enjoy ourselves while we wait. What do you think?"

James backed toward the door. He wasn't sure how long he had to get the others away, but he had to try. "Me? What? Why me?"

"I told you. Andres is grateful. And intrigued."

"Tell him I said he's welcome to you and I'm truly sorry I couldn't heal what's really wrong with you." Turning, James yanked open the door and ran down the street back toward Union Station. He ran as if all of hell were chasing him.

New Babylon, Iraq

The drapes were drawn tightly, and only a small sliver of light from the adjoining room illuminated the space. Stephen stifled a moan, knowing Luca would not approve of how little control he had over the pain. He moved in the bed to sit upright and caught his breath in pain as one of the boils on his back burst. He could feel the pus ooze through his shirt and onto the bed sheets. He would have to wait until they were done with their planning session to have his nurse clean him up.

Billings Mason paced at the foot of the bed. Stephen could see that the smells of the sickroom were offensive to the man now called the Prophet. His predictions and their fulfillments were daily fare in the media. He had successfully foretold the explosion of Mount Rainier in North America. The nearby cities of Seattle and Tacoma had been forcibly evacuated by President Quinteros' troops before the devastating eruptions. The pyroclastic flow hit the snowpack and began a catastrophic tide of boiling mud, creating a lahar that took out most of the Puget Sound region. Because of his prophecy, the death rate was under one hundred, rather than the tens of thousands who would have been entombed in the molten current.

Luca was congratulating Billings on this latest prophetic word. "This is just the thing, Billings! You are making a tremendous impact. I believe OneFaith membership has increased over 80 percent." Luca sat next to the open window. "Do you have any more indications of impending doom?"

Billings stopped pacing and stood still for a moment. "Not at this time, but I'm confident your Father's associates will tell me. These prophecies, along with the miracles, are making great headway for your kingdom, Luca. It will not be long before the way has been made ready for your total revelation."

"Yes, Master! Your time has come! I rejoice to see the day approaching!" Stephen tried to keep his voice from cracking with pain, but he could not.

"Damn it, Billings! Can't you do something to help him?" Luca shouted, his face suddenly red with anger and annoyance.

Stephen noted the fear in Billings' eyes and felt sorry for his friend, but he was also relieved that he was not the source of Luca's irritation. He was gratified by the display of Luca's affection for him and concern for his condition.

ONE WILL BE LEFT

Billings looked down at the carpet, unable to meet his master's eyes. "No. I cannot. It wasn't the blind woman after all. It must be your sister, sir. No matter what I do, there is no change in Stephen's condition. The doctors are baffled. None of their treatments are effective."

"Then we must do something with my sister, but what?" Luca caught Stephen's gaze. "Perhaps we must cut our losses, Stephen. The media still has not been told about her amazing survival. She can be the next offering, and that will surely end your suffering."

Licking his lips carefully, Stephen answered. "Master, I'm grateful for your care and concern. You've done everything possible to alleviate my condition. But Teo is mine. You promised that I could have her. I don't want her dead." Despite himself, his tone was groveling.

"Yes, I did. But I had no idea this would happen to you! Stephen, you've been my greatest advocate and friend. I will not have you suffering! My sister has always been a sniveling, whiny fool. She's fearful and weak, and if I am honest, unbearably annoying. I don't know what it is you see in her." Luca grimaced in disgust.

"I'll give you one week," Luca continued. "When I go to Jerusalem, you will be at my side. You've worked just as hard for this as I have. You will watch me ratify that treaty with the Israelis, which gives you one week to heal or get rid of the problem."

Amman, Jordan

The room was cool and quiet—delightful after a stressful night with little sleep followed by an early game of tennis with his two sisters. Since they didn't have enough people to play doubles, Zayd had taken turns playing each of his sisters, and he was worn out after all the exertion. He leaned his head back against the supple leather of the chair, noting that his sisters sat with Uncle Rasheed in the small alcove next to him. Closing his eyes, Zayd relaxed as Rasheed lec-

ONE WILL BE LEFT

tured the young women. His uncle's warm baritone was pleasant.

"The history of this city is a rich one. As you know, Amman was built on seven hills originally, like Rome. It became one of the cities in the Decapolis around AD 106, when it went by the name Philadelphia. It was a powerful city until several earthquakes devastated it.

"Not until an Ottoman sultan decided to build a railway to link Damascus and Medina—with Amman as a main station—did the city begin to truly regain its glory. Later on, your ancestor, King Abdullah I, chose Amman as his capital. You know, there was nothing here to begin with, so he lived in a train car!"

Zayd opened one of his eyes to see if his sisters were paying attention; Uncle Rasheed had been speaking to them for quite a while. They had all come in hot and tired and wanting refreshments. Both of his sisters were sitting on the carpet, legs tucked under them, listening attentively to the old man.

"Uncle, do we not have a gracious history?" Rania asked. Zayd noted how her red highlights glistened in the sun streaming in the window behind her. Although he would never admit it, Rania was his favorite sister. He watched the scene with both eyes opened. When his young sister spoke, it was always worth hearing.

"What do you mean by 'gracious?'" Rasheed asked.

"Almost from the beginning, our ancestors have welcomed those escaping the horrors of war. I can think of no other nation that has been as gracious as Jordan. Think of all of the refugees that have come here over the past century and added to our culture."

Uncle Rasheed nodded his head thoughtfully in agreement.

"So, dear Uncle, it would be in keeping with the gracious tradition of our ancestors to prepare for the coming days with the thought of what the refugees would need," Rania said.

"Indeed, Rania! Your brother has already begun to do so. We were going to talk about it tonight over dinner with you and your sister. His Majesty, your brother, would like to have your help in the preparations."

ONE WILL BE LEFT

Zayd silently thanked God. He wanted to get his sisters out of Amman without alarming them. Providing humanitarian aid was a means they could use to get the girls out of the capital without any questions.

His uncle continued, "We've debated where best to have you both help. Your brother feels his greatest need will be for aid in the south, and he'd like your assistance in establishing camps there in preparation for the coming times."

"Uncle, I too have been studying." Rania spoke quietly, but there was such radiance about her that Zayd sat up and leaned forward. His heart began to beat more quickly, and he heard, *Listen to her*, whispered in his head.

"I overheard you and Zayd talking about the prophecies concerning Jordan a few months ago. Truly, I did not mean to eavesdrop. I was sitting on the balcony reading when you entered the garden. I was so comfortable; it did not occur to me that I should let you know I could hear you. Once I heard you were speaking about biblical prophecy, I didn't want to miss a word." She stopped speaking for a moment to collect her thoughts. She smoothed out a wrinkle in her tennis skirt and continued.

"I was so afraid after that. It was difficult to sleep, and I didn't have an appetite. I started praying, but day after day I was so afraid. I tried to search through information on the Internet, but you know how much religious content OneFaith restricts now—I couldn't find anything helpful. I decided to fast, as well.

"Four days later, Alia wanted me to go with her to the Taj Mall, so I went with her. While she was trying on some clothes, a woman approached me. She was middle-aged, wearing the same clothing the rest of the store staff was wearing. She held out a card and told me all I wanted to know was available at the link written on the card.

"I took the card and looked at it. There was a short series of instructions telling how to log on and find access to a subnet. I looked up to ask her about it, but she was gone.

ONE WILL BE LEFT

"Alia came out of the dressing room at that moment, so I just shrugged and put the card in my purse. We went to dinner, and it wasn't until late that night, when I woke up from a troubling dream, that I remembered the card."

Rania stopped for a moment and took a sip of her lemon water from the crystal glass. "I got my laptop out and the card. Following the steps carefully, I was led to a different sort of internet."

"Different in what way?" Rasheed asked, obviously intrigued.

Rania scrunched up her face and shook her head. "I'm not sure how to describe it, except as a unique homepage. There were many links with titles like 'So Now What?' and 'You've Been Left Behind,' and others that were about Jesus Christ. There was a place to search, so I typed in 'Jordan in the end days.' It was unbelievable. Article after article about Jordan—our own country! Many were written long ago. It seems that whoever put this subnet together was able to upload information before OneFaith deleted it from the Internet."

Alia rubbed her forehead. "Rania, this is giving me a headache. Can you get to the point?"

Rania smiled at her younger sister gracefully and then looked Zayd in the eyes. "Somehow you're going to have to stand up against the Antichrist, brother."

A tremor of fear rippled down his spine. "Why do you say that, Rania?" he asked. His voice cracked at the end of his question.

"Because apparently the Bible says Jordan will be the one nation the Antichrist will not have power over. That is a sure prediction." Her face radiated with joy.

Zayd stood up and moved into the alcove closer to his sisters and uncle. He knew that Rania was correct. He had seen the prophecies himself in the old books Uncle Rasheed had collected, but he still had so many questions and fears. He'd pushed it to the back of his mind for the longest time, possibly in denial of what lay ahead in his future.

"But how? And what about the other predictions about the destruction of southern Jordan, Edom? And it's been predicted that

Moab and Ammon will suffer the same fate.... How can we stand in the midst of that kind of devastation?" he asked.

"Those prophecies will not come about until the very end of the seven years, Zayd. And there will be a believing remnant of us that will enter the kingdom age. I believe that there is a key to our people having hope in that promise."

"What is that?" he asked. "What is the key?"

Rania turned to their uncle. "Uncle Rasheed, what did you teach us about the consequences of the war our ancestors fought against Israel? The one prophesied in Psalm 83?"

Rasheed started smiling, his teeth gleaming as he spoke. "That the economic crash and the earthquakes, floods, and other natural disasters that hit us were God's rebuke."

"Uncle, you told us there was a promise the Lord made to Abraham and his descendants—that He would bless those who blessed Israel and curse those who cursed her, yes?" Rania looked at her uncle intently, clearly on to something.

"Yes, I see it. I do see it!" he exclaimed.

"What do you see? I'm confused," Zayd said.

Rasheed answered, "You must find a way to bless Israel, Zayd. God's blessing will then be on you and on many in our nation! The Bible speaks of a place of refuge for the Jewish people to flee to when the Evil One seeks to kill them."

Zayd thought about the information he had just received. He was grateful for his sister's revelation. Despite the fact that there were many in Jordan who favored Israel, there were still many who did not. In fact, a significant number in Zayd's army had an intense hatred of Israel. He thought back to a conversation he'd had with his uncle earlier in the day, when they'd discussed how the reordering of the World Union signaled the coming revelation of the Antichrist. The unified world system was being reorganized into ten kingdoms, something Scripture had predicted would occur. Zayd's stomach churned with anxiety over the huge responsibility on his shoulders for his kingdom and all the people in it.

ONE WILL BE LEFT

Rania stood up and looked toward him. Something about her demeanor had suddenly changed. Wonder lightened her face and she fell on her knees. Zayd was about to go to her when he heard his name spoken by a voice behind him. He turned around in response. There before him was a shimmering man who could be no one other than the Lord Jesus! Zayd fell to his knees, and in his peripheral vision, he saw Alia and his uncle do the same. He was overcome with emotion and felt his body weaken in surrender as he lifted his hands in the air. He could not speak as he gazed at the Savior.

"Zayd, I have made you king of this nation for this very reason. You will be My emissary to the leader of Israel and to the Son of Perdition. There is a place where you will prepare refuge for those whom I have called by name out of Israel, the remnant.

"Many will fall, but you will stand. Stand fast and prepare yourself; I will be with you always. Though many will come against you, I will cause you to hold strong, and you will enter into the kingdom age as an overcomer."

Zayd bowed low before the King of Kings and felt a hand upon his head. He heard the blessing and instructions the Lord Himself spoke over him. All of his fears and questions vanished in that touch, and he was overcome with an incredible sense of confidence and faith. The Lord finished speaking, and then he was gone.

They all sat back on the floor in silence for a moment, dazed. Zayd looked at each of his sisters and his uncle and could see the glory of the Lord still shimmering on each of their faces.

Alia spoke, "I believed, but now I have seen! Oh, we have seen him!" She clapped her hands in joy.

"Did you hear what he said? He told us we are to go and prepare a place for his remnant. There is much to do; we must make plans," Uncle Rasheed exclaimed in wonder to his brother's children.

Zayd stood up. "Yes, Uncle, I want the three of you to make preparations. In fact, I would like you to take my sisters there, to Petra. I am going to Jerusalem."

19

VIRGINIA

Elena sat on the rock by the pool, the sun warming her body, which was cool after splashing around in the natural pool outside of the cave complex. She saw her young friend, Annabel, navigate her way along the poolside, avoiding the splash attacks from the children.

"Your lips are blue!" Annabel arrived breathlessly and stood over Elena.

Elena chuckled. "I don't know how the children can stay in there so long! Are you going in for a swim?"

"No, I'm going hunting in the morning with Brant. I have to get things ready for that. I prefer warmer baths anyway!" Annabel squatted down beside the older woman.

"Me too! But Livie is having fun 'swimming' with the other girls." She nodded toward where the younger children played in the shallows. The toddler was busy filling a pitcher with water and pouring it on the dog that stood in the pool with the children.

"I see Mozart is on guard duty again!" The women chuckled together. Mozart had followed the family for days as they made their way to the cave home. No one knew where he came from. The Australian Shepherd had obviously been a favored pet, because his name was proudly etched on a tag shaped in the form of a music note. He'd quickly become a favorite in the community. The kids loved that he had one blue eye and one brown eye.

"You know he chased off a cougar yesterday."

"Really? What happened?" Elena asked.

ONE WILL BE LEFT

"The Philips girl was out by herself collecting mushrooms. Brant took a look at the tracks and recognized that it had been stalking her for a while. She had no idea there was any danger until Mozart streaked past her, growling. The cougar was hidden in a bush just to her right. It ran away from the dog! Who knows what might have happened to her if Mozart hadn't shown up."

Elena shook her head. "You know, I'm grateful that so many believers are finding their way here, and we certainly have plenty of room, but it's getting to the point where I think we need to choose some leaders and others to enforce community rules. We need to maintain safety the best we can." Her voice grew more strident. "Sadie Philips has been told not to go out alone. That was foolish, and it's not just wild animals roaming around these mountains. We have to be careful not to draw attention to our location."

"Brant said the same thing. I think a meeting is being planned for after worship tomorrow," Annabel informed her friend.

"That's good! In the months since you arrived, we've gone from under ten people to over forty. We need some sort of organization."

They sat in companionable silence for a few minutes. The sun's warmth made Elena feel sleepy, so she closed her eyes. Annabel picked at the grass beneath her feet. There were other women sitting at the water's edge with the children, watching them play.

Elena noticed that she was dozing off. *I can indulge in a short snooze...Annabel won't mind...* she let herself drift off.

A shadow passed over, blocking the sunlight and making everything suddenly dark. Elena opened her eyes again, but she was no longer by the pool with Annabel. Her heart started pounding quickly, because suddenly she was nowhere near the cave, or even in Virginia. Instead, somehow, she was in New Babylon!

Large crowds milled about on either side of Processional Street. Everyone was dressed in white clothing and was waving branches of some kind. Palm branches! Barricades had been erected on either side of the street to keep the masses at bay. Elena was standing in the middle of the street, but no one seemed to notice her.

ONE WILL BE LEFT

A policeman walked right past her, oblivious to her presence.

Am I dreaming? Elena wondered. It didn't seem like a dream. She turned to survey the crowds. A man to her right had a curious tattoo on his forehead, some strange mark she didn't recognize. Others had the same pattern on the backs of their hands. In fact, the majority of the people she saw had the same mark, most on their right hands, but some had it on their foreheads.

She heard music blaring and turned to see a band winding its way up the street toward her, leading a parade. Elena stepped back as the spectacle wove along the street. After a minute or two, she made out a long black convertible limousine rolling forward in the middle of the procession. The crowd around her saw it too and went wild with shouts and clapping. She recognized Billings Mason perched on the backseat, waving, the same tattoo decorating his forehead. As he came closer, she stared in horror. His hands were dripping with bright red blood. He handed a gold wine goblet to the man seated next to him. She realized it was Luca.

Luca accepted the golden cup with a regal nod and held it aloft for the crowd's attention. The parade stopped, and the crowd hushed all at once in anticipation. Luca stood up on the backseat of the limousine, his resonant voice carried through the crowded streets by the microphone barely visible on the side of his face.

"What you once worshipped in ignorance, I now proclaim to you with all wisdom and knowledge. I am the Messiah, the Savior of mankind!

"Born of a virgin, I am the fulfillment of all prophecies concerning the Christ. He is here among you!"

The crowd went wild in enthusiasm, and Luca waited, his smile gleaming in approval of their adulation. "There have been others who have come, hoping to be the One, the Savior. But none succeeded in bringing about the promised peace, did they? The one who was called Jesus tried, but we know all that was done in that name, do we not?"

Elena cringed at the crowd's vehement anger. Her stomach

twisted in fear, although she realized no one could see her.

"He turned water into wine and walked on water. I've done so much more, have I not? The world is at peace. Although the earth has experienced some tragic sufferings, I have brought healing. My government has provided for you all. Life is good for every citizen.

"To celebrate my victory over death, you'll find barrels of water at each corner of the city. Prophet Mason will offer a prayer of dedication, and he will change the water into wine." Luca waited for the crowd to stop cheering and applauding, but their enthusiasm continued unabated.

Elena noted that he had stopped the procession in front of a bank of cameras. She saw reporters standing by, reverently listening. She scanned their faces, recognizing some of them. The scene in front of her was sparkling in the wavy heat, and the chaos of the crowd was overwhelming. Her ears began to ring, and she swayed.

"Do not fear, Elena. I am with you." She felt a hand touch her shoulder, steadying her. Immediately, the ringing stopped, the faintness passed. Realizing this was some kind of vision, she turned back to see that Luca had begun speaking again.

"My inauguration will be consecrated. We must rid the earth of all that is evil and negative. By releasing the spirits of those who oppose the new world order, we free human society to become all that my Father intended it to be from the beginning.

"There can be no peace among men without sacrifice. It is no longer survival of the fittest, but of the faithful. Those who are not faithful hinder and harm this world. The sacrifices are a sacred event, part of your service of worship to me. As such, they will be televised for all to see, because this is a solemn and holy occasion, something we want everyone to see. As we free the earth from the negative presence of dissenters, we also free them. Remember, there is no death—only freedom."

Luca nodded to someone unseen, and moments later, huge Jumbotrons on the buildings along the street lit up. Each screen revealed a bright courtyard filled with men and women dressed in red robes, their hands tied behind their backs. The camera panned across the faces of the terrified prisoners before centering on a huge wooden machine.

Elena heard the voice speak to her again. She turned. The scene in the streets of Babylon faded in front of her, and she realized she was suddenly on a blustery mountain. Before her was someone she'd never seen before, yet she knew him as soon as he spoke her name. Falling to her knees, she bowed before him.

His hands raised her up. Tears ran down her cheeks and intense joy raced through her.

"Elena, I've shown you what the Evil One has in store for My followers because I do not want you to fear. The nations rage and kingdoms will totter, including this final kingdom of men. I will bring desolation on the earth. Mountains like this one will be moved into the heart of the sea and the seals of the scroll will be opened at the appointed time.

"Yet, do not fear, for I will be with you. I will be your fortress and your deliverer. Do not fear men who can destroy the body but cannot kill the soul. You've put your life in My care, and I am faithful and true. I am with you always, even to the end of this age."

Elena closed her eyes as he embraced her.

"Are you okay? Elena, what's wrong?" Someone was shaking her violently.

Annabel. With a start, Elena opened her eyes. The children still played in the pool nearby while the dog nipped at fish in the water. It was peaceful and idyllic—for now.

She sat up and gripped her friend's hands. "I had a vision. Oh, Annabel! I saw the Lord! I saw Jesus!"

"I thought you'd fallen asleep until you started crying. Are you sure you weren't dreaming?" Annabel asked.

"I'm sure. I need to find John and Brant. They need to know what I saw. We need to be prepared for what is coming soon."

She stood up and grabbed the towel she'd been sitting on. Wrapping it around her body, she went over to the pool and got her granddaughter, Olivia. Elena briskly dried the girl off, picked her up, and carried her back to Annabel.

"Would you go find Brant and bring him to our rooms? I think John is in the caverns organizing a new space for the latest arrivals. I need to tell all of you what the Lord has revealed to me.

There was a warning and a promise I have to share."
Turning, Elena made her way to the cave to find her husband.

New Babylon, Iraq

The room was dark; not a single shape could be made out. It was still so early that the sun had not risen in the sky. Teo rolled over in bed and pulled the covers up over her face. She knew Luca had cameras monitoring her at all times. There were guards at her door and a "companion" who never left her side.

Luca had brought her in the day after Rhetta died. His soft voice had dripped with insincere concern for Teo as he told her he didn't want her to be "alone in her grief." He'd brought in Tali to be her companion. The woman was terrible in so many ways, which Teo was certain was the reason Luca chose her. She had greasy hair that hung around her scarred face in snarled strands. It had obviously once been a beautiful face, but now it was disfigured with bizarre tattoos. The large one on her forehead was the same Teo had observed on many others in Stephen's villa. Her nose and the area around her eyes were tattooed completely black. The rest of her face and body, from what Teo could see, was tatted to appear skeletal. Tali slept on a mat at the foot of Teo's bed. Teo could hear the woman breathing rhythmically.

Good, Teo thought. *She's still asleep!*

Teo was not allowed to have a Bible. She'd asked Tali for one last week and had been slapped across the face and then kicked viciously in the stomach as a response, without a word or expression of anger. That had been the beginning of the beatings. If Teo tried to bow her head to pray before a meal, or ask for anything, she was beaten. If Tali suspected Teo was praying, she was beaten. Day after day they sat in the room doing nothing; the only distractions were the times she was given food.

Teo wondered how her brother had become this monster. She lay in bed and prayed that God would rescue her somehow, that He would let her see her girls again. It did not seem likely she would be able to escape. She moaned in pain as she tried to adjust her position in bed. Her largest bruises were on her back and torso.

Controlling her breathing, she prayed again that God would give her strength to trust Him and courage to face whatever the day held for her. Because of the strength He miraculously supplied, she'd been able to endure the beatings. She froze when she heard a soft tapping on the door.

She knew better than to get up. Instead, she held her breath as Tali rolled over slowly and lumbered across the large room to the door, yanking it open.

"What do you want?" Tali demanded, her eyes half-open.

"Mr. Amona wants to see the woman. Now. Get her dressed and out here right away."

Teo recognized the voice of one of the guards, Howell. He was the one who always tried to touch her. She began praying in earnest. Tali taunted her daily with stories of Howell's brutal attacks on her and other women who served Stephen. When Teo tried to express concern and sorrow for Tali's experience, the woman had only laughed at her and punched her in the face.

Something sharp hit her in the back. "Get up!" Tali screeched. "You're wanted. I have no idea why, but you are."

Quickly, Teo got out of bed and pulled the robe she was already wearing tighter around her. She went to the door. Howell sneered at her and grabbed her arm. The guard sitting by the door laughed and mockingly reminded him that they had orders not to touch her.

ONE WILL BE LEFT

Teo had no idea where Howell was taking her. She struggled to keep up with him as he hurriedly ushered her through the large villa. He yanked her down a corridor, digging his long nails painfully into her arm. At the end of the dark hallway, they turned and entered a large foyer dominated by black-and-white marble. Howell pulled her aggressively up the stairs behind him. When she tripped and fell, he did not allow her to regain her footing, but dragged her up the stairs behind him, laughing when she cried out in pain as her body thumped over each tread.

He pulled her up to her feet at the top of the stairs and grabbed a handful of her hair. "How about doing that again? I'll toss you down and drag you back up." He put a foot behind her legs causing her to lose her footing. The only thing keeping her from tumbling back down the stairs was his grip on her hair.

"Howell, stop that!" A voice barked out the command. "The master is waiting."

Somehow she was on her feet again, her hair free from Howell's grip, and was allowed to walk on her own the last few feet to the door. Teo knew the man standing by it. He had been her executive assistant for years.

"Teo, you look well." His tone was sarcastic.

"Perez, how disappointing to see you here." She looked at his face with sympathy. He, too had the emblem on his forehead. It seemed like some kind of special distinction to have it placed there, perhaps an honor. She recalled what DC had told her about the mark of the beast. Those who took on that mark had no chance of salvation. Their souls were sealed for doom by their allegiance to the Son of Perdition, her brother.

She entered the dim room. A massive bed sat in the middle of it, reminding her of something in a castle from the Middle Ages. The white, sheer curtains surrounding the bed were closed, obscuring whoever was lying in it.

"Come closer." She recognized Stephen's voice, although it was weak.

Moving closer, the small lamp next to the bed allowed her to see the dark shape sitting up in the bed.

"Please sit in the chair, Teo."

She sat down, wincing as she did. Her whole body ached from Tali's last beating and her ascent up the marble staircase.

"Are you unwell?" She could see Stephen move his head forward through the sheer curtains.

"A bit sore from Luca's hospitality, courtesy of my companion," she joked.

She saw him put a hand to his mouth. "But you are mine! No one is to touch you but me!" He whined, "Master, you promised her to me!"

Teo watched and listened as Stephen spoke to Luca as if he were there. In the silences and utterances that went on for the next few minutes, she realized that Stephen was speaking to Luca and hearing a response. It stunned her.

She noticed a slight gap in the curtains and tried to look through it without Stephen noticing. Holding back a gasp of horror, Teo saw the dreadfulness the curtains attempted to hide.

Huge pustules and lesions covered his face. His eyes were hardly open due to the swelling around them. His hair remained only in wisps between vile sores that dripped yellow pus. He had a towel clipped around his shoulders. It was covered with the same substance.

"What's happened to you?" she whispered raggedly. The smell was fetid.

"Apparently you. Ever since you were brought to my home, I have endured these sores. At first, we thought it was a curse brought on by your friend. We were wrong.

"Luca says it's you, Teo. You are the source of my pain. He said it is the manifestation of my unhealthy affection for you." He was quiet for a long moment. "My lord needs me by his side. He told me that today is the last day I will suffer."

Teo looked at him. "No, the source of your pain is not me. I don't have the power to inflict that on you, Stephen, but God does.

He is giving you an opportunity to repent, by keeping you from using me for your own pleasure." She begged God to help Stephen hear her.

"You've not taken the mark yet. It is not too late for you! Please, please turn to the Lord Jesus now. He is powerful enough to save you!"

"How has He saved you, Teo? You're here—without your children, without DC—and you are going to die tonight. Your brother is going to kill you in front of your father. He has it all planned. And the moment you die, I will be free of this and of my sick, twisted need for you."

"But Stephen, you don't know what Luca is, who he is! You weren't there. He could not take the life of my friend Rhetta. God did. God kept her from Luca's sacrifice and He's kept me from you.

"If I die tonight, I'll be with the Lord Jesus in heaven. I'll be at peace. You may or may not be healed from your skin condition, but you will still be a dead man walking. I beg of you, please turn to God. Repent of all this wickedness. It's not too late."

"Teo, if only you'd come to me willingly before! Now it *is* too late—too late for you, that is." His voice softened slightly. "But listen. I want to show my love for you one last time. Perez is going to take you to see your father. You may visit with him for a few hours, and then you will be prepared for the sacrifice. Luca insists I be there." Stephen stopped talking and moaned in pain. Teo waited quietly, detached from his suffering.

"Be assured, my dear love, that I will rejoice when you are set free from your misery," Stephen said. "Luca has shown me how captive you are to the sentimental foolishness of faith in your Jesus. He failed, you know that? Dying on some cross was not a victory. Your brother, though! If only you'd placed your faith in him. He loved you so much, and looked up to you, but you turned your back on him and deceived him.

"You can't help it, I suppose. Luca says all women deceive. It's been that way since the beginning of mankind. I was blinded by your charm, but these days spent in agony have helped me to understand that the feelings I allowed myself to have for you corrupted me. Tonight, my true savior will set me free. Then I will take his mark so all will know my trust is in him."

Abruptly, hands grabbed her from behind and jerked her roughly out of the chair. Perez escorted her down the stairs, thankfully with much less force than Howell had taken her up them.

As they went out the front door, the dazzling glare of the sun blinded Teo temporarily and she had to close her eyes from its rays. She struggled along as Perez yanked her by her forearm, led her to a car, and pushed her into the backseat. She was annoyed to find Tali sitting on the other side. Tali bashed Teo in the face as she was seated, and the abuse continued for the entire drive. Finally, the car pulled into the gates of Luca's residence.

Perez opened the door and wrenched Teo away from Tali, snarling at the woman to stop.

He escorted Teo around the side of the stately mansion, where they entered through what appeared to be a servant's entrance. Heading down the hall, they stopped in front of an elevator. Perez pushed her inside as soon as the metal doors opened. She was quiet as the elevator doors closed, and Perez pushed a button. She watched carefully.

"You're not going to escape, Teo," Perez laughed, noticing her watchfulness. "Tonight's the last night for you. Your brother has some great treats for you before you go, though." He leaned over and brushed her hair away from her face. "You're going to love the one I've got for you." He chuckled suggestively.

She balled her hands up on either side of her body and shook with rage.

When the elevator doors opened, Perez led her to a large wooden door. There was no guard, no lock. Perez told her to go in, so she turned the knob and entered alone.

"Teo!" Arturo Giamo sat by the window in his wheelchair.

Teo rushed into her father's opened arms and began to weep.

20

JERUSALEM, ISRAEL

Michael Benari stretched out on the leather chaise in his office, his eyes closed as he listened to the audio of the video clip playing on his computer. He had not listened to Devorah's music since the day she died. Although his eyes were closed, he could see the video in his memory. His exquisite wife had been eight months pregnant with Micah when she had performed her original compositions at the annual piano festival in Tel Aviv. In his memory, he could see the sparkle of her black gown under the stage lights and the way her body swayed as she played.

The music was intricate, vivacious, and uplifting—just as she had been. *Paradise Pool.* He remembered when she had composed it. They had spent part of their honeymoon hiking through Yehudia Canyon in the Golan Heights. The hike down to Paradise Pool was amazing. Following the dirt path down into the canyon's open desert was not for the fainthearted. Between the heat and clambering over rocks along the mountain path, they had reached the pool ready to drop. They'd both dove into the cool water and swum near the waterfall, kissing breathlessly. Later they had enjoyed a picnic lunch in the cool shade of the canyon trees. When they'd returned to the cabin in Moshav Ramot later that day, Devorah had gone straight to the piano and sat composing for hours.

The music ended. Reluctantly, Michael got up and went to the computer where Devorah's image remained frozen on the screen. "What would you think of me now?" he asked the image. Glancing at the time on the screen, he quickly switched off the monitor, left his office, and headed to the storage facility on the Temple Mount.

The walk took only a few minutes, but by the time he stood in front of the entrance of the storage facility and showed his badge to the guards, the back of his shirt was soaked. As he entered the air-conditioned building, he murmured a quick thanks to the guard who opened the door for him.

He was stopped several times along the way to the bank of elevators. There were questions from some of the builders about a meeting they had later in the week to go over the final lists. The consecration ceremonies were next week, and everyone was determined for the work to be completed on time. There was a lot of hustle and bustle in every corner of the building.

Pushing the elevator button, Michael looked around. Even the storage facility was attractive. The commission in charge of rebuilding the Temple had determined that the Mount be an example of all the finest Israeli ingenuity and creativity. The walls around him held an impressive mural depicting Israel's history. From Abraham to the Diaspora, from the sacking of Jerusalem by Titus to the rebirth of Israel after the Holocaust, the artist had captured the unique history of the chosen people.

The elevator bell dinged. The door opened, and Michael entered. He put his key into a small lock above the floor buttons and twisted it. A hidden panel in the wall illuminated, and he pressed in the sequence of numbers that would allow him to take the elevator to the floor housing the Ark of the Covenant.

When he arrived at the correct floor, he exited the elevator and walked down a brightly lit hallway to a steel door. He put his eye over the biometric device, waiting ten seconds for verification as the light levels in the scan changed to authenticate the presence of a live eye. When the head of security had first walked him through the process, Michael thought that bit was quite clever, especially after considering why a "live eye" would have to be verified.

The metal door slid open into the wall, revealing a guard sitting behind a desk and another next to the small chamber where the Ark rested. Michael knew the guards had monitored his approach; there was no way to enter the room undetected. He pulled at the lanyard around his neck to lengthen it so the guard at the door could scan his card.

Mumbling his thanks as his ID was verified, Michael entered the room, and the door closed behind him. He sighed in wonder at the treasure before him. The Ark was awe-inspiring. Bezalel had faithfully crafted the acacia-wood box as described in the Scriptures thousands of years ago, then plated it with gold, inside and out. Michael paced around the small room, circling the box and admiring its gleaming surface. Two carved cherubs sat upon the *kapporeth*, a pure gold covering for the top of the box, also known as the Mercy Seat. The cherubs faced one another, their wings outstretched and touching. The Jewish people considered the Ark to be the only man-made object that was holy, the spiritual manifestation of the *shekinah* glory of God.

Michael wondered what the world would think of the artifact that stood against the wall across from the Ark. The seven-branched menorah was a surprise for the Jewish nation at the dedication ceremony of the Temple; only a select few knew it had been discovered along with the Ark of the Covenant. The huge candle stand had been hammered from one solid piece of gold. It had once stood in Solomon's Temple; now it would grace the Third Temple.

Michael picked up a pen and started tapping the end of it on the desk as he considered the Ark. At first, Kate had pressured him to open it because she wanted an exclusive interview. They had fought about it for several days before she finally gave in and gave up. It was still a sore point with her. He sighed. He was finding out that his charming wife was a contentious woman. Kate would argue with him about almost everything. How difficult it must be for Micah! Michael thought. His son was gentle and reserved, while his wife was anything but. Kate was loud, opinionated, and vivacious. Their family dinners had become tense lately, when Kate wasn't traveling.

ONE WILL BE LEFT

When he was honest with himself, Michael realized he found work a relief from the pressures at home, and he often stayed there fifteen or sixteen hours to avoid going home. He felt guilty for leaving Micah alone so much with Kate, but the atmosphere of their home was more than he wanted to handle. Retreat was better than constant attack.

Michael walked over to the small desk that had been set up for him in the room. He clicked the computer on and sat behind it. Leaning back, he considered the Ark before him.

The high priest and the government leaders had finally decided that, in respect of the historical and spiritual significance of the Ark, it would not be opened. The Gentile world had exploded in condemnation and disapproval. People wanted to know what was inside.

But Michael had found another way—at least, he hoped he had. He opened the drawer to his right and pulled out the device his inventor friend, Dov Yanai, had given to him a few days before. It was an invention based on a camera that Israelis had developed early in the twenty-first century. Dov told him that he would be able to "see" through the Ark with the device if he chose to use it. As he scanned the Ark, the high-resolution image would be transmitted to the screen on the device. He could even record the process—all without the possibility of damage to the artifact or its contents.

Unfortunately, the high priest had been adamant that the Ark's holiness prohibited any kind of violation. Michael had argued politely that there was little chance of harming the Ark using modern x-ray technology, but the high priest was insistent. He had said it was not the idea of harming the Ark that convinced him to leave its contents undisturbed, but the intrinsic holiness the object possessed, since it had once held the glory of God. Michael would not be permitted to answer the questions he, and the rest of the world, had about the Ark.

But after Dov gave him the device, Michael immediately set about planning on how he would get it past the guards. It looked like a high-tech camera, which was what he passed it off as. No one would know what it really was, even if they saw him on their security videos.

Michael switched on the device, recalling with a bit of trepidation what had happened in ancient times when anyone dared to touch the Ark—they dropped dead! *But I don't need to touch it*, he reassured himself. *I won't touch it.* He picked up the gift from his friend, got up from the desk, and began pointing his specialized camera at the Ark.

Staring intently at the screen, he could just make out the shape of a pot. After he ensured that the recorder was turned on, he followed the curve of the pot. It looked the right size to hold an omer, the portion of manna for one man. *Incredible!* he marveled. He could make out what appeared to be a long piece of wood: the staff of Aaron. God had miraculously caused it to burst forth with buds as a sign to remind the Israelites that they had rejected His authority when they rebelled against their high priest, Aaron. The thought occurred to him that that was exactly what he was doing now, but he pushed the notion aside and continued the recording.

To the right of the pot were two objects stacked on top of each other. According to the built-in measuring system on the camera, the length and width were forty-six centimeters by twenty-three centimeters. They had to be the legendary tablets inscribed with the Ten Commandments! He could make out some faint inscription on one of the stones. His hand started to tremble, and he shut off the device.

His heart pounding violently, Michael sat on the floor in front of the Ark and let the device fall to the floor. His mind was beginning to register what he had just seen. In his memory, he could hear his father speaking to him, again reminding him that God had commanded that those three items be put into the Ark to remind Israel of some of its most disgraceful events. The manna because they had grumbled about God's provision in the desert, the staff because they had rejected His authority, and the stone tablets because they had rejected His laws.

ONE WILL BE LEFT

I have rejected Him, too, Michael thought. *Yet still, He sent Elijah to me so I could find Micah. He let me find the Ark, and now I see everything that was said to be inside is truly there. What else should God do to convince me that He is real and powerful?*

Michael bowed his head and began to pray.

Upstate New York

"Listen, I have *got* to get to Israel!" Andie protested. "My mother has been taken. My brother, Ari, says no one can find her. She begged me to come home, and I refused. If only I had been at that store with her, I could have—" She broke down in sobs.

James tried to console her. "There is no way you could have known this was going to happen. Ari told you there is nothing you can do to help. I'm not sure how we'd even get you out."

Bess sat on the other side of Andie and kept a hand on her shoulder. James knew that Bess was praying quietly. Bess never offered a word of advice unless she prayed first and asked God what He wanted her to say.

Jack came in from the kitchen with a glass of water and offered it to Andie. They all waited while she sipped and slowly calmed down. She wiped her eyes with the end of her plaid flannel shirt.

"Ari still has no clue who took her. There's been no ransom demand, nothing. Surely she was targeted because of our family's wealth? Why else would anyone take her? Do you think she's even alive?" Andie's face was red and patchy from crying.

"Listen, sweetie," Bess began, "I know it's hard not knowing. Believe me, I know! But the thing is that all these questions are what-ifs. We just don't know what's going on, but God knows where your mother is. She loves Him; you told me she does, right?"

"Yes." Andie wiped her face again.

"So, since she loves God and He knows where she is, what

can you think about instead of the maybes and what-ifs?" Bess asked gently.

Andie thought for a moment. "Well, God is in control. He loves my mother. But, Bess, what if the worst happens?"

There was a strained silence for a moment before Bess gently said, "What would be the worst?"

"You know, if she dies," Andie whispered.

Bess sat up a bit straighter and pursed her lips before she began. "If we lived in a different time, I would be a lot gentler with you now, Andie. But we are about to enter the darkest era of human history, the end of days. From what Pastor James says, according to the prophecies in the Bible, only about a third of us are going to make it through to the end. That means two-thirds of us won't." She patted the younger woman's hand affectionately.

"But we have a promise, don't we? Is death the worst thing? No! Not at all. You are young, so you think so, but I know. I've thought long and hard on it because even apart from the times we live in, Jack and I aren't going to live much longer on this earth.

"The worst thing is being dead—spiritually dead—and then dying. Those folks who don't know Jesus, they are dead. If they die without turning to Him, they're going to experience eternal separation from God—and from everything good. That's the worst thing. So there is no worst thing for us, Andie, and not for your mother, either." Bess put her arm around Andie and squeezed her shoulder.

"Why don't we pray for your mom now, Andie?" James asked.

"Yes, please," she answered. They paused their conversation and asked God for His protection over Andie's mother and for His strength and peace to comfort her wherever she was. When they finished, Bess bustled Andie outside with her to milk the goats and help the younger woman take her mind off things.

"Bess will do her best to keep Andie busy," Jack remarked.

James sat down next to him on the couch. "I admit, I do feel guilty that I didn't encourage her to go back to Israel when her mother asked."

"She wouldn't have left you and David anyway."

"No, she really loves David," James agreed.

"She's in love with you, James. You must realize that," Jack said.

James looked at the older man astonished. "What? No, you have it all wrong, Jack. She and I are just friends. She's not in love with me. That's just not possible."

"Well, I hate to disagree with you, Pastor, but you're wrong. Andie Singleton is in love with you. Bess said you were too dim to realize it, but I thought you were just ignoring the issue."

James felt sick to his stomach. "Bess was right. I'm dim, I guess. I really had no clue!" James sat for a moment and contemplated before he continued.

"If it's true, I have no idea what to do about it! I don't love Andie like that. She's a good friend. I totally trust her with David, but I've never considered her, or anyone else, after Cynthia. That part of my life is just…over. I'm a father and a pastor, but romance is just not an option for me.

"Jack, what should I do?"

Jack smiled. "Do? Why do you have to do anything? You know, one thing I used to love to do was to mock all those pithy sayings Christians like my son used. I would just rake him over the coals because I could tell it got under his skin.

"But now I see that the reason folks are attracted to pithy sayings, whether they're Christian ones or not, is that there's some truth in them. While you were talking, this one came to my mind: 'Let go and let God.'"

"What's that supposed to mean?" James asked.

"Well, I think in this situation it means, don't plan out what your life is going to be like. Let God bring His plan about instead, without you trying to orchestrate it. What if He wants you to get married again?"

"There's no way after what happened with Cynthia," James insisted.

"But God is an expert in making a way through impossible

situations, isn't He? Aren't you fond of quoting 'with God all things are possible,' James?" Jack asked humorously.

"But—" James began to protest again.

"Listen, I'm not saying it will happen for you again, James. I'm not even telling you that you have to like her that way. I don't know what's in God's plan. I'm just saying, don't limit Him. Andie is a wonderful young woman. She loves you, and she loves your boy. Why not pray and ask God to show you if it's something He wants for you and for David?"

James was at a loss for words. He thought of how much Andie had done for David—and for him. He recalled how he had been relieved when she'd decided not to return to Israel when she'd had the chance. Was it only because of David?

"Thanks, Jack. I appreciate all you've said to me. I think I'll go for a walk. I promise I'll pray about it." James patted Jack's shoulder and headed out the door.

As he walked along the trail from Jack and Bess's house to the resort grounds, he saw Bess and Andie out in the field next to the barn. Bess had the kids in the pen where she kept them from their mothers at night. Andie was milking one of the mothers on the other side of the fence. James stopped for a minute and watched.

Andie was sitting on a small stool at the back of the goat. He smiled as she brushed back her hair with the back of her hand. Her hair was always coming loose and falling into her eyes. He wondered for a minute what it would look like if it were all loose instead of pulled back in the bun she always wore.

He laughed out loud when the goat kicked over the bucket and all of the milk splattered across the grass. Milking goats was not one of Andie's favorite things to do. He could guess what she was saying to Bess! His laughter died on his lips.

"There just is no way, Lord! I sinned against You with Cynthia. I fell hard because of the weakness of my own flesh, and I sure don't want to go there again. I know there's nothing wrong with marriage, but I have my ministry. I have so many people depending on me. There's no way I could add one more." He prayed out loud as he walked back toward the cabin where David was sleeping.

It is not good for man to be alone. Let Us make him a helper. The words he had read only yesterday in the book of Genesis screamed at him from his own mind—or were they really from his own mind?

"You surely didn't mean me, Lord!" He looked up at the sky, searching for an answer as the wispy clouds moved slowly across the crystal sky. Silence. James thought back to his short marriage to Cynthia. Already by their wedding reception, he'd realized he'd made a mistake, but he had been determined to make it work. He sighed. *If only she were different! Even after You healed her, Lord, her heart was so hard. Was that what You were showing me? Was that why I saw her in New York? Why did You use me to heal her? What is it I'm supposed to do now?*

As he walked along the path, James heard a quiet voice speak to his heart as the Spirit of God reminded him of God's unending love. He could feel the tug in his heart between enjoying the sweetness of Andie's character and detesting the bitterness of Cynthia's. He sank down to his knees.

"I could marry Andie. I know before You, I am free to do that," he told God quietly. "I know I would be happy with her, but I'm afraid." James felt his heart race at the thought of opening himself up to someone else.

"I'm so confused, Father," he whispered, "show me what to do. In the meantime, help me set aside bitterness towards Cynthia. You've been so good to forgive me; help me to forgive her. Save her…"

James got up from the ground. His eyes were gritty with the tears he'd shed as he prayed, but his heart felt peaceful and hopeful.

ONE WILL BE LEFT

Jerusalem, Israel

Mara took the bottle out of the mug of hot water she'd been warming it up in. She swirled the milk and then tested the heat on her wrist over the sink. She could hear the men speaking in low tones in the living room behind her. As she walked into the room, her husband, Ari, started speaking louder about some new experiment he was working on.

She snorted. "You'll have to do better than that, Ari Singleton! You know I have the hearing of a bat. I heard what you two were talking about.

"Here's Juliana's bottle." She handed the bottle to DC.

"I want to know what you found out from the prime minister too." She sat on the couch next to her husband and curled her feet up, snuggling close to him.

DC shook his head at Ari. "I told you we had to tell her." He looked down at his daughter as he fed her, enamored with her beauty and how much she looked like her mother. "Mara, we are going to get Teo and Rhetta back."

Mara looked at her husband. "We? Are you going with DC?"

"Yes, I know you want me to stay here, but I can help DC get into New Babylon. You know that Giamo International is setting up its flagship clinic boutique, Metamorphosis, right? I can call my liaison there and ask for a private tour for a VIP from Israel."

"Who's the VIP?" she asked.

"Angelina Rogov, the prime minister's daughter," DC answered.

"I can't believe the prime minister would allow his daughter to do that. You know about the kidnapping attempt on her and her daughter a few months ago," Mara protested.

"Actually, it was DC who thwarted the attempt, not the police as was reported. That story was put out to help protect DC and Teo

ONE WILL BE LEFT

from being discovered. DC just finished telling me the whole story," Ari explained.

"The prime minister is extremely grateful, as is his daughter," Ari continued. "They both have great affection for DC because he saved little Charlie. Angelina feels responsible for not being able to stop Teo and my mother from being taken."

Mara interrupted her husband. "Well, there was nothing she could have done to stop it! Then Juliana would be gone, too!"

They all looked at the baby. DC noticed the bottle was already empty and Juliana had fallen asleep still sucking on it. Pulling the bottle slowly out of her mouth, he tipped her gently up over his shoulder and patted her back until he heard the soft burp. He continued to rub her back as he spoke in a soft tone.

"I'm grateful to both Angelina and her father. Prime Minister Rogov recruited his best advisors in the Mossad to plan the operation. We cannot explain everything, but the part you can know is that Ari will be escorting Angelina, along with her security team, to the new clinic in New Babylon. Because she is the prime minister's daughter and the New World Union is trying to negotiate a treaty with Israel, we expect that the Italian ambassador will invite her to his home."

"DC! You know what he is!" Mara protested.

"I do, and I know he has them there. The agent the Mossad has planted in Luca's household knows there are two women being kept in Stephen Amona's residence. There have been rumors about some mysterious illness plaguing Amona. Just about every doctor in New Babylon has made a house call to his residence."

"The two women have to be my mother and Teo!" Ari exclaimed. "So, you see, we have to do this, Mara. We have to try and rescue them."

"I know you do. I wish there were some way I could help you."

"You can," DC assured her. "You can take care of Juliana for me and pray for us. We need a lot of prayer for this to work, and we can't tell anyone else. The fewer people in the loop, the less chance we have of being found out."

"So I can't tell Andie when I talk to her online?" Mara asked. "You know she's frantic about your mother."

Ari shook his head negatively. His twin sister lived in upstate New York in an enclave of believers. One of them was James Martin, one of the most well-known Christian leaders in the world, thanks to the development of the subnet. Pastor James' teaching videos and blog were some of the first to be broadcast through the Deep Web on a secret intranet site. Andie had been in Washington, DC, when the rapture took place and had become a follower of Christ not long after. Although their mother had begged her to come back to Jerusalem, Andie wouldn't leave New York. Ari sensed his twin sister was in love with someone in her new community, even if she refused to acknowledge it.

"No, we can't chance it. I know it's supposed to be secure, but we just don't know what the enemy can access, either through the Web or in other ways," Ari explained.

"What other ways could there be?" Mara asked, a bit uneasy.

"We're not sure," DC answered. "Think about it, though. The Antichrist gets help from something powerful to do all that he's going to be able to do—or is able to do already."

"You mean the devil and his demons?"

"Yes, and although Angelina is not a believer in Jesus, she has described just such creatures to me. She's seen them several times and describes them as fierce-looking, evil men, large and physically imposing. She saw some just before Teo was taken."

"We don't know if or how they communicate with Luca Giamo," Ari added.

"What prevents them from hearing whatever we say then?" Mara asked, pulling her sweater a bit tighter around her narrow shoulders.

"I believe God protects us, but that doesn't mean we're always going to outwit the enemy. We all know how few people will survive the next few years. Regardless of the danger, we have to try to rescue them." DC finished speaking, stood up, and handed the baby carefully to Mara.

"I know she'll be safe in your care, Mara. The prime minister has assigned men to guard the house while we're gone and watch you and Juliana when you go out. You will not be alone."

He bent over and kissed his daughter's head. "I love you, Jules," he murmured affectionately, then turned to Mara and Ari. "I'll leave the two of you alone to say good-bye. Thank you, Mara." He smiled down at her and left the room.

Ari took her free hand. "I'm sorry I have to leave."

"No, you have to try to get your mother back, and Teo. This baby needs her mother."

"This is our best shot. With Angelina there, we should have access to where Teo's being kept."

"Does Angelina know what she's facing there?" Mara asked quietly.

"What do you mean?"

"Has DC told her who Luca is?"

"No. I mean, he's told her that Luca is evil. If she can see demons, she'll see that for herself. We decided not to reveal what we know about him to nonbelievers. There's no point, really. What help would it be? It makes us look nutty."

"I suppose, but I'd want to know!" Mara whispered fiercely.

"But you believe the Scriptures. They don't. To them it's foolishness, and if we talk about it, they'll only think we are as well. Remember, we are to be wise as serpents!"

"Yes, Ari, as long as you are innocent as doves, too! I just don't like the idea of that young woman going into the viper's den and not knowing what she is facing. It feels like you are using her."

"This was her idea! One of us will be with her at all times. It will be fine. Really, soon we'll be back here with Teo and my mother. Let's pray now before I go. Please?"

Together, they implored God for His help in rescuing the women they loved so dearly, Teo and Rhetta.

21

WASHINGTON, DC

The satin sheets slipped to the floor when Cynthia stood up. She stretched slowly, aware that Andres Quinteros, the most powerful man in North America, was admiring her slender, taut figure.

She turned to face him. "That was incredible, my love! You surprise me every time!"

He got up from the bed and embraced her. "I've never met such an intoxicating woman! Truly. I have eyes for no one else."

"Not even your wife?" Cynthia was careful to keep her tone light and teasing. Andres was easily angered. His wrath hadn't been directed at her—yet. But she would never forget the sight of him choking a woman to death because she spilled coffee on him during one of their intimate dinners at the Ritz-Carlton apartment. They'd been out on the balcony enjoying dessert. Andres had asked for more coffee, and the young woman's hand shook as she poured, spilling some on Andres's shirtsleeve. Cynthia had been too horrified even to protest when he threw the dead woman's body over the roof.

She looked up at him now with a charming smile.

Andres pushed her away gently. "Listen, my Thia, Patricia is my wife and is expecting our first son, my only child. There will never be a place for you by my side in public. But I promise you that I will not have anyone else but you by my side in private."

He pulled her back into his arms and kissed her passionately, then left the bedroom to take a shower.

Cynthia sat down on the bed. She'd been seeing Andres for

months. When they'd first met, she'd played hard to get. She knew men well, and the president of the North American sector was no different than any other man, except his temper was more unpredictable. She knew for a fact that he'd had many mistresses when they'd first met, but she believed he had been honest about his fidelity this morning. She knew, because she'd befriended one of the maids who worked at the White House, Doris. Oh, sweet Doris.

Cynthia stood up and cinched her silk robe tightly around her waist as she recalled how she'd orchestrated the initial meeting with Doris at a grocery store. She'd been careful to disguise herself, wearing a brown wig and heavy makeup. As Doris wheeled her cart down the aisle, Cynthia had knocked a jar of pickles on the floor. Doris had offered to help right away, and Cynthia had invited her to have coffee at the small café in the store. They met for coffee every week now.

She walked over to the mirror and picked up the hairbrush. Brushing her hair, she considered her next move. According to Doris, Andres never slept in the same bedroom as his wife. Doris said she never saw them together in the private apartments at the White House. The heavily pregnant Patricia spent much of her days meeting with staff regarding the rebuilding projects around the city. The First Lady was intent on restoring Washington, indeed improving it. Doris said there was a lot of work being done inside of the White House and on the grounds.

Cynthia stared at herself in the mirror, dispassionately evaluating her reflection. She knew she was beautiful. Her golden red hair cascaded over her shoulders and down her back. The media celebrated her pale green eyes and her luscious figure. She was rich. She was a celebrity. "It's not enough," she whispered at her reflection. Emptiness gnawed at her thoughts as she considered her options.

Andres came back into the bedroom, grabbed his cell phone and briefcase, said good-bye to her, and left. She migrated out of the bedroom and onto the terrace. It was another hot, humid summer day in DC. She loved this weather. Taking off her robe, she stretched out on one of the canvas lounge chairs and mulled over her situation. Picking up the phone on the table next to her, she rang one of the staff to bring her a mimosa.

As she lay out in the gleaming sun, she thought of a friend who might be of help. He was a bit of a troubled soul—a cousin of hers, Maxwell Adams. They'd been lovers for awhile in high school, but had remained good friends when Cynthia had grown tired of him romantically. She recalled the first time he'd showed her his secret room. The walls and ceiling were painted black and had strange emblems embossed on them in gold and red. Chunky, large candles sat on tables, and torches hung along the walls; the room had no electric lights. Maxwell was a Satan worshipper. He had introduced her to the occult. She'd practiced for a time, but grew bored of the exaggerated drama of the black candles, Ouija boards, and tarot cards. Nothing ever really happened. It kind of seemed like a charade.

Maxwell insisted that he did have powerful experiences, especially when he found the right method of contacting the spirit world. He was cagey about what it was, but from the veiled comments he had made over the years, she suspected it involved a sacrifice of some kind. *To each his own!* she thought.

The heat of the sun made her skin feel taut. Maxwell was an interior decorator of some renown. If she could convince him to apply to the White House project, he might be able to strike up a friendship with the First Lady. Maxwell could be quite charming. Cynthia smiled as her plans took shape. Her cousin was also quite knowledgeable about poisons.

She doesn't have to die, Cynthia told herself, *just lose that damned baby. He's the only obstacle to me living in the White House, at Andres's side as his wife. All Maxwell needs to do is find the right thing and wait for an opportunity to put it in her drink.*

Maxwell had said something once about child sacrifice being one of the most potent offerings to the spirits, that there was great power to be gained from it. In fact, his current wife, Vera, a famous abortionist, had been the one to introduce the idea to Maxwell.

ONE WILL BE LEFT

Cynthia recalled a conversation between the two that she'd heard when she'd been at their house for a cocktail party. The striking doctor was the center of attention. Cynthia could see why her cousin was so smitten; Vera was charismatic and very charming. The inebriated crowd listened in silence as she spoke.

Vera boasted that her spirit guide, Elihiel, grew more powerful with every "offering" the doctor made in her clinic. Since the women were usually sedated, they didn't hear her offering the child's life to her guide in prayer. When she first started offering to Elihiel, nothing happened. But after a few weeks, the spirit guide began manifesting in the clinic room where the abortions took place. After a few more weeks, the spirit would actually unite himself with Vera and perform the task using her body.

Now Vera was able to summon the spirit at will, and she actually did so right in front of the crowd in her own living room. Cynthia recalled rolling her eyes at the mysticism, only to stare in disbelief as she saw the guide materialize next to Vera. The spirit guide was massive. At first, its body was misty, but it took on substance and grew thicker and more tangible with every second.

Cynthia didn't remember much of what happened after that. There had been screaming, and things flew around the room; vases smashed against walls. The rest was a blur. She'd woken up the next morning on the floor. Others were passed out throughout the house.

Cynthia had picked her way through the unconscious bodies on the floor, looking for her cousin and Vera. She found them drinking coffee in the kitchen.

"I want one, Vera," she'd said.

"A coffee?"

"No, I want a guide like yours." Cynthia held Vera's dark gaze and trembled a bit, sensing that more than Vera was looking back at her.

It had taken her months to find a guide and persuade it to take her as its servant. Vera and Maxwell had led her through the appropriate ceremonies and experiences. Some had been humiliating, others painful; but finally, Hiliah had joined himself with her.

ONE WILL BE LEFT

He never manifested himself to her the way Elihiel did with Vera, though. He was not as powerful, but Cynthia saw him in her dreams every night. She would ask Hiliah about her plan. He wanted her to succeed. Indeed, it was his power and influence that gave her such favor with Andres and others. He would show her what to do.

Cynthia rolled over on the lounge chair and went to sleep.

Prime Minister's Residence, Jerusalem, Israel

The prime minister's home was completely packed; even the foyer was full. As King Zayd bin Asem made his way through the crowd with his uncle trailing behind, he greeted news anchor Kate Benari. Her world-renowned archaeologist husband was with her as well. They were standing close to the patio door leading to the garden. Zayd could hear "The Impossible Duet" being played somewhere in the gardens. In his opinion, the passacaglia seemed like menacing background music for such a festive occasion. He turned to his uncle and introduced him to the archaeologist, speaking loudly to be heard over the music and the crowd around them.

"Mr. Benari!" Rasheed had to practically shout. "I must ask you if the Israeli government is still quite firm in its decision not to open the Ark or explore its contents in any way?"

"I'm sorry, sir, that is the case. The Ark will be carried into the Holy of Holies unexamined," Michael replied. Zayd noted the look of irritation on Kate's face.

"Ah, you disagree with this, Mrs. Benari?" he asked.

"Yes, Your Highness, I do disagree. I think this relic belongs to the world, not just Israel. I've tried my best to change the minds of the governing authorities, believe me!" Kate pursed her lips tightly.

The music stopped for a moment, and the crowd quieted as the prime minister entered the room with his entourage. Suddenly, a loud burst of laughter punctuated the quieted room, and people turned to see who it was.

Zayd stared at the woman laughing across the room, a look of bemusement on his face. The slender woman was looking down at a small, dark-haired toddler. The child had a cat by the tail and was dragging it toward the garden door. Everyone in the room watched and chuckled as the little girl scolded the cat for coming in the house. Zayd kept his eyes on the woman. The mass of freckles that dusted the nose and cheeks of the brunette woman were striking. Rather than detracting from her beauty, they highlighted the intense brown of her eyes.

"Who is that?" he asked Kate, nodding in the direction of the young woman.

"That's the prime minister's daughter, Angelina Rogov. The little girl is her daughter, Charlie. Charlie is the prime minister's pride and joy."

"Oh, she's married." He turned back to face the others, disappointed.

"No, she's not. Her husband died under some rather strange circumstances a few months ago. No one is sure what happened. It was a boating accident, but there were no witnesses," Kate explained.

"What was strange about it?" Uncle Rasheed asked.

"Well, someone had tried to kidnap the prime minister's granddaughter earlier in the week. There was a huge custody battle for the girl going on between Angelina and her husband, and some think he was behind the kidnapping attempt and that he was neutralized by Israeli agents as a consequence."

"Kate, I really wish you would not say such things here," Michael whispered to his wife in a strained tone.

"Oh, it's quite alright, Mr. Benari. I'm aware of all the gossip going on about me."

Zayd turned to see that the young woman he had been admiring was standing by his side. She was even more delightful up close. He took her hand in greeting, kissed it, and let his hand linger on hers.

ONE WILL BE LEFT

"Ms. Rogov, it is my pleasure to meet you," he said.

"And I you, Your Highness." Angelina made a curtsy that revealed her impeccable upbringing. She gently pulled her hand from his, extending it to his uncle. "A pleasure to meet you as well, Mr. Rasheed bin Jamil." She smiled up at him, revealing dimples on either side of her mouth. Zayd had never found a woman so intriguing. He listened to her speak to his uncle in fluid Arabic, quoting from a passage in one of the older man's historical novels. Rasheed was quite flattered by her interest, and Zayd waited impatiently for a break in their conversation.

When his uncle stopped speaking to take a breath, Zayd quickly asked her if she would show him the gardens. Nodding in agreement, Angelina led the way through the crowded room out to the garden at the back of the residence. She laughed again when she saw her daughter in one of the flowerbeds, her white chiffon dress covered with dirt. Charlie turned toward them, and Zayd could see the dirt was smeared on her face too. Charlie ran across the grass toward them, holding out a bunch of flowers she'd picked.

"Mama! Mama! Look here! These are for you!" She handed them up to her mother.

Zayd watched with interest as Angelina bent over and picked up her daughter, careless of her own dress.

"Oh, Charlie! Those are so beautiful!" Angelina kissed the toddler's dirty cheek.

The little girl hugged her mother, then turned in her arms and faced Zayd.

"Who you?" she demanded. Zayd saw she had the same eyes and dusting of freckles, a perfect miniature of her mother, and completely charming.

"Charlie, this is King Zayd bin Asem. He is the King of Jordan," Angelina said.

"Oh, hi." The little girl offered her hand to him.

Zayd took it and shook it with a serious expression on his face. "It is a pleasure to meet you, Miss Charlie."

ONE WILL BE LEFT

Just then, an older woman came out from the house, scolding both the daughter and her mother. She clucked, took the toddler away from Angelina, and went back into the house, shaking her head and calling out reproofs.

Angelina chuckled, "That's my Yona! She is very determined Charlie will not turn out like her mother!" She craned her neck back to look up at him. It wasn't something Zayd was used to, but Angelina was extremely petite. "How are you enjoying Jerusalem, Your Highness?"

"Please call me Zayd," he insisted. "It's a beautiful city, the eternal city." He gestured to the view of the Old City they had from the terrace.

"It's a troubled city," she said. "Despite all the movement toward peace in the world, through the World Union and now the New World Union, Jerusalem still is a place of conflict, as is all Israel. I often wonder why it is that the world hates us."

Zayd looked down at her, wondering at the depths behind those brown eyes.

"My Uncle Rasheed says it will be so until the 'times of the Gentiles' are over," he found himself saying, without thinking.

"What is that?"

"Forgive me, I know that as a Jewish woman, the name of Yeshua may be distasteful to you, but the phrase is from a prophecy that He gave concerning Jerusalem."

She snorted. "Oh, I'm not bothered by what others believe. I've had some experiences recently that have caused me to explore my faith, but I've not been observant at all. My father, of course, is. What is the prophecy?"

Closing his eyes, Zayd recited from memory, "And they will fall by the edge of the sword, and will be led captive into all the nations; and Jerusalem will be trampled underfoot by the Gentiles until the times of the Gentiles are fulfilled."

"But we have had Jerusalem in our control for decades now!" Angelina protested.

ONE WILL BE LEFT

"Yes, that is so." Zayd closed his mouth tightly, not wanting to upset her. He turned away to view the city again.

Out of the corner of his eye he could see Angelina scrutinize him intently before asking, "What exactly does this prophecy mean? I've seen some incredibly unbelievable things in the last few months, and I don't want to discount anything that might be helpful to my country. What does the phrase 'times of the Gentiles' refer to?"

Still looking at the view before them, Zayd replied, "My uncle, Rasheed, has been studying this intently. He told me that this time period began long ago, when Nebuchadnezzar destroyed Jerusalem."

Angelina cut in. "Yes, the prophet Daniel talked about him. I remember. He was a Babylonian king and he had a dream about a large statue. A head of gold, I think?"

"That's right. Those statue parts represent various Gentile nations that have dominated this area for millennia. We are now at the point of time represented by the feet of clay and iron." He turned again to her. "The feet—"

"Ten toes!" she exclaimed. "And now there are ten rulers! The World Union reorganized into ten sectors. It bothered me for a while, and I couldn't think of why, but I do remember that story from long ago. Now I know why it didn't sit right! But you're saying that now we're at the point in history represented by the toes?"

"That's right. Do you recall what happened to the statue in the dream?"

"It fell and smashed to pieces?" she guessed, wrinkling her nose. Zayd found it delightful and admired her for a moment before he answered.

"No, a small stone struck it, and it broke into pieces and became like chaff in the wind. The stone became a great kingdom that will never end."

"Since the dream was recorded in Daniel, and he was a great prophet in Israel, surely the stone must be Israel?" she asked.

"I suppose one might think so." Zayd wanted to be diplomatic. This was the daughter of the Israeli prime minister, after all.

"It seems you don't think so," Angelina remarked. "What do you think? You can be honest with me, really."

"Well, Uncle showed me how, in the Old Testament, the term 'rock' was used to represent God. And this 'rock' in Daniel's prophecy was cut out, but not by human hands. Uncle believes the rock represents the Messiah."

Angelina stared up at him intently, her eyes full of genuine emotion. Zayd couldn't read what she was feeling. "I used to think the Messiah was a fairy tale told to children to give them false hope that God would rescue Israel."

"Has He not? Surely you can see His hand in destroying the armies who massed against Israel, and that He destroyed the Dome of the Rock, allowing the Temple to be rebuilt?" Zayd looked incredulous.

"I've seen some things myself," Angelina responded in a hushed tone, "and a good friend has told me more. He's talked with me about Yeshua, too. He believes that Yeshua was the Messiah." She sighed. "That's hard for me to believe, though, because of who I am and how I was raised." She spoke softly, looking around to make sure there was no one around to overhear. "But if we are truly living in the time where we are at the base of that statue in Daniel, and that destruction is coming, I must know the truth."

Angelina patted Zayd's hand on the balustrade. "Enough heavy talk! Let's change the subject. I'm going to New Babylon tomorrow. Have you ever been there?"

"Yes, indeed, I have." Zayd followed her lead. "It's an astonishing place. The architects and builders succeeded in making it a world wonder, that's for sure. What will you be doing there?"

"Oh, sightseeing, shopping, and attending the opening of Giamo International's new clinic, Metamorphosis." She noticed the crowd was heading back indoors. "I think dinner is ready. Shall we go in?" Angelina took his arm casually.

22

WASHINGTON, DC

Patricia looked around the nursery with satisfaction. The glider on which she was sitting on was upholstered in creamy white velvet and decorated with lush, blue throw pillows. White, wispy curtains fluttered over the windows, and the floor was covered in a luxurious handwoven Moroccan rug in a blue ikat pattern. The walls were tinted with a special paint her designer had concocted. Patricia looked at the rich, old-world color with satisfaction. Who knew milk could be used as paint? Not only was the effect charming, but there were no harsh chemicals that could adversely affect her son. She patted her stomach fondly. *Six more weeks*, she thought.

"Are you counting the days, sister?" Marc walked into the nursery unannounced.

Patricia nodded, feeling very agreeable. "I am indeed! What are the reports from Florida?"

Marc's face grew somber. "It's not good. The southern part of the state is completely devastated. The hurricane stalled over the area. There were two hundred-mile-an-hour winds whipping across it! Buildings collapsed and houses were blown right off their foundations, not to mention major flooding. The flood waters still haven't receded." He paused to open the bottle of water in his hand and tipped it back to drink. Wiping his mouth with the back of his hand, he shared his concerns about Andres with his sister.

"Andres decided not to allow National Broadcasting to air video of the devastation. He's ordered his own news team to produce reports."

"Why's that?" Patricia asked.

"The storm has killed thousands of people. Tens of thousands. Whole towns have been wiped away by the wind gusts and flooding, and from what the weather forecasters tell, this hurricane isn't weakening or going away any time soon. It's now heading back out to the Gulf, toward New Orleans. He's afraid people will panic and begin looting.

"The storm has also spawned tornadoes. The National Weather Service is still trying to get a count, but there's only a skeleton crew left of that agency in the Silver Spring office in Maryland. We're relying on the group in Fort Worth. Apparently, there's not been a storm like this in recorded history." Marc quickly left the room to pour himself a glass of scotch, then came back and plopped down on a chair next to his sister. He sipped on his drink and admired the nursery artwork for a moment. "Andres wants to keep people calm, I guess. He said there's no way they can evacuate everyone. He's sending in teams of soldiers to rescue essential personnel."

"Well, that's certainly cold-blooded," she remarked, her green eyes snapping with anger.

"That's your husband. How long do we have to wait, Patricia?"

Patricia noticed Marc run his hand through his hair the way he had as a boy whenever he was afraid, and her anger intensified. "I don't know. Luca promised that he would take care of Andres. Know this, I will rule with much more compassion than my husband! My son will have a vigorous and wealthy nation to rule one day, and this sort of ruthlessness will only cause our sector go the way of other totalitarian regimes. We'll see to it that things will change once Luca has removed Andres." She patted her stomach affectionately. "He moves a lot, unless Andres is around. It's almost as if he senses Andres is dangerous."

"How could an unborn child sense anything, Patricia? I think your hormones are affecting your reasoning," he joked.

Patricia glared at her brother. "This is not just any human being. I'm telling you, he's aware even now."

"How could you possibly know that?"

She closed her eyes and her expression softened. "I don't know how to explain it, Marc. I can touch him with my thoughts.

"The first time it happened, I was just waking up. I could feel someone trying to communicate with me mentally, the way Luca does. So I opened up my mind to the experience, and my baby began to communicate with me." The corners of her eyes filled with warm tears, but they didn't spill over.

"What does he say?" Marc asked quietly. His sister was not a woman given to fantasies.

"There are no real words, just impressions of things. When Andres is around, the baby stops communicating with me. It's as if he's afraid Andres will hear."

Marc downed the rest of the scotch quickly and could feel it warming his stomach. He felt fearful. "Is Andres able to communicate with others telepathically too? Can he read minds?" His voice cracked.

Patricia opened her eyes and stared at her brother. "I don't know. He grows stronger every day, and I cannot always read his thoughts now. There's some sort of psychic cloud covering him. I sense there is some danger to us, but I don't know where it comes from.

"I've been trying to discern when this shrouding happened, which will enable me to better figure out the source. Andres is dangerous enough, but if he has the ability to read our thoughts, you know what he's capable of doing."

Marc leaned closer to his sister and whispered, "I do. We've seen him do it to others. He lulls his victims into a false sense of security, fattening them with his friendship and affection. At the time when they feel the most honored and valued by Andres, he strikes in the most vicious way possible.

"If he finds out that Luca has promised to remove him from power and give the North American sector to you, Andres will kill us all—including the child!"

ONE WILL BE LEFT

Patricia paled. She could feel the fear emanating from her baby. There was a real threat to their welfare. She might not be able to wait for Luca to intervene, but he had been extremely clear about his agenda. She thought back to what he'd told her.

"I am going to gain considerable power in the New World Union when I broker a peace treaty between the Union and Israel," he had confided in her. "Once I've done that, I will remove those who stand in my way. Andres is one who opposes me. He will be removed, but in my time and manner."

Closing her eyes, she repeated Luca's words to her brother.

"Do you have confidence that Luca is able to protect you at this great distance?" Marc asked. "He's in New Babylon, after all!"

Patricia stood up and began pacing, caressing her burgeoning belly protectively. "He is more powerful than you can imagine, Marc, but he has not yet come into his kingdom. There are pockets of resistance even among those we serve. They are united in their hatred of our enemy, but still not a cohesive group."

Marc was perplexed. "What do you mean? Who is this 'enemy?' This is the first time you've mentioned such a thing. And whom are you serving besides Luca? I don't understand."

Patricia stopped pacing and looked her brother in the eyes. "This world did not 'evolve,' Marc. It was seeded with life long ago by beings much more advanced than mankind. Mankind was meant to honor and serve these beings for eternity.

"Some sort of coup happened, and my ancestors valiantly fought against a tyrant, who took control over their realm. This tyrant planted false ideas within the human consciousness, making himself out to be the progenitor of the human race and thus their god. He even went so far as to have one of his cohorts become human and pose as mankind's savior."

Marc sat stunned. "You mean the God of the Bible, and Jesus Christ?"

"That's what they call themselves, but in reality, it is Luca's Father who is the rightful god. Now, after many battles throughout the solar system, he has finally regained enough power to challenge this usurper. Luca is the true messiah, the savior of mankind.

"My siblings and I are linked to him, unique among humanity, as he is. I'm bound to obey and serve him, but until he is in complete control, there are still dangers facing us."

Marc stood up and walked over to his sister, his brows furrowed in confusion. "This sounds like science fiction."

"I know," she smiled tiredly at him, "but it's true. How arrogant mankind has been to ever suppose they are the only intelligent beings in the universe."

"I guess that's true. I've never thought much about it, but even if all you're saying is correct, we still have to deal with Andres," he insisted.

"No, we can't 'deal' with Andres. Luca made it clear that he will take care of Andres at the right time. He needs a strong man to dominate this sector until he's able to take his rightful place."

Marc shuddered. "Trish, we can't take the chance. If he knows what's being planned…"

"Let me communicate with Luca. I'm sure he can discover the source of the threat. Once he does, you and I will take care of it—together, as we always have."

Marc took his sister's hand and kissed it. "Together, as always."

New Babylon, Iraq

"So you see, Father, everything you railed about for years as being foolish was really true. God does exist. He created the world and all that's in it. Those who followed Jesus were right."

Arturo looked down at his daughter. There was no way to tell exactly how long it had been since Luca had left them, but it had to have been many hours. Arturo wasn't sure how much time they had left. He assumed the sacrifice would happen at night, like the others.

He reached forward and stroked her cheek. "I've known for quite some time that I'm a fool."

"Oh no, Father, that's not what I meant!"

"I know you didn't. I have rejected God all of my life. Instead, I made myself a god. I took what I wanted, did what I wanted. I loved your mother, Teo, but I destroyed her. When I did that, part of me was devastated, but another part relished doing it." He sighed, pulling his hand away and rocking back and forth slightly in his chair.

"When my only son died, I knew deep down in my heart that God existed, and I hated Him for taking my son to punish me for my sins. I found a way to get my boy back, but your mother refused to cooperate with my plans. That's why our marriage ended.

"My good friend Stephen convinced me that I could have a son, a perfect son made in the image I designed. In all of the time I've suffered here, I've seen the result of my pride. Luca is a monstrosity, pure evil." Arturo's voice lowered to a whisper. "But I found out he is nothing I created, Teo. He's not just human. He is the son of the devil."

Teo knelt on the floor by her father's side. She pulled herself up higher, her hands grasping the arms of his wheelchair, and put her head against his forehead, the way she had as a young girl when she'd wanted to share a secret with him.

"He's the Antichrist warned about in the Bible," she whispered. "Luca is going to rule the world, bringing more destruction on it than history has ever recorded."

"Then we have to kill him," Arturo whispered fiercely, adamant about his decision. Slowly, he pulled something out from under his right leg. "I've made this over the past few months. I believe they call it a 'shank' in American prisons." He chuckled wryly.

"They accidentally gave me two spoons one day, so I kept this one." He showed her the spoon. The handle was sharpened to a ragged point, and the round part was wrapped with fibers he'd meticulously pulled from his robe to make a better grip.

ONE WILL BE LEFT

"No, I don't think he can be killed, unfortunately. It's written that he will rule the world for seven years. Besides, there are all of the guards to get past, and you can't..." Teo shook her head and sank back onto the floor.

Arturo put his weapon down carefully, placed both hands on the wheelchair and stood up. He hobbled quickly up and down the room, demonstrating his dexterity on his feet, before sitting back down in the wheelchair.

"I've been able to walk for some time now. I get up at night and practice. They don't bother monitoring me anymore. I've used my time well."

Teo opened her mouth to respond, but there was a sound outside of the door. Arturo quickly made sure his weapon was not visible and then hunched down in his chair, putting on a melancholic, dejected expression.

Brempton entered with Howell. Teo stood up and moved beside her father.

"It's almost time now!" Brempton's voice was high-pitched as he squealed, "Master's coming! Dinner is over, and now it's time for dessert! Howell and Brempton get dessert tonight. Master promised us!" Teo swore he was foaming at the mouth like a rabid dog.

Arturo moved his right hand slowly down and grasped the weapon in his hand under the blanket that covered his legs. He pondered his next move as the two men gabbled back and forth about what they intended to do to his daughter.

"That will be enough." Luca entered the room, elegantly attired in a custom-made tuxedo. "I'm sorry for the delay. The Israeli prime minister's daughter is here in New Babylon and I had to extend hospitality to her. I'm hoping to get her father to sign a special treaty with me soon." He laughed. "Not that you will be around to see it, Teo. But you, Father, will see me take my rightful place very soon."

Teo snapped at her younger brother. "You know you won't win, Luca. It's prophesied, and every word will be fulfilled. Birds will feast on the carcasses of your followers, and the Lord Jesus Himself will cast you and that false prophet Billings Mason into the lake of fire."

"That is not what my true Father has told me," he sneered at her.

"Your true father? He's been a liar and a murderer from the beginning. He will be dealt with, too. This is futile, Luca! I'm sure you can still repent. Please, turn away from—"

He interrupted her, snickering. "From what? To what? You follow that Nazarene, but he died on a bloody piece of wood millennia ago. A dead man cannot stop me. I'm immortal."

Luca turned from her to his faithful followers. "Brempton and Howell, you can do what you want to her while I'm gone. I've decided to take the prime minister's daughter on a night tour of New Babylon. She's quite an attractive young woman." He snickered. "When you are finished with Teo, you can prepare her for the sacrifice. I'll return later tonight for the festivities." Luca turned and bowed formally to his sister and Arturo and left the room.

Brempton went to the door and shut it. As the door clicked, Howell approached Teo, grabbing her roughly and yanking her to the bed. Arturo screamed in rage and Teo kicked at the man, tenaciously fighting back. Brempton barreled over to help his friend control her. Arturo waited until Brempton moved right in front of him. With a quick motion, he pummeled the sharpened spoon into Brempton's abdomen and knew instantly he'd hit the aorta. He pulled the shank out and watched with satisfaction as his tormentor fell to the floor, bleeding and gasping.

Strong arms grasped Arturo from behind. *It was Howell!* Arturo made himself go limp, and Howell grunted as both men fell to the ground, Howell on top. Teo jumped on the fiend and grabbed fistfuls of his hair, pulling him back off of her father.

When Howell pulled away, screaming in a frenzied fury, Arturo was able to slide the shank into his gut, cutting his aorta in the same way he had sliced Brempton's.

"Move back, Teo," Arturo commanded. When she moved, he pushed the younger man off him. Howell rolled on the ground, grabbing his abdomen.

ONE WILL BE LEFT

"How?" Howell gasped, blood seeping out between the fingers he had clutched against his stomach.

Arturo and Teo watched in silence as Howell bled to death.

"What do we do now, Father?" she asked. She felt no remorse.

"I don't know. There are other guards out there. I think I've seen six other men during the time I've been here, but there could be more," Arturo answered.

They heard a thud outside in the hallway, and Arturo motioned Teo to move behind him. He stood ready to defend his daughter, the shank gripped tightly in his right hand. The door opened slowly, and a dark-haired man dressed in a tuxedo peered around the door.

"Ari!" Teo rushed to him and flung herself into his arms.

Arturo recognized the young man. Ari Singleton was the scientist who had developed the serum that restored youthful vitality to aging people. His invention had made Giamo Enterprises even more successful.

"What are you doing here?" Arturo asked, suspicious.

Other men, military by the look of them, entered the room. One of them checked for a pulse on one of the two men on the floor while another stood guard at the door.

"We don't have much time. Teo, where are they keeping my mother?" Ari asked.

Teo clutched Ari's arms, looked down, and shook her head in sorrow. Arturo realized with a start that the woman Luca had tried to sacrifice was Ari's mother. *How many more would Luca kill?* the older man wondered.

"We have to move now," one of the men told them, before turning to Ari and clapping him on the back. "I'm sorry, man."

Ari stood motionless, paralyzed by shock and grief.

Everyone else started moving out of the room, but Arturo sat back in his wheelchair, carefully placing his weapon under his right leg.

"Father, what are you doing?" Teo asked. "We have to go now."

"I'm not going. You go, Teo. I created this monster, and I'm going to kill him," Arturo said.

"But we can get out of here. You can come with me. Please!" she begged her father.

"I wish I could, Teo, but I've seen what Luca is. I know what he is planning, and I know that now I'll have a perfect opportunity to stop him when he comes back here tonight. If I'm successful, I'll make my way to you somehow. Now go. I assume DC is somewhere nearby?" he asked Ari.

"Yes," Ari said, snapping back to the present from his daze of sorrow. "We need to go now, Teo. DC couldn't come in here. He would have been recognized, so he's with the exit team waiting."

Teo embraced her father, tearfully kissing his cheek. Arturo watched her leave the room. He sat in the chair, waiting for his son to return.

Jerusalem, Israel

Micah stood in front of the gravestone with his father and best friend. The heat of the morning sun caused sweat to bead on his upper lip. He wiped it off with the back of his hand.

"Are you sure this is his grave?" Joel asked.

"Yes, it is," Michael answered. "The grave of the man who brought the Hebrew language back from its death and made it a living language once again—Eliezer Ben-Yehuda. They say that before Ben-Yehuda, Jews *could* speak Hebrew, and after him, they *did* speak Hebrew!"

Micah pulled the customary small, white stone out of his pocket and placed it on the tomb in front of him to symbolize the permanence of Eliezer's legacy.

"What else would you like to see while we're here, boys?" Michael took a couple of water bottles out of the backpack on the ground and handed one to each of them.

"We'd like to go to Bethany," Joel answered.

Michael took a swig from his own bottle and checked his watch. "Sure. Let's go." They made their way back to the car. "Now that all of Jerusalem is under Israel's control, it's easier to visit these places. I have never been to Bethany. It was always under Palestinian control, at least as long as I've been alive. Mostly Christians wanted to go there; Jews were not allowed," Michael remarked to the boys.

Micah pulled open the passenger door and got into the car. The cloth seat was warm, so he left the door ajar while his father started the car and turned on the air-conditioning.

"Well, you're a Christian now, Papa."

Michael rolled his eyes. "I told you, Micah. I'm a Jew who has accepted that Yeshua is the Messiah. I'm not a—"

"A Christian is a Jew or a Gentile who has chosen to follow Yeshua. Have you not done so?"

"Ah, I guess it is so. You must know that it's a humbling thing for a rational man like me to even admit that there is a God. I've always dealt in what is factual, things I can prove." Michael took a deep breath, wanting to speak carefully.

"I have not been a religious man since your mother died. Now I can't deny there is a God. The God of Israel being a reality is the only reasonable explanation for the events that have taken place in our nation."

He leaned his head on the headrest of his seat as he continued.

"When I read the pages in the New Testament you gave me, Micah, I was moved by the authority with which Jesus spoke. He's the fulfillment of all that the prophets foretold. But I've had to ask myself how I, as a Jew, can become a Christian and truly follow Yeshua, in whose name my people have suffered for thousands of years."

Michael shifted his eyes over to see how his son was responding. He was surprised to see a grin on his face.

"Papa, Yeshua never taught hate. The more you read and

study about Him, and come to know His followers, you will see that His message is one of love and sacrifice. Being a follower of Yeshua makes you more of a true Jew, not less."

After a while, they arrived in Bethany. Their car was covered in a thick layer of gray, dusty dirt. Michael turned the car into a gravel parking lot, pulling in behind another car parked by the curb. He turned off the engine and twisted in his seat so he could see both his son in the front and Joel sitting behind. "I do believe. It's just difficult. And I don't think we should continue our conversation outside the car."

The boys nodded and got out, making their way up the street. Michael followed the boys, who had mapped out their hike the day before. They wanted to follow the path they believed Yeshua had taken from Bethany to the hilltop where he had ascended into heaven. The security fence that had kept people from walking from Bethany over the crest of the Mount of Olives had been torn down and removed.

Michael and the boys left the village behind and climbed the summit of Mount Olivet to the western side. As they scrambled along the path, Joel started singing a song and Micah joined him. Michael listened as they harmonized.

While he walked, Michael noticed the shoelace on his left boot was flailing in the dirt, so he stooped to tie it and fell behind. Suddenly, the boys stopped singing. Michael looked up and saw them kneeling, heads bowed.

Quickly, he made his way to them. He looked around but could not tell what had caused them to stop singing and bow down.

He whispered to Micah, "What happened? Are you okay?"

Micah turned his face upward. "This is where Yeshua ascended into heaven, and this is where he will return. Right here on Mount Olivet."

"Right on this spot?" Michael whispered doubtfully.

"How would we know, Papa?" Micah poked at him playfully. "But in this area, yes, and here He will return. This mountain will be split north to south, opening up a valley in between running east to west."

"Yes, and He will come with his holy ones!" Joel added.

"Who are they?" Michael asked.

"Those followers who have already left the earth," Joel answered again.

Michael thought about that. "Interesting. What are they doing now?"

Micah ran his hand through his hair, grinning. "They are with Yeshua in heaven."

Michael sat down with his back against a rock, next to where his son knelt. He closed his eyes. It occurred to him that those who did not believe in Yeshua would not be in heaven. *I'll never see Devorah again, and if Kate will not believe, she will be separated from me forever, too*, he thought. He sighed.

He felt a hand on his leg. Opening his eyes, he saw Micah was crying. "I've never seen her except in pictures, but one day, here maybe, I will see her!"

Michael held his breath in awe. This was too much of a coincidence. Slowly he asked, "Who?"

"My mother."

Michael did not know how to respond. How could he tell his son that Devorah was not in heaven? He could not speak.

"She was a follower, Papa. Savta found her journal when I was a baby. She was a secret follower because Mother wanted to honor her parents. She knew how unhappy they would be, so she kept it a secret.

"Savta said that after she read Mother's journal, she began to explore her own faith. Saba, too. They both believed on Yeshua because of Mother's journal."

Michael shook his head in disbelief. "Your grandmother found a journal your mother kept? But surely she would have told me!"

Shrugging his shoulders, Micah turned to Joel and began asking him questions about what he felt like eating for dinner. Michael thought back over his time with Devorah. How could she not share with him such an important aspect of her life?

As he sat there pondering, he recalled all of his many jokes and derisive comments about the gullible Christians that toured the Holy City to see the footsteps of Jesus and the place he was buried.

He gazed at the clear sky and quietly thanked God for the assurance that he would see his beloved Devorah again. Then he began praying for Kate.

23

VIRGINIA

John set the last of the venison down on the counter. Elena and some of the other women were preparing the evening meal, and there was a great deal of activity in the kitchen. He leaned back against the counter and watched his wife. She was still such a beautiful woman. He gave her a playful slap on the bottom as she moved past him.

"Hey, you! You'd better watch those hands!" she scolded jokingly. Grabbing some onions from the pantry, she went past him again, skipping just out of his reach.

"That's the last of the deer meat," he told her. "I hope Brant and Annabel were able to find another one today."

Elena handed the onions to one of the newcomers. They now had over forty people in the caves. At the last community meeting, John and Elena had been chosen as leaders for the community. He and Elena had organized people into groups. Some, like Brant and Annabel, were responsible to find food, while others foraged the surrounding area looking for useful items. Elena wanted to prepare for the days ahead, so they had designated storage areas in parts of the underground caverns.

"Let's go into the storage room, John. I want to look at the inventory." She led the way out of the kitchen and into the hallway that led to the caves. John followed her, grabbing a lantern.

They walked in silence for a few minutes. Finally, they stood in front of the cave where the food was stored. Metal shelves lined the walls and stood in rows inside the vast subterranean room. Every shelf was full of canned goods and other nonperishable food items.

"There's a lot here," John remarked. "The foraging team has done a great job."

"They have," she acknowledged, "but it's not going to be enough. We need a more constant supply of protein. You know over half of the community are children, John. They need protein. Most of the canned foods here are vegetables and fruits. We have some canned meats— tuna and such—but not nearly enough."

John thought for a few minutes. "All of our cash is gone. I'm not sure what else we can do. We've gone through all of the homes that were abandoned, and now that Quinteros has restored order to the continent, people are starting to move back into this area. Remember, I told you that anyone who swears allegiance to the North American Republic is guaranteed a home and a job? Many people are heading this way because of that promise."

Elena looked at him; her eyes sparkling in the dim light. "That can be to our advantage. Now that there is peace and order, luxuries are starting to matter again.

"I brought all of my jewelry with me in that backpack, remember? Arturo was extremely generous. I know a few of the other women have some valuable things too. Maybe we can find some way to barter now for items we need, before that treaty is signed. You know that's when the seven-year countdown starts."

"Yes. And Brant told me he heard that Luca and Billings are headed to Israel soon to negotiate a treaty. So if we're able to barter, what is it you want to get?" John asked her.

"Chickens. I've been researching, and I think we could get the right materials and keep the chickens in one of the caves closer to the surface. Then we'd have plenty of protein for everyone."

"Diamonds for chickens?" he asked teasingly.

"Yes, and goats."

"Where are you going to keep goats, Elena? I can see keeping chickens in here, but goats?"

"I'm sure we can do it. We'll have to have assigned goat herders. But think about it! We can have milk and cheese if we have goats." She smiled teasingly at him. "You remember how much you love goat cheese."

John chuckled because he couldn't stand the stuff. "It's hard to believe my city girl is talking about milking goats. Does anyone here have any experience with animals? I can't think of anyone who does off of the top of my head."

"Yes, Annabel does. Remember, her parents were preppers so she has experience with all of this. She and I have been brainstorming about it for the last few days."

"Okay, great. I like the idea, babe. Brant, Philip Jeffries, and I can get the truck and make a few trips. We'll have to make sure that we go far out and work our way back toward home. We don't want to draw too much attention." John started thinking about where he would start his search.

"Also, if you can find some solar power bars for our computers, that would be ideal," Elena added. "Now that stores are opened again, they shouldn't be too hard to find. You may even find there are places you can go to hawk the jewelry. Is that the right word?"

John chuckled. "You mean *pawn*. I'm sure that if things are really getting back to normal, we should be able to find something. Anything else?" he asked.

"Doc Reynolds has a list for you. He's written out prescriptions, if you can find any pharmacies open. He wants supplies, especially for the children. He explained that certain things would be helpful to keep them healthy, like fluoride we can add to their water."

John shook his head. "That's going to be hard, Elena. Since Quinteros came to power, the new health care system is government-run. All of the pharmacies are under the auspices of the military. Only government-approved doctors can write scripts."

"When did you find that out?" she asked, turning to a shelf and shuffling a few cans around.

"I was talking to a guy on the radio last night." John had

found a ham radio on a scavenging hunt, and ever since, he had been making friends all over the country. He was careful, however, never to disclose any identifying information.

"Did you hear anything else?" she asked.

"No, we were just shooting the breeze. I've been praying for an opportunity to share the gospel with him. He's a crusty old guy. He served in the Gulf War and is quite a patriot. He hates what's happened with the United States."

"I can understand that. Have you seen photos of the new flag?" Elena turned back to face him.

"Ugh, yes," John replied. "I just can't believe how quickly everything is changing." "From being a world superpower, to not, then part of the one world government, now one of the ten sectors. It's happened fast."

Elena shivered involuntarily and moved into John's arms, laying her head against his chest. They stood like that for a moment before he bent his head down and tenderly kissed her soft lips.

"We know how it ends," he encouraged her. She nodded in agreement, her blue eyes sparkling up into his.

"Are you ready to go back now?" she asked, reaching out her hand for his.

They headed back to the house at the front of the entrance to the caves. As they walked hand in hand through the caverns, John thanked God for providing so perfectly for them. With His help, they might be able to weather the next seven years.

New Babylon, Iraq

Kate and Christopher sat in the shade provided by the umbrella that rose from the center of their table. The hotel's terrace café was crowded with wealthy clientele enjoying the sunset. Ribbons of red in the sky wove between the white clouds. Exotic birds swooped over the water. Kate gazed at the view, elated with the beauty of nature and the elegance of her surroundings. After all of the devastation she and Christopher had covered in the last few weeks, New Babylon was nothing but paradise.

"I can't believe how beautiful this city is, Christopher! I could stay here forever!" Kate exclaimed. "Everything has been perfection! Our rooms, the food, the wine! And the interview! We got an amazing interview with an incredible man.

"You know he is going to do it! Luca Giamo is going to do what no world leader has been able to accomplish. He is going to bring peace to the Middle East. And we get to see it happen! Can you believe it?"

"I can, Kate, because the moment he saw you, he was captivated. You have that charisma about you that makes every man want to give you whatever you want." Christopher toasted her with his wineglass. "Not only do we have this interview, but we get to be right there in the room as he negotiates with Israel's prime minister."

Kate smiled triumphantly, dimples framing her mouth. "At least my professional life is going well." She picked up her glass and clinked it against Christopher's.

"Kate, you know the first year of marriage is the hardest. You both have a lot to work through, but you can make it." He liked Michael, and Kate wasn't the most steadfast person when it came to her love life.

"I'm not sure. I haven't told you, but now Michael has decided that he's a Christian Jew, just like his son. I swear it's just to appease the kid." She drained her wineglass and motioned for another to the waiter walking past them.

"Appease? Micah seems like a nice boy to me." Christopher gave her a questioning look. "I think you're being a bit harsh."

"You know, I'm just about at the point where I don't care. Michael doesn't care about my career. It's all about him and Micah," she complained.

The waiter brought over a bucket and a bottle of expensive

champagne. "What's this?" Kate asked him.

"Compliments of Ambassador Giamo," he informed her.

"Oh, great! Thank you!" she exclaimed to the waiter, looking around.

"Kate, I'm warning you!" Christopher whispered to her, watching as the handsome young man made his way over to their table. Kate kicked friend hard under the table.

Her pulse quickened as Luca Giamo reached their table and took her right hand in his. "I was at the hotel for diplomatic reasons and realized it was dinnertime. What a pleasant surprise to find you here, Ms. Benari," Luca said. He was dressed in a dark-blue suit. His blonde hair fell over his forehead as he bent over to kiss her hand.

"Why, I'm so glad! This is fortunate for me because Christopher has an emergency at home and he was just leaving to deal with it. Now I don't have to eat alone!" Kate smiled at Luca coyly and kicked Christopher again under the table.

"Uhhh, yeah. This is great. I felt terrible about leaving poor Kate all alone. I'll just head back to my room and deal with the issue." He stood up and shook Luca's hand.

As Luca turned his back to Christopher and pulled out a chair, Christopher shook a finger at Kate in warning. He turned around abruptly and walked out of the dining room, shaking his head and muttering.

Luca sat back in the chair, his eyes running over the woman in front of him, obviously intrigued. Kate felt the familiar thrill of attraction—and something else she couldn't put her finger on.

"What brings you to the hotel?" she asked.

"I escorted the charming daughter of the Israeli prime minister back to her room." He leaned forward and picked up her glass of wine, smelled the bouquet, took a sip, and licked his lips.

Kate's stomach flipped and she felt a bit breathless. "Oh?" She shook her head to clear it. "I've met the charming Angelina Rogov. She's unforgettable, all those delightful freckles on her cheeks. My husband thinks she's quite an unusual beauty."

"Ah yes, I'd forgotten you have a husband," Luca stroked the back of her hand slowly. "How is Dr. Benari? Quite the achievement for him, finding the Ark of the Covenant! I would love to see that when I visit Israel."

"They won't let you," Kate said flatly. "I tried to convince Michael to look inside—to let me record the contents for the world. The Israelis insist it is holy and the rest of the world is not fit to see it. Do you know they are putting it in the Temple at the rededication ceremony?"

"Yes, on their holy day, Yom Kippur. It's quite an exciting time for Israel. They are dwelling in the land, fairly securely, for the first time since they became a nation," he commented, leaning in toward her.

Kate could smell his cologne. *He smells delicious.* "Yes, they are, which makes me wonder how on earth you were able to convince them to sign that treaty. Israel has always refused to make accommodations."

"I can be quite persuasive," he whispered, his hand moving up her arm to stroke the back of her neck. "I always get what I want."

Despite the buzz she felt from the alcohol and the thrill of Luca's touch, something in Kate was repelled by his comment. She moved her chair back from the table, out of reach, and smiled.

"And I usually get what I want," she said lightly, with a grin. She wanted a little space, but she wasn't quite sure she was ready to refuse him.

"Not always?" Luca asked.

Kate sighed and took a sip of her wine. "No, I wanted to go to the dedication ceremony with Michael, but I can't because I'm a Gentile. He is going inside."

"Into the Holy of Holies? That's something I would like to see." Luca murmured the last part so softly that she almost missed it.

"Oh no! Priests will carry the Ark into the Holy of Holies. Only the high priest is allowed usually, but it needs to be placed in there and he can't do it by himself. Michael will be in the Court of the

Israelites, with his son, Micah. Since I'm not Jewish, I can't go in."

"Have you even seen it?"

"Michael did let me look at it, but only because I raised such a stink about them not looking at the contents. You would think that an archaeologist of his caliber would want to see what is inside! There was nothing I could do to convince him!" Kate rolled her eyes and flicked her wrist in disdain.

Luca poured champagne into the glass in front of him and toasted her. "I would enjoy being convinced by you, Kate."

The look in his eyes made her quiver. For some reason, a memory from childhood made her close her eyes. She'd been walking down the path from her parent's cottage to play with a friend when a man had driven up alongside her in a shiny convertible. He'd slowed down and said something softly. She had stopped walking and asked him to repeat his question. When he spoke, something inside her had screamed, *Run!* and she'd taken off, running off of the pathway, through the neighbor's garden. She'd run all the way home, not stopping until she was in the house with the door latched. Right now she felt the exact same way.

She swayed a bit in her seat, unnerved. "You know, I think I've had too much to drink. I'm sorry, Mr. Ambassador. I don't think dinner is a good idea for me. I think I need to sleep…alone."

Luca stood up politely as she got up from the table and moved to give her a farewell embrace. He kissed both of her cheeks. "I can think of some more exciting pastimes."

Kate pulled away. "I'm sure you can," she said, teasingly, "I take it this is a new experience for you."

Luca laughed. "Until tonight it was! But the charming Angelina put me off, and now you. I must be losing my touch."

Kate thought of a few choice responses to the handsome ambassador, but her interview with him after the treaty signing was a possible Pulitzer in the making. She could not afford to offend such a powerful man—and her ticket to sit at the negotiating table with Israel.

She leaned into him and kissed him softly on the lips. "I don't think you're losing anything, Ambassador." Kate gave him a look that made most men pant with desire, turned on her heels, and left the dining room alone.

Upstate New York

James sat at the desk in the makeshift studio, looking over his notes while Eric got the equipment ready. It was time for his daily broadcast. He felt a heavy burden to get believers as ready as possible for the Tribulation, and they had no idea how long they would be able to broadcast, even with their secure Internet.

Eric shook his head. "Listen, James. This mic is not working. I'll be right back. I think I can fix it, but the part I need is in my cabin." He got out of his chair and left the room.

James opened the laptop next to him and logged in. He might as well get caught up on his correspondence while Eric was gone. There was a lot to do. He was scrolling through e-mails when the subject line on one of the messages caught his eye. "The Antichrist."

Reading through the e-mail, he pursed his lips. Another one asking if it would be murder to kill the man the book of Revelation called the "man of perdition." He typed back a response. *Yes!* It would not work anyway; the prophecy was clear. The man would be killed sometime in the middle of the Tribulation, but he would be resurrected.

"Satan is such a mocker! Resurrected. Unholy trinity: Giamo and that false prophet, Billings Mason. I won't be surprised to find out they found some way to fake a virgin birth." James spoke aloud as he typed, provoked by the enemy's bold sacrilege.

Eric came back through the door and closed it carefully behind him. There was no lock, but everyone knew not to enter when it was closed. He went over to the equipment and began working on the broken part.

"Did you find what you needed?" James asked.

"Yup, it'll take just a minute." Eric plopped back in his chair and flipped some switches. James switched off the laptop to conserve power and closed it. He put his Bible and notes in front of him.

Eric gave him a thumbs-up and pushed the recording button, signaling "go" with another thumbs-up. James made sure to speak slowly. Andie told him he had a habit of speaking too quickly when he was "stirred up," as she put it. He prayed again quickly for God's help, then began to speak.

"This is James Martin, again, bringing you the Word of Truth. Today we're going to focus on the time ahead of us. I've talked about it before, but as we know, events are proceeding in the Middle East. Israel's prime minister is indeed considering signing the peace treaty with the New World Union. Ambassador Giamo is headed to Jerusalem soon.

"Daniel chapter 9 makes it clear that treaty signing marks the start of the Tribulation. We are about to enter the darkest, most evil days mankind has ever known." He paused.

"I know many of you are terrified. You've written to me and expressed your fears. I have to tell you, I'm afraid, too. What many of you have experienced in the last few weeks has been horrifying.

"The entire south part of Florida is essentially gone, while the Philippines have been hit by a devastating typhoon. Millions are dead there. Japan had another major earthquake early this week, and the ensuing tsunami destroyed much of the Big Island in Hawaii.

"Some of you have asked me where God is in all of this. All I can answer is that He is where He always has been. Mankind has been warned of this time for generations. Unfortunately, we are the ones who are living through it."

He paused, glancing at his notes. "God has made it clear why this is happening. He is just and justified in bringing this judgment to the world. Think along with me about the state the world is in.

ONE WILL BE LEFT

"But God has not left us as orphans. We have the Spirit with us. We also have angels ministering to us. I've read many e-mails from brothers and sisters throughout the world, amazing stories about angels leading you out of dangers to safe havens, even to faith in Jesus Christ. He's made many promises to those who overcome and persevere!

"It seems that in this next season of time, we're going to see many supernatural events and supernatural beings. I'm unsure how long we will be able to communicate, but we will try as long as the Lord allows.

"If you have a Bible, open it with me now to the fourth chapter of Revelation. I'm going to read through the whole chapter, then explain verse by verse." James began reading.

Eric checked on a few settings and then pulled out his own Bible to read along.

24

NEW BABYLON, IRAQ

DC sat in the van with the leader of the rescue team. He had wanted to go in with the team and get Teo, but the risk that someone would recognize him and alert her captors was too great.

He saw the leader, Omer, tap his right ear and listen intently. Nodding his head, the man began responding rapidly in Hebrew. DC could not follow what he was saying, so he waited impatiently to hear the status of the mission.

Omer looked him in the eye. "They are in transit."

"Teo? They got Teo?"

"Yes, my friend. She is with the extraction team and Ari, your friend."

DC bowed his head and prayed, thanking God for rescuing his wife. Omer clapped him on the back. "Don't be downcast! They have her. She's safe!"

DC looked up, his eyes misty with relief. "No man, I was praying, thanking the Lord for saving my wife."

"Oh! I guess I don't see many people pray. I apologize if I interrupted you."

"No, thank you, man! Omer, you and your team are risking your lives for this. I owe you all a great debt."

There was a sharp rap on the door, and Omer opened it. Teo was standing outside in a long, white nightgown. The men on either side of her pushed her gently into the van and DC's open arms.

She began sobbing, grasping tightly to her husband. DC

didn't say a word and just let his wife cry. Ari entered the van next, followed by the other members of the team.

"Let's go!" Omer ordered.

The driver pulled the van away from the curb. DC knew they were going to the airport, where a private jet waited for them. He hugged his wife and looked at Ari, puzzled.

"Where is your mother?" DC asked his friend.

Ari shook his head. "She wasn't there. They killed her."

Teo picked her head up from her husband's shoulder and looked at Ari. "No, Ari, no. You must understand. They were going to kill her, but God took her. They were going to hurt her, but she died before they could harm her.

"She saw Him, Ari! She saw the Lord before she died. The most beautiful smile stayed on her face, even after." Teo's voice broke. "I'm so sorry. I loved her so, so much. I don't know how I could have made it without her. You know, she chose to be taken with me. She could have stayed with Juliana at the store, but she left her with a woman and came with me."

Before Teo could ask, DC explained who the woman in the store had turned out to be, and that their baby was safe with Mara, Ari's wife.

"You mean the prime minister's daughter? The same one you helped? That can't be a coincidence!" she exclaimed.

"No, it could only be God," DC agreed.

Teo sat up a little on the bench seat and looked at her husband. "Luca lied, DC—about so many things, of course, but especially about my dad. He didn't die of that supposed stroke. He's been imprisoned in Luca's basement all this time. Luca made some sort of hospital setup for him down there, with a medical team and everything."

"What! Where is he?"

"He wouldn't come with us," Ari inserted, his face grim. "He wants to kill Luca."

DC eyed the soldiers around them in the van and whispered, "Is it even possible to kill the Antichrist?"

"I don't know, but Father insisted on staying. He feels responsible for creating a monster. I begged him to come with me," Teo whispered back.

Ari moved away from the couple to give them some privacy. They sat quietly in their embrace for the rest of the ride to the airport. Once they were on the tarmac, the Mossad team hustled them into the small jet. DC and Teo sat together in the back row of seats, their hands intertwined and resting on the armrest between them.

"I can't believe you rescued me from Luca again," Teo said.

DC grinned. "I can't really claim that! Mossad rescued you. The prime minister and Angelina were involved, too, but ultimately it was God."

"I wish I knew that He will keep us safe through the Tribulation. So many won't make it. I try not to think about it too much, but I'm so scared. Do you think there's any way you can convince the prime minister not to sign that treaty with Luca?"

"No. I did try to warn him. He's sure that the only way Israel can survive is to do what the Jordanian king did and sign the treaty Luca wrote. The Jordanians keep their sovereignty and are not required to join the New World Union, but they must allow peacekeepers to guard all access points on the borders and in airports, to combat global terrorists," DC said. "I talked with Angelina about it when we flew here to rescue you, hoping she could convince her father. She listened, but I'm not sure she believed me."

Teo pulled her hand out of her husband's and rested it on his thigh. "Do you think there's any way we can make it to Virginia? Can we join Mom and John and Olivia?" Her voice broke, and she leaned her head on DC's shoulder. She missed her daughter so much.

He hesitated before replying. "I don't know how we can with Jules, sweetie. I've thought about it a lot. I just can't think of any way we can do it that would be safe for her. But hey, just because I can't think of a way doesn't mean God can't. We're just going to have to pray and wait to see if He will make a way for us."

"Olivia won't know us. She hears our voices once in a while, but that's it. She sees our pictures, but she won't really know us, DC! It breaks my heart."

"But she's safe," DC interrupted. "She's safe. I have to hope that we're all going to make it through the next seven years, but even if we don't, we know what the end is. We know who wins. We know what comes next. We have to trust God."

Teo looked at her husband. "Rhetta did. She trusted Him even at the very end. She was so brave! I have to tell Ari and Mara how brave she was. You should have heard her warn Luca. It was truly God speaking through her.

"I need to remember that God gave Rhetta the courage she needed and He'll do the same for me."

DC rested his head on top of hers as she continued. "I had a lot of time to think and pray when I was captive. It was horrible, like a forecast of hell. The ones who follow Luca are evil. It was easier when Rhetta was alive, but after her death, it was so hard…worse than any nightmare you could imagine. Sometimes it was hard to pray, as if I were fighting through barriers of some kind. I couldn't get words out. All I could do was say Jesus's name over and over.

"Stephen never even came near me after he saw me the first day. I found out later that he was struck with boils. That surely was God protecting me. After Rhetta died, Luca made sure I was never alone, not even for a minute."

DC gripped her hand tighter. In the dim light he had noticed the bruises on her face. He clenched his free hand into a fist and gritted his teeth.

"It was terrible, but I never felt hopeless or alone. I have to keep remembering all that God has done for us. I need to keep it all in my heart," Teo finished and sighed.

"That's right, love, the end of the Book says the best is yet to be," DC responded. Teo turned her face up toward him, closing her eyes as DC's firm lips touched hers in soft, feathery kisses. She began to weep out of sweet relief as he brought his free hand up and ran it through her silky hair.

She pulled away and whispered into his ear, "DC, every moment with you is the best."

Jerusalem, Israel

The Knesset chamber was full. Kate stood next to Christopher, who was filming the proceedings. They'd prerecorded her introduction earlier, before the ceremony began. The prime minister was just finishing his comments. Kate listened with interest as he introduced the head of state from eastern Europe, Sergey Koslov. *This isn't on the agenda,* Kate thought.

The Israeli prime minister shook hands with the European leader and then returned to his seat by the podium facing the Knesset. Governor-in-Council Koslov waited for the polite applause to end.

"It is with great effort that the World Union has worked during this past year to restructure itself. The ten regions each have duly appointed leaders. As you are surely aware, we elected to appoint a legal institution to oversee the governors-in-council, a triumvirate. The governors have elected three officials, one of whom is with us here today. He is the architect of this peace accord and has been instrumental in helping the World Union establish and later restructure itself. His gifts and abilities are an important asset to our government. In is my pleasure to announce that Ambassador Luca Giamo will be the third magistrate for the World Union." The room erupted in deafening applause, and the entire assembly stood in homage to the young leader.

Sergey Koslov stood waiting to finish, but the enthusiastic applause continued. Luca stood and acknowledged the endorsement of the Knesset, modestly motioning with his hand for everyone to sit down.

"We certainly have Ambassador Giamo to thank for tirelessly

working to bring both the Israeli people and the World Union together," Koslov added as he waited for the thunderous applause and shouts to end. "I think it is no exaggeration to state that this one man, this one incredible man, is part of the reason we have hope for our future.

"Therefore, it is my great pleasure to give Ambassador Giamo the World Union's seat at this historic table before us where this peace agreement will be signed." Koslov gestured to the table set up in the middle of the Knesset chamber.

Kate looked to where Michael was sitting at the second grouping of seats that surrounded the "peace table." His face was grim, despite the buoyant atmosphere that filled the room. As those around him stood up again applauding, she watched him stare to the right of the prime minister. Following her husband's gaze, she saw Luca standing, his golden hair glowing in the light like a halo. Luca was smiling and nodding acknowledgement to his supporters in the room. He and the prime minister of Israel made their way to the table, where they took their seats next to one another.

What's with Michael? Kate thought scornfully. She shook her head slightly in disgust before turning her attention back to the scene in front of her. As the only reporter allowed in the chamber, she was scheduled for an interview by major news outlets later in the day. *I can't let his fanaticism ruin my career.*

Each of the men had a platinum Tibaldi pen, handcrafted by one of the company's top jewelers to commemorate this historic occasion. Kate watched intently as each man picked up his pen and signed his name to the document before them. When they finished, they exchanged pens and shook hands. The onlookers went wild, shouting and applauding. Israel was now at peace with the rest of the world.

PREVIEW

ONE WILL STAND

Michael Benari waited for the prime minister to exit the limousine first before he stepped out onto the sidewalk. He looked up at the Temple before him with foreboding. The rest of the dignitaries had already arrived for the official dedication of the third Jewish Temple. He could see them standing in line ahead of him, waiting to go through the security checkpoint. The ceremony would take place in the Court of the Gentiles.

Michael followed the prime minister and his entourage up the stairs, bypassing the group waiting to enter the Temple. He was surprised as he entered the Court of the Gentiles to see his son, Micah, and Micah's friend, Joel, standing on the dais that had been erected for today's ceremony. *What are they doing here?* Michael wondered.

As he hurried over to question the boys, he noticed the air seemed thicker, much more humid than was normal for the summer. Looking up, Michael gasped. A massive, fierce-looking shelf cloud hovered ominously above the Temple Mount. *It doesn't rain in the summer,* he thought anxiously, walking faster toward the boys. It looked like the supercell thunderstorm was about to unleash its fury.

Before he could reach the boys, hail started hitting the pavement around him. From the corner of his eye, he saw the prime minister being hustled to cover under the colonnades. Michael ran to the boys, who stood alone in the middle of the raised platform.

"Father, you will be safe if you stay here by us," Micah spoke first. Michael opened his mouth to respond, but Joel shouted into the microphone before the archaeologist could say anything. Joel's voice echoed through the Temple, resounding powerfully.

"Woe to you! Woe to you! You scoffers have signed a covenant of death. Now the decree of destruction has gone out, and the time of Jacob's trouble is upon you!"

Michael watched dumbstruck as Temple guards came running toward them, guns drawn menacingly. The wind picked up forcefully, and huge balls of hail smashed into the pavement around them, driving the guards back. One of the guards was hit on the shoulder and crumpled to the ground. Another man dragged him back to the colonnades. A bolt of lightning hit nearby; the shock wave knocked Michael to the ground. Instinctively, he curled up in the fetal position and closed his eyes in terror. All hell was breaking loose around him.

Also by Dawn Morris:
ONE WILL BE TAKEN
Insidious evil grows; time is running out ...

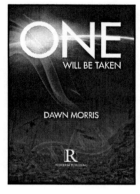

Arturo Giamo is a renowned visionary whose pioneering methodology in genetic engineering has established him as the world's foremost expert in his field. It also puts within his grasp the realization of his life's dream: to design children who are not just intelligent beyond imagination, but capable of leading mankind to the next level of evolutionary development, to solve the gravest problems in the world—and usher in an age of lasting unity, peace, and prosperity.

With the birth of his son, Luca Romano Giamo, Arturo attains his greatest personal triumph and the crowning achievement for Giamo Infertility Associates—the "miraculous" birth of the perfect child, his own son. As Luca matures, his fawning mentor, Billings Mason, rises to world renown as a man of faith, able to perform extraordinary miracles. After the mysterious disappearance of the world's Christians, Mason is named as the new pope of the Catholic Church. As the miracle-working pontiff draws the world into a unified faith system, Luca's power is consolidated governmentally, positioning both men as key leaders on the new world scene.

Global crises multiply and natural disasters are unleashed on the earth, while Israel's enemies mass on her borders. As evil gains dominion throughout the world, what will God do? What will become of His people? Can faith endure in such times?

"...*this is the spirit of the antichrist, of which you have heard that it is coming, and now is already in the world.*" (1 John 4:3, NASB)

Available at www.DawnMorris.net
Or at www.amazon.com

CPSIA information can be obtained at www.ICGtesting.com
Printed in the USA
LVOW07s1355200515
439087LV00002B/2/P